F. SCOTT FITZGERALD was born in 1896 in St. Paul, Minnesota, and educated at the St. Paul Academy in St. Paul, Minnesota, and Newman Academy in Hackensack, New Jersey and at Princeton. *This Side of Paradise,* his first novel, was published in 1920 and transformed him virtually overnight into a hero of his generation and the writer who named and captured the spirit of the "Jazz Age." That same year, he married Zelda Sayre and the two became America's most glamorous expatriates, dividing their time between New York and Paris, and traveling throughout Europe. Fitzgerald's most accomplished novel, *The Great Gatsby,* was published in 1925, and *Tender Is the Night* in 1934. Fitzgerald was also a prolific writer of short stories which were published in magazines like *The Saturday Evening Post* and *Esquire* throughout the 1920s and 1930s. When money and health problems finally forced Scott and Zelda to return to the States, Fitzgerald became a contract writer for a Hollywood movie studio. He died in 1940 while working on his unfinished novel of Hollywood, *The Last Tycoon.* His other works include *Flappers and Philosophers* (1920), *The Beautiful and Damned* (1922), *Tales of the Jazz Age* (1922), *All the Sad Young Men* (1926), and *Taps at Reveille* (1935).

F. SCOTT FITZGERALD

Bernice Bobs
Her Hair
and
Other Stories

EDITED AND WITH AN INTRODUCTION
BY BARBARA H. SOLOMON

A SIGNET CLASSIC

SIGNET CLASSIC
Published by the Penguin Group
Penguin Books USA Inc., 375 Hudson Street,
New York, New York 10014, U.S.A.
Penguin Books Ltd, 27 Wrights Lane,
London W8 5TZ, England
Penguin Books Australia Ltd, Ringwood,
Victoria, Australia
Penguin Books Canada Ltd, 10 Alcorn Avenue,
Toronto, Ontario, Canada M4V 3B2
Penguin Books (N.Z.) Ltd, 182–190 Wairau Road,
Auckland 10, New Zealand

Penguin Books Ltd, Registered Offices:
Harmondsworth, Middlesex, England

Published by Signet Classic, an imprint of Dutton Signet,
a division of Penguin Books USA Inc.

First Signet Classic Printing, January, 1996
10 9 8 7 6 5 4 3 2 1

Introduction copyright © Barbara H. Solomon, 1996
All rights reserved

Ⓒ REGISTERED TRADEMARK—MARCA REGISTRADA

Library of Congress Catalog Card Number: 95-74614

Printed in the United States of America

This book is for Connie and Jack

Acknowledgments

I would like to thank Adrienne Franco and Sr. Mary Eucharia Carrigan of Ryan Library at Iona College for securing the numerous Fitzgerald materials needed for my editing of this collection. A great deal of assistance was provided by Mary Bruno and the staff of the College's Information Technology Resource Center: Teresa Alifante, Patti Besen, and Nancy Girardi.

At the Department of English, I was greatly assisted by Liisa Chider and Terence Fitzgerald, graduate student assistants, and by Catherine Donato, Daniel O'Melia, and Patricia Varol, undergraduate student assistants.

Contents

Introduction

I

All of the stories in this collection were written or published during F. Scott Fitzgerald's extraordinary first year as a professional writer. During the early months of 1919, Fitzgerald was earning $90 a month writing advertising copy to be placed on streetcars, was trying desperately to convince Zelda Sayre, a beautiful and exciting young woman, to marry him, and had written nineteen stories and received 122 rejection slips.

Like some of the young men he was writing about, the twenty-three-year-old Fitzgerald had lived an elitist, upper-class life, attending Newman Academy in Hackensack, New Jersey, and Princeton University. He had been invited to country club dances where the daughters of America's wealthy families shimmered in organdy dresses with slippers of gold or silver. He had enjoyed swimming, tennis, and card parties with other popular young singles, had walked across the golf courses and through the rose-scented gardens, and had dined on the verandas and in the hotels and restaurants where wealthy people gathered, people without concern for the cost of their pleasures.

But unlike most of his friends and Princeton classmates, Fitzgerald had no family fortune to sustain the lifestyle he had been experiencing in tantalizing glimpses. He was an outsider who, deep down, knew that he was merely passing for an insider. When he was discharged from the army in February 1919, he returned not to the secure family estate or to the promising position in his father's solid business of his imagination, but to the reality of the need to earn his living by his wits and his words in a competitive, bustling New York City, a place ferociously indifferent to the dreams of an ambitious and talented Midwesterner.

His need to succeed, and to do so quickly, was intensified by the pressure he felt to claim the most desirable debutante, "the top girl" he had wooed as a second lieutenant stationed in Montgomery, Alabama. Zelda, the daring and witty daughter of a Southern judge, had already expressed her expectation that the man she married must be able to support her not merely in comfort, but in a style of life free from daily cares and filled with the stimulation, pleasure, and endless possibility that wealth can provide. She was not prepared to wait very long for a struggling young writer who, as her disapproving family pointed out, had not even been graduated from Princeton.

Made desperate by Zelda's breaking off their engagement and by the prospect of endless years of producing advertising slogans such as "We Keep You Clean in Muscatine" for the Barron Collier Advertising Company, Fitzgerald quit his job and returned home to St. Paul in July 1919. There, he revised the manuscript titled "The Romantic Egoist" that he had been working on for the past two years. Amazingly, by September 1919, the rewritten novel, now titled *This Side of Paradise*, was accepted for publication by Scribner's, appearing in March 1920. In September 1920, Scribner's also published Fitzgerald's first collection of stories, a volume containing eight works and titled *Flappers and Philosophers*.

Fitzgerald's career as a writer of short stories advanced by leaps and bounds. "Babes in the Woods," his first commercially published story, was sold to the magazine *The Smart Set* in June 1919 for $30. A few months later, "Head and Shoulders" was sold to *The Saturday Evening Post* (America's most widely read magazine at the time) for $400. It appeared in the February 21, 1920, issue, and Hollywood's Metro Company quickly purchased the movie rights to the story for $2,250, producing it under the title *The Chorus Girl's Romance*. (Two additional stories in this volume were also made into films: "The Offshore Pirate" and "Myra Meets His Family," which was released by Fox with the title *The Husband Hunter.*) During 1920, Fitzgerald published a total of fifteen stories, six in the *Post*, five in *The Smart Set*, two in *Scribner's Magazine*, and one each in *Metropolitan Magazine* and the December 12 *Chicago Tribune*. He earned a total of $18,000 during his first year as an author and accomplished his major goal.

With the assurance that he could now earn significant sums through his writing, and with the status of a successful author making him a literary as well as a romantic figure, Scott convinced Zelda that he was ready to take care of her and, equally important, to offer her the kind of life she craved. On March 20, 1920, Zelda Sayre's parents announced the engagement of their daughter to F. Scott Fitzgerald, about a week prior to the appearance of *This Side of Paradise,* and the couple were married in the rectory of New York's St. Patrick's Cathedral on April 3, 1920.

One of the major reasons for the instant popularity of Fitzgerald's fiction was that it reflected the far-reaching changes in values, behavior, and appearance of the generation coming of age after World War I. Along with the considerable disillusionment of young people after the war, came a sense of living in extravagant and daring times. Fitzgerald perceptively dramatized the new ways in which males and females related to one another, the kinds of conversations taking place and the new attitudes behind them, as well as conveying vivid details of clothes, entertainments, cars, houses, and hotels. In the American "Jazz Age," the name Fitzgerald coined to describe the decade of the 1920s, young people with a sense of the piquancy and the possibility of life rooted in an awareness of the devastation the war had created throughout Europe determined to lead lives very different from those of their parents. More straightforward about sexual feelings and more openly active sexually, they were highly romantic and expressed their pleasure-seeking behavior as a new ethic of their era. More mobile than their parents because of the increasing production of automobiles throughout the decade of the 1920s, more sophisticated in their pleasures as they frequented cocktail parties, urban theaters, and night clubs, and more affluent as factories churned out a range of desirable goods, youthful American readers found in Fitzgerald's stories the themes and characters that they identified with intensely.

A number of topics, themes, and situations recur both in Fitzgerald's stories and in his novels. Many of his tales are concerned with romantic young love and identity. In a nation that often idealized itself as a classless society, Fitzgerald would return again and again, as in "May Day" and "The Jelly-Bean," as well as in the novel *The Great Gatsby,* to dramatize the attraction of a poor or middle-class young man for a "golden girl," a beautiful, self-confident, and highly desirable upper-class young woman. He would depict vividly the gulf that separates those born into wealthy and "good" families from those who lack these advantages.

Weaving the hero's quest for the affluent and prized debutante into fiction about the elusive American Dream, Fitzgerald examined the nation's insistent optimism that success was within the grasp of every determined and energetic young man. He raised troubling questions about American ideals of success and the materialistic goals of his generation.

Closely connected to these themes is Fitzgerald's portrayal of "the new woman" who emerged in the 1920s. For the most part, Fitzgerald heartily approved of the transformation that had been occurring among American young women as he came of age. He chronicled what might well be described as a revolution in the appearance, manners, and morals of the type of girls he and his friends had been dating for a period of five or six years. He noted their blatant use of lipstick and rouge, hitherto considered not socially respectable, the changing fashions by which ankle-length skirts and layers of petticoats were being replaced by knee-length dresses, and the process by which long, elaborate hair styles gave way throughout the decade to bobbed hair, a straight, short, boyish style.

In behavior as well as appearance, Fitzgerald's emerging young flapper differed radically from the young woman of only a decade earlier. If the young woman of 1910 prided herself on being demure and refined, the debutante of 1920 prided herself on being a lively companion for men, funloving, provocative, and spunky. Freed from the restrictive corsets and long dresses of her mother's generation, she played golf and tennis and went swimming, boating, and horseback riding. Whereas her mother might have danced waltzes and polkas, Fitzgerald's "golden girl" did the Charleston, the toddle, the black bottom, and the shimmy.

Several distinctive qualities of Fitzgerald's belles and flappers characterized the heroines he created in a wide range of stories. Intelligent as well as beautiful, they occasionally proclaim that they have "masculine" minds. Like Marjorie in "Bernice Bobs Her Hair" they are not prone to be silly or to giggle. And like Marjorie, the only relationships that they truly value are those with males. They have little interest in other women, who are merely rivals for a man's attention, and generally find other women to be dull.

Unashamedly egotistical, they are demanding, stubborn,

and selfish as is Ardita Farnam in "The Offshore Pirate."
Like Edith Bradin in "May Day" and Nancy Lamar in "The
Jelly-Bean," these upper-class women would never consider
marrying an impoverished or even a middle-class suitor.
Brought up in luxurious circumstances, they have expensive
tastes and require a "background" of wealth. Curiously, in
several works Fitzgerald defends his heroines from the accu-
sation that they are spoiled. He seems to believe that like his
own wife, Zelda, the beautiful flappers of his stories are right
to value themselves highly and are justified in demanding
that their suitors have the affluence and social status they
need to maintain their lifestyle. In many of the stories, the
women believe that plentiful money is a key element in keeping romance alive. Surprisingly, Fitzgerald often seems to af-
firm this attitude, believing that the golden girl's beauty, high
self-image, egotism, and blunt speech make her desirable and
entitle her to dominate others.

II

Four of the stories in this collection, "Bernice Bobs Her
Hair," "Babes in the Woods," "The Ice Palace," and "Benediction," are concerned with the character, problems, actions,
and values of attractive young women. In one of the best of
these stories, "Bernice Bobs Her Hair," Fitzgerald dramatizes
the relationship and contrast between two eighteen-year-old
cousins, Marjorie Harvey and Bernice. Whereas Marjorie is
extremely popular and pleased with herself, Bernice is somewhat old-fashioned and has not been very astute in analyzing
or acquiring the qualities that attract young men. The story
depicts the way in which Bernice consciously transforms herself into a flapper, rejecting many of the ideals of femininity
that characterized her behavior when she first arrived at
Marjorie's house for a month-long visit. Offended by her
cousin's indifferent treatment of her, Bernice tells Marjorie:
"I think you're hard and selfish, and you haven't a feminine
quality in you."

Like many young women of her age, when Bernice thinks of
femininity she thinks of the values and guidelines for behavior
that were handed down by mothers and other relatives of the
generation that came of age at the turn of the century. Those
authorities praised feminine virtues such as modesty, charity,
spirituality, self-sacrifice, and domestic competence. They de-

cried traits such as vanity and egotism. When, for example, Marjorie discusses Bernice with her mother, the daughter anticipates the comment Mrs. Harvey will very likely make about her niece: "Oh, I know what you're going to say! So many people have told you how pretty and sweet she [Bernice] is, and how she can cook! What of it? She has a bum time. Men don't like her." Clearly, mother and daughter evaluate Bernice by very different standards.

Bernice begins to complain to Marjorie in terms of traditional womanly values, asking her:

"Don't you think common kindness—"
"Oh, please don't quote 'Little Women'!" cried Marjorie impatiently. "That's out of style."
"You think so?"
"Heavens, yes! What modern girl could live like those inane females?"
"They were models for our mothers."
Marjorie laughed. "Yes they were—not! Besides, our mothers were all very well in their way, but they know very little about their daughters' problems."

After Bernice's admission that she would be willing to make some changes, Marjorie gives her a series of directions. They include improving upon her personal appearance, dancing in a manner that will be more comfortable for her partner, and inventing or culling amusing and provocative remarks, known by Fitzgerald's contemporaries as "a line."

Marjorie's advice to Bernice is based on assessing and consciously developing the personality that will enable a woman to attract and hold the attention of young men. It has nothing to do with the discovery or nurturance of one's own individual traits or needs, it has nothing to do with sincere feelings, but it has all to do with a new and exciting courtship game that the clever young woman can manipulate to her advantage. The successful flapper such as Marjorie, thus, will have a crowd of suitors, referred to as "beaux," will enjoy dances and parties, and will be invited to dinners, teas, and matinées by attractive college men. Marjorie's lessons have a twofold goal. First, Bernice will lead the very pleasant life of the popular belle and have a calendar filled with enjoyable social activities. Second, as both girls tacitly understand, the final result of their attractiveness and popularity, at some future time, will be an appropriate marriage proposal from an affluent young man of their own social class. Thus, in spite of her apparent independence, intelligence, self-confidence, and daring, Fitzgerald's "new woman" generally had an old-fashioned goal: making a good marriage. Under Marjorie's tutelage, Bernice discovers that she has a real aptitude for being a popular debutante, and she leaves the Harvey household a very different girl from the guest whose idea of small talk consisted of remarks about the weather.

"Babes in the Woods" is a story Fitzgerald slightly revised to make into a scene in his first novel, *This Side of Paradise*. The character called Stephen Palms in the story became the novel's central character, Amory Blaine. Interestingly, in both the novel and the story Fitzgerald chose Isabelle's point of view for the narrative's center of consciousness. Sixteen and a half years old, Isabelle is an emerging "golden girl" or "popular daughter" or desirable debutante. Extremely attractive, with "intense physical magnetism" like Marjorie, Isabelle has developed the ability to capture and hold the attention of the young men with whom she wishes to flirt:

> What Isabelle could do socially with one idea was remarkable. First, she repeated it rapturously in an enthusiastic contralto with a trace of a Southern accent; then she held it off at a distance and smiled at it—her wonderful smile; then she delivered it in variations and played a sort of mental catch with it, all this in the nominal form of dialogue.

Completely focused on whether she will find Stephen attractive and whether she will be able to impress him with her beauty and personality, Isabelle both enjoys herself and cleverly works at creating the desired effect.

One of Fitzgerald's great talents is the skill with which he depicts the cultivated charm and courtship strategies of young people. He well understood their passionate need to be exciting and desirable and to distinguish themselves from their peers and rivals. He simultaneously celebrates the intensity and vitality of their social encounters and reflects the perspective of a detached and critical adult who observes of his heroine that Isabelle's "capacity for love affairs was limited only by the number of boys she met." Yet, he believes that his characters are admirable for investing so much of their energy and intelligence in making the most of their poignant youth. He is charmed by their attempts to appear more sophisticated than they are, but also conveys the fact that they are not naive or innocent. Falling in love or making someone fall in love with you is both their serious pursuit and the stuff their dreams are made of.

In "The Ice Palace," one of three stories Fitzgerald set in Tarleton, Georgia, two of the author's recurring themes are developed at the same time. The first concerns the choices and identity of an emerging "golden girl," Sally Carrol Happer; the second contrasts the culture, history, values, and way of life of the North and the South. Raised in St. Paul, Minnesota, married to a distinctly Southern young woman, and with paternal family roots in Maryland, Fitzgerald clearly was intrigued by the geographical differences he perceived.

Nineteen-year-old Sally Carrol with "bobbed corn-colored hair" has grown up in the South. When she discusses her future with Clark Darrow, a childhood friend, she explains that she does not want to marry a Southerner and settle down in Tarleton. She tells him that

> "tied down here I'd get restless. I'd feel I was—wastin' myself. There's two sides to me, you see. There's the sleepy old side you love; an' there's a sort of energy—the feelin' that makes me do wild things. That's the part of me that may be useful somewhere, that'll last when I'm not beautiful any more."

Sally Carrol, intelligent as well as beautiful, understands that her reign as a belle and the pleasures associated with it will diminish with the passage of time and the loss of her beauty. Significantly, she longs, as do several other Fitzgerald debutantes, for a future in which her vitality and intelligence will continue to be valued after her loveliness has faded. Her concern for such a future partly motivates her to engage herself to Harry Bellamy, who comes from an unnamed Northern city and has "everything she wanted."

Traveling by train on a January visit to meet Harry's family, Sally Carrol has high expectations: "She experienced a surging rush of energy and wondered if she was feeling the bracing air of which Harry had spoken. This was the North, the North—her land now!"

After meeting Harry's family, Sally Carrol discovers she has feelings of antipathy for both her future mother-in-law and Myra, her future sister-in-law. The Bellamy women, Sally Carrol observes, lack "charm and assurance." She reaches an unexpected conclusion: " 'If those women aren't beautiful,' she thought, 'they're nothing. They just fade out when you look at them. They're glorified domestics. Men are the centre of every mixed group.' "

Equally important, during her first dinner party she notices that "the men seemed to do most of the talking while the girls sat in a haughty and expensive aloofness." Also, Sally Carrol resents the treatment she is accorded as an engaged woman by the Northern men she meets. They wrongly assume that the only topic that will interest her is Harry, and she receives none of the playful compliments that would be considered appropriate for an engaged debutante or newly married woman in Tarleton.

One effect of the visit is that Sally Carrol has been disabused of her idea that the role of the married woman in the North is less ornamental and more meaningful than that of the Southern belle. As Fitzgerald intuitively knew, throughout America of the 1920s the interesting young woman all too soon would be viewed as an aging wife, a person with little status in much of the community, and one who was generally expected to live vicariously, through the experiences of her husband and children. Fitzgerald is surprisingly astute and clearly ahead of his time in diagnosing the inevitable problem of the bright and lively "new woman." What will her options be for a fulfilling and active adult life after the flush of youthful beauty has faded and the excitement of competing suitors is just a memory? Trained from childhood to believe that marriage and motherhood will be her full-time career, treated as an expensive ornament, and valued for her appearance above all else, it is little wonder that a perceptive woman of the era, such as Fitzgerald's heroine Sally Carrol, would fear that marriage will diminish her.

It is important to note that "The Ice Palace" raises an issue for contemporary readers that was not an issue at the time of its publication. In describing the characteristics of Sally Carrol's Southern life, Fitzgerald refers to "noisy niggery streets fairs" and to "scantily clothed pickaninnies." Here and in several other stories such as "The Jelly-Bean" and "The

Offshore Pirate," Fitzgerald employs descriptions of African-Americans that are highly offensive to a modern audience.

Coming of age in the 1920s, in an America complacent about its Jim Crow laws and plagued by anti-black violence following World War I, Fitzgerald reflected some of the attitudes of a racist society. He wrote for a white audience, and his many magazine editors were clearly indifferent to or approving of his descriptions.

We know that great writers are not necessarily great men nor astute social critics. However, Fitzgerald's negative characterization of the bigoted Tom Buchanan in *The Great Gatsby* is one indication of the author's distaste for people who espoused racist views. Then, too, Fitzgerald did seem to be growing in awareness as America itself moved away from a policy of official approval of segregation throughout the nation. In his unfinished novel *The Last Tycoon,* Fitzgerald dramatizes a scene between his central character, Monroe Stahr, and a very individualized African-American man who has read Ralph Waldo Emerson and who is highly critical of the movies. This character is not a stereotype and Stahr rebukes an Englishwoman who tries to demean the man by referring to him as a "poor old Sambo."

In the fourth story that depicts a young, unmarried woman, "Benediction," Lois is introduced as "nineteen and very romantic and curious and courageous." The structure of the story is somewhat unusual in that Fitzgerald dramatizes Lois's visit to her brother, a seminarian, during the time when she is making a crucial decision. The process by which she decides whether she will travel to Wilmington to meet Howard, the young man who claims to be deeply in love with her, is only obliquely portrayed.

Lois's relationship with Howard is suggested through only a few details. In a letter to her, he indicates that because of a lack of money they can not marry, but immediately he declares that "we can't lose each other and let all this glorious love end in nothing." Her thoughts about him are distinctly tinged with sexual excitement as she recalls "the furtive, restless excitement she felt sometimes when he talked to her, his dreamy sensuousness that lulled her mind to sleep." She telegraphs Howard that she will meet him in Wilmington within the next day or two as he had asked in his letter, presumably to initiate an affair. During the interval, Lois travels to the seminary where her brother, Kieth, is preparing for ordination as a Roman Catholic priest.

The central action of the story revolves around this meeting of Lois with Kieth, who had left home seventeen years earlier to pursue his vocation. Lois has not seen her brother for fourteen years, and Fitzgerald chronicles their afternoon visit from his point of view. Kieth is now thirty-six, almost perhaps a father figure, and Lois seems to value his judgments, but she never mentions her relationship with Howard or her plans to meet him. Instead, Lois asks her brother a number of questions about his way of life as a novitiate in an attempt to understand him better. She clearly wants to learn about his character and beliefs.

Among their exchanges is a brief discussion of the kind of person each of them would find comforting or helpful in a time of crisis. Kieth believes that "real help comes from a stronger person whom you respect." Lois disagrees, arguing that "people want human sympathy." She adds an explanation: "They want to feel the other person's been tempted."

Towards the end of their afternoon together Lois does reveal something of her inner life to her brother with a blunt statement about religion: she characterizes Catholicism as "inconvenient." Although brother and sister discuss Lois's lack of religious belief as well as experience and life in general terms, Lois's reunion with her brother and her unusual sensations at the seminary's Benediction service that she attends with him may well serve as an indirect commentary on both Lois's planned rendezvous with Howard and on Lois as a representative of a generation that has become alienated from traditional religious values.

Fitzgerald often chronicled the sexual revolution of his generation, which partially resulted from this alienation. As he well knew, the respectable American young woman of his parents' generation was expected to have a courtship that was, by and large, free of physical contact. She would be proposed to first and kissed afterward, and a lover's kiss would be construed as a serious pledge of commitment. But Fitzgerald's heroines come of age after World War I and at the beginning of a new decade. Often dating numerous suitors at the same time, the "popular daughters" might decide to kiss on a first date, might be found in parked cars, and certainly know about "petting parties." But provocative and liberated as Fitzgerald's heroines might seem, they were essentially virginal. When Fitzgerald uses the phrases "to have affairs" or "to be made love to" he is not describing sexual relations but stages in dating relationships. Thus, "Benediction" is a somewhat unusual Fitzgerald story in both its structure and in the behavior of its heroine.

III

"May Day," "The Jelly-Bean," and "Dalyrimple Goes Wrong" are concerned with the lives of poor young men: Gordon Sterrett, Jim Powell, and Bryan Dalyrimple. The first two stories are very typical of Fitzgerald's themes and settings, but the third depicts rather atypical behavior on the part of one of his characters.

"May Day," published in July 1920, is among the best of Fitzgerald's works of fiction. Sometimes described as a novella rather than a story, it is a tale of two intertwining actions set against a backdrop of the social and political unrest that characterized America in the years immediately following the end of World War I. One of the two plots is a variant of Fitzgerald's almost obsessive treatment of the "poor boy" and "golden girl" encounter. But the impoverished young man in this instance is Gordon Sterrett, a Yale graduate who has returned to America after the war to find that he cannot earn enough money as an artist to permit him to live among the upper-class people with whom he was raised and educated. Unlike the males of "Winter Dreams" and *The Great Gatsby*, Gordon is not a lower- or middle-class youth inspired by glimpses of the lives of the wealthy to struggle to become one of them. Instead, he was one of the leisured, but has become bitter, dissipated, and weak-willed. His period of suffering as a failed artist in New York has lasted all of three months. During that time, he has become involved with Gloria Hudson, a lower-class, sexually active young woman. She is now blackmailing him to marry her because of the promises contained in letters he had written her during their brief affair.

Sterrett is not a particularly sympathetic character. His artistic goal, as he tells Philip Cory, his former college roommate, is to draw illustrations for magazines because "there's a pile of money in it." Fitzgerald also casts doubt on the degree of ability Gordon possesses as he tells Cory: "My stuff's crude. I've got talent, Phil; I can draw—but I just don't know how. I ought to go to art school and I can't afford it."

Another rather pathetic excuse he offers is that he hasn't been able to afford materials for drawing. Possibly Gordon's most understandable description of his situation is his statement to Cory, "I can't draw when I'm tired and discouraged and all in." Significantly, Sterrett has a serious drinking problem. He wrote the inappropriate letters to Gloria while drunk, and throughout the evening of the story he becomes increasingly dishevelled and incoherent. Although many of Sterrett's remarks and his behavior are off-putting, some sympathy for him is generated through the contrast between his desperate need for money, represented by his shabby suit, faded tie, and frayed sleeves, with the nonchalant extravagance of Cory who, with almost a dozen silk shirts, and expensive ties, and socks spread on the chairs of his hotel room, chooses a dozen new ties at a haberdashery. While Gordon's request for a loan of $500 might prove somewhat inconvenient or annoying to Philip Cory, there is no doubt that this freely spending and pleasure-seeking young man can afford that sum. Openly criticizing Gordon as being "bankrupt—morally as well as financially," Cory does not perform a single action except those necessary to provide him with pleasure. In depicting these two college friends, Fitzgerald seems to indicate that the possession of wealth by one and the extreme need of the other divides them irrevocably.

If Gordon Sterrett is an unpleasant "poor boy," Edith Bradin is one of Fitzgerald's most off-putting debutantes. She is visiting New York and has a date for the Yale fraternity dance at Delmonico's restaurant that Cory and Sterrett attend. Calculating, self-assured, and beautiful, she thinks about the entertaining small talk with which she will greet the stream of young men who will dance with her:

> She would talk the language she had talked for many years— her line—made up of the current expressions, bits of *journalese* and college slang strung together into an intrinsic whole, careless, faintly provocative, delicately sentimental.

Whereas Fitzgerald clearly enjoys and approves of the efforts of Marjorie and Bernice in "Bernice Bobs Her Hair" to create an interesting series of "lines" to raise Bernice from the ranks of the wallflowers and transform her into a desirable popular daughter, he views Edith as blatantly superficial, cold, and egotistical. Even her decision to pay a surprise visit to her brother, Henry, at the socialist newspaper office where he works late into the night is connected to negative traits. Edith pictures herself as floating "in on him, a shimmering marvel in her new crimson opera cloak" and revels in her plan to do "an unconventional, jaunty thing." Her impulse has little to do with the pleasure of seeing a loved family member.

Her encounter with Gordon Sterrett at the dance is disappointing, because she has grown tired of the round of dances and parties and would like to get married. Half in love with her memories of Gordon, she had determined to use the evening's opportunity to turn him from a one-time prom date into a serious candidate for marriage. Like Philip Cory, however, Edith has little patience for a Gordon who is less than physically robust, who is troubled, and filled with self-pity. Usually, Edith prefers dance partners who have had a few drinks because it makes them "so much more cheerful and appreciative and complimentary," but she is disconcerted to find that Gordon is unpleasantly drunk. His drinking and his problems have changed him: "He wasn't at all light and gay and careless—a great lethargy and discouragement had come over him." Given the egotistical perspective and shallow character that Edith has generally displayed throughout the evening, her reaction to a diminished and desperate Sterrett is consistent with her values. "Revulsion seized her, followed by a faint, surprising boredom." And after his assertion that he has become a failure and a poor man, she can barely wait a decent interval to be rid of the man she addresses as her "old friend." Clearly there is no place in Edith or Cory's glittering world for a young man who does not contribute to the carefree gaiety they are determined to pursue.

When Fitzgerald turns to the lives and activities of the two discharged soldiers Carrol Key and Gus Rose, he introduces them as "two human beings" who are "ugly, ill-formed, devoid of all except the very lowest form of intelligence, and without even that animal exuberance that in itself may bring color to the struggle of life." The physical description that continues is laden with unpleasant details and the goal of the two consists of trying to "getta holda some liquor." Fitzgerald clearly does not identify with these drafted soldiers of the working class who have returned from overseas. Perhaps one of the few flaws in "May Day" is in the naturalistic portrayals of the two servicemen, depictions that render the men so unpleasant, unintelligent, and unfocused, that readers can hardly be expected to care greatly about what happens to them. Fitzgerald may have identified in an intellectual way with those condemned to a round of toil and to cheap and readily available amusements, but he was, generally, unable or unwilling to create detailed portraits of engaging or likable working- or lower-middle-class individuals.

"The Jelly-Bean" is an early example of Fitzgerald's theme of the love of a poor or middle-class young man for a beautiful, popular, and wealthy young woman. The girl, desired by many other men, is generally highly self-confident, self-absorbed, and rude or indifferent to others. An onlooker less sympathetic than Fitzgerald would call her "spoiled." Her actions are daring and challenge old-fashioned values, but that behavior makes her all the more exciting and valuable in the eyes of her suitor. Like Daisy Buchanan of *The Great Gatsby* and Judy Jones of "Winter Dreams," the girl is an emblem of the upper class, the flower of an entire social system. In the usual course of events, she will be won by a male of similar status, one who can afford to support her in the extravagant style she assumes to be her birthright.

Jim Powell, the Jelly-Bean of the story, is something of an idler, a "corner loafer," who lives in a small Georgia city. At the age of twenty-one, he lives above Tilly's garage where he helps to fix cars in exchange for his rent. Occasionally he drives a taxi and adds to his income by gambling. Jim describes himself as "the champion crap-shooter" of the town.

In some of Fitzgerald's stories on this theme, the poor boy comes from an immigrant or lower-middle-class background with no claims to social status. Jim Powell, however, is carefully presented as a young Southerner whose family had been distinguished in the past. Much of the land around the white house on Elm Street in which he was born to impoverished parents had once belonged to the Powells, but after the death of his father when he was five, it became a boarding house run by a woman Jim called "Aunt Mamie." Clark Darrow, Nancy Lamar, Joe Ewing, Marylyn Wade, and the other young people who regularly attend the country club dances to which Jim is never invited are, according to Fitzgerald, "the old crowd, the crowd to which, by right of the white house sold long since, and the portrait of the officer in gray over the mantel, Jim should have belonged. Lacking an education, money, and family, "Jim was an outsider—a running mate of poor whites."

On the one occasion he is invited by Clark Darrow, "one of the best beaux of the town," to a country club dance, he is intensely attracted to Nancy Lamar, one of the town's most desirable debutantes. Jim's emotion, "a pull of breathless interest [that] took him completely out of himself" is stirred by this girl who "had left a trail of broken hearts from Atlanta to New Orleans."

Nancy is one of Fitzgerald's beautiful, dark-haired and self-destructive heroines. She has "a mouth like a remembered kiss and shadowy eyes and blue-black hair inherited from her mother who had been born in Budapest." Like Eleanor in *This Side of Paradise,* she has a tarnished reputation, the result of a wild streak and a series of "crazy stunts." Discontented with a parade of infatuated American males who are not worth "doing sensational things for," Nancy has adopted some vague and silly ideals of an exciting life that she has culled from English novels. Clearly an immature and romantic young woman, she drinks excessively and gambles recklessly. But Powell, far from ridiculing Nancy's ideals, is inspired by the love he feels for her to make plans for overhauling his entire life. As part of his quest to be worthy of this jaded and discontented young beauty, Jim wants to change his identity and social status. Deciding that he has been "bummin' too long," he makes plans to work for his uncle, so that he can return home transformed into a gentleman, that is, into an acceptable suitor for Nancy.

An important, but underdeveloped, character in this germinal story of Fitzgerald is Ogden Merritt, the wealthy suitor from Savannah who has been avidly courting Nancy for a year. No doubt, the author intends a pun on the suitor's name, since the only merit the young man seems to have is the enormous wealth of his father, a fortune built on the success of Merritt safety razors.

When Powell thinks about his rival, the image that represents Ogden Merritt in his mind is that of "white trousers." In this image of a young man empowered by family wealth, Fitzgerald employs the color white as he would later use it throughout his fiction. In a recurring motif of white clothing and white homes, Fitzgerald manipulates the traditional association of that color with purity and stainlessness. Connected to wealth because in the 1920s white clothing often required expensive laundering and care, the color is used by Fitzgerald to symbolize affluence as well as surface stainlessness or seeming purity. However, wealthy characters who wear white are often essentially corrupt and merely deceiving others through their pristine appearance.

Once again, in "Dalyrimple Goes Wrong," Fitzgerald has his finger on the pulse of his generation and its problems. Bryan Dalyrimple, the central character, is a highly decorated World War I hero who has just returned to his home town. Twenty-three years old, with two years at the state university, he needs to get a job and earn his living. Like Fitzgerald and most of his young, male contemporaries, Dalyrimple has no capital to invest or family business connections, and along with thousands of returning jobless soldiers, he faces a highly competitive workplace. A celebrity at his homecoming, Bryan finds that the vague promises of positions made to him have come to nothing. With only $14 in his pockets, he will have to settle quickly for any job that is offered.

The theme of disillusionment is introduced by Fitzgerald in a prelude to a story even before any characters have appeared. He asserts that an appropriate, philosophical book with "the flavor of Montaigne's essays and Samuel Butler's notebooks—and a little of Tolstoi and Marcus Aurelius" will, at some future time, be presented "to every young man on the date of his disillusion."

Dalyrimple's disillusionment begins almost immediately at his job interview with Theron G. Macy, the prosperous and smug owner of the town's biggest wholesale grocery house. Bryan's interview with Macy dramatizes the humiliation of needing to ask for work, since Macy feels free to criticize the young man's poor timing and to disparage his past experience. Bryan regrets thanking his prospective employer at the end of their conversation, and clearly the nature of their relationship has been established. It is that of a young subordinate addressing the person who has power over him.

Bryan's situation may well have paralleled that of Fitzgerald's father, Edward Fitzgerald, with his father-in-law, Philip McQuillan, a wealthy wholesale grocer in St. Paul. Edward was fired by Proctor and Gamble when Scott was twelve years old, and the traumatized boy feared they would end up in the "poorhouse." The family returned to St. Paul, where Edward, probably through his relationship to the McQuillans, became a wholesale grocery salesman who eked out a minimal living.

Fitzgerald's resentment of the undeserved privilege and power of the wealthy appeared early in his work and was neither casual nor superficial. He recalled scenes of his early childhood in Buffalo in which his father's lack of money had humiliating social ramifications. Fitzgerald commented: "I did not understand at all why men that I knew were vulgar and not gentlemen made him stand up or give the better chair on our veranda. But I know now."

Bryan Dalyrimple's experience with Theron Macy's firm intensifies his disillusionment. He had been told by Macy that he would learn the stockroom, then work in the office, then travel for the company. A fellow employee who has worked at the concern for four years, Charley Moore, enlightens Bryan that Macy promises all his new employees those opportunities to learn the business, but nothing comes of the promises. Additionally, Dalyrimple finds that his monthly salary of $40 is insufficient and will barely cover his expenses. In order to earn even this subsistence amount, he is compelled to work from 7:00 A.M. to 5:30 P.M. and, occasionally, to stay until 9:00 P.M. As a Macy employee, he is prohibited from going out to enjoy a cigarette and threatened that, if he does so, he will be reported to his employer.

Bryan accidentally discovers, in contrast, that Tom Everett, Macy's nephew, had been hired for $60 a month, and within three weeks had been promoted from the packing room to the office. Dalyrimple's frustration and anger lead to a problematic series of actions and the surprising offer of a new career. Certainly, in this story of one young man's "American Dream," Fitzgerald dramatizes the inevitable disillusionment of those who believe that ability, hard work, virtue, and high principles are always the qualities that earn respect and rewards in America.

IV

"Myra Meets His Family," "The Offshore Pirate," and "The Camel's Back" have three elements in common. All are stories of courtship of wealthy young people, all involve some element of disguise or deception, and all have surprise endings. Some of Fitzgerald's theatrical experiences while he was a student at Princeton may have inspired his depiction of elaborate costumes, makeup, and disguised characters. At the university, he was an influential member of the Triangle Club, the respected extracurricular drama organization whose members produced and acted in elaborate musicals. All of the roles, male and female, were performed by the young male students, and Fitzgerald himself posed for publicity photographs as the "Most Beautiful 'Show Girl' in the Princeton Triangle Club's New Musical Play 'The Evil Eye.'" Thus, the motif of creating and acting out a character role probably seemed much less far-fetched to the young writer than it might seem to modern readers.

In the best of the three tales, "Myra Meets His Family," Myra Harper, a pretty and spirited debutante from Cleveland, has been attending dances and going to matinées with Ivy League bachelors for five years. Now twenty-one years old, she feels that she has become jaded and is aware that she is getting a reputation as a husband hunter. She explains to her married friend, who was her roommate at school, that she has grown tired of her round of pointless dates:

> "Funny, Lilah, but I do feel ancient. Up at New Haven last spring men danced with me that seemed like little boys—and once I overheard a girl say in the dressing room, 'There's Myra Harper! She's been coming here for eight years.' Of course she was about three years off, but it did give me the calendar blues."

Myra's attraction to Knowleton Whitney seems to be based on a real appreciation of his good traits as well as a calculated appraisal of his affluent family and social position. She notes that "he's smart as a whip, and shy—rather sweetly shy," and she speedily accomplishes her objective of becoming engaged to this highly eligible bachelor.

When Myra journeys to Westchester County, New York, for a week's visit to the estate of her wealthy fiancé's parents, she finds a household that is both extraordinary and unpleasant. Her response to one unexpected situation is a good index to her spunky character. When she is called upon to perform in an amateur vaudeville show organized by Knowleton's father, she brushes aside her feelings of embarrassment and confusion. Angered by the rude treatment she has received as a guest, she nevertheless decides to perform:

> As she sang a spirit of ironic humor slowly took possession of her—a desire to give them all a run for their money. And she did. She injected an East Side snarl into every word of slang; she ragged; she shimmied; she did a tickle-toe step she had learned once in an amateur musical comedy; and in a burst of inspiration finished up in an Al Jolson position, on her knees with her arms stretched out to her audience in syncopated appeal.

As this scene demonstrates, when Myra is angry, she employs her sense of humor and innovation to cope with the situation.

Fitzgerald portrays Myra with some ambiguity. Clearly not overwhelmed by romantic love for Knowleton, she does find him attractive. Her fiancé describes the effect Myra had on him during their whirlwind courtship: "You were the first girl in my life whom I ever thought of marrying. You intoxicated me, Myra. It was just as though you were making me love you by some invisible force." In response to this declaration, Myra murmurs, "I was."

Is Myra a manipulative gold digger who deserves to fail in her aim of marrying Knowleton, or is she a beautiful, lively flapper worthy of our admiration? With her good self-image, pride, and sense of humor, Myra emerges from her adventures at the Whitneys' estate as an undaunted, imaginative young woman, ready to face the future. Fitzgerald seems to have grown increasingly fond of his heroine as the story progresses, and so do we.

In "The Offshore Pirate," Fitzgerald's debutante heroine, Ardita Farnam, has been raised in luxurious surroundings by her aunt and uncle. A nineteen-year-old blonde, she is "slender and supple, with a spoiled alluring mouth and quick gray eyes full of a radiant curiosity." At first she appears to be an enviable flapper. But she and her uncle are engaged in an unpleasant battle of wills over whether she will marry the man she has chosen, a suitor whom Mr. Farnam considers a notorious libertine. During one of their heated arguments about her infatuation, Ardita tells her uncle to shut up, then throws a book at him, and finally hits him in the neck with half a lemon.

A major problem with this story centers about Fitzgerald's attitude towards this young "golden girl." Certainly she is beautiful, determined, intelligent, and rebellious. As the story opens, she is reading Anatole France's *The Revolt of the Angels* in French. Later in the story, she demonstrates the kind of physical courage that Fitzgerald admired in his wife, Zelda, when she dives gracefully from a rock ledge some forty feet above the ocean.

She is hardly a sympathetic character, however. Her rude behavior with her uncle seems less a glorious attempt to revolt against the older generation than a crude and ugly show of temper. Fitzgerald here, as elsewhere in his fiction, seems to overvalue a girl's physical attractiveness. In the midst of their heated exchange, Mr. Farnam looks at Ardita "and then all at once something in the utter childishness of her beauty seemed to puncture his anger like an inflated tire and render him helpless, uncertain, utterly fatuous."

"The Offshore Pirate," highly popular in its time and turned into a Hollywood film of the same title, has not stood the test of time as well as many of the other early stories of Fitzgerald. Some of the flaws in the story are inherent in the material the author chose. He possibly considered the story a farce with literary roots in novels such as *Treasure Island* and *Peter Pan.* He also may have intended the story as a parody of the popular romances of his youth in which a wealthy girl's lowly suitor is really an aristocrat or a millionaire's son in disguise. In that case, Fitzgerald's problems with characterization result from a conflict between his intention to satirize Ardita and Curtis Carlyle and his desire to make them appealing and exciting so that readers would identify with them and enjoy their adventure.

The third story in this group, "The Camel's Back," like "Myra Meets His Family" and "The Offshore Pirate," depicts the behavior of affluent young people with assured social status. Perry Parkhurst is a Harvard graduate, a twenty-eight-year-old lawyer who lives in Toledo. He has been secretly engaged to the belle of Toledo society, Betty Medill. A typical lovely Fitzgerald debutante, she has "tawny eyes and hair." The costume she wears to the Townsends' circus ball, that of an Egyptian snake charmer, is a good index of her beauty and self-assurance, tinged with a touch of the flapper's rebellion against old-fashioned standards of modesty and decorum:

> Her tawny hair was braided and drawn through brass rings, the effect crowned with a glittering Oriental tiara. Her fair face was stained into a warm olive glow and on her bare arms and the half moon of her back writhed painted serpents with single eyes of venomous green. Her feet were in sandals and her skirt was slit to the knees, so that when she walked one caught a glimpse of other slim serpents painted just above her bare ankles. Wound about her neck was a huge, glittering, cotton-stuffed cobra, and her bracelets were in the form of tiny garter snakes. Altogether a very charming and beautiful costume— one that made the more nervous among the older women shrink away from her when she passed, and the more troublesome ones to make great talk about "shouldn't be allowed" and "perfectly disgraceful."

The flirtation she initiates with the camel, believing it to be the costume of an interesting bachelor guest of the Tates, Warren Butterfield, is typical of the attitudes of a number of Fitzgerald's heroines towards men.

Early in the story, Fitzgerald supplies a catalogue of the social activities available to Perry and Betty during the Christmas holiday season of 1919. They include "forty-one dinner parties, sixteen dances, six luncheons, male and female, twelve teas, four stag dinners, two weddings, and thirteen bridge parties." On the evening of the story, the Howard Tates are hosting an elaborate party for a college-age crowd while the guests at the Townsends' circus ball have emptied the shelves of the local costume rental shop. Although this Fitzgerald tale relies heavily on plot, with only sketchy character development, it provides yet another glimpse into the pleasure-filled world of the wealthy.

V

Two of the less successful stories in this collection, "The Smilers" and "The Four Fists," have two features in common: they are episodic in structure and moralistic in content. The episodes of "The Smilers" are scenes of Sylvester Stockton's brief encounters on the same day with three people: Betty Tearle, Waldron Crosby, and Jerry, who is Sylvester's hotel waiter. Next, three additional scenes depicting crises in the lives of these individuals illustrate the gulf between outward appearance and the reality of the characters' lives. Thus, the themes of the story are about the unhappiness people endure, the superficiality of relationships, and the extent to which people purposely protect their hidden, personal lives. The themes are somewhat parallel to those of E. A. Robinson's well-known poem "Richard Cory." Unfortunately, Fitzgerald's sketches of the characters are too perfunctory to involve the reader very deeply. But even in this brief story of diverse characters, the author introduces one of his central preoccupations: the destructive consequences when a man lacks the money to win the woman of his choice.

"The Four Fists" is a sort of miniature *bildungsroman*, a tale of a young man's coming of age and of his education about appropriate social behavior as well as humane and moral values. The earliest of Samuel Meredith's four encounters occurs when he is fourteen years of age and arrives with all his snobbish pretentions at an exclusive preparatory school. The last of the encounters occurs when he is thirty-five, and that experience, in San Antonio, does not so much teach Meredith about moral behavior as give him an opportunity to discover how principled a person he has become. There is, perhaps, a poignant simplicity about Meredith's real estate negotiations and his direct relationship with his employer. Readers familiar with today's levels of impersonal corporate plans and contracts may well find the depiction of Meredith's personal business influence to reflect an idealistic, less complicated—almost quaint—era.

It is also interesting to note that throughout his career, Fitzgerald had a somewhat odd view about physical blows as a corrective to immoral or repulsive behavior. "The Four Fists" is a germinal story in that it anticipates two scenes in his later fiction: the beating administered to Anthony Patch in *The Beautiful and Damned* and that of Dick Diver in *Tender Is the Night*.

VI

Three of the stories in this collection, "Head and Shoulders," "The Lees of Happiness," and "The Cut-Glass Bowl," are histories of marriages. Although the experiences of the three married couples are very different, all have one thing in common.

Each marriage turns out, sooner or later, to be disappointing or even destructive, a far cry from the ideal of marital happiness that spurred these characters to marry. Intriguingly, these portraits of married life were written either during the months when Fitzgerald was pressing Zelda to resume their broken engagement or during the first few months after their marriage. Perhaps some of Fitzgerald's reservations about the effects of marriage on a writer or about Zelda's suitability for wifehood are expressed in these stories.

"Head and Shoulders" depicts the meeting, courtship, and married life of Horace Tarbox, almost eighteen years old, and Marcia Meadow, a nineteen-year-old actress. Marcia has a number of the desirable qualities of the typical Fitzgerald heroine. Beautiful and high-spirited, with natural blond hair, she astonishes Horace with "the freshness and originality of her mind, her dynamic, clear-headed energy and her unfailing good humor."

But Marcia is not a true "golden girl," not really the appropriate spouse in Fitzgerald's cosmos for a brilliant young man working on a Yale master's degree. She does not come from the right social class, and the author employs several telltale characteristics as reminders that although Marcia is a successful Broadway musical star, she began as a waitress in a Trenton, New Jersey, tearoom. First, the apartment she has furnished for herself reveals her lack of good taste. There is a glaring lack of harmony in her possessions, and the "nice things" she has bought are "unrelentingly hostile to each other, offsprings of a vicarious, impatient taste acting in stray moments."

The second signal that Marcia comes from an inferior social sphere is her occasional lapse in pronunciation or word choice. She substitutes "ats" for "that's," "I got" for "I've got," pronounces "American" as "Amuricum," "remember" as "member," and "couple of" as "cupla." At one point, she tells Horace "I wish we was there [in his room] now."

Most important, although Horace has become obsessed with Marcia, he is also disgusted by the shimmy she performs on stage. She has always thought of her shaking her shoulders as a kind of acrobatic stunt, but Horace sees her dance as erotic and degrading. He tells her bluntly that when he attended the show, "the people behind me were making remarks about your bosom."

Interestingly, Fitzgerald has an important double standard for his male and female characters. He has considerable sympathy for lower- or middle-class males, such as Jim Powell of "The Jelly-Bean" or Dexter Green in "Winter Dreams," when they become strongly attracted to wealthy debutantes. On the other hand, working-class women almost always have an unsavory or tainted element about them and are a destructive force in the lives of the men attracted to them. Gloria Hudson of "May Day" and Dorothy Raycroft of *The Beautiful and Damned* are two typical examples of this sort of woman.

Marcia, however, fares much better than most of the other Fitzgerald women of her social status. Her husband's reaction to the far-reaching changes in his life might well be interpreted as a reaction to the demands of marriage rather than as an indictment of Marcia.

In "The Lees of Happiness," Fitzgerald depicted the married lives of two couples, Roxanne and Jeffrey Curtain, the central characters, and their close friend Harry Cromwell and his wife, Kitty. After a year of marriage, Jeffrey, the successful author of a novel and a number of short stories, and his beautiful wife, Roxanne, a talented actress who has given up her stage career, decide to buy a house and settle down outside of Chicago. Fitzgerald idealizes their intensely romantic first year of marriage, explaining that they

> loved and quarreled gently, and kissed and gloried in the golden triflings of his wit and her beauty—they were young and gravely passionate; they were companions inseparable; they yielded all and demanded all and then yielded again in ecstasies of unselfishness and pride. She loved the swift tones of his voice, his summer tan, his frantic, unfounded jealousy. He loved her dark radiance, the white irises of her eyes, the warm, lustrous enthusiasm of her smile.

In contrast, Harry's marriage, now in its second year, is an example of the dream turned into a nightmare. When Roxanne visits Kitty Cromwell for the first and only time, she finds a superficially pretty woman, but she is revolted by the dirt and vulgar taste displayed by her friend's wife. The kimono Kitty wears is "vilely unclean." Roxanne is certain that the woman's neck is also dirty. When Harry and Kitty's little son, George, joins them Roxanne is outraged to see that this slovenly woman has failed to care for the toddler. He is dressed in "dirty pink rompers," his shoes are torn, his face is smudged, and his nose needs wiping.

By the second year of his marriage, Harry is in despair and knows the relationship must end: "Suddenly he hated her. He wanted to throw her down and kick at her—to tell her she was a cheat and a leech—that she was dirty. Moreover, she must give him his boy."

Clearly the dedicated and charming wife, Roxanne, and the unpleasant and selfish wife, Kitty, are foils for one another. In fact, Roxanne might well be described as a male fantasy of the perfect, selfless, angelic spouse, and although she is in no way responsible for the tragedy that befalls her husband, it is interesting that both he and Horace Tarbox of "Head and Shoulders" have married beautiful actresses and that both never experience the kind of fulfilling married life they had joyfully anticipated.

In "The Cut-Glass Bowl," the least artistic of the three stories of marriages, Fitzgerald employs a large punch bowl as a symbol. It was a wedding gift that a rejected suitor, Carleton Canby, had given Evylyn upon her marriage to Harold Piper seven years before the opening of the story. At the time, Canby told Evylyn that the present he would choose for her would be "as hard as you are and as beautiful and as empty and as easy to see through."

The structure of the story is episodic, with scenes in the Piper household that occur when Evylyn is twenty-seven, thirty-five, and forty-six years of age. Fitzgerald chronicles the death of love between the couple as well as three tragedies, but his attempt to depict the punch bowl as an active agent causing all of Evylyn's misery seems far-fetched. And although Evylyn's behavior before the story opens in carrying on an affair for six months renders her somewhat unsympathetic, she is never the "hard" and "empty" beauty of her onetime suitor's description. In fact, one failing of the tale appears to be that Evylyn Piper's suffering seems so unconnected to her actions or decisions in the story. On the other hand, it is possible that Fitzgerald's 1920s audience may well have viewed the series of disasters that befall the Piper family as Evylyn's inexorable punishment for having been an adulteress. In American literature, until recent decades, the price exacted of women for sexual transgressions, or even the appearance of sexual misconduct, has been death, as the fates of Henry James's Daisy Miller and Edith Wharton's Lily Bart will attest.

Prophetically, in "The Cut-Glass Bowl" as in "May Day" and several other stories, Fitzgerald dramatizes the destructive consequences of alcoholism. Several of his unhappy characters such as Harold Piper seek solace in drinking, while others, usually college boys at parties, drink excessively in order to have a good time. But the drunk man often becomes a social embarrassment.

Scott and Zelda discovered early in their marriage that they often consumed too much liquor when they went out as well as when they entertained guests. They resented the debilitating consequences of evenings of heavy drinking, but craved the excitement of those evenings and felt that they needed the stimulation of alcohol to be at their best and to live as fully as they could. Thus, Fitzgerald's alcoholic binges were followed by vows of sobriety aimed at creating a quiet, productive lifestyle.

VII

After publishing the fifteen stories collected in this volume— stories that reflect an amazing period of imaginative fecundity and literary energy—F. Scott Fitzgerald enjoyed only two decades as one of America's best-known writers. In one way, the promise of his glittering career in 1920 was fulfilled with his publication of 145 additional stories and four novels, *This Side of Paradise*, *The Beautiful and Damned*, *The Great Gatsby*, and *Tender Is the Night.* But the strain of supporting Zelda and himself, and later their daughter, Scottie, by his writing took a terrible toll. Trying to combine an idealized extravagant and carefree existence with that of a disciplined and productive writer, Fitzgerald suffered chronic disillusionment and disappointment. In 1930, a decade after their exuberant marriage, Zelda was hospitalized with schizophrenia, which would prove incurable, and Scott was plagued by problems with alcoholism, bankruptcy, and an inability to write as he wished. In 1940, while at work on a novel he never finished, *The Last Tycoon,* Fitzgerald suffered a fatal heart attack. Zelda died in 1948 in a fire at the mental hospital where she was staying.

The lives of the Fitzgeralds have, ironically, become intertwined with those of Scott's heroes and heroines who dreamed "The American Dream," who gloried in the changes the 1920s brought about, who believed in the quest for true love, and who faced the future with a zest for life and high hopes for golden days to come. They have become poignant emblems of the era that Scott Fitzgerald depicted so vividly in his early short stories.

—Barbara H. Solomon
Iona College
New Rochelle, New York

A Note on the Text

The first seven of the stories in this volume are reprinted from the 1919–20 magazines and newspaper in which they originally appeared. The other eight stories comprise *Flappers and Philosophers*, Fitzgerald's first collection of stories, published in 1920, and have been reprinted from that book.

Collections of Fitzgerald's Stories

Flappers and Philosophers (1920)
Tales of the Jazz Age (1922)
All the Sad Young Men (1926)
Taps at Reveille (1935)
The Stories of F. Scott Fitzgerald (1951)
Afternoon of an Author: A Selection of Uncollected Stories and Essays (1958)
The Pat Hobby Stories (1962)

Selected Works About
F. Scott Fitzgerald

Allen, Joan M. *Candles and Carnival Lights: The Catholic Sensibility of F. Scott Fitzgerald.* New York: New York University Press, 1978.

Bruccoli, Matthew J. *Some Sort of Epic Grandeur: The Life of F. Scott Fitzgerald.* New York: Harcourt Brace Jovanovich, 1981.

Bryer, Jackson R., ed. *F. Scott Fitzgerald: The Critical Reception.* New York: Burt Franklin, 1978.

———. *The Short Stories of F. Scott Fitzgerald: New Approaches in Criticism.* Madison: University of Wisconsin Press, 1982.

Cowley, Malcolm, and Robert Cowley. *Fitzgerald and the Jazz Age.* New York: Charles Scribner's Sons, 1966.

Cross, K.G.W. *F. Scott Fitzgerald.* New York: Capricorn, 1971.

Donaldson, Scott. *Fool for Love: F. Scott Fitzgerald.* New York: Congdon & Weed, 1983.

Eble, Kenneth. *F. Scott Fitzgerald,* rev. ed. Boston: Twayne, 1977.

Gallo, Rose Adrienne. *F. Scott Fitzgerald.* New York: Frederick Ungar, 1978.

Goldhurst, William. *F. Scott Fitzgerald and His Contemporaries.* New York: World, 1963.

Higgens, John A. *F. Scott Fitzgerald: A Study of the Stories.* Jamaica, New York: St. John's University Press, 1971.

Kazin, Alfred, ed. *F. Scott Fitzgerald: The Man and His Work.* New York: Collier, 1962.

Kuehl, John Richard. *F. Scott Fitzgerald: A Study of the Short Fiction.* Boston: Twayne, 1991.

Lehan, Richard D. *F. Scott Fitzgerald and the Craft of Fiction.* Carbondale: Southern Illinois University Press, 1966.

LeVot, Andre. *F. Scott Fitzgerald: A Biography.* Garden City, New York: Doubleday, 1983.

Mangum, Bryant. *A Fortune Yet: Money in the Art of F. Scott Fitzgerald's Short Stories.* New York: Garland, 1991.

Mellow, James R. *Invented Lives: F. Scott & Zelda Fitzgerald.* Boston: Houghton Mifflin, 1984.

Meyers, Jeffrey. *Scott Fitzgerald: A Biography.* New York: HarperCollins, 1994.

Milford, Nancy. *Zelda.* New York: Avon, 1970.

Miller, James E., Jr. *F. Scott Fitzgerald: His Art and His Technique.* New York: New York University Press, 1964.

Mizener, Arthur. *The Far Side of Paradise: A Biography of F. Scott Fitzgerald,* 2d ed. Boston: Houghton Mifflin, 1965.

Perosa, Sergio. *The Art of F. Scott Fitzgerald,* trans. Charles Matz and Sergio Perosa. Ann Arbor: University of Michigan Press, 1965.

Petry, Ann Hall. *Fitzgerald's Craft of Short Fiction: The Collected Stories, 1920–1935.* Ann Arbor: UMI Research Press, 1989.

Piper, Henry Dan. *F. Scott Fitzgerald: A Critical Portrait.* New York: Holt, Rinehart and Winston, 1965.

Shain, Charles E. *F. Scott Fitzgerald.* Minneapolis: University of Minnesota Press, 1961.

Sklar, Robert. *F. Scott Fitzgerald: The Last Laocoon.* New York: Oxford University Press, 1967.

Stavola, Thomas J. *Scott Fitzgerald: Crisis in an American Identity.* New York: Barnes and Noble, 1979.

Stern, Milton R. *The Golden Moment: The Novels of F. Scott Fitzgerald.* Urbana: University of Illinois Press, 1970.

Turnbull, Andrew. *Scott Fitzgerald.* New York: Scribner's, 1962.

Way, Brian. *F. Scott Fitzgerald and the Art of Social Fiction.* New York: St. Martin's, 1980.

May Day

There had been a war fought and won and the great city of the conquering people was crossed with triumphal arches and vivid with thrown flowers of white, red and rose. All through the long Spring days the returning soldiers marched up the chief highway behind the strump of drums and the joyous, resonant wind of the brasses, while merchants and clerks left their bickerings and figurings and, crowding to the windows, turned their white-bunched faces gravely upon the passing battalions.

Never had there been such splendor in the great city, for the victorious war had brought plenty in its train, and the merchants had flocked thither from the South and West with their households to taste of all the luscious feasts and witness the lavish entertainments prepared—and to buy for their women furs against the next winter and bags of golden mesh and vari-coloured slippers of silk, satin, and marvelously-wrought leather.

So gayly and noisily were the peace and prosperity impending hymned by the scribes and poets of the conquering people that more and more spenders had gathered from the provinces to drink the wine of excitement, and faster and faster did the merchants dispose of their trinkets and slippers until they sent up a mighty cry for more trinkets and more slippers in order that they might give in barter what was demanded of them. Some even of them flung up their hands helplessly, shouting:

"Alas! I have no more slippers! and alas! I have no more trinkets! May heaven help me for I know not what I shall do!"

But no one listened to their great outcry for the throngs were far too busy—day by day, the foot-soldiers trod jauntily the highway and all exulted because the young men returning were pure and brave, sound of tooth and pink of cheek, and the young women of the land were virgins and comely both of face and of figure.

So during all this time there were many adventures that happened in the great city and it is one of these that is here set down.

CHAPTER I

At nine o'clock on the morning of the first of May, 1919, a young man spoke to the room clerk at the Biltmore Hotel, asking if Mr. Philip Cory were registered there, and if so, could he be connected with Mr. Cory's rooms. The inquirer was dressed in a well-cut but quite shabby suit. He was slender and darkly handsome; his eyes were framed above with unusually long eyelashes and below with the blue semi-circle of ill health, this latter effect heightened by an unnatural glow which colored his face like a low incessant fever.

Mr. Cory was staying there. The young man was directed to a telephone at the side.

After a second his connection was made; a sleepy voice hello'd from somewhere above.

"Mr. Cory?"—this very eagerly—"It's Gordon, Phil. It's Gordon Sterrett. I'm down stairs. I heard you were in New York and I had a hunch you'd be here."

The sleepy voice became gradually enthusiastic. Well, how was Gordy, old boy! Well, he sure was surprised and tickled! Would Gordy come right up, for Pete's sake!

A few minutes later Cory, dressed in blue silk pajamas, opened the door and they greeted each other with a half-embarrassed exuberance still vaguely collegiate. They were both about twenty-four, Yale graduates of the year before the war, but there the resemblance stopped abruptly. Cory was blond, ruddy, and rugged under this thin pajamas. Everything about him from his firm step as he moved about the room to the hard grip of his hand radiated fitness and bodily comfort. He smiled frequently, showing large and prominent teeth.

"I was going to look you up," he cried enthusiastically. "I'm taking a couple of weeks off. If you'll sit down a sec I'll be right with you. I'm going to take a shower."

As he vanished into the bathroom his visitor's dark eyes roved nervously around the room, resting for a moment on a great English traveling bag in the corner and on a family of thick silk shirts littered on the chairs amid impressive neckties and soft-ribbed woolen socks.

Gordon rose nervously and, picking up one of the shirts, gave it a minute examination. It was of very heavy silk, yellow, with a pale blue stripe—and there were nearly a dozen of them. He glanced involuntarily at his own shirt-cuffs—they were ragged and linty at the edges and soiled to a faint gray. Dropping the silk shirt he held his coat sleeves down and worked the frayed shirt-cuffs up 'til they were out of sight. Then he went to the mirror and looked at himself with a listless, unhappy interest. His suit had once been excellent; at present it shone with use; his tie, also of former glory, was faded and thumb-creased—it served no longer to hide the jagged button-holes of his collar. He thought, quite without amusement, that only three years before he had received a scattering vote in the senior elections at college for being the best-dressed man in his class.

Cory emerged from the bathroom polishing his body with hearty meticulousness.

"Saw an old friend of yours last night," he commenced jovially. "Passed her in the lobby and couldn't think of her name to save my neck. That girl you brought up to New Haven senior year."

Gordon started.

"Edith Bradin? That who you mean?"

"'At's the one. Damn good looking. She's still sort of a pretty doll—you know what I mean: 'if you touch her she smears.'"

He surveyed his shining self complacently in the mirror and smiled faintly, exposing a section of teeth.

"She must be twenty-three anyway," he continued.

"Twenty-two last month," said Gordon absently.

"What? Oh, last month. Well, I imagine she's down for the Gamma Psi dance. Did you know there's a Gamma Psi dance tonight at Delmonico's? You better come up, Gordy. Half of New Haven'll probably be there. I can get you an invitation."

Draping himself reluctantly in B. V. D.'s, Cory lit a cigarette and sat down in a big chair by the open window, inspecting his calves and knees carelessly in the morning sunshine which poured into the room.

"Sit down, Gordy," he suggested, "and tell me all about what you've been doing and what you're doing now and everything."

Gordon collapsed unexpectedly upon the bed; lay there inert and spiritless, a picture of utter misery. His mouth, which habitually dropped a little open when his face was in repose, became suddenly helpless and pathetic.

"What's the matter?" asked Cory quickly.

"Oh, God!"

"What's the matter?"

"Everything," he said miserably, "every damn thing in the world. I've absolutely gone to pieces, Phil. I'm all in."

"Huh?"

"I'm all in." His voice was shaking.

Cory scrutinized him more closely with appraising blue eyes.

"You certainly look all shot."

"I am. I've made one hell of a mess of everything." He paused. "I'd better start at the beginning—or will it bore you?"

"Not at all; go on." There was, however, a hesitant note in Cory's voice. This trip east had been planned for a holiday—to find Gordon Sterrett in trouble ruffled him a little, exasperated him.

"Go on," he repeated, and then added half under his breath, "Get it over with."

"Well," began Gordon unsteadily, "I got back from France in February, went home to Harrisburg for a month and then came down to New York to get a job. I got one—with an export company. They fired me yesterday."

"Fired you?"

"I'm coming to that, Phil. I want to tell you frankly. You're about the only man I can turn to in a matter like this. You won't mind if I just tell you frankly, will you, Phil?"

Cory stiffened a bit more. The pats he was bestowing on his knees grew perfunctory. He felt vaguely that he was being unfairly saddled with responsibility; he was not even sure he wanted to be told. Though never surprised at finding Gordon Sterrett in some sort of difficulty, there was something in this present misery that repelled him and hardened him, even though it excited his curiosity.

"Go on."

"It's a girl."

"Hm." Cory made a quick resolution that nothing was going to spoil his trip. If Gordon was going to be depressing, then he'd just have to see less of Gordon—that was all.

"Her name is Gloria Hudson," went on the distressed voice from the bed. "She—used to be decent, I guess, up to about a year ago. Lived here in New York—poor family. Her people are dead now and she lives with an old aunt. You see it was just about the time I met her that all my friends and acquaintances began to come back from France in droves—and all I did was to welcome the newly arrived and go to parties with 'em. That's the way it started, Phil, just from being glad to see everybody and having them glad to see me."

"You ought to've had more sense."

"I know," Gordon paused, and then continued listlessly, "but everything seemed to go wrong. I'm on my own now, you know, and Phil, I can't stand being poor. I'd get a few drinks in me and somehow, somehow the struggle'd seem a little more dignified. Then came this darn girl. She sort of fell in love with me for awhile and, though I never intended to get so involved, whenever I'd get a little tight I'd run into her somewhere. You can imagine the sort of work I was doing for those exporting people—sometimes I'd come into that office white as a sheet without even having closed my eyes all night. Of course, I always intended to draw; do illustrating for magazines; there's a pile of money in it."

"Why didn't you?"

"Why, I never seemed to get around to it."

"You've got to buckle down if you want to make good," suggested Cory coolly.

"I tried, a little, but my stuff's crude. I've got talent, Phil; I can draw—but I just don't know how. I ought to go to art school and I can't afford it. Well, things came to a crisis about a week ago. Just as I was down to about my last dollar this girl began bothering me. She wants some money; claims she can make trouble for me if she doesn't get it."

"Can she?"

"I'm afraid she can. That's one reason I lost my job—she kept calling up the office all the time, and that was sort of the last straw down there. She's got a letter all written to send to my family. Oh, she's got me, all right. I've got to have some money for her."

There was an awkward pause.

Gordon lay very still, his hands clenched by his side, his eyes showing up large and dark in his feverish face.

"I'm all in," he continued, his voice trembling. "I'm half crazy, Phil. If I hadn't known you were coming east, I think

I'd have killed myself. I want you to lend me five hundred dollars."

Cory's hands, which had been absently patting his bare ankle, suddenly stopped—and the curious uncertainty playing between the two became strained and taut.

After a second Gordon continued:

"I've bled the family until I'm ashamed to ask 'em for another nickel."

Still Cory made no answer.

"Gloria says she's got to have two hundred dollars."

"Tell her where she can go."

"Yes, that sounds easy, but she's got a couple of drunken letters I wrote her. Unfortunately she's not at all the flabby sort of person you'd expect."

Cory made an expression of distaste.

"I can't stand that sort of woman. You ought to have kept away."

"I know," admitted Gordon wearily.

"You've got to look at things as they are. If you haven't got money you've got to work and stay away from liquor and women."

"That's easy for you to say," began Gordon, his eyes narrowing, "you've got all the money in the world."

"I most certainly have not. My family keep darn close tab on what I spend. Just because I have a little leeway I have to be extra careful not to abuse it."

Gordon laughed bitterly.

"I don't know," he said, "maybe you're right. But it just seems as if everything had combined against me—everything. I didn't want to get stewed most of the time, but I got so damn lonely and before I knew it I'd be thinking what's the use, why not be happy this evening anyhow."

Cory raised the blind and let in a further flood of sunshine.

"I'm no prig, Lord knows," he said deliberately. "I like a highball—and I like a lot of 'em on a vacation like this, but you're—you're in awful shape. I never heard you talk just this way before. There's an air about you of—of weakness."

"I know."

"You seem to be sort of bankrupt—morally as well as financially."

"Don't they usually go together?"

Cory shook his head impatiently.

"There's a regular aura about you that I don't understand. It's a sort of evil."

"It's an air of poverty and sleepless nights and too much liquor," said Gordon, rather defiantly.

"I don't know."

"Oh, I admit I'm depressing. I depress myself. But, my God, Phil, a week's rest and a new suit and some ready money and I'd be like—like I was. Phil, I can draw like a streak, and you know it. But half the time I haven't had the money to buy decent drawing materials—and I can't draw when I'm tired and discouraged and all in. With a little ready money I can take a few weeks off and get started."

"How do I know you wouldn't use it to get drunk with?"

"Why rub it in?" said Gordon quietly.

"I'm not rubbing it in. I hate to see you this way."

"Will you lend me the money, Phil?"

"I can't decide right off. That's a lot of money and it'll be darn inconvenient for me."

"It'll be hell for me if you can't—oh, I know I'm whining, and it's all my own fault but—that doesn't change it."

"When could you pay it back?"

This was encouraging. Gordon considered. It was probably wisest to be frank.

"Of course, I could promise to send it back next month, but—I'd better say three months. Just as soon as I start to sell drawings."

"How do I know you'll sell any drawings?"

Some new quality of hardness in Cory's voice sent a faint chill of doubt over Gordon. Was it possible that he wouldn't get the money?

"I supposed you had a little confidence in me."

"I did have—but when I see you like this I begin to wonder. I'm hanged if I'll help you to make a drunken bum of yourself."

"Do you suppose if I wasn't at the end of my rope I'd come to you like this? Do you think I'm enjoying it?" He broke off and bit his lip, feeling that he had better subdue the rising anger in his voice. After all, he was the suppliant.

"You seem to manage it pretty easily," said Cory angrily. "You put me in the position where, if I don't lend it to you, I'm a sucker—oh, yes you do. And let me tell you it's no easy thing for me to get hold of five hundred dollars. My income isn't so big but that a slice like that won't play the deuce with it."

He left his chair and began to dress, choosing his clothes very carefully. Gordon stretched out his arms and clenched the edges of the bed, fighting back a desire to cry out. His head was splitting and whirring, his mouth was dry and bitter and he could feel the fever in his blood resolving itself into innumerable regular counts like a slow dripping from a roof.

Cory tied his tie carefully, brushed his eyebrows and removed a piece of tobacco from his teeth with an air of critical solemnity. Next he filled his cigarette case, tossed the empty box thoughtfully into the waste basket and settled the case in his vest pocket.

"Had breakfast?" he demanded, turning to Gordon.

"No; I don't eat it any more."

"Well, we'll go out and have some. We'll decide about that money later. I'm sick of the subject. I came east to have a good time."

"Let's go over to the Yale Club," he continued moodily, and then added with an implied reproof. "You've given up your job. You've nothing else to do."

"I'd have a lot to do if I had a little money," said Gordon pointedly.

"Oh, for heaven's sake drop the subject for a while. No point in glooming on my whole trip. Here, here's some money."

He took a five-dollar bill from his wallet and tossed it over to Gordon, who folded it carefully and put it in his pocket. There was an added spot of colour in his cheeks, an added glow that was not fever. For an instant before they turned to go out their eyes met and in that instant each found something that made him lower his own glance quickly. For in that instant they quite definitely and completely hated each other.

CHAPTER II

Fifth Avenue, Forty-fourth Street and Madison Avenue swarmed with the noon crowd. A bright sun had shot through two days' cloudiness and glittered in transient gold through the thick windows of the smart shops, lighting upon mesh bags and purses and strings of pearls laid in grey velvet cases; upon gaudy feather fans of many colours; upon the laces and silks of expensive dresses; upon the great paintings and period furniture in the elaborate show rooms of interior decorators.

Gossiping shop-girls, in pairs and groups and swarms, loitered by these windows, choosing their future boudoirs from some resplendent display which included even a man's silk pajamas laid domestically across the bed. They stood in front of the jewelry stores and picked out their engagement rings and their wedding rings and their platinum wrist watches and then drifted on to inspect the feather fans and opera cloaks; most of them meanwhile digesting the sandwiches and sundaes that had comprised their lunch.

All through the crowd were men in uniform, sailors from the great fleet anchored in the Hudson, soldiers with divisional insignia from Massachusetts to Maine, wanting fearfully to be noticed and finding the great city perhaps a little fed up with soldiers unless they were nicely massed into pretty formations and staggering under the weight of a pack and rifle.

Through this medley Cory and Gordon wandered; the former interested, made alert by the display of humanity at its frothiest and gaudiest; the latter morose, blind to all except the ugliness that, to him, lay just beneath. He could not enjoy this crowd on the Avenue. Too often he had been one of the crowd, tired, casually fed, overworked and dissipated. To Cory the struggle was significant, young, cheerful; to Gordon it was dismal, meaningless, endless.

In the Yale Club they met a group of their former classmates who greeted Cory vociferously, and sitting around in a semi-circle of lounges and great chairs they had a highball all around.

Gordon, who took nothing to drink, found the conversation tiresome and interminable. They lunched together *en masse,* warmed with liquor as the afternoon began. They were all going to the Gamma Psi dance that night. It promised to be the best party since the war.

"Edith Bradin's coming," said someone, and turning to Gordon he added, "Didn't she used to be an old flame of yours? Aren't you both from Harrisburg?"

"Yes." He tried to change the subject—"I see her brother occasionally. He's sort of a socialistic nut. Runs a paper or something here in New York."

"Not like his gay sister, eh?"

"No."

"Well," continued his eager informant, "she's coming to-night with some undergraduate named Barton."

Gordon was to meet Gloria at eight o'clock—he had promised to have some money for her. Several times he glanced nervously at his wrist watch. At four o'clock, to his relief, Cory rose and announced that he was going over to Rivers Brothers to buy some collars and ties. But to Gordon's great dismay, as they left the Club another of the party joined them. Cory was in a jovial mood now, happy, expectant of the evening's party, faintly hilarious. Over in Rivers' he chose a dozen neckties, selecting each one after long deliberation and consultations with the other man. Did they think narrow ties were coming back? And wasn't it a shame that Rivers couldn't get any more Welsh Margotson collars? There never was a collar like the "Livingston."

Gordon was in something of a panic. He wanted the money right away. A vague idea of attending the Gamma Psi dance was becoming intermixed with his misery. He wanted to see Edith—Edith whom he hadn't met since one fairy night at the Harrisburg Country Club just before he went to France. Somehow the affair had died, drowned in the turmoil of the war and quite forgotten in the arabesque of these three months, but a picture of her, laughing, debonnaire, rambling on in her inconsequential chatter, flashed before him and brought a dozen memories with it. It was Edith's face that he had cherished through college with a sort of detached yet affectionate admiration. He had loved to draw her—around his room had been a dozen sketches of her—playing golf, in bathing—he could draw her pert, kindly profile with his eyes shut.

Yes, if he could get this money he could buy the essentials that would enable him to go to the dance and talk to her. That was what he needed after all, he thought—a good woman. But he must first have his dinner coat pressed, buy a dress shirt and some dancing slippers, redeem his pawned studs—and before all, he must settle with Gloria.

They left Rivers' at five-thirty and paused for a minute on the sidewalk.

"Well," said Cory genially, "I'm all set now. Think I'll go back to the hotel and get a shave, haircut and massage."

"Good enough," said the other man, "I think I'll join you."

Gordon wondered if he was to be beaten after all. With difficulty he restrained himself from turning to the man and

snarling out a "Go on away, damn you!" In despair he suspected that perhaps Cory had spoken to him, was keeping
him along in order to avoid a dispute about the money.

They went into the Biltmore—a Biltmore gay with girls;
Western girls with high colour and erect bodies, Southern
girls with soft voices and limpid intriguing eyes, Eastern
girls, bored and fashionable, and around them all stood the
men, very well set up and correctly dressed for the parade of
beauty. For these girls were in a measure the pick of East and
South, and West, the stellar débutantes of many cities gathered for the dance of a famous fraternity of a famous university.

But to Gordon they were faces in a dream. He gathered
together his forces for a last appeal, was about to come out
with he knew not what, when Cory suddenly excused himself
to the other man and taking Gordon's arm led him aside.

"Gordy," he said quickly, "I've thought the whole thing
over carefully and I've decided that I can't lend you that
money. I'd like to oblige you, but I don't feel I ought to—it'd
put a crimp in me for a month."

Gordon was watching him dully, wondering why he had
never before noticed how much those upper teeth projected.
If he hit him now he would catch him just on the point of the
two center ones.

"—I'm mighty sorry, Gordon," continued Cory, "but that's
the way it is."

He took out his wallet and hurriedly counted out seventy-
five dollars in bills.

"Here," he said, holding them out, "here's seventy-five;
that makes eighty all together. That's all the actual cash I
have with me besides what I'll actually spend on the trip."

Gordon raised his clenched hand automatically, opened it
as though it were a tongs he was holding, and clenched it
again on the money.

"I'll see you at the dance," continued Cory. "I've got to get
shaved now."

"So long," said Gordon in a strained and husky voice.

"So long."

Cory began to smile but seemed to change his mind. He
nodded briskly and disappeared.

But Gordon stood there, his handsome face awry with dis-
tress, the roll of bills clenched tightly in his hand. Then

blinded by sudden tears he stumbled clumsily down the Biltmore steps.

CHAPTER III

About nine o'clock of the same night two human beings came out of a cheap restaurant in Sixth Avenue. They were ugly, ill-formed, devoid of all except the very lowest form of intelligence and without even that animal exuberance that in itself may bring colour to the struggle of life; they were lately vermin-ridden, cold and hungry in a dirty town of a strange land; they were poor, friendless, and tossed as driftwood from their births, would be tossed as driftwood to their deaths. They were dressed in the uniform of the United States Army and on the shoulder of each was the insignia of a drafted division from New Jersey, landed three days before.

The taller of the two was named Carrol Key, a name hinting that in his veins, however thinly diluted by generations of degeneration, ran the blood of distinguished forebears. But one could stare endlessly at the long chinless face, the dull watery eyes and high cheekbones without finding a suggestion of either ancestral worth or native intelligence.

His companion was swart and bandy-legged with rat-eyes and a much broken hooked nose. His defiant air was obviously a pretense, a weapon of protection, borrowed from that world of snarl and snap, of physical bluff and physical menace, in which he had always lived. His name was Gus Rose.

Leaving the café they sauntered down Sixth Avenue, wielding toothpicks with great gusto and an air of complete detachment.

"Where to?" asked Rose in a tone which implied that he would not be surprised or opposed if Key mentioned the South Sea Islands.

"Whatcha say we see if we can getta holda some liquor?" The ginger in this suggestion was caused by the law forbidding the selling of liquor to soldiers.

Rose agreed enthusiastically.

"I got an idea," continued Key, after a moment's thought, "I got a brother somewhere."

"In New York?"

"Yeah. He's an old fella. He's a waiter in a hash joint."

"Let's us go there and maybe he can get us some."

"I'll say he will."

"B'lieve me, I'm goin' to get this darn uniform off me tomorra an' never get it on again, neither. I'm goin' to get me some regular clothes."

"Say, maybe I'm not."

As their combined finances were something less than five dollars, this intention can be taken largely as a pleasant game of words, harmless and consoling. It seemed to please both of them, however, for they reinforced it with chuckles and mentionings of people high in biblical circles, adding such further emphasis as "Oh, Boy!" "You know!" and "I'll say so!" repeated many times over.

The entire mental pabulum of these two men consisted of a pessimistic nasal comment extended through the years upon the attitude toward them of the institution—army, business or poorhouse—which kept them alive, and toward their immediate superior in that institution. Until that very morning the institution had been the "government" and the immediate superior had been the "Cap'n"—from these two they glided out and were now in the vaguely uncomfortable state before they should adopt their next bondage. They were uncertain, resentful and somewhat ill at ease. This they hid by pretending an elaborate relief at being out of the army, and by assuring each other that military discipline should never again rule their stubborn, liberty-loving wills. Yet, as a matter of fact, they would have felt more at home in a prison than in this complete and unquestioned new-found liberty.

Suddenly Key increased his gait. Rose, looking up and following his glance, discovered a crowd that was collecting fifty yards down the street. Key chuckled and began to run in the direction of the crowd; Rose thereupon also chuckled and broke into a run, his short bandy legs seeming to twinkle beside the long, awkward strides of his companion.

Reaching the outskirts of the crowd they immediately became an indistinguishable part of it. It was composed of ragged civilians somewhat the worse for liquor, and of soldiers representing many divisions and many stages of sobriety, all clustered around a gesticulating little Jew with long black whiskers, who was waving his arms and delivering an excited but quiet succinct harangue. Key and Rose, having wedged themselves into the approximate parquet, scrutinized him with acute suspicion as his words penetrated their consciousness.

"—What have you got outa the war?" he was crying

fiercely. "Look arounja, look arounja! Are you rich? Have you got a lot of money offered you?—no; you're lucky if you're alive and got both your legs; you're lucky if you came back an' fin' your wife ain't gone off with some other fella that had the money to buy himself out of the war! That's when you're lucky! Who got anything out of it except J. P. Morgan an' John D. Rockerfeller?"

At this point the little Jew's oration was interrupted by the hostile impact of a fist upon the point of his bearded chin and he toppled backward to a sprawl on the pavement.

"The damn Bolsheviki!" cried the big soldier with the arm of a blacksmith who had delivered the blow. There was a rumble of approval, the crowd closed in nearer.

The Jew staggered to his feet, and immediately went down again before a half-dozen reaching-in fists. This time he stayed down, breathing heavily, blood oozing from his lip where it was cut within and without.

There was a riot of voices.

"Too many of those damn suckers!"

"We ought to kill the dirty bums!"

"Damn filthy Russian Jews."

In a minute Rose and Key found themselves flowing with the jumbled crowd down Sixth Avenue under the leadership of a thin civilian in a slouch hat and the brawny soldier who had summarily ended the oration. The crowd had swollen marvelously to formidable proportions and a stream of more non-committal citizens followed it along the sidewalks lending their moral support by intermittent huzzas.

"Where we goin'?" yelled Key to the man nearest him.

His neighbour pointed up to the leader in the slouch hat.

"That guy knows where there's a lot of 'em! We're goin' to show 'em!"

"We're goin' to show 'em!" whispered Key delightedly to Rose, who repeated rapturously to a man on the other side.

Down Sixth Avenue swept the procession, joined here and there by soldiers and marines, and now and then by civilians, who came up with the inevitable cry that they were just out of the army themselves, as if presenting it as a card of admission to a newly-formed Sporting and Amusement Club.

Then the procession swerved down a cross street and headed for Fifth Avenue and the word filtered here and there that they were bound for a Red meeting at Tolliver Hall.

"Where is it?"

The question went up the line and a moment later the answer floated back. Tolliver Hall was down in Tenth Street. There was a bunch of other sojers who was goin' to break it up and was down there now!

But Tenth Street had a faraway sound and at the word a general groan went up and a score of the procession dropped out. Among these were Rose and Key, who slowed down to a saunter and let the more enthusiastic sweep on by them.

"I'd rather get some liquor," said Key as they halted and made their way to the sidewalk amid cries of "Shell hole!" and "Quitters!"

"Does your brother work around here?" asked Rose, assuming the air of one passing from the superficial to the eternal.

"He oughta," replied Key. "I ain't seen him for a coupla years. I been out to Pennsylvania since. Maybe he don't work at night anyhow. It's right along here and he can get us some o'right, if he ain't gone."

They found the place after a few minutes' patrol of the street—a shoddy table cloth restaurant between Fifth Avenue and Broadway. Here Key inquired for his brother George while Rose waited outside.

"He ain't here no more," said Key as he emerged. "He's a waiter up to Delmonico's."

Rose nodded wisely as if he'd expected as much. One should not be surprised at a capable man changing jobs occasionally. He knew a waiter once—there ensued a long conversation as they walked as to whether waiters made more in actual wages than in tips—it was decided that it depended on the social tone of the joint wherein the waiter labored. After having given each other vivid pictures of millionaires dining at Delmonico's and throwing away fifty-dollar bills after their first quart of champagne, both men thought privately of becoming waiters. In fact, behind Key's narrow brow was secretly forming a resolution to ask his brother about the profession and see if he could get him a job.

"A waiter can drink up all the champagne those fellas leave in bottles," suggested Rose with some relish and then added as an afterthought, "Oh, boy!"

By the time they reached Delmonico's it was half past ten and they were surprised to see a stream of taxis driving up to the door one after the other and emitting marvelous young ladies in opera cloaks of blue and yellow and rose, hatless and elaborately coiffured, each one attended by a stiff young gentleman in evening clothes.

"It's a party," said Rose with some awe. "Maybe we better not go in. He'll be busy."

"No he won't. He'll be o'right."

After some hesitation they entered what appeared to them to be the least elaborate door and, indecision falling upon them immediately, they stationed themselves nervously in an inconspicuous corner of the small dining room in which they found themselves. They took off their caps and held them in their hands. A cloud of gloom fell upon them and they both started when a door at one end of the room crashed open, emitted a comet-like waiter who streaked across the floor and vanished through another door on the other side.

There had been three of these lightning passages before the seekers mustered the acumen to hail a waiter. He turned, looked at them suspiciously and then approached with soft, catlike steps as if prepared at any moment to turn and flee.

"Say," began Key, "say, do you know my brother? He's a waiter here."

"His name is Key," annotated Rose.

Yes, the waiter knew Key. He was upstairs he thought. There was a big dance going on in the main ball room. He'd tell him.

Ten minutes later George Key appeared and greeted his brother with the utmost suspicion; his first and most natural thought being that he was going to be asked for money.

George was tall and weak chinned, but there his resemblance to his brother ceased. The waiter's eyes were not dull, they were alert and twinkling and his manner was suave, indoor and faintly superior. They exchanged formalities. George was married and had three children. He seemed faintly interested, but not impressed by the fact that Carrol had been abroad in the army, which latter fact disappointed Carrol.

"George," said the younger brother, these amenities having been disposed of, "we want to get some liquor and they won't sell us any. Can you get us some?"

George considered.

"Sure. Maybe I can. It may be half an hour, though."

"All right," agreed Carrol, "we'll wait."

He started to sit down in a convenient chair, but was hailed to his feet by the indignant George.

"Hey! Watch out, you! Can't sit down here! This room's all set for a midnight banquet."

"I ain't goin' to hurt it," said Carrol. "I been through the delouser."

"Never mind," said George sternly, "if the head waiter seen me here talkin' he'd romp all over me."

"Oh."

The mention of the head waiter was full explanation to the other two; they fingered their overseas caps nervously and waited for a suggestion.

"I tell you," said George, after a pause, "I got a place you can wait; you just come with me."

They followed him out the far door, through a deserted pantry and up a pair of dark winding stairs, emerging finally into a small room chiefly furnished by piles of pails and stacks of used and unused scrubbing brushes and illuminated by a single dim electric light. There he left them, after soliciting two dollars and agreeing to return in half an hour with a quart of whiskey.

"George is makin' money, I bet," said Key gloomily as he seated himself on an inverted pail. "I bet he's making fifty dollars a week."

Rose nodded his head and spat.

"I bet he is, too."

"What'd he say the dance was of?"

"A lot of college fellas. Yale College."

They both nodded solemnly at each other.

"Wonder where that crowda sojers is now?"

"Maybe they're there. I don't know. I know that's too darn long to walk for me."

"Me too. You don't catch me walkin' that far."

Ten minutes later restlessness seized them.

"I'm goin' to see what's out here," said Rose, stepping cautiously toward the other door.

It was a swinging door of green baize and he pushed it cautiously open an inch.

"See anything?"

For answer Rose drew in his breath sharply.

"Doggone! Here's some liquor I'll say!"

"Liquor?"

Key joined Rose at the door and looked eagerly.

"I'll tell the world that's liquor," he said, after a moment of concentrated gazing.

It was a room about twice as large as the one they were in—and in it was prepared a radiant feast of spirits. There were long walls of alternating bottles set along two white covered tables; whiskey, gin, brandy, French and Italian vermouths, and orange juice, not to mention an array of syphons and two great empty punch bowls. The room was as yet uninhabited.

"It's for this dance they're just starting," whispered Key; "hear the violins startin' playin'? Say boy, I wouldn't mind havin' a dance."

They closed the door softly and exchanged a glance of mutual comprehension. There was no need of feeling each other out.

"I'd like to get my hands on a coupla those bottles," said Rose emphatically.

"Me too."

"Do you suppose we'd get seen?"

Key considered.

"Maybe we better wait till they start drinkin' em. They got 'em all laid out now and they know how many of them there are."

They debated this point for several minutes. Rose was all for getting his hands on a bottle now and tucking it under his coat before anyone came into the room. Key, however, advocated caution. He was afraid he might get his brother in trouble. If they waited till some of the bottles were opened it'd be all right to take one and everybody'd think one of the guests had taken it.

While they were still engaged in argument George Key hurried through the room and barely grunting at them disappeared by way of the green baize door. A minute later they heard several corks pop and then the sound of cracking ice and splashing liquid. George was mixing the punch.

The soldiers exchanged delighted grins.

"Oh, boy!" whispered Rose.

George reappeared.

"Just keep low, boys," he said quickly. "I'll have your stuff for you in five minutes."

He disappeared through the door by which he had come.

As soon as his footsteps receded down the stairs, Rose, after a cautious look, darted into the room of delights and reappeared with a bottle in his hand.

"My idea is this," he said, as they sat radiantly digesting

their first drink. "We'll wait till he comes up and we'll ask him if we can't just stay here and drink what he brings us—see. We'll tell him we haven't got any place to drink it—see. Then we can sneak in there whenever there ain't no one in that room and tuck a bottle under our coats. We'll have enough to last us a coupla days—see."

"Sure," agreed Rose enthusiastically. "Oh, boy! And if we want to we can sell it to soldiers any time we want to."

They were silent for a moment thinking rosily of this idea. Then Key reached up and unhooked the collar of his O. D. coat.

"It's hot in here, ain't it?"

Rose agreed earnestly.

"Hot as hell."

CHAPTER IV

She was still *quite* angry when she came out of the dressing room and crossed the intervening parlour of politeness that opened onto the hall—angry not so much at the actual happening which was, after all, the merest commonplace of her social existence, but because it had occurred on this particular night. She had no quarrel with herself. She had acted with that correct mixture of dignity and reticent pity which she always employed. She had succinctly and deftly snubbed him.

It had happened when their taxi was leaving the Biltmore—hadn't gone half a block. He had lifted his left arm awkwardly—she was on his right side—and attempted to settle it snugly around the crimson fur-trimmed opera cloak she wore. This in itself had been a mistake. It was inevitably more graceful for a young man attempting to embrace a young lady of whose acquiescence he was not certain, to first put his far arm around her. It avoided that awkward movement of raising the near arm.

His second *faux pas* was unconscious. She had spent the afternoon at the hairdresser's; the idea of any calamity overtaking her hair was extremely repugnant—yet as Peter made his unfortunate attempt the point of his elbow had just faintly brushed it. That was his second *faux pas*. Two were quite enough.

He had begun to murmur. At the first murmur she had decided that he was nothing but a college boy and that she was in love with another man—a man she had not seen for three

years. A man for whom she had so far only a sad-eyed, adolescent mooniness. Edith Bradin was in love with Gordon
Sterrett.

So she came out of the dressing room at Delmonico's and
stood for a second in the doorway looking over the shoulders
of a black dress in front of her at the groups of Yale men who
flitted like dignified black moths around the head of the
stairs. From the room she had left drifted out the heavy fragrance left by the passage to and fro of many scented young
beauties—rich perfumes and the fragile memory-laden dust of
fragrant powders. This odour drifting out acquired the tang of
cigarette smoke in the hall and then settled sensuously down
the stairs and permeated the ball room where the Gamma Psi
dance was to be. It was an odour she knew well, exciting,
stimulating, restlessly sweet—the odour of a fashionable
dance.

She thought of her own appearance. Her bare arms and
shoulders were powdered to a creamy white. She knew they
looked very soft and would gleam like milk against the black
arms and shoulders that were to silhouette them tonight. The
hairdressing had been a success: her reddish mass of hair was
piled and crushed and creased to an arrogant marvel of mobile curves. Her lips were finely made of deep carmine; her
nose was pert; the irises of her eyes were delicate, breakable
blue, like china eyes. She was a complete, infinitely delicate,
quite perfect thing of beauty, flowing in an even line from a
complex coiffure to two small slim feet.

She thought of what she would say tonight at this revel,
faintly presaged already by the sounds of high and low laughter and slippered footsteps and movements of couples up and
down the stairs. She would talk the language she had talked
for many years—her line—made up of the current expressions, bits of *journalese* and college slang strung together into
an intrinsic whole, careless, faintly provocative, delicately
sentimental. She smiled faintly as she heard a girl sitting on
the stairs near her say: "You don't know the half of it,
dearie!"

And as she smiled her anger melted for a moment, and
closing her eyes she drew in a deep breath of pleasure. She
dropped her arms to her sides until they were faintly touching
the sleek sheath that covered and suggested her figure. She
had never felt her own softness so much nor so enjoyed the
whiteness of her own arms.

"I smell sweet," she said to herself simply and then came another thought—"I'm made for love."

She liked the sound of this and thought it again; then in inevitable succession came her newborn riot of dreams about Gordon. An unexpected, unexplainable twist of her imagination two months before had disclosed to Edith that she wanted Gordon more than she wanted anything in the world.

For all her sleek beauty, Edith was a grave, slow-thinking girl. There was a streak in her of that same desire to ponder, of that adolescent idealism that had turned her brother socialist and pacifist. Henry Bradin had left Cornell, where he had been an assistant in economics, and came to New York to pour the dissatisfaction of his active mind into the columns of a radical weekly newspaper. He was managing editor of the *New York Trumpet*. Ostensibly, brother and sister had no more in common than a beaver and a peacock; at heart the springs of Harold's idealism were twin to the motive power of Edith's fancies.

She was twenty-one, with a faint weariness. There was a quality of weakness she had always seen in Gordon that she wanted to take care of; there was a quality of helplessness in him that she wanted to protect. And she wanted someone she had known a long while, someone who had loved her a long while. She was a little tired; she wanted to get married. Out of a pile of letters, half a dozen pictures and as many memories, and, somehow, this tiredness, she had decided that next time she saw Gordon their relations were going to be changed. She would say something that would change them. There was this evening. This was her evening. All evenings were her evenings.

Then her thoughts were interrupted by a solemn undergraduate with a hurt look and an air of strained formality presenting himself before her and bowing unusually low. It was the man she had come with. Peter Barton. He was tall and humorous, with horned-rimmed glasses and an air of attractive whimsicality. She suddenly rather disliked him—probably because he had not succeeded in kissing her.

"Well," she began, "are you still furious at me?"

"Not at all."

She stepped forward and took his arm.

"I'm sorry," she said softly. "I don't know why I snapped out that way. I'm in a bum humour tonight, I guess, for some strange reason. I'm sorry."

"S'all right," he mumbled, "don't mention it."

He felt disagreeably embarrassed. As if she was rubbing in the fact of his late failure.

"It was a mistake," she continued, on the same consciously gentle key. "We'll both forget it."

A few minutes later they drifted out on the floor while the dozen swaying, sighing members of the specially hired jazz orchestra informed the crowded ballroom that if a saxophone is left alone it's more than enough for me.

A man with a light mustache cut in.

"Hello," he began reprovingly. "You don't remember me."

"I can't just find your name," she said lightly—"and I know you so well."

"I met you up at—" His voice trailed disconsolately off as a man with very fair hair cut in. Edith murmured a conventional "Thanks, loads—cut in later," to the *inconnu*.

The very fair man insisted on shaking hands enthusiastically. She placed him as one of the numerous Jims of her acquaintance—last name a mystery. She remembered even that he had a peculiar rhythm in dancing; found as they started that she was right.

"Going to be here long?" he breathed confidentially.

She leaned back and looked up at him.

"Couple of weeks."

"Where are you?"

"Biltmore. Call me up some day."

"I mean it—I will. We'll go to tea."

"So do I—do."

A dark man cut in with intense formality.

"You don't remember me, do you?" he said gravely.

"I should say I do. Your name's Harlan."

"No—ope. Barlow."

"Well, I knew there were two syllables anyway. You're the boy that played the ukulele so well up at Jim Marshall's house party."

"I played—but not—"

A light-haired man with prominent teeth cut in. Edith inhaled a slight cloud of whiskey. It made her feel quite at home. She liked men to have had something to drink; they were so much more cheerful and appreciative and complimentary—much easier to talk to.

"My name's Cory, Philip Cory," he said cheerfully. "You don't remember me, I know; but you used to come up to New

Haven with a fellow I roomed with senior year, Gordon Sterrett."

Edith looked up quickly.

"Yes, I went up with him twice—to the Pump and Slipper and the Junior prom."

"You've seen him, of course," said Cory carelessly. "He's here tonight. I saw him just a minute ago."

Edith started. Yet she had felt quite sure he would be here.

"Why no, I haven't—"

A little man with black hair cut in.

"Hello Edith," he began.

"Why—hello there—"

She slipped, stumbled lightly.

"I'm sorry, dear," she murmured mechanically.

She had seen Gordon—Gordon very white and listless, leaning against the side of a doorway, smoking and looking into the ballroom. Edith could see that his face was thin and wan—that the hand he raised to his lips with a cigarette was trembling. They were dancing quite close to him now.

"—They invite so darn many extra fellas that you—" the short man was saying.

"Hello, Gordon," said Edith over her partner's shoulder. Her heart was pounding wildly.

His large dark eyes were fixed on her. He took a step in her direction. Her partner turned her away—she heard his voice bleating—

"—but half the stags get lit and leave long before, so—"

Then a low tone at her side.

"May I, please?"

She was dancing suddenly with Gordon; one of his arms was around her; she felt it tighten spasmodically; felt his hand on her back with the fingers spread. Her hand holding the little lace handkerchief was crushed in his.

"Why Gordon," she began breathlessly.

"Hello Edith."

She slipped again—was tossed forward by her recovery until her face touched the black cloth of his dinner coat. She loved him—she knew she loved him—then for a minute there was silence while a strange feeling of uneasiness crept over her. Something was wrong.

Of a sudden her heart wrenched and turned over as she realized what it was. He was pitifully and wretchedly drunk.

"Oh—" she cried involuntarily.

His eyes looked down at her. She saw suddenly that they were bloodstreaked and rolling uncontrollably.

"Gordon," she murmured, "we'll sit down; I want to sit down."

They were nearly in mid-floor, but she had seen two men start toward her from opposite sides of the room, so she halted, seized Gordon's limp hand and led him bumping through the crowd, her mouth tight shut, her face a little pale under her rouge, her eyes trembling with tears.

She found a place high up on the soft-carpeted stairs and he sat down heavily beside her.

"Well," he began, staring at her unsteadily. "I certainly am glad to see you, Edith."

She looked at him without answering. The effect of this on her was immeasurable. For years she had seen men in various stages of intoxication, from uncles all the way down to chauffeurs, and her feelings had varied from amusement to disgust, but here for the first time she was seized with a new feeling—an unutterable horror.

"Gordon," she said accusingly and almost crying, "you're drunk."

He nodded. "I've had trouble, Edith."

"Trouble?"

"All sorts of trouble. Just big mess. Don't you say anything to the family, but I'm all gone pieces. I'm a mess. I'm a mess, Edith."

His lower lip was sagging. He seemed scarcely to see her.

"Can't you—can't you," she hesitated, "can't you tell me about it, Gordon. You know I'm always interested in you."

She bit her lip—she had intended to say something stronger, but found at the end that she couldn't bring it out.

Gordon shook his head dully. "I can't tell you. You're a good woman. I can't tell a good woman the story."

"Rot," she said defiantly. "I think it's a perfect insult to call anyone a good woman in that way. It's a slam."

"You're a good woman," he repeated.

"You're drunk, Gordon."

"Thanks." He inclined his head gravely. "Thanks for the information."

"Why do you drink?"

"Because I'm so damn miserable."

"Do you think drinking's going to make it any better?"

"What you doing—trying to reform me?"

"No; I'm trying to help you, Gordon. Can't you tell me about it?"

"What do you mean? I'm in an awful mess. Best thing you can do is to pretend not to know me."

"Why, Gordon?"

"That's it—pretend not know me. I'm *sorry* I cut in on you—unfair to you. You're pure woman—I'm a bad man. Now on we pretend not know each other. Here. I'll get some-one else to dance with you."

He half rose clumsily to his feet, but she reached up and pulled him down beside her on the stairs.

"Here, Gordon. You're ridiculous. You're hurting me. You're acting like a—like a drunken man—"

"Admit it. I'm drunken. I'm not worthy look at you. Some-thing's wrong with me, Edith, from bottom up. There's some-thing left me. It doesn't matter."

"It does, tell me."

"Just that. I was always queer—li'l bit different from other boys. All right in college, but now it's all wrong. Things have been snapping inside me for four months like li'l hooks on a dress and it's about to come off when a few more hooks go. I'm very gradually going crazy."

He turned his eyes full on her and began to laugh, and she shrank away from him.

"What *is* the matter?"

"Just me," he repeated. "I'm going crazy. This whole place is like a dream to me—this Delmonico's—"

As he talked she saw he had changed utterly. He wasn't at all light and gay and careless—a great lethargy and discour-agement had come over him. Revulsion seized her, followed by a faint, surprising boredom. His voice seemed to come out of a great void.

"Edith," he said, "I used to think I was clever, talented, an artist. Now I know I'm nothing. Can't draw, Edith. Don't know why I'm telling you this."

She nodded absently.

"I can't draw, I can't do anything. I'm poor as a church mouse." He laughed, bitterly and rather too loud. "I've be-come a damn beggar, a leech on my friends. I'm a failure. I'm poor as hell."

Her distaste was growing. She barely nodded this time, waiting for her first possible cue to rise.

Suddenly Gordon's eyes filled with tears.

"Edith," he said, turning to her with what was evidently a strong effort at self-control, "I can't tell you what it means to me to know there's one person left who's interested in me."

He reached out and patted her hand and unconsciously she drew it away.

"It's mighty fine of you," he repeated.

"Well," she said slowly, looking him in the eye, "anyone's always glad to see an old friend—but I'm sorry to see you like this, Gordon."

There was a pause while they looked at each other and the momentary eagerness in his eyes wavered. She rose and stood looking at him, her face quite expressionless.

"Shall we dance?" she suggested coolly.

—Love is fragile—she was thinking—but perhaps the pieces are saved. The new love words, the tendernesses learned, are treasured up for the next lover.

CHAPTER V

Peter Barton, unaccustomed to being snubbed, having been snubbed, was hurt and embarrassed and ashamed of himself. For a matter of two months he had been on special delivery terms with Edith Bradin and, knowing that the one excuse and explanation of the special delivery letter is its value in sentimental correspondence, he had believed himself quite sure of his ground. He searched in vain for any reason why she should have taken this attitude in the matter of a simple kiss.

Therefore when he was cut in on by the fair-haired man he went out into the hall and, making up a sentence, said it over to himself several times. Considerably deleted, this is it:

"Well, if any girl ever led a man on and then jolted him, she did—and she has no kick coming if I go out and get beautifully boiled."

So he walked through the supper room into a small room adjoining it, which he had located earlier in the evening. It was a room in which there were several large bowls of punch flanked by many bottles. He took a seat beside the table which held the bowls.

At the second highball, boredom, disgust, the monotony of time, the turbidity of events, sank into a vague background before which glittering cobwebs formed. Things became reconciled to themselves, lay quietly on their shelves: the troubles of the day arranged themselves in trim formation and at his curt wish of dismissal, marched off and disappeared. And with the departure of worry came brilliant permeating symbolism. Edith became a flighty, negligible girl, not to be worried over; rather to be laughed at. She fitted like a figure of his own dream into the surface world forming about him. He himself became in a measure symbolic, a type of the continent bacchannal, the brilliant dreamer at play.

Then the symbolic mood faded and as he sipped his third highball his imagination yielded to the warm glow and he lapsed into a state similar to floating on his back in pleasant water; and it was at this point that he noticed that a green baize door near him was open about two inches and through the aperture a pair of eyes were watching him intently.

"Hm," murmured Peter, somewhat startled.

The green door closed—and then opened again—a bare half inch this time.

"Hm," murmured Peter.

The door remained stationary and then he became aware of a series of tense intermittent whispers.

"One guy."

"What's he doin'?"

"He's sittin' lookin'."

"He better beat it off. We gotta get another li'l bottle."

Peter listened while the words filtered into his consciousness.

"Now this," he thought, "is most remarkable."

He was excited. He was jubilant. He felt that he had stumbled upon a mystery. Affecting an elaborate carelessness he arose and walked around the table—then, turning quickly, pulled open the green door, precipitating Private Rose into the room.

Peter bowed.

"How do you do," he said.

Private Rose set one foot slightly in front of the other, poised for fight, flight or compromise.

"How do you do," repeated Peter politely.

"I'm o'right."

"Can I offer you a drink?"

Private Rose looked at him searchingly, suspecting possible sarcasm.

"O'right," he said finally.

Peter indicated a chair.

"Sit down."

"I got a friend," said Rose. "I got a friend in there." He pointed to the green door.

"By all means let's have him in."

Peter crossed over, opened the door and welcomed in Private Key, very suspicious and uncertain and guilty. Chairs were found and the three took their seats around the punch bowl. Peter gave them each a highball and offered them a cigarette from his case. They accepted both with some diffidence.

"Now," continued Peter easily, "may I ask why you gentlemen prefer to lounge away your leisure hours in a room which is chiefly furnished, as far as I can see, with scrubbing brushes, when the human race has progressed to the stage where seventeen thousand chairs are manufactured on every day except Sunday?"

Rose and Key regarded him vacantly. Key grunted.

"Will you tell me," went on Peter, "why you chose to rest yourselves on articles intended for the transportation of water from one place to another?"

At this point Rose contributed a grunt to the conversation.

"And lastly," finished Peter, "will you tell me why, when you are in a building beautifully hung with enormous candelabra, you prefer to spend these mellow evening hours under one anemic electric light?"

Rose looked at Key; Key looked at Rose. They laughed; they laughed uproariously; they found it was impossible to look at each other without laughing. But they were not laughing with this man—they were laughing at him. To them a man who talked after this fashion was either raving drunk or raving crazy.

"You are Yale men, I presume," said Peter, finishing his highball and preparing another.

They laughed again.

"Na-ah."

"So? I thought perhaps you might be members of that obscure section of the university known as the Sheffield Scientific School."

"Na-ah."

"Hm. Well, that's too bad. No doubt you are Harvard men, anxious to preserve your incognito in this—this paradise of violet blue, so to speak."

"An-ah," said Key scornfully, "we was just waitin' for somebody."

"Ah," exclaimed Peter, rising and filling their glasses, "very interestin'. Had a date with a scrub-lady, eh?"

They both denied this indignantly.

"S'all right," Peter reassured them, "don't apologize. S'all right. Scrub-lady's as good as any lady in the world. Kipling says "Any lady and Julie O'Grady under the skin.' One woman's as bad as another. Isn't she?"

"Sure," said Key, winking broadly at Rose.

"My case, for instance," continued Peter, finishing his glass. "I got a girl up here tha's spoiled. Spoildest darn girl I ever saw. Refuse to kiss me; no reason whats'ever. Led me on deliberately to think sure I want to kiss you and then plunk! Threw me over! Wha's younger generation comin' to."

"Say tha's hard luck," said Key—"that's awful hard luck."

"Oh boy!" said Rose.

"Have another?" said Peter.

"We got in a sort of fight for awhile," said Key after a pause, "but it was too far away."

"A fight?—tha's stuff!" said Peter, seating himself unsteadily. "Fight 'em all! I was in the army."

"This was with a Bolshevik fella."

"Tha's stuff!" exclaimed Peter, enthusiastic. "That's what I say! Kill Bolshevik! Exterminate 'em!"

"We're Americuns," said Rose, implying a sturdy, defiant patriotism.

"Sure," said Peter. "Greates' race in the world! We're all Americuns! Have another."

They had another.

CHAPTER VI

At one o'clock a special orchestra, special even in a day of special orchestras, arrived at Delmonico's, and its members, seating themselves arrogantly around the piano, took up the burden of providing music for the Gamma Psi Fraternity. They were headed by a famous flute player, distinguished throughout New York for his feat of standing on his head and shimmying with his shoulders while he played the latest jazz on his flute. During his performance the lights were extinguished except for the spotlight on the flute player and another roving beam that threw flickering shadows and changing kaleidoscopic colours over the massed dancers.

Edith had danced herself into that tired, dreamy state possible only to débutantes, a state equivalent to the glow felt by a man after several long highballs. Her mind floated vaguely on the bosom of her music: her partners changed with the unreality of phantoms under the colourful shifting dusk, and to her present coma it seemed as if days had passed since the dance began. She had talked on many subjects with many men. She had been kissed once and made love to six times. Earlier in the evening different undergraduates had danced with her, but now, like all the more popular girls there she had her own entourage—that is, half a dozen gallants had singled her out or were alternating her charms with those of some other chosen beauty; they cut in on her in regular inevitable succession.

Several times she had seen Gordon—he had been sitting a long time on the stairway with his palm to his head, his dull eyes fixed at an infinite speck on the floor before him, very depressed, he looked, and quite drunk—but Edith each time had averted her glance hurriedly. All that seemed long ago; her mind was passive now, her senses were lulled to trance-like sleep; only her feet danced and her voice talked on in hazy sentimental banter.

But Edith was not nearly so tired as to be incapable of moral indignation when Peter Barton cut in on her quite sublimely and happily drunk. She gasped and looked up at him.

"Why, *Peter!*"

"I'm a li'l stewed, Edith."

"Why, Peter, you're a peach, you are! Don't you think it's a bum way of doing—to drink when you're with me?"

Then she smiled unwillingly, for he was looking at her with owlish sentimentality varied with a silly spasmodic smile.

"Darlin' Edith," he began earnestly, "you know I love you, don't you?"

"You tell it well."

"I love you—and I merely wanted you to kiss me," he added sadly.

His embarrassment, his shame were both gone. She was a mos' beautiful girl in whole worl'. Mos' beautiful eyes, like stars above. He wanted to 'pologize—firs', for presuming try to kiss her; second, for drinking—but he'd been so discouraged 'cause he had thought she was mad at him—

The very dark man cut in, and looking up at Edith smiled radiantly.

"Did you bring anyone?" she asked.

No. The very dark man was a stag.

"Well, would you mind—would it be an awful bother for you to—to take me home tonight (this extreme diffidence was a charming affectation on Edith's part—she knew that the dark man would immediately dissolve into a paroxysm of delight).

"Bother? Why, good Lord. I'd be darn glad to! You know I'd be darn glad to."

"Thanks *loads*! You're awfully sweet."

She glanced at her wrist-watch. It was half-past one. And, as she said "half-past one" to herself, it floated vaguely into her mind that she had heard that very hour mentioned lately in some significant connection. Where?

Then she remembered, her brother had told her at luncheon that he worked in his Weekly office until after one-thirty every evening.

Edith turned suddenly to her current partner.

"What street is Delmonico's on, anyway?"

"Street? Oh, why Fifth Avenue, of course."

"I mean, what cross street?"

"Why—let's see—it's on Forty-fourth Street."

This verified what she had thought, Henry's office must be across the street and just around the corner, and it occurred to her immediately that she might slip over for a moment and surprise him, inspect his office, cheer him up, float in on him, a shimmering marvel in her new crimson opera cloak. It was exactly the sort of thing Edith revelled in doing—an unconventional, jaunty thing. The idea reached out and gripped at her imagination—after an instant's hesitation she had decided.

"My hair is just about to tumble entirely down," she said pleasantly to her partner, "would you mind if I go and fix it?"

"Not at all."

"You're a peach. I'll meet you at the door of the dressing room in about fifteen minutes."

Wrapped in her crimson opera cloak she flitted down a sidestairs, her cheeks glowing with excitement at her little adventure. She ran by a couple who stood at the door,—a weak-chinned waiter and an over-rouged young lady, in hot dispute—and opening the outer door stepped into the warm May night.

The over-rouged young lady followed her with a brief, bitter glance,—then turned again to the weak-chinned waiter and took up her argument.

"You better go up and tell him I'm here," she said defiantly, "or I'll go up myself."

"No, you don't!" said George sternly.

The girl smiled sardonically.

"Oh, I don't, don't I? I'm not good enough, eh? Well, let me tell you I know more college fellas and more of 'em know me and are glad to take me out on a party, then you ever saw in your whole life."

"Maybe so—"

"Maybe so," she interrupted, mimicking him. "Oh, it's all right for any of 'em like that little lady that just ran out— Lord knows where she went—it's all right for them that are asked here to come or go as they like—but when I want to see a friend they have some cheap, ham-slinging, bring-me-a-doughnut waiter to stand here and keep me out."

"See here," said the elder Key indignantly, "I can't lose my job. Maybe this fella you're talkin' about doesn't want to see you."

"Oh, he wants to see me all right."

"Anyways, how could I find him in all that crowd?"

"Oh, he'll be there," she asserted confidently. "You just ask anybody for Gordon Sterrett and they'll point him out to you. They all know each other, those fellas."

She produced a mesh bag and taking out a dollar bill handed it to George.

"Here," she said, "here's a bribe. You find him and give him my message. You tell him if he isn't here in five minutes I'm coming up."

George shook his head pessimistically, considered the question for a moment, wavered violently and then withdrew.

In less than the allotted time Gordon came downstairs. He was quite as drunk as he had been earlier in the evening but in somehow a different way. The liquor seemed to have hardened on him like a crust. He was heavy and lurching,— almost incoherent when he talked.

" 'Lo Gloria," he said thickly, "come righ' away. Gloria, I couldn't get tha' money. Tried my best."

"Money nothing!" she snapped. "You haven't been near me for ten days. What's the matter?"

He shook his head slowly.

"Been very drunk, Gloria. Been sick."

"Why didn't you tell me if you were sick. I don't care about the money that bad. I didn't start botherin' you about it at all until you began neglecting me."

Again he shook his head.

"Haven't been neglecting you. Not t'all."

"Haven't! You haven't been near me for three weeks, unless you been so drunk you didn't know what you were doing."

"Been sick, Gloria," he repeated, turning his eyes upon her wearily.

"You're well enough to come and play with your débutante friends here all right. You told me you'd meet me for dinner and you said you'd have some money for me. You didn't even bother to ring me up."

"I couldn't get any money."

"Haven't I just been saying that doesn't matter. I wanted to see you, Gordon, but you seem to prefer your Yale girls."

He denied this bitterly.

"Then get your hat and come with me," she suggested.

Gordon hesitated—and she came suddenly close to him and slipped her arms around his neck.

"Come on with me, Gordon," she said in a half whisper. "We'll go over to Devineries and have a drink, and then we can go up to my apartment."

"I can't, Gloria,—"

"You can," she said intensely.

"I'm sick as a dog!"

"Well, then, you oughtn't to stay here and dance."

With a glance around him in which relief and despair were mingled, Gordon hesitated and then suddenly pulled her to him clumsily and kissed her soft, pulpy lips.

"All right," he said heavily. "I'll get my hat."

CHAPTER VII

When Edith came out into the clear blue of May night she found the Avenue deserted. The windows of the great shops were dark; over their doors were drawn great iron masks until they were only shadowy tombs of the day's past splendour.

Glancing down toward Forty-second Street she saw a com-mingled blur of lights from the all-night restaurants. Over on Sixth Avenue the elevated, a flare of fire, roared across the street between the glimmering parallels of light at the station and streaked along into the crisp dark. But at Forty-fourth Street it was very quiet.

Pulling her cloak close about her Edith darted across the Avenue and hurried along Forty-fourth Street. She started ner-vously as a solitary man passed her and said in a hoarse whisper—"Where bound kiddo?" She was reminded of a night in her childhood when she had walked around the block in her pajamas and a big dog had howled at her from a mystery-big back yard.

In a minute she had reached her destination, a two-story, comparatively old building in the upper window of which she thankfully detected a wisp of light. It was bright enough out-side for her to make out the sign beside the window "The New York Trumpet." She stepped inside a dark hall and after a second saw the stairs in the corner.

Then she was in a long, low room furnished with many desks and hung on all sides with file copies of newspapers. There were only two inhabitants. They were sitting at differ-ent ends of the room, each wearing a green eye-shade and writing by a solitary desk light.

For a moment she stood uncertainly in the doorway and then both men turned around simultaneously and she recog-nized her brother.

"Why, Edith!" He rose quickly and approached her in amazement, removing his eyeshade. He was tall, lean and dark, with black, piercing eyes under very thick glasses. They were far-away eyes that seemed always fixed just over the head of the person he was talking to.

He put his hands on her arms and kissed her cheek.

"What is it?" he repeated in some alarm.

"I was at a dance across at Delmonico's, Henry," she said excitedly, "and I couldn't resist tearing over to see you."

"I'm glad you did." His alertness gave way quickly to a habitual vagueness. "You oughtn't to be out alone at night though, had you?"

The man at the other end of the room had been looking at them curiously but at Henry's beckoning gesture he ap-proached. He was loosely fat with little twinkling eyes, and, having removed his collar and tie, he gave the impression, somehow, of a middle western farmer on Sunday afternoon.

"This is my sister," said Henry. "She dropped in to see me."

"Dropped in to see you, eh?" said the fat man smiling. "My name's Bartholomew, Miss Bradin. I know your brother has forgotten it long ago."

Edith laughed politely.

"Well," he continued, "not exactly gorgeous quarters we have here, are they?"

Eleanor looked around the room.

"They seem very nice," she replied. "Where do you keep the bombs?"

"The bombs?" repeated Bartholomew, laughing. "That's pretty good,—the bombs. Did you hear her, Henry? She wants to know where we keep the bombs."

Edith swung herself on to a vacant desk and sat dangling her feet over the edge. Her brother took a chair beside her and produced his pipe.

"Well," he asked, "how do you like New York this trip?"

"Not bad."

"How's your dance?"

"Not bad, and, Henry, I'll be over at the Biltmore with the Hoyts until Sunday. Can't you come to luncheon tomorrow?"

He thought a moment.

"I'm especially busy," he objected, "and I hate women in groups."

"All right," she agreed unruffled. "Let's you and me have luncheon together."

"Very well."

"I'll call for you at twelve."

Bartholomew was obviously anxious to return to his desk, but apparently considered that it would be rude to leave without some parting pleasantry.

"Well"—he began awkwardly.

They both turned to him.

"Well, we—we had an exciting time earlier in the evening."

The two men exchanged glances and laughed.

"You should have come earlier," continued Bartholomew, somewhat encouraged. "We had a regular vaudeville."

"Did you really?"

"A serenade," put in Henry. "A lot of soldiers gathered down there in the street and began to yell at the sign."

"Why?" she demanded.

"Just a crowd," said Henry, abstractedly. "All crowds have to howl. They didn't have anybody with much initiative in the lead or they'd probably have forced their way in here and smashed things up."

"Yes," said Bartholomew, turning again to Edith, "you should have been here."

He seemed to consider this a sufficient cue for withdrawal, for he turned abruptly and went back to his desk.

"Are the soldiers all set against the Socialists?" demanded Edith of her brother. "I mean do they attack you violently and all that?"

Henry replaced his eye-shade and yawned.

"There always have been a lot of fools," he said casually. "The human race has come a long way, but most of us are throw-backs; the soldiers don't know what they want or what they hate or what they like. They're used to acting in large bodies and they seem to have to make demonstrations. So it happens to be against us. There've been riots all over the city tonight. It's May Day, you see—some sort of holiday."

"Was the disturbance here pretty serious?"

"Not a bit," he said scornfully. "About twenty-five of them stopped in the street about nine o'clock and began to bellow at the moon."

"Oh"—She changed the subject. "You're glad to see me, Henry?"

"Why, sure."

"You don't seem to be."

"I am."

"I suppose you think I'm a—a waster. Sort of the World's Worst Butterfly."

Henry laughed.

"Not at all. Have a good time while you're young. Why? Do I seem like the priggish and earnest youth?"

"No—" She paused, "—but somehow I began thinking how absolutely different the party I'm on is from—from all your purposes. It seems sort of—of incongruous, doesn't it?—me being at a party like that and you over here working for a thing that'll make that sort of party impossible ever any more."

"I don't think of it that way. You're young and you're acting just as you were brought up to act. Go ahead—have a good time."

Her feet, which had been idly swinging, stopped and her voice dropped a note.

"I wish you'd—you'd come back to Harrisburg and have a good time. Do you feel sure that you're on the right track—"

"You're wearing beautiful stockings," he interrupted. "What on earth are they?"

"They're embroidered," she replied, glancing down. "Aren't they cunning?" She raised her skirts and uncovered slim, silk-sheathed calves. "Or do you disapprove of silk stockings?"

He seemed slightly exasperated, bent his dark eyes on her piercingly.

"Are you trying to make me out as criticizing you in any way, Edith?"

"Not at all—"

She paused. Someone had uttered a grunt. She turned and saw that Bartholomew had left his desk and was standing at the window.

"What is it," demanded Henry.

"Some people," said Bartholomew, and then after an instant, "a whole jam of them. They're coming from Sixth Avenue."

"People?"

The fat man pressed his nose to the pane.

"Soldiers, by God!" he said emphatically. "I had an idea they'd come back."

Edith jumped to her feet and running over joined Bartholomew at the window.

"There's a lot of them!" she cried excitedly, "Come here, Henry!"

Henry readjusted his shade, but kept his seat.

"Simple apes," he commented contemptuously.

"Hadn't we better turn out the lights?" suggested Bartholomew.

"No. They'll go away in a moment."

"They're not," said Edith, peering from the window. "They're not even thinking of going away. There's more of them coming. Look—there's a whole crowd turning the corner of Sixth Avenue."

By the yellow glow and blue shadows of the street lamp she could see that the sidewalk was crowded with men. They were mostly in uniform, some sober, some enthusiastically drunk, and over the whole swept an incoherent clamour and shouting.

Henry rose and going to the window exposed himself as a long silhouette against the office lights. Immediately the shouting became a steady yell, and a rattling fusilade of small missles, corners of tobacco plugs, cigarette boxes and even pennies beat against the window. The sounds of the racket which had hitherto come through the front windows now began floating up the stairs as the folding doors revolved.

"They're coming up!" cried Bartholomew.

Edith turned anxiously to Henry.

"They're coming up, Henry."

From downstairs in the lower hall their cries were now quite audible.

"—damn Socialists!"

"We'll go get those Bolsheviks!"

"Pacifists!—Aah—h-h!"

"Pro-Germans! Boche-lovers!"

The next five minutes passed in a dream.

Edith was conscious that the clamour burst suddenly upon the three of them like a cloud of rain, that there was a thunder of many feet on the stairs, that Henry had seized her arm and drawn her back toward the rear of the desk. Then the door opened and an overflow of men were forced into the room— not the leaders, but simply those who happened to be in front.

"Hello Bo!"

"Hello you yellow Bolshevik!"

"Up late, ain't you?"

"You an' your girl. Damn *you*!"

She noticed that there were two very drunken soldiers in front,—one of them short and dark, the other tall and weak-chinned.

Henry stepped forward and raised his hand.

"Friends!" he said.

The clamour faded into a momentary stillness, punctuated with mutterings.

"Friends!" he repeated, his far-away eyes fixed over the heads of the crowd. "You're injuring no one but yourselves by breaking in here tonight. Do we look like rich men? Do we look like Germans? I ask you in all fairness—"

"Pipe down!"

"I'll say you do!"

"Say, who's your lady friend, buddy?"

A man in civilian clothes who had been pawing over a table suddenly held up a newspaper.

"Here it is!" he shouted. "Here's the greasy sheet!"

A new overflow from the stairs was shouldered in and of a sudden the room was full of men all closing in around the little pale group at the back. Edith saw that the tall man with the weak chin was still in front. The little dark man had disappeared.

She edged slightly backward, stood close to the open window through which came a clear breath of cool night air.

Then the room was in riot. She realized that the soldiers were surging forward, glimpsed the fat man swinging a chair over his head—instantly the lights went out, and she felt the push of warm bodies under rough cloth and her ears were full of shouting and trampling and hard breathing.

A figure flashed by her out of nowhere, tottered, was edged sideways and of a sudden disappeared helplessly out through the open window a frightened, fragmentary cry that died staccato on the bosom of the clamour. By the faint light streaming from the building backing on the area Edith had a quick impression that it had been the tall soldier with the weak chin.

Anger rose astonishingly in her. She swung her arms wildly, edged blindly toward the thickest of the scuffling. She heard grunts, curses, the muffled impact of fists.

"Henry!" she called frantically. "Henry!"

Then, it seemed minutes later, she felt suddenly that there were other figures in the room. She heard a voice, deep, bullying, authoritative; she saw yellow rays of light sweeping here and there in the fracas. The cries became more scattered. The scuffling increased and then stopped.

Suddenly the lights were on and the room was full of policemen, clubbing left and right. The deep voice boomed out:

"Here now! Here now! Here now!"

And then:

"Quiet down and get out! Here now!"

The room seemed to empty like a wash bowl. A policeman fast-grappled in the corner released his hold on his soldier antagonist and started him with a shove toward the door. The deep voice continued—Edith perceived now that it came from a bull-necked police captain standing near the door.

"Here now! This is no way! One of your own sojers got shoved out of the back window an' killed hisself!"

"Henry!" called Edith. "Henry!"

She beat wildly with her fists on the back of the man in front of her; she brushed between two others; fought, shrieked and beat her way to a very pale figure sitting on the floor close to a desk.

"Henry," she cried passionately, "What's the matter!" "What's the matter! What's the matter! Did they hurt you?"

His eyes were shut. He groaned and then looking up complained dismally—"They broke my leg, hell take their stupid souls!"

"Here now!" called the police captain. "Here now! Here now!"

CHAPTER VIII

"Childs', Fifty-ninth Street" at eight o'clock of any morning differs from its sisters by less than the width of a marble table or the degree of polish on a frying pan. You will see there a crowd of poor people with sleep in the corners of their eyes, trying to look straight before them at their food so as not to see the other poor people. But Childs', Fifty-ninth, four hours earlier is quite unlike any Childs' restaurant from Portland, Oregon, to Portland, Maine. Within its pale but sanitary walls one finds a noisy medley of chorus girls, college boys, débutantes, rakes, *filles de joie*—a not unrepresentative mixture of the gayest of Broadway's evening population.

In the early morning of May the second it was unusually full. Over the marble-topped tables were bent the excited faces of flappers whose fathers owned individual villages. They were eating buckwheat cakes and scrambled eggs with relish and gusto, an accomplishment that it would have been utterly impossible for them to repeat in the same place four hours later.

Almost the entire crowd were from the Gamma Psi dance at Delmonico's except for several chorus girls from a midnight revue who sat at a side table and wished they'd taken off a little more make-up after the show. Here and there a drab mouse-like figure, quite out of place, watched the butterflies with a weary, puzzled curiosity. But the drab figure was the exception. This was the morning after May Day and celebration was still in the air.

Gus Rose, sober but a little dazed, must be classed as one of the drab figures. How he had gotten from Forty-fourth Street to Fifty-ninth Street after the riot was only a hazy half-memory. He had seen the body of Carrol Key put in an ambulance and driven off, and then he had started up town with two or three soldiers. Somewhere between Forty-fourth Street and Fifty-ninth Street the other soldiers had met some women and disappeared. Rose had wandered to Columbus Circle and chosen the gleaming lights of Childs' to minister to his craving for coffee and doughnuts.

So he walked in and sat down. All around him floated airy, inconsequential chatter and high-pitched laughter.

At first he failed to understand, but after a puzzled five minutes he realized that this was the aftermath of some gay party. Here and there a restless, hilarious young man wandered fraternally and familiarly between the tables, shaking hands indiscriminately and pausing here and there for a facetious chat. Excited waiters bearing cakes and eggs aloft swore at them silently as they bumped them out of the way on their imperious course. To Rose, seated at the most inconspicuous and least crowded table, the whole scene was a colorful circus of young beauty and riotous pleasure.

He became gradually aware, after a few moments, that the couple seated diagonally across from him with their backs to the crowd were not the least interesting pair in the room. The man was drunk. He wore a dinner coat with a dishevelled tie and shirt swollen by spillings of water and wine. His eyes, dim and bloodshot, roved unnaturally from side to side. His breath came short between his lips.

"I'll say he's been on some spree!" thought Rose.

The woman was almost if not quite sober. She was pretty, with dark eyes and feverish high colour, and she kept her active eyes fixed on her companion with the alertness of a hawk. From time to time she would lean and whisper intently to him and he would answer by inclining his head heavily or by a particularly ghoulish and repellant wink.

Rose scrutinized them carefully for some minutes, until the woman gave him a quick, resentful look; then he shifted his gaze to the most conspicuously hilarious of the promenaders who were on a protracted circuit of the tables. To his surprise he recognized in one of them the young man by whom he had been so ludicrously entertained at Delmonico's. This started him thinking of Key with a vague sentimentality, not unmixed with awe. Key was dead. He had fallen thirty-five feet and split his skull like a cracked cocoanut.

"He was a darn good guy," thought Rose mournfully. "He was a darn good guy, o'right. That was awful hard luck about him."

The two promenaders approached and started down between Rose's table and the next, addressing friends and strangers alike with jovial familiarity. Suddenly Rose saw the fair haired one with the prominent teeth stop, look unsteadily at the man and girl opposite and then begin to move his head disapprovingly from side to side.

The man with the blood-shot eyes looked up.

"Gordy," said the promenader, "Gordy."

"Hello," he said thickly.

The man shook his finger pessimistically at the pair, giving the woman a glance of aloof condemnation.

"What'd I tell you Gordy?"

Gordon stirred in his seat.

"Go to hell!" he said.

Cory continued to stand there shaking his finger. The woman began to get angry.

"You go way!" she cried fiercely; "you're drunk, that's what you are!"

"So's he," suggested Cory, staying the motion of his finger and pointing it at Gordon.

Peter Barton ambled up, very owlish now and oratorically inclined.

"Here now," he began as if called upon to deal with some petty dispute between children. "Wha's all trouble?"

"You take your friend away," said Gloria tartly. "He's bothering us."

"Wha's at?"

"You heard me!" she said shrilly. "I said to take your drunken friend away."

Her rising voice rang out above the clatter of the restaurant and a waiter came hurrying up."

"You gotta be more quiet!"

"That fella's drunk," she cried. "He's insulting us."

"Ah—ha, Gordy," persisted the accused, "wha'd I tell you." He turned to the waiter. "Gordy an' I friends. Been tryin' help him, haven't I, Gordy?"

Gordy looked up.

"Help me? Hell no!"

Gloria rose suddenly and seizing Gordon's arm assisted him to his feet.

"Come on, Gordy!" she said, leaning toward him and speaking in a half whisper. "Let's us get out of here. This fella's got a mean drunk on."

Gordon allowed himself to be urged to his feet and started toward the door. Gloria turned for a second and addressed the provoker of their flight.

"I know all about you!" she said fiercely. "You're Mr. Philip Cory, that's who! Nice friend you are. I'll say. He told me about you."

Then she seized Gordon's arm and together they made their way through the curious crowd, paid their check and went out.

"You'll have to sit down," said the waiter to Peter after they had gone.

"Wha's 'at? Sit down?"

"Yes—or get out."

Peter turned to Cory.

"Come on," he suggested. "Le's beat up the waiter."

"All right."

They advanced toward him, their faces grown very stern. The waiter retreated.

Peter suddenly reached over to a plate on the table beside him and picking up a handful of hash tossed it into the air. It descended as a languid parabola in snowflake effect on the heads of those near by.

"Hey! Ease up!"

"Put him out!"

"Sit down, Peter!"

"Cut out that stuff!"

Peter laughed and bowed.

"Thank you for your kind applause, ladies and gents. If some one will lend me some more hash and a tall hat we will go on with the act."

The bouncer bustled up.

"You've gotta get out!" he said.

"Hell, no!"

"He's my friend!" put in Cory indignantly.

A crowd of waiters were gathering. "Put him out!"

"Better go, Peter."

There was an instant struggle and the two were edged and pushed toward the door.

"I got a hat and a coat here!" cried Peter.

"Well, go get 'em and be spry about it!"

The bouncer released his hold on Peter, who, adopting a ludicrous air of extreme cunning, rushed immediately around to the other table, where he burst into derisive laughter and thumbed his nose at the exasperated waiters.

"Think I just better wait a l'il longer," he announced.

The chase began. Four waiters were sent around one way and four another. Cory caught hold of two of them by the coat and another struggle took place before the pursuit of Peter could be resumed, when he was finally pinioned after overturning a sugar bowl and several cups of coffee. A fresh argument ensued at the cashier's desk, where Peter attempted to buy another dish of hash to take with him and throw at policemen.

But the commotion upon his exit proper was dwarfed by another phenomenon which drew admiring glances and a prolonged involuntary "Oh-h-h!" from every person in the restaurant.

The great plate glass front had turned to a deep creamy blue, the colour of a Maxfield Parrish moonlight—a blue that seemed to press close upon the pane as if to crowd its way into the restaurant. Dawn had come up for Columbus Circle, magical, breathless dawn, silhouetting the great statue of the immortal Christopher and mingling in a curious and uncanny manner with the fading yellow electric light inside.

CHAPTER IX

Mr. In and Mr. Out are not listed by the census taker. You will search for them in vain through the social register or the births, marriages and deaths, or the greengrocer's credit list. Oblivion has swallowed them a long year since and the testimony that they ever existed at all is very vague and shadowy and inadmissable on a court of law. Yet I have it upon the best authority that for a brief space Mr. In and Mr. Out lived, breathed, answered to their names and radiated vivid personalities of their own.

During the brief span of their lives they walked in their native garments down the great highway of a great nation; were laughed at, sworn at, chased and fled from. Then they passed and were heard of no more.

They were already taking form dimly when a taxicab with

the top open breezed down Broadway in the faintest glimmer
of May dawn. In this car sat the souls of Mr. In and Mr. Out
discussing with amazement the blue light that had so precip-
itately coloured the sky behind the statue of Christopher Columbus, discussing with bewilderment the old grey faces of
the early risers who skimmed palely along the street like
blown bits of paper on a grey lake. They were agreed on all
things, from the absurdity of the bouncer in Childs' to the absurdity of the business of life. They were dizzy with the extreme maudlin happiness that the blue dawn had awoken in
their glowing souls. Indeed, so fresh and strong was their
pleasure in living that they felt it should be expressed by loud
cries.

"Ye-ow-ow!" hooted Peter, making a megaphone with his
hands—and Cory joined in with a call that, though equally
significant and symbolic, derived its resonance from its very
inarticulateness.

"Yo-ho! Yea! Yoho! Yo-buba!"

Fifty-third Street was a bus with a dark, bobbed-hair
beauty atop; Fifty-second was a street cleaner who dodged,
escaped and sent up a yell of, "Look where you're aimin' at!"
in a pained and grieved voice. At Fiftieth Street a group of
men on a very white sidewalk in front of a very white building turned to stare after them and shouted:

"Some party, boys!"

At Forty-ninth Street Peter turned jubilantly to Cory.
"Beautiful morning," he said gravely, squinting up his owlish
eyes.

"Probably is."

"Go get some breakfast, hey?"

Cory agreed—with additions.

"Breakfast and liquor."

"Breakfast and liquor," repeated Peter, and they looked at
each other, nodding. "Tha's logical."

Then they both burst into loud laughter.

"Breakfast and liquor! Oh gosh!"

"No such thing," announced Peter.

"Don't serve it? Ne'min. We force 'em serve it. Bring
pressure bear."

"Bring logic bear. I drink—therefore I am."

The taxi cut suddenly off Broadway, sailed along a cross
street and stopped in front of a heavy tomb-like building in
Fifth Avenue.

"Wha's idea?"

The taxi-driver informed them that this was Delmonico's.

This was somewhat puzzling. They were forced to devote several minutes to intense concentration if such an order had been given there must have been a reason for it.

"Somep'm 'bouta coat," suggested the taxi-man.

That was it. Peter's coat and hat. He had forgotten them at Delmonico's when he left there about three-thirty. Having decided this, they disembarked from the taxi and strolled toward the entrance arm in arm.

"Hey!" said the taxi-driver.

"Huh?"

"You better pay me."

They shook their heads in shocked negation.

"Later, not now—we give orders, you wait."

The taxi-driver objected; he wanted his money now. With the scornful condescension of men exercising tremendous self-control they paid him.

Inside Peter groped in vain through a dim, deserted checkroom in search of his coat and derby.

"Gone, I guess. Somebody stole it."

"Some Sheff student."

"All probability."

"Never mind," said Cory nobly, "I'll leave mine here too— then we'll both be dressed same."

He removed his coat and hat and was about to hang them up when his roving glance was caught and held magnetically by two large squares of cardboard tacked to the two coatroom doors. The one on the left hand door bore the word "In" in big black letters, and the one on the right hand door flaunted the equally emphatic word "Out."

"Look!" he exclaimed happily—

Peter's eyes followed his pointing finger.

"What?"

"Look at the signs. Let's take 'em."

"Good idea."

"Probably pair very rare an' valuable signs. Probably come in handy."

Peter removed the left hand sign from the door and endeavored to conceal it about his person. The sign being of considerable proportions, this was a matter of some difficulty. An idea flung itself at him and with an air of dignified mystery he turned his back. After an instant he wheeled dramatically around and stretching out his arms displayed himself to the admiring Cory. He had inserted the sign in his vest, completely covering his shirt front. The effect given was that the word "In" had been painted upon his shirt in large black letters.

"Yoho!" cheered Cory. "Mister In."

He inserted his own sign in like manner.

"Mister Out!" he announced triumphantly. "Mr. In meet Mr. Out."

They advanced and shook hands. Again laughter overcame them and they rocked in a shaken spasm of mirth.

"Yoho!"

"We probably got a flock of breakfast."

"We'll go—go to the Commodore."

Arm in arm they sailed out the door and turning east in Forty-fourth Street set out for the Commodore.

As they came out, a short dark soldier, very pale and tired, who had been wandering listlessly along the sidewalk, turned to look at them.

He started over as though to address them, but as they immediately bent on him glances of withering unrecognition, he waited until they had started unsteadily down the street, and then followed at about forty paces, chuckling to himself and saying "Oh boy!" over and over under his breath, in delighted, anticipatory tones.

Mr. In and Mr. Out were meanwhile exchanging pleasantries concerning their future plans.

"We want liquor; we want breakfast. Neither without th' other. One an' indivisible."

"We want both 'em!"

"Both 'em!"

"Both 'em."

It was quite light now, and passers-by began to bend curious glances at the pair. Obviously they were engaged in a discussion, which afforded each of them intense amusement, for occasionally a fit of laughter would seize upon them so violently that, still with their arms interlocked, they would bend nearly double.

Reaching the Commodore, they exchanged a few spicy epigrams with the sleepy-eyed doorman, navigated the revolving door with some difficulty and then made their way through a thinly populated but quite startled lobby to the dining-room where a puzzled waiter showed them to an obscure table in a corner. They studied the bill of fare help-lessly, telling over the items to each other in puzzled mumbles.

"Don't see any liquor here," said Peter reproachfully.

The waiter became audible but unintelligible.

"I repeat," continued Peter, with a sort of forced tolerance, "that there seems to be unexplained and quite distasteful lack of liquor upon this bill of fare."

"Here!" said Cory confidently. "Lem-me handle him." He turned to the waiter—"Bring us—bring us—" he scanned the bill of fare anxiously. "Bring us a quart of champagne and a—a—probably ham sandwich."

The waiter looked doubtful.

"Bring it!" roared Mr. In and Mr. Out in chorus.

The waiter coughed and disappeared. There was a short wait during which they were subjected without their knowl-edge to a careful scrutiny of the head-waiter. Then the champagne arrived, and at the sight of it Mr. In and Mr. Out became jubilant.

"Imagine their objecting to us having champagne for breakfast—jus' imagine."

They both concentrated upon the vision of such an awe-some possibility, but the feat was too much for them. It was impossible for their joint imaginations to conjure up a world where anyone might object to anyone else having champagne for breakfast. The waiter drew the cork with an enormous *pop*—and their glasses immediately foamed with pale yellow froth.

"Here's health, Mr. In."

"Here's same to you, Mr. Out."

The waiter withdrew; the minutes passed; the champagne became low in the bottle.

"It's—it's mortifying," said Cory suddenly.

"Wha's mortifying?"

"The idea their objecting us having champagne breakfast."

"Mortifying?" Peter considered. "Yes, tha's word—mortifying."

Again they collapsed into laughter, howled, swayed, rocked back and forth in their chairs, repeating the word "morti-fying" over and over to each other—each repetition seeming to make it only more brilliantly ironic.

After a few more gorgeous minutes they decided on an-other quart. Their anxious waiter consulted his immediate superior, and this discreet person gave implicit instructions that no more champagne should be served. Their check was brought.

Five minutes later, arm in arm, they left the Commodore and made their way through a curious, staring crowd along Forty-second Street, and up Vanderbilt Avenue to the Biltmore. There, with sudden cunning, they rose to the occasion and traversed the lobby, walking very fast and standing very erect.

Once in the dining-room they repeated their performance. They were torn between intermittent convulsive laughter and sudden spasmodic discussions of politics, college and the sunny state of their dispositions. Their watches told them that it was now nine o'clock and a dim idea was born in them that they were on a memorable party, something that they would remember always. They lingered over the second bottle. Either of them had only to mention the word "mortifying" to send them both into riotous gasps. The dining-room was whirring and shifting now; a curious lightness permeated and rarified the heavy air.

They paid their check and walked out into the lobby.

It was at this moment that the exterior doors revolved for the thousandth time that morning, and admitted into the lobby a very pale young beauty with dark circles under her eyes, attired in a much rumpled evening dress. She was accompanied by a plain stout man, obviously not an appropriate escort.

At the top of the stairs this couple encountered Mr. In and Mr. Out.

"Edith," began Mr. In, stepping toward her hilariously and making a sweeping bow. "Darling, good morning."

The stout man glanced questioningly at Edith, as if merely asking her permission to throw this man summarily out of the way.

" 'Scuse familiarity," added Peter, as an afterthought. "Edith, good morning."

He seized Cory's elbow and impelled him into the foreground.

"Meet Mr. In, Edith, my bes' frien'. Inseparable. Mr. In and Mr. Out."

Mr. Out advanced and bowed, in fact he advanced so far and bowed so low that he tipped slightly forward and only kept his balance by placing a hand lightly on Edith's shoulder.

"I' Mr. Out," he mumbled pleasantly. "S'misterin Misterout."

"'Smisterinanout," rejoined Peter proudly.

But Edith stared straight by them, her eyes fixed on some infinite speck in the gallery above her. She nodded slightly to the stout man, who advanced bull-like and with a sturdy brisk gesture pushed Mr. In and Mr. Out to either side. Through this alley he and Edith walked.

But ten paces further on Edith stopped again—stopped and pointed to a short dark soldier who was eyeing the crowd in general and the tableau of Mr. In and Mr. Out in particular with a sort of puzzled spell-bound awe.

"There," cried Edith, "see there!"

Her voice rose, became somewhat shrill. Her pointing finger shook slightly.

"There's the soldier who broke my brother's leg."

There were a dozen exclamations; a man in a cutaway coat left his place near the desk and advanced alertly; the stout person made a sort of lightning-like spring and then the lobby closed around the little group and blotted them from the sight of Mr. In and Mr. Out.

But to Mr. In and Mr. Out this event was merely a particoloured iridescent segment of a whirring, spinning world.

They heard loud voices; they saw the stout man spring; the picture suddenly blurred.

Then they were in an elevator bound skyward.

"What floor, please?" said the elevator man.

"Any floor," said Mr. In.

"Top floor," said Mr. Out.

"This is the top floor," said the elevator man.

"Have another floor put on," said Mr. Out.

"Higher," said Mr. In.

"Heaven," said Mr. Out.

CHAPTER X

In a bedroom of a small hotel just off Sixth Avenue Gordon Sterrett awoke with a pain in the back of his head and a sick throbbing in all his veins. He saw the dusky-gray shadows in the corners of the room, a raw place on a large leather chair in the corner where it had long been in use. He saw clothes, dishevelled, rumpled clothes on all the chairs and he smelt cigarette smoke and stale liquor. The windows were tight shut—outside a bright sunlight had thrown a dust-filled beam across the sill—a beam broken by the head of the wide wooden bed in which he had slept. He lay very quiet—comatose, drugged, his eyes wide, his mind clicking wildly like an unoiled machine.

It must have been thirty seconds after he perceived the sunbeam with the dust on it and the rip on the large leather chair that he had the sense of life close beside him, and it was another thirty seconds after that before he realized that he was irrevocably married to Gloria Hudson.

The clerk in charge of the fishing tackle trade at "J. C. Fowler's, Sporting Goods and Accessories," entered the little back room where they count the money, and going up to J. C. Fowler himself, addressed him in a low tone.

"There's a fella out here just bought a automatic—an' he wants some forty-four ammunition."

J. C. Fowler was busy.

"Well, what about it?" he said. "Sell it to him. Business is bad enough, God knows!"

The Jelly-Bean

Jim Powell was a Jelly-bean. Much as I desire to make him
an appealing character, I feel that it would be distinctly unscrupulous to deceive you on that point. He was a bred-in-
the-bone, dyed-in-the-wool, ninety-nine three-quarters per
cent Jelly-bean and he grew lazily all during Jelly-bean season, which is every season, down in the land of the Jelly-
beans well below the Mason-Dixon line.

Now if you call a Memphis man a Jelly-bean he will quite
possibly pull a long sinewy rope from his hip pocket and
hang you to a convenient telegraph pole. If you call a New
Orleans man a Jelly-bean he will probably grin and ask you
who is taking your girl to the Mardi Gras ball. The particular
Jelly-bean patch which produced the protagonist of this history lies somewhere between the two—a little city of thirty
thousand that has dozed sleepily for thirty thousand years in
southern Mississippi, occasionally stirring in its slumbers and
muttering something about a war that took place sometime,
somewhere, and that everyone else has forgotten long ago.

Jim was a Jelly-bean. I write that again because it has such
a pleasant sound—rather like the beginning of a fairy
story—as if Jim were nice. It somehow gives me a picture of
him with a round, appetizing face and all sorts of leaves and
vegetables growing out of his cap. But Jim was long and thin
and bent at the waist from stooping over pool-tables, and he
was what might have been known in the indiscriminating
North as a corner loafer. "Jelly-bean" is the name throughout
the undissolved Confederacy for one who spends his life con-
jugating the verb to idle in the first person—I am idling, I
have idled, I will idle.

Jim was born in a white house on a green corner. It had
four weather-beaten pillars in front and a great amount of
lattice-work in the rear that made a cheerful criss-cross background for a flowerly sun-drenched lawn. Originally the

dwellers in the white house had owned the ground next door and next door to that and next door to that, but that had been so long ago that even Jim's father scarcely remembered it. He had, in fact, thought it a matter of so little moment that when he was noisily and alcoholicly dying he neglected even to tell little Jim who was five years old and quite miserably frightened.

The white house became a boarding-house run by a tight-lipped lady from Macon, whom Jim called Aunt Mamie and detested with all his soul.

He became fifteen, went to high-school, wore his hair in a tangle of black snarls and was afraid of girls. He hated his home where four women and one old man prolonged an interminable chatter from summer to summer about what lots the Powell place had originally included and what sort of flowers would be out next.

Sometimes the parents of little girls in town, remembering Jim's mother and fancying a resemblance in the dark eyes and hair, invited him to parties, but parties made him shy and he much preferred sitting on a disconnected axle in Tilly's Garage, rolling the bones or exploring his mouth endlessly with a long straw. For pocket money, he picked up odd jobs, and it was due to this that he stopped going to parties. At his third party little Marjorie Haight had whispered indiscreetly and within hearing distance that he was the boy who brought the groceries sometimes. So instead of the two-step and polka, Jim had learned to throw any number he desired on the dice and had listened to spicy tales of all the shootings that had occurred in the surrounding country for the last fifty years.

He became eighteen. The war broke out and he enlisted as a gob and polished brass in the Charleston Navy-yard for a year. Then, by way of variety, he went North and polished brass in the Brooklyn Navy-yard for a year.

The war over he went home. He was twenty-one, his trousers were too short and too tight. His buttoned shoes were long and narrow. His tie was an alarming conspiracy of purple and pink marvellously scrolled, and over it were two blue eyes faded like a piece of very good old cloth long exposed to the sun.

In the twilight of one April evening when a soft gray had drifted down along the cottonfields and over the sultry town, he was a vague figure leaning against a board fence, whistling and gazing at the moon's rim over the lights of Jackson street. His mind was working succinctly and persistently on a problem that had held his attention for an hour.

The Jelly-bean had been invited to a party.

Back in the days when all the boys had detested all the girls, Peter Delanoy and Jim had sat side by side in school. But, while Jim's social aspirations had died in the oily air of the garage, Peter had alternately fallen in and out of love, gone to college, taken to drink, given it up and, in short, become one of the best beaux of the town. Nevertheless Peter and Jim had retained a friendship that, though casual, was quite definite. Jim took a certain conscious pride in knowing Peter, and Peter on his side, felt somehow that Jim would be a good man to have with him in a fight. Peter was Jim's hand in the air. Jim was Peter's foot on the ground.

That afternoon Peter's ancient flivver had slowed up beside Jim on the sidewalk and, out of a clear sky, he had invited Jim to a party at the country club. The impulse that made him do this was no stranger than the impulse which made Jim accept. It was probably an unconscious ennui, a half-frightened sense of adventure. And now Jim was very soberly thinking it over.

He began to sing, drumming his long foot idly on a stone block in the sidewalk till it wobbled up and down in time to the low throaty tune:

> "One mile from Home in Jelly-Bean town,
> Lives Jeanne, the Jelly-bean Queen.
> She loves her dice and treats 'em, nice;
> No dice could treat her mean."

He broke off and agitated the sidewalk to a bumpy gallop. "Daggone!" he muttered, half aloud.

They would all be there—the old crowd, the crowd to which, by right of the old white house, sold long since, and the portrait of the officer in gray over the mantel Jim should have belonged. But that crowd had grown up together into a tight little set as gradually as the girls' dresses had lengthened inch by inch, as definitely as the boys' trousers had dropped suddenly to their ankles. And to that society of first names and dead puppy-loves Jim was an outsider—a running mate of poor whites. Most of the men knew him, half-contemptuously; he tipped his hat to three or four girls. That was all.

When the dusk had thickened into a blue setting for the moon, he walked through the hot, pleasantly-pungent town to Jackson Street. The stores were just closing and the last shoppers were drifting homeward as if borne on the dreamy revolution of a slow merry-go-round. Further down a street-fair made a brilliant alley of vari-colored booths and contributed a blend of music to the night—an oriental dance on a calliope, a melancholy bugle in front of a freak show, a cheerful rendition of "Back Home in Tennessee" on a hand-organ.

The Jelly-Bean stopped in a dusty store and bought a collar. Then he sauntered along toward Soda Sam's where he found the usual three or four cars of a summer evening parked in front and the little darkies running back and forth with sundaes and lemonades.

"Hello, Jim."

It was a voice at his elbow—that of Ben Arrot in the front seat of a car beside Evylyn Ware; Nancy Lamar and a strange man were in the back.

The Jelly-bean tipped his hat quickly.

"Hi, Ben—" then, after an almost imperceptible pause—"How y' all?"

Passing, he ambled on toward the garage where he had a room up-stairs. His "How y' all" had been said to Nancy Lamar to whom he had not spoken in fifteen years.

Nancy had a mouth like a remembered kiss and shadowy eyes under blue-black hair inherited from her mother who had been born in Budapest. Jim passed her often in the street, walking small-boy fashion with her hands in her pockets and he knew that with her inseparable Celia Larrabee she had left a trail of broken hearts from Atlanta to New Orleans.

For a few fleeting moments Jim wished he could dance. Then he laughed and as he reached his door began to sing softly to himself:

> "Her Jelly Roll can twist your soul,
> Her eyes are big and brown,
> She's the Queen of the Queens of the Jelly-beans—
> My Jeanne of Jelly-bean Town."

At nine-thirty Jim and Peter met in front of Soda Sam's and started for the Country Club in Peter's flivver.

"Jim," asked Peter casually, as they drove along through the jasmine-scented night, "can you satisfy my curiosity by casting a stray sidelight on your method of keeping alive?"

The Jelly-bean paused and considered.

"Well," he said finally, "I got a room over Tilly's garage. I help him some with the cars in the afternoon an' he gives it to me free. Sometimes I drive one of his taxies and pick up a little that away. I get fed up doin' that regular though."

"That all?"

"Well, when there's a lot of work I help him by the day— Saturdays usually—and then there's one main source of revenue I don't generally mention. Maybe you don't recollect I'm about the champion crap-shooter of this town. They make me shoot from a cup now because once I get the feel of a pair of dice they just roll for me."

Peter chuckled appreciatively.

"I never could learn to set 'em so's they'd do what I wanted. Wish you'd shoot with Nancy Lamar some day and take all her money away from her. She's going get into trouble 'cause she will roll 'em with the boys and she loses more money than her daddy can afford to give her. I happen to know she sold a good ring last month to pay a debt."

The Jelly-bean was silent.

"The white house on Elm Street still belong to you?"

Jim shook his head.

"Sold. Got a pretty good price seein' it wasn't in a good part of town no more. Lawyer told me to put it into liberty bonds. But Aunt Mamie got so she wasn't no good any more so it takes all the interest to keep her up at Great Farms Sanitarium. I guess her mind just gave out from sheer contrariness."

"Hm."

"I got an old uncle up-state an' I reckon I kin go up there if ever I get sure enough pore. Nice farm but nobody much to work it. Many the time he's asked me to come up and help him but I don't guess I'd take much to farm life. It's too doggone lonesome—" He broke off suddenly. "Peter, I want to tell you I'm much obliged to you for askin' me out but I'd be a lot happier if you'd just stop the car right here an' let me walk back into town."

"Shucks!" Peter scoffed. "Do you good to step out. You don't have to dance—just get out there on the floor and shake."

"Hold on," exclaimed Jim in terror, "Don't you go leadin' me up to any girls and leavin' me there so I'll have to dance with 'em."

Peter laughed.

" 'Cause," continued Jim desperately, "without you swear you won't do that I'm agoin' to get out right here an' my good legs goin' carry me back to Jackson Street."

They agreed after some argument that Jim, unmolested by females, was to view the spectacle from a secluded settee in the corner where Peter would join him whenever he wasn't dancing.

So ten o'clock found the Jelly-bean with his legs crossed and his arms conservatively folded, trying to look casually at home and politely uninterested in the dancers. At heart he was torn between overwhelming self-consciousness and an intense curiosity about all that went on around him. He saw the girls emerge one by one from the dressing-room, stretching and pluming themselves like bright birds, smiling over their powdered shoulders at the chaperones, casting a quick glance around to take in the room and simultaneously the room's reaction to their entrance—and then, again like birds, alighting and nestling in the sober arms of their waiting escorts. Celia Larrabee, slim, blonde and lazy-eyed, appeared clad in her favorite pink and blinking like an awakened rose. Marjorie Haight, Evylyn Ware, Harriet Cary, all the girls he had seen loitering down Jackson Street by noon, now, curled and brilliantined and delicately tinted for the overhead lights, were miraculously strange dresden figures of pink and blue and red and gold, fresh from the shop and not yet fully dried.

He had been there half an hour, totally uncheered by Peter's jovial visits which were each one accompanied by a "Hello, old boy, how you making out?" and a slap at his knee. A dozen or so males had spoken to him or stopped for a moment's chat but he knew instinctively that they were each one surprised at finding him there and fancied that one or two were even slightly resentful. But at half past ten his embarrassment suddenly left him and a pull of breathless interest took him completely out of himself—Nancy Lamar had come out of the dressing-room.

She was dressed in yellow organdie, a costume of a hundred cool corners, with three tiers of ruffles and a big bow in back until she shed black and yellow around her in a sort of phosphorescent luster. The Jelly-bean's eyes opened wide and a lump arose in his throat. For a minute she stood beside the door until her partner hurried up. Jim recognized him as the stranger who had been with her in Ben Arrot's car that afternoon. He saw her set her arms akimbo and say something in a low voice and laugh. The man laughed too and Jim experienced the quick pang of a weird new kind of pain. Some ray had passed between the pair, a shaft of beauty from that sun that had warmed him a moment since. The Jelly-bean felt suddenly like a weed in a shadow.

A minute later Peter approached him, bright-eyed and glowing.

"Hi, old man," he cried with some lack of originality. "How you making out?"

Jim replied that he was making out as well as could be expected.

"You come along with me," commanded Peter, "I've got something that'll put an edge on the evening."

Jim followed him awkwardly across the floor and up the stairs to the locker-room where Peter produced a flask of nameless yellow liquid.

"Whiskey. Good old corn."

Ginger ale arrived on a tray. Such potent nectar needed some disguise beyond seltzer.

"Say, boy," exclaimed Peter breathlessly, "doesn't Nancy Lamar look beautiful."

Jim nodded.

"Mighty beautiful," he agreed.

"She's all dolled up to a fare-you-well tonight," continued Peter, tasting his concoction with the appreciative pride of ownership. "Notice that fellow she's with?"

"Big fella? White pants?"

"Yeah. Well, that's Ogden Merritt from Savannah. Old man Merritt makes the Merritt safety razors. This fella's crazy about her. Been chasing after her all year.

"She's a wild baby," continued Peter, "but I like her. So does everybody. But she sure does do crazy stunts. She usually gets out alive but she's got scars all over her reputation from one thing or another she's done."

"That so?" Jim passed over his glass. "That's good corn."

"Not bad. Oh, she's a wild one. Shoots craps, say boy! And she do like her high-balls. Promised I'd give her one later on."

"She in love with this—Merritt?"

"Damned if I know. Seems like all the best girls around here marry fellas and go off somewhere."

He poured himself one more drink and carefully corked the bottle.

"Listen, Jim, I got to go dance and I'd be much obliged if you just stick this corn right on your hip as long as you're not dancing. If a man notices I've had a drink he'll come up and ask me and before I know it it's all gone and somebody else is having my good time."

So Nancy Lamar was going to marry. This toast of a town was to become the private property of an individual in white trousers, to bear his children and humor his whims—and all because white trousers' father had made a better razor than his neighbor. As they descended the stairs Jim found that the idea was depressing him inexplicably. For the first time in his life he felt a vague and romantic yearning. A picture of her began to form in his imagination—Nancy walking boylike and debonnaire along the street, taking an orange as tithe from a worshipful fruit-dealer, charging a dope on a mythical account at Soda Sam's, assembling a convoy of beaux and then driving off in triumphal state for a gorgeous afternoon of splashing and singing.

The Jelly-bean walked out on the porch to a deserted corner, dark between the moon on the lawn and the single lighted door of the ballroom. There he found a chair and, lighting a cigarette, drifted into the thoughtless reverie that was his usual mood. Yet now it was a reverie made sensuous by the night and the hot smell of damp powder puffs, tucked in the fronts of low dresses, distilling a thousand rich scents to float out through the open door. The music itself, blurred by a loud trombone, became hot and shadowy, a languorous overtone to the scraping of many shoes and slippers.

Suddenly the square of yellow light that fell through the door was obscured by a dark figure. A girl had come out of the dressing-room and was standing on the porch not more than ten feet away. Jim heard a low-breathed "doggone" and then she turned and saw him. It was Nancy Lamar.

Jim rose to his feet.

"Howdy."

"Hello—" she paused, hesitated and then approached. "Oh, it's—Jim Powell."

He bowed slightly and tried to think of a casual remark.

"Do you suppose," she began quickly, "I mean—do you know anything about gum?"

"What?"

"I've got gum on my shoe. Some utter ass left his or her gum on the floor and of course I stepped in it."

Jim blushed quite inappropriately.

"Do you know how to get it off?" she demanded petulantly. "I've tried a knife. I've tried every darn thing in the dressing-room. I've tried soap and water—and even perfume and I've ruined my power-puff trying to make it stick to that."

Jim considered the question in some agitation.

"Why—I think perhaps gasolene—"

The words had scarcely left his lips when she grasped his hand and pulled him at a run off the low verandah, over a flower bed and at a gallop toward a group of cars parked in the moonlight by the first hole of the golf course.

"Turn on the gasolene," she commanded breathlessly.

"What?"

"For the gum of course. I've got to get it off. I can't dance with gum on."

Obediently Jim turned to the cars and began inspecting them with a view to obtaining the desired solvent. Had she demanded a cylinder he would have done his best to wrench one out without an instant's hesitation.

"Here," he said after a moment's search. "Here's one that's easy. Got a handkerchief?"

"It's upstairs wet. I used it for the soap and water."

Jim laboriously explored his pockets.

"Don't believe I've got one either."

"Doggone it! Well, we can turn it on and let it run on the ground."

He turned the spout; a dripping began.

"More!"

He turned it on fuller. The dripping became a flow and formed an oily pool that glistened brightly, reflecting a dozen tremulous moons on its quivering bosom.

"Ah," she sighed contentedly, "let it all out. The only thing to do is to wade in it."

In desperation he turned on the tap full and the pool suddenly widened sending tiny rivers and trickles in all directions.

"That's fine. That's something like."

Raising her skirts she stepped gracefully in.

"I know this'll take it off," she sighed.

Jim smiled inadvertently.

"There's two more cars."

She stepped daintily out of the gasolene and began scraping her slippers, side and bottom, on the running board of the car. The Jelly-bean contained himself no longer. He bent double with explosive laughter and after a second she joined in.

"You're here with Peter Delanoy, aren't you?" she asked as they walked back toward the verandah.

"Yes."

"You know where he is now?"

"Out dancin', I reckon."

"The deuce. He promised me a highball."

"Well," said Jim, "I guess that'll be all right. I got his bottle right here in my pocket."

She smiled at him radiantly.

"I guess maybe you'll need ginger ale though," he added.

"Not me. Just the bottle."

"Sure enough?"

She laughed scornfully.

"Try me. I can drink anything any man can. Let's sit down."

She perched herself on the side of a table and he sank luxuriously into one of the wicker chairs beside her. Taking out the cork she held the flask to her lips and took a long drink. He watched her fascinated.

"Like it?"

She shook her head breathlessly.

"No, but I like the way it makes me feel. I think most people are that way."

Jim agreed.

"My daddy liked it too well. It killed him."

"American men," said Nancy gravely, "don't know how to drink."

"What?" Jim was distinctly startled.

"In fact," she went on carelessly, "they don't know how to do anything very well. The one thing I regret in my life is that I wasn't born in England."

"In England?"

"Yes. It is the one regret of my life that I wasn't."

"Do you like it over there?"

"Yes. Immensely. I've never been there in person but I've

met a lot of Englishmen who were over here in the army, Oxford and Cambridge men—you know, that's like Sewanee and University of Georgia are here—and of course I've read a lot of English novels."

Jim was interested, amazed.

"D' you ever hear of Lady Diana Manners?" she asked earnestly.

No, Jim had not.

"Well, she's what I'd like to be. Dark, you know, like me, and wild as sin. She's the girl who rode her horse up the steps of some cathedral or church or something and all the novelists made their heroines do it afterwards."

Jim nodded politely. He was out of his depths.

"Pass the bottle," suggested Nancy, "I'm going to take another little one. A drink wouldn't hurt a baby."

"You see," she continued, again breathless after a draught. "People over there have style. Nobody has style here. I mean the boys here aren't really worth dressing up for or doing sensational things for. Don't you know?"

"I suppose so—I mean I suppose not," murmured Jim confusedly.

"And I'd like to do 'em an' all. I'm really the only girl in town that has style."

She stretched out her arms and yawned pleasantly.

"Pretty evening."

"Beautiful," agreed Jim.

"Like to have boat," she suggested dreamily. "Like to sail out on a silver lake, say the Thames for instance. Have champagne and ca-caviarre sandwiches along. Have about eight people. And one of the men would jump overboard to amuse the party and get drowned like a man did with Lady Diana Manners once."

"Did he do it to please her?"

"Didn't mean drown himself to please her. He just meant to jump overboard and make everybody laugh."

"I reckin they just died laughin' when he drowned."

"Oh, I suppose they laughed a little," she admitted. "I imagine she did, anyway. She's pretty hard, I guess—like I am."

"You hard?"

"Like nails." She yawned again and added, "Give me a little more from that bottle."

Jim hesitated but she held out her hand defiantly.

"Don't treat me like a girl," she warned him, "I'm not like any girl *you* ever saw." She hesitated. "Still, perhaps you're right. You got—you got old head on young shoulders."

She rose to her feet and moved toward the door. The Jelly-bean rose also.

"Good-bye," she said politely, "good-bye. Thanks, Jelly-bean."

Then she stepped inside and left him wide-eyed upon the porch.

At twelve o'clock a procession of cloaks issued single file from the women's dressing-room and, each one pairing with a coated beau like dancers meeting in a cotillion figure, drifted through the door with sleepy happy laughter—through the door into the dark where autos backed and snorted and parties called to one another and gathered around the water-cooler.

Jim, sitting in his corner, rose to look vaguely around for Peter. They had met at eleven; then Peter had gone in to dance. So, seeking him, Jim wandered into the soft-drink stand that had once been a bar. The room was deserted except for a sleepy negro dozing behind the counter and two boys lazily fingering a pair of dice at one of the tables. He was about to leave when he saw Peter. At the same moment Peter spied him.

"There he is," he cried and then, turning to his party, "C' mon over and help us with this bottle. I guess there's not much left, but there's one all around."

Nancy, the man from Savannah, Evylyn Ware and Ben Arrot were lolling and laughing in the doorway. Nancy caught Jim's eye and winked at him broadly.

They drifted over to a table and arranging themselves cheerfully around it began a casual badinage as they waited for the colored boy to bring ginger ale. Jim, faintly ill-at-ease, turned his eyes on Nancy who had drifted into a nickel crap game with the two boys at the next table.

"Bring them over here," suggested Peter.

Ben looked around.

"We don't want to draw a crowd. It's against club rules."

"Nobody's around," insisted Peter, "except Mr. Taylor. He's walking up and down like a wild-man trying to find out who let all the gasolene out of his car."

There was a general laugh.

"I bet a million Nancy got something on her shoe again. You can't park when she's around."

"O Nancy, Mr. Taylor's looking for you!"

Nancy's cheeks were glowing with excitement over the game. "I haven't seen his fussy little flivver in two weeks," she flashed.

Jim felt a sudden silence. He turned and saw an individual of uncertain age standing in the doorway, an individual who he knew instinctively was married, played poker till he began to lose, and danced because he liked telling naughty stories to young girls.

Peter's voice punctuated the embarrassment.

"Won't you join us, Mr. Taylor?"

"Thanks."

Mr. Taylor spread his unwelcome presence over a chair. "Have to, I guess. I'm waiting till they dig me up some gasolene. Somebody got funny with my car."

His eyes narrowed and he looked quickly from one to the other. Jim wondered what he had heard from the doorway—tried to remember what had been said.

"I'm right tonight," Nancy sung out, "and my four bits is in the ring."

"Faded!"

"Why, Mr. Taylor, I didn't know you shot craps!" Nancy was surprised to find that he had seated himself and instantly covered her bet. They had openly disliked each other since the night she had definitely discouraged a series of rather insinuating advances.

"All right, babies, do it for your mamma. Just one little seven." Nancy was cooing to the dice. She rattled them with a brave underhand flourish, then rolled them out on the table.

"Ah-h! I knew it. And now again with the dollar up."

Nancy *was* right. Five passes to her credit, and Mr. Taylor was a bad loser. She was making it personal, after each success Jim watched a look of triumph flutter across her face. She was doubling with each throw—her luck could never last.

"Better go easy," he cautioned timidly.

"Ah, but watch this one," she breathed in a tense whisper. It was eight this time, and Nancy was calling her number.

"Little Ada, this time we're going South."

Ada from Decatur rolled over the table. Nancy was flushed and half-hysterical, but her luck was holding. She drove the pot up and up, refusing to drag. Taylor was drumming with his fingers on the table, but his determined eyes showed that he was in to stay.

Then Nancy tried for a ten. She lost the dice.

Taylor seized them nervously. He shot in silence, and in the hush of excitement the clatter of one pass after another on the table was the only sound.

Now Nancy had the dice again, but her luck had broken. Back and forth it went. Taylor was at it again—and again and again. Was the man never going to lose? They were even at last—Nancy lost her last five dollars.

"Will you take my check," she said quickly, "for fifty, and we'll shoot it all." Her voice was a little unsteady and her hand shook as she reached for the money.

Peter exchanged an uncertain but alarmed glance with Ben.

Taylor shot again. He had Nancy's check.

"How 'bout another?" she said wildly. "Jes' any bank'll do—money everywhere as a matter of fact."

Light dawned on Jim—the hot room—the drinks he had given her—the ones she had taken since. He wished he dared interfere—a girl of that age and position would hardly be likely to have two bank accounts. What was the matter with Merritt? Jim saw him start to speak but so thoroughly had he applied himself to a new bottle that had appeared from nowhere that his attention was wandering.

When the clock struck two Jim could contain himself no longer.

"May I—can't you let me roll 'em for you?" he suggested anxiously, his low, lazy voice a little strained.

Suddenly sleepy and listless, Nancy flung the dice down before him.

"All right—old boy! As Lady Diana Manners says, 'Shoot 'em, Jelly-bean'—My luck's gone."

"Mr. Taylor," said Jim, carelessly, "we'll shoot for one of those checks against the cash."

Half an hour later Nancy swayed forward and clapped him on the back.

"Stole my luck, you did." She was nodding her head sagely.

Jim swept up the last check and putting it with the others tore them into confetti and scattered them on the floor.

Someone started singing, and Nancy kicking her chair backward rose to her feet.

"Ladies and gentlemen," she announced. "Ladies—that's you Evylyn. I want to tell the world that Mr. Jim Powell, who is a well-known Jelly-bean of this city, is an exception to a great rule—'lucky in dice—unlucky in love.' He's lucky in dice, and as matter fact I—I *love* him. Ladies and gentlemen, Nancy Lamar, famous dark haired beauty often featured in the Herald as one th' most popular members th' younger set as other girls are often featured in this particular case. Wish to announce—wish to announce—anyway, Gentlemen—" She tipped suddenly. Jim caught her and restored her balance.

"My error," she laughed, "she stoops to—stoops to—anyways—We'll drink t' Jelly-bean—Mr. Jim Powell, King of th' Jelly-beans."

And a few minutes later as Jim waited hat in hand for Peter in the darkness of that same corner of the porch where she had come searching for gasolene, she appeared suddenly beside him.

"Jelly-bean," she said, "are you here, Jelly-bean? I think—" and even her slight unsteadiness seemed part of an enchanted dream—"I think you deserve one of my sweetest kisses for that, Jelly-bean."

For an instant her arms were around his neck—her lips were pressed to his.

"I'm a wild part of the world, Jelly-bean, but you did me a good turn."

Then she was gone, down the porch, over the cricket-loud lawn. Jim saw Merritt come out the front door and say something to her angrily—saw her toss her head and turning away walk with averted eyes to the car. Evylyn and Ben followed singing a drowsy song about a Jazz baby.

Peter came out and joined Jim on the steps. "All pretty lit, I guess," he yawned, "and Merrit's in a mean mood. He's certainly off Nancy."

Over east along the golf course a faint rug of gray spread itself across the feet of the night. The party in the car began to chant a chorus as the engine warmed up.

"Good night everybody," called Peter.

"Good night, Peter."

"Good night."

There was a pause, and then a soft, happy voice added, "Good night, Jelly-bean."

The car drove off to a burst of singing. A rooster on a farm across the way took up a solitary mournful crow and behind them a last negro waiter turned out the porch light. Jim and Peter strolled over toward the flivver, their shoes crunching raucously on the gravel drive.

"Oh, boy!" sighed Peter softly, "How you can set those dice!"

It was still too dark for him to see the flush on Jim's thin cheeks—or to know that it was a flush of sudden and unexpected shame.

Over Tilly's garage a bleak room yawned all day to the rumble and snorting downstairs and the singing of the negro washers as they turned the hose on the cars outside. It was a cheerless square punctuated with bed, bureau and green topped table. On the table were half a dozen books—Joe Miller's "Slow Train thru Arkansas," "Lucille" in an old edition very much annotated in an old-fashioned hand, "The Eyes of the World" by Harold Bell Wright, and an ancient prayer book of the Church of England with the name of Alice Powell and the date 1831 written on the fly-leaf.

The East, gray when the Jelly-bean entered the garage, became a rich and vivid blue as he turned on his solitary electric light. He snapped it out again and going to the window rested his elbows on the sill and stared into the deepening morning.

With the awakening of his mind Jim's first perception was a sense of futility, a dull ache at the utter grayness and insignificance of life. A wall sprang up suddenly around him hedging him in, a wall as definite and tangible as the white wall of his bare room. And with his perception of this wall all that had been the romance of his existence, the casualness, the lighthearted improvidence, the miraculous openhandedness of life faded out. The Jelly-bean strolling up Jackson Street humming a lazy song, known at every shop and street stand, cropfull of easy greeting and local wit, sad sometimes for only the sake of sadness and the flight of time—that Jelly-bean was suddenly dead. The very name was a reproach, a triviality. With a flood of insight he knew that Merritt must despise him, that even Nancy's kiss in the dawn would have awakened not jealousy but only a contempt for Nancy's so lowering herself. And on his part the Jelly-bean had used for her a dingy subterfuge learned from the garage. He had been her moral laundry; the stains were his.

As the gray became blue, brightened and filled the room he

crossed to his bed and threw himself down on it gripping the edges fiercely.

"I love her," he cried aloud, "God!"

As he said this something gave way within him like a lump melting in his throat. The air cleared and became radiant with dawn and turning over on his face he began to sob dully into the pillow.

In the sunshine of three o'clock Peter Delanoy chugging painfully along Jackson Street was hailed by the Jelly-bean who stood on the curb with his fingers in his vest pockets.

"Hi!" called Peter, bringing his flivver to an astonishing stop alongside. "Just get up?"

The Jelly-bean shook his head.

"Never did go to bed. Felt sorta restless so I took a long walk this morning out in the country. Just got into town this minute."

"Should think you would feel restless. I been feeling that-away all day—"

"I'm thinkin' of leavin' town," continued the Jelly-bean, evidently absorbed by his own thoughts. "Been thinkin' of goin' up on the farm and takin' a little that work off Uncle Jack. Reckin I been bummin' too long."

Peter was silent and the Jelly-bean continued.

"I reckin maybe after Aunt Mamie dies I could sink that money of mine in the farm and make somthin' out of it. All my people originally came from that part up there. Had a big place."

Peter looked at him curiously.

"That's funny," he said. "This—this sort of affected me the same way."

The Jelly-bean hesitated.

"I don't know," he began slowly, "somethin' about—about that girl last night talkin' about a lady named Diana Manners—an English lady, sorta got me thinkin'!" He drew himself up and looked oddly at Peter, "I had a family once," he said defiantly.

Peter nodded.

"I know."

"And I'm the last of 'em," continued the Jelly-bean his voice rising slightly, "and I ain't worth shucks. Name they call me by means jelly—weak and wobbly like. People who weren't nothin' when my folks were a lot turn up their noses when they pass me on the street."

Again Peter was silent.

"So I'm through. I'm goin' today. And when I come back to this town it's going to be like a gentleman."

Peter took out his handkerchief and wiped his damp brow.

"Reckon you're not the only one it shook up," he admitted gloomily. "All this thing of girls going round unchaperoned is going to stop right quick. Too bad too but everybody'll have to see it thataway."

"Do you mean," demanded Jim in surprise, "that all that's leaked out?"

"Leaked out? How on earth could they keep it secret. It'll be announced in the papers tonight. Dr. Lamar's got to save his name somehow."

Jim put his hands on the sides of the car and tightened his long fingers on the metal.

"Do you mean Taylor investigated those checks?"

It was Peter's turn to be surprised.

"Haven't you heard what happened?"

Jim's startled eyes were answer enough.

"Why," announced Peter dramatically, "those four got another bottle of corn, got tight and decided to shock the town—so Nancy and that fella Merritt were married in Rockville at seven o'clock this morning."

A tiny indentation appeared in the metal under the Jelly-bean's fingers.

"Married?"

"Sure enough. Nancy sobered up and rushed back into town, crying and frightened to death—claimed it'd all been a mistake. First Doctor Lamar went wild and was going to kill Merritt but finally they got it patched up some way and Nancy and Merritt went to Savannah on the two-thirty train."

Jim closed his eyes and with an effort overcame a sudden sickness.

"It's too bad," said Peter philosophically, "I don't mean the wedding—reckon that's all right, though I don't guess Nancy cared a darn about him. But it's a crime for a nice girl like that to hurt her family that way."

The Jelly-bean let go the car and turned away. Again something was going on inside him, some inexplicable but almost chemical change.

"Where you going?" asked Peter.

The Jelly-bean turned and looked dully back over his shoulder.

"Got to go," he muttered. "Been up too long; feelin' right sick."

"Oh."

The street was hot at three and hotter still at four, the April dust seeming to enmesh the sun and give it forth again as a world-old joke forever played on an eternity of afternoons. But at half past four a first layer of quiet fell and the shades lengthened under the awnings and heavy foliaged trees. In this heat nothing mattered. All life was weather, a waiting through the hot where events had no significance for the cool that was soft and caressing like a woman's hand on a tired forehead. Down in Mississippi everyone knows that this is the greatest wisdom of the south—so after awhile the Jelly-bean turned into a pool-hall on Jackson Street where he was sure to find a congenial crowd who would make all the old jokes—the ones he knew.

Myra Meets His Family

Probably every boy who has attended an Eastern college in the last ten years has met Myra half a dozen times, for the Myras live on the Eastern colleges, as kittens live on warm milk. When Myra is young, seventeen or so, they call her a "wonderful kid"; in her prime—say, at nineteen—she is tendered the subtle compliments of being referred to by her name alone; and after that she is a "prom trotter" or a "the famous coast-to-coast Myra."

You can see her practically any winter afternoon if you stroll through the Biltmore lobby. She will be standing in a group of sophomores just in from Princeton or New Haven, trying to decide whether to dance away the mellow hours at the Club de Vingt or the Plaza Red Room. Afterward one of the sophomores will take her to the theater and ask her down to the February prom—and then dive for a taxi to catch the last train back to college.

Invariably she has a somnolent mother sharing a suite with her on one of the floors above.

When Myra is about twenty-four she thinks over all the nice boys she might have married at one time or other, sighs a little and does the best she can. But no remarks, please! She has given her youth to you; she has blown fragrantly through many ballrooms to the tender tribute of many eyes; she has roused strange surges of romance in a hundred pagan young breasts; and who shall say she hasn't counted?

The particular Myra whom this story concerns will have to have a paragraph of history. I will get it over with as swiftly as possible.

When she was sixteen she lived in a big house in Cleveland and attended Derby School in Connecticut, and it was while she was still there that she started going to prep-school dances and college proms. She decided to spend the war at Smith College, but in January of her freshman year, falling violently in love with a young infantry officer, she failed all her midyear examinations and retired to Cleveland in disgrace. The young infantry officer arrived about a week later.

Just as she had about decided that she didn't love him after all he was ordered abroad, and in a great revival of sentiment she rushed down to the port of embarkation with her mother to bid him good-by. She wrote him daily for two months, and then weekly for two months, and then once more. This last letter he never got, for a machine-gun bullet ripped through his head one rainy July morning. Perhaps this was just as well, for the letter informed him that it had all been a mistake, and that something told her they would never be happy together, and so on.

The "something" wore boots and silver wings and was tall and dark. Myra was quite sure that it was the real thing at last, but as an engine went through his chest at Kelly Field in mid-August she never had a chance to find out.

Instead she came East again, a little slimmer, with a becoming pallor and new shadows under her eyes, and throughout armistice year she left the ends of cigarettes all over New York on little china trays marked "Midnight Frolic" and "Coconut Grove" and "Palais Royal." She was twenty-one now, and Cleveland people said that her mother ought to take her back home—that New York was spoiling her.

You will have to do your best with that. The story should have started long ago.

I

It was an afternoon in September when she broke a theater date in order to have tea with young Mrs. Arthur Elkins, once her roommate at school.

"I wish," began Myra as they sat down exquisitely, "that I'd been a señorita or a mademoiselle or something. Good grief! What is there to do over here once you're out, except marry and retire!"

Lilah Elkins had seen this form of ennui before.

"Nothing," she replied coolly; "do it."

"I can't seem to get interested, Lilah," said Myra, bending forward earnestly. "I've played round so much that even while I'm kissing the man I just wonder how soon I'll get tired of him. I never get carried away like I used to."

"How old are you, Myra?"

"Twenty-one last spring."

"Well," said Lilah complacently, "take it from me, don't get married unless you're absolutely through playing round. It means giving up an awful lot, you know."

"Through! I'm sick and tired of my whole pointless existence. Funny, Lilah, but I do feel ancient. Up at New Haven last spring men danced with me that seemed like little boys—and once I overheard a girl say in the dressing room, 'There's Myra Harper! She's been coming up here for eight years.' Of course she was about three years off, but it did give me the calendar blues."

"You and I went to our first prom when we were sixteen—five years ago."

"Heavens!" sighed Myra. "And now some men are afraid of me. Isn't that odd? Some of the nicest boys. One man dropped me like a hotcake after coming down from Morristown for three straight weekends. Some kind friend told him I was husband hunting this year, and he was afraid of getting in too deep."

"Well, you are husband hunting, aren't you?"

"I suppose so—after a fashion." Myra paused and looked about her rather cautiously. "Have you ever met Knowleton Whitney? You know what a wiz he is on looks, and his father's worth a fortune, they say. Well, I noticed that the first time he met me he started when he heard my name and fought shy—and, Lilah darling, I'm not so ancient and homely as all that, am I?"

"You certainly are not!" laughed Lilah. "And here's my advice: Pick out the best thing in sight—the man who has all the mental, physical, social and financial qualities you want, and then go after him hammer and tongs—the way we used to. After you've got him don't say to yourself 'Well, he can't sing like Billy,' or 'I wish he played better golf.' You can't have everything. Shut your eyes and turn off your sense of humor, and then after you're married it'll be very different and you'll be mighty glad."

"Yes," said Myra absently; "I've had that advice before."

"Drifting into romance is easy when you're eighteen," continued Lilah emphatically; "but after five years of it your capacity for it simply burns out."

"I've had such nice times," sighed Myra, "and such sweet men. To tell you the truth I have decided to go after someone."

"Who?"

"Knowleton Whitney. Believe me, I may be a bit blasé, but I can still get any man I want."

"You really want him?"

"Yes—as much as I'll ever want anyone. He's smart as a whip, and shy—rather sweetly shy—and they say his family have the best-looking place in Westchester County."

Lilah sipped the last of her tea and glanced at her wrist watch.

"I've got to tear, dear."

They rose together and, sauntering out on Park Avenue, hailed taxicabs.

"I'm awfully glad, Myra; and I know you'll be glad too."

Myra skipped a little pool of water and, reaching her taxi, balanced on the running board like a ballet dancer.

" 'By, Lilah. See you soon."

"Good-by, Myra. Good luck!"

And knowing Myra as she did, Lilah felt that her last remark was distinctly superfluous.

II

That was essentially the reason that one Friday night six weeks later Knowleton Whitney paid a taxi bill of seven dollars and ten cents and with a mixture of emotions paused beside Myra on the Biltmore steps.

The outer surface of his mind was deliriously happy, but just below that was a slowly hardening fright at what he had done. He, protected since his freshman year at Harvard from the snares of fascinating fortune hunters, dragged away from several sweet young things by the acquiescent nape of his neck, had taken advantage of his family's absence in the West to become so enmeshed in the toils that it was hard to say which was toils and which was he.

The afternoon had been like a dream: November twilight along Fifth Avenue after the matinee, and he and Myra looking out at the swarming crowds from the romantic privacy of a hansom cab—quaint device—then tea at the Ritz and her white hand gleaming on the arm of a chair beside him; and suddenly quick broken words. After that had come the trip to the jeweler's and a mad dinner in some little Italian restaurant where he had written "Do you?" on the back of the bill of fare and pushed it over for her to add the ever-miraculous

"You know I do!" And now at the day's end they paused on the Biltmore steps.

"Say it," breathed Myra close to his ear.

He said it. Ah, Myra, how many ghosts must have flitted across your memory then!

"You've made me so happy, dear," she said softly.

"No—you've made me happy. Don't you know—Myra—"

"I know."

"For good?"

"For good. I've got this, you see." And she raised the diamond solitaire to her lips. She knew how to do things, did Myra.

"Good night."

"Good night. Good night."

Like a gossamer fairy in shimmering rose she ran up the wide stairs and her cheeks were glowing wildly as she rang the elevator bell.

At the end of a fortnight she got a telegraph from him saying that his family had returned from the West and expected her up in Westchester County for a week's visit. Myra wired her train time, bought three new evening dresses and packed her trunk.

It was a cool November evening when she arrived, and stepping from the train in the late twilight she shivered slightly and looked eagerly round for Knowleton. The station platform swarmed for a moment with men returning from the city; there was a shouting medley of wives and chauffeurs, and a great snorting of automobiles as they backed and turned and slid away. Then before she realized it the platform was quite deserted and not a single one of the luxurious cars remained. Knowleton must have expected her on another train.

With an almost inaudible "Damn!" she started toward the Elizabethan station to telephone, when suddenly she was accosted by a very dirty, dilapidated man who touched his ancient cap to her and addressed her in a cracked, querulous voice.

"You Miss Harper?"

"Yes," she confessed, rather startled. Was this unmentionable person by any wild chance the chauffeur?

"The chauffeur's sick," he continued in a high whine. "I'm his son."

Myra gasped.

"You mean Mr. Whitney's chauffeur?"

"Yes; he only keeps just one since the war. Great on

economizin'—regelar Hoover." He stamped his feet nervously and smacked enormous gauntlets together. "Well, no use waitin' here gabbin' in the cold. Le's have your grip."

Too amazed for words and not a little dismayed, Myra followed her guide to the edge of the platform, where she looked in vain for a car. But she was not left to wonder long, for the person led her steps to a battered old flivver, wherein was deposited her grip.

"Big car's broke," he explained. "Have to use this or walk." He opened the front door for her and nodded.

"Step in."

"I b'lieve I'll sit in back if you don't mind."

"Surest thing you know," he cackled, opening the back door. "I thought the trunk bumpin' round back there might make you nervous."

"What trunk?"

"Yourn."

"Oh, didn't Mr. Whitney—can't you make two trips?"

He shook his head obstinately.

"Wouldn't allow it. Not since the war. Up to rich people to set 'n example; that's what Mr. Whitney says. Le's have your check, please."

As he disappeared Myra tried in vain to conjure up a picture of the chauffeur if this was his son. After a mysterious argument with the station agent he returned, gasping violently, with the trunk on his back. He deposited it in the rear seat and climbed up front beside her.

It was quite dark when they swerved out of the road and up a long dusky driveway to the Whitney place, whence lighted windows flung great blots of cheerful, yellow light over the gravel and grass and trees. Even now she could see that it was very beautiful, that its blurred outline was Georgian Colonial and that great shadowy garden parks were flung out at both sides. The car plumped to a full stop before a square stone doorway and the chauffeur's son climbed out after her and pushed open the outer door.

"Just go right in," he cackled; and as she passed the threshold she heard him softly shut the door, closing out himself and the dark.

Myra looked round her. She was in a large somber hall paneled in old English oak and lit by dim shaded lights clinging like luminous yellow turtles at intervals along the wall. Ahead of her was a broad staircase and on both sides there were several doors, but there was no sight or sound of life, and an intense stillness seemed to rise ceaselessly from the deep crimson carpet.

She must have waited there a full minute before she began to have that unmistakable sense of someone looking at her. She forced herself to turn casually round.

A sallow little man, bald and clean shaven, trimly dressed in a frock coat and white spats, was standing a few yards away regarding her quizzically. He must have been fifty at the least, but even before he moved she had noticed a curious alertness about him—something in his pose which promised that it had been instantaneously assumed and would be instantaneously changed in a moment. His tiny hands and feet and the odd twist to his eyebrows gave him a faintly elfish expression, and she had one of those vague transient convictions that she had seen him before, many years ago.

For a minute they stared at each other in silence and then she flushed slightly and discovered a desire to swallow.

"I suppose you're Mr. Whitney." She smiled faintly and advanced a step toward him. "I'm Myra Harper."

For an instant longer he remained silent and motionless, and it flashed across Myra that he might be deaf; then suddenly he jerked into spirited life exactly like a mechanical toy started by the pressure of a button.

"Why, of course—why, naturally. I know—ah!" he exclaimed excitedly in a high-pitched elfin voice. Then raising himself on his toes in a sort of attenuated ecstasy of enthusiasm and smiling a wizened smile, he minced toward her across the dark carpet.

She blushed appropriately.

"That's awfully nice of—"

"Ah!" he went on. "You must be tired; a rickety, cindery, ghastly trip, I know. Tired and hungry and thirsty, no doubt, no doubt!" He looked round him indignantly. "The servants are frightfully inefficient in this house!"

Myra did not know what to say to this, so she made no answer. After an instant's abstraction Mr. Whitney crossed over with his furious energy and pressed a button; then almost as if he were dancing he was by her side again, making thin, disparaging gestures with his hands.

"A little minute," he assured her, "sixty seconds, scarcely more. Here!"

He rushed suddenly to the wall and with some effort lifted

a great carved Louis Fourteenth chair and set it down carefully in the geometrical center of the carpet.

"Sit down—won't you? Sit down! I'll go get you something. Sixty seconds at the outside."

She demurred faintly, but he kept on repeating "Sit down!" in such an aggrieved yet hopeful tone that Myra sat down. Instantly her host disappeared.

She sat there for five minutes and a feeling of oppression fell over her. Of all the receptions she had ever received this was decidedly the oddest—for though she had read somewhere that Ludlow Whitney was considered one of the most eccentric figures in the financial world, to find a sallow, elfin little man who, when he walked, danced was rather a blow to her sense of form. Had he gone to get Knowleton! She revolved her thumbs in interminable concentric circles.

Then she started nervously at a quick cough at her elbow. It was Mr. Whitney again. In one hand he held a glass of milk and in the other a blue kitchen bowl full of those hard cubical crackers used in soup.

"Hungry from your trip!" he exclaimed compassionately. "Poor girl, poor little girl, starving!" He brought out this last word with such emphasis that some of the milk plopped gently over the side of the glass.

Myra took the refreshments submissively. She was not hungry, but it had taken him ten minutes to get them so it seemed ungracious to refuse. She sipped gingerly at the milk and ate a cracker, wondering vaguely what to say. Mr Whitney, however, solved the problem for her by disappearing again—this time by way of the wide stairs—four steps at a hop—the back of his bald head gleaming oddly for a moment in the half dark.

Minutes passed. Myra was torn between resentment and bewilderment that she should be sitting on a high comfortless chair in the middle of this big hall munching crackers. By what code was a visiting fiancée ever thus received!

Her heart gave a jump of relief as she heard a familiar whistle on the stairs. It was Knowleton at last, and when he came in sight he gasped with astonishment.

"Myra!"

She carefully placed the bowl and glass on the carpet and rose, smiling.

"Why," he exclaimed, "they didn't tell me you were here!"

"Your father—welcomed me."

"Lordy! He must have gone upstairs and forgotten all about it. Did he insist on your eating this stuff? Why didn't you just tell him you didn't want any?"

"Why—I don't know."

"You musn't mind father, dear. He's forgetful and a little unconventional in some ways, but you'll get used to him."

"Show Miss Harper to her room and have her bag carried up—and her trunk if it isn't there already." He turned to Myra. "Dear, I'm awfully sorry I didn't know you were here. How long have you been waiting?"

"Oh, only a few minutes."

It had been twenty at least, but she saw no advantage in stressing it. Nevertheless it had given her an oddly uncomfortably feeling.

Half an hour later as she was hooking the last eye on her dinner dress there was a knock on the door.

"It's Knowleton, Myra; if you're about ready we'll go in and see mother for a minute before dinner."

She threw a final approving glance at her reflection in the mirror and turning out the light joined him in the hall. He led her down a central passage which crossed to the other wing of the house, and stopping before a closed door he pushed it open and ushered Myra into the weirdest room upon which her young eyes had ever rested.

It was a large luxurious boudoir, paneled, like the lower hall, in dark English oak and bathed by several lamps in a mellow orange glow that blurred its every outline into misty amber. In a great armchair piled high with cushions and draped with a curiously figured cloth of silk reclined a very sturdy old lady with bright white hair, heavy features, and an air about her of having been there for many years. She lay somnolently against the cushions, her eyes half closed, her great bust rising and falling under her black negligee.

But it was something else that made the room remarkable, and Myra's eyes scarcely rested on the woman, so engrossed was she in another feature of her surroundings. On the carpet, on the chairs and sofas, on the great canopied bed and on the soft Angora rug in front of the fire sat and sprawled and slept a great army of white poodle dogs. There must have been almost two dozen of them, with curly hair twisting in front of their wistful eyes and wide yellow bows flaunting from their necks. As Myra and Knowleton entered a stir went over the dogs; they raised one-and-twenty cold black noses in the air and from one-and-twenty little throats went up a great clatter of staccato barks until the room was filled with such an uproar that Myra stepped back in alarm.

But at the din the somnolent fat lady's eyes trembled open and in a low husky voice that was in itself oddly like a bark she snapped out: "Hush that racket!" and the clatter instantly ceased. The two or three poodles round the fire turned their silky eyes on each other reproachfully, and lying down with little sighs faded out on the white Angora rug; the tousled ball on the lady's lap dug his nose into the crook of an elbow and went back to sleep, and except for the patches of white wool scattered about the room Myra would have thought it all a dream.

"Mother," said Knowleton after an instant's pause, "this is Myra."

From the lady's lips flooded one low husky word: "Myra?"

"She's visiting us, I told you."

Mrs. Whitney raised a large arm and passed her hand across her forehead wearily.

"Child!" she said—and Myra started, for again the voice was like a low sort of growl—"you want to marry my son Knowleton?"

Myra felt that this was putting the tonneau before the radiator, but she nodded. "Yes, Mrs. Whitney."

"How old are you?" This very suddenly.

"I'm twenty-one, Mrs. Whitney."

"Ah—and you're from Cleveland?" This was in what was surely a series of articulate barks.

"Yes, Mrs. Whitney."

"Ah—"

Myra was not certain whether this last ejaculation was conversation or merely a groan, so she did not answer.

"You'll excuse me if I don't appear downstairs," continued Mrs. Whitney; "but when we're in the East I seldom leave this room and my dear little doggies."

Myra nodded and a conventional health question was trembling on her lips when she caught Knowleton's warning glance and checked it.

"Well," said Mrs. Whitney with an air of finality, "you seem like a very nice girl. Come in again."

"Good night, mother," said Knowleton.

" 'Night!" barked Mrs. Whitney drowsily, and her eyes

sealed gradually up as her head receded back again into the cushions.

Knowleton held open the door and Myra feeling a bit blank left the room. As they walked down the corridor she heard a burst of furious sound behind them; the noise of the closing door had again roused the poodle dogs.

When they went downstairs they found Mr. Whitney already seated at the dinner table.

"Utterly charming, completely delightful!" he exclaimed, beaming nervously. "One big family, and you the jewel of it, my dear."

Myra smiled, Knowleton frowned and Mr. Whitney tittered.

"It's been lonely here," he continued; "desolate, with only us three. We expect you to bring sunlight and warmth, the peculiar radiance and efflorescence of youth. It will be quite delightful. Do you sing?"

"Why—I have. I mean, I do, some."

He clapped his hands enthusiastically.

"Splendid! Magnificent! What do you sing? Opera? Ballads? Popular music?"

"Well, mostly popular music."

"Good; personally I prefer popular music. By the way, there's a dance to-night."

"Father," demanded Knowleton sulkily, "did you go and invite a crowd here?"

"I had Monroe call up a few people—just some of the neighbors," he explained to Myra. "We're all very friendly hereabouts; give informal things continually. Oh, it's quite delightful."

Myra caught Knowleton's eye and gave him a sympathetic glance. It was obvious that he had wanted to be alone with her this first evening and was quite put out.

"I want them to meet Myra," continued his father. "I want them to know this delightful jewel we've added to our little household."

"Father," said Knowleton suddenly, "eventually of course Myra and I will want to live here with you and mother, but for the first two or three years I think an apartment in New York would be more the thing for us."

Crash! Mr. Whitney had raked across the tablecloth with his fingers and swept his silver to a jangling heap on the floor.

"Nonsense!" he cried furiously, pointing a tiny finger at his son. "Don't talk that utter nonsense! You'll live here, do you understand me? Here! What's a home without children?"

"But, father—"

In his excitement Mr. Whitney rose and a faint unnatural color crept into his sallow face.

"Silence!" he shrieked. "If you expect one bit of help from me you can have it under my roof—nowhere else! Is that clear? As for you, my exquisite young lady," he continued, turning his wavering finger on Myra, "you'd better understand that the best thing you can do is to decide to settle down right here. This is my home, and I mean to keep it so!"

He stood then for a moment on his tiptoes, bending furiously indignant glances first on one, then on the other, and then suddenly he turned and skipped from the room.

"Well," gasped Myra, turning to Knowleton in amazement, "what do you know about that!"

III

Some hours later she crept into bed in a great state of restless discontent. One thing she knew—she was not going to live in this house. Knowleton would have to make his father see reason to the extent of giving them an apartment in the city. The sallow little man made her nervous; she was sure Mrs. Whitney's dogs would haunt her dreams; and there was a general casualness in the chauffeur, the butler, the maids and even the guests she had met that night, that did not in the least coincide with her ideas on the conduct of a big estate.

She had lain there an hour perhaps when she was startled from a slow reverie by a sharp cry which seemed to proceed from the adjoining room. She sat up in bed and listened, and in a minute it was repeated. It sounded exactly like the plaint of a weary child stopped summarily by the placing of a hand over its mouth. In the dark silence her bewilderment shaded gradually off into uneasiness. She waited for the cry to recur, but straining her ears she heard only the intense crowded stillness of three o'clock. She wondered where Knowleton slept, remembered that his bedroom was over in the other wing just beyond his mother's. She was alone over here—or was she?

With a little gasp she slid down into bed again and lay listening. Not since childhood had she been afraid of the dark, but the unforeseen presence of someone next door startled her and sent her imagination racing through a host of mystery stories that at one time or another had whiled away a long afternoon.

She heard the clock strike four and found she was very tired. A curtain drifted slowly down in front of her imagination, and changing her position she fell suddenly to sleep.

Next morning, walking with Knowleton under starry frosted bushes in one of the bare gardens, she grew quite light-hearted and wondered at her depression of the night before. Probably all families seemed odd when one visited them for the first time in such an intimate capacity. Yet her determination that she and Knowleton were going to live elsewhere than with the white dogs and the jumpy little man was not abated. And if the near-by Westchester County society was typified by the chilly crowd she had met at the dance—

"The family," said Knowleton, "must seem rather unusual. I've been brought up in an odd atmosphere, I suppose, but mother is really quite normal outside of her penchant for poodles in great quantities, and father in spite of his eccentricities seems to hold a secure position in Wall Street."

"Knowleton," she demanded suddenly, "who lives in the room next door to me?"

Did he start and flush slightly—or was that her imagination?

"Because," she went on deliberately, "I'm almost sure I heard someone crying in there during the night. It sounded like a child, Knowleton."

"There's no one in there," he said decidedly. "It was either your imagination or something you ate. Or possibly one of the maids was sick."

Seeming to dismiss the matter without effort he changed the subject.

The day passed quickly. At lunch Mr. Whitney seemed to have forgotten his temper of the previous night; he was as nervously enthusiastic as ever; and watching him Myra again had that impression that she had seen him somewhere before. She and Knowleton paid another visit to Mrs. Whitney—and again the poodles stirred uneasily and set up a barking, to be summarily silenced by the harsh throaty voice. The conversation was short and of inquisitional flavor. It was terminated as before by the lady's drowsy eyelids and a paean of farewell from the dogs.

In the evening she found that Mr. Whitney had insisted on organizing an informal neighborhood vaudeville. A stage had been erected in the ballroom and Myra sat beside Knowleton in the front row and watched proceedings curiously. Two slim and haughty ladies sang, a man performed some ancient card tricks, a girl gave impersonations, and then to Myra's astonishment Mr. Whitney appeared and did a rather effective buck-and-wing dance. There was something inexpressibly weird in the motion of the well-known financier flitting solemnly back and forth across the stage on his tiny feet. Yet he danced well, with an effortless grace and an unexpected suppleness, and he was rewarded with a storm of applause.

In the half dark the lady on her left suddenly spoke to her.

"Mr. Whitney is passing the word along that he wants to see you behind the scenes."

Puzzled, Myra rose and ascended the side flight of stairs that led to the raised platform. Her host was waiting for her anxiously.

"Ah," he chuckled, "splendid!"

He held out his hand, and wonderingly she took it. Before she realized his intention he had half led, half drawn her out on to the stage. The spotlight's glare bathed them, and the ripple of conversation washing the audience ceased. The faces before her were pallid splotches on the gloom and she felt her ears burning as she waited for Mr. Whitney to speak.

"Ladies and gentlemen," he began, "most of you know Miss Myra Harper. You had the honor of meeting her last night. She is a delicious girl, I assure you. I am in a position to know. She intends to become the wife of my son."

He paused and nodded and began clapping his hands. The audience immediately took up the clapping and Myra stood there in motionless horror, overcome by the most violent confusion of her life.

The piping voice went on: "Miss Harper is not only beautiful but talented. Last night she confided to me that she sang. I asked whether she preferred the opera, the ballad or the popular song, and she confessed that her taste ran to the latter. Miss Harper will now favor us with a popular song."

And then Myra was standing alone on the stage, rigid with embarrassment. She fancied that on the faces in front of her she saw critical expectation, boredom, ironic disapproval. Surely this was the height of bad form—to drop a guest unprepared into such a situation.

In the first hush she considered a word or two explaining that Mr. Whitney had been under a misapprehension—then anger came to her assistance. She tossed her head and those in front saw her lips close together sharply.

Advancing to the platform's edge she said succinctly to the orchestra leader: "Have you got 'Wave That Wishbone'?"

"Lemme see. Yes, we got it."

"All right. Let's go!"

She hurriedly reviewed the words, which she had learned quite by accident at a dull house party the previous summer. It was perhaps not the song she would have chosen for her first public appearance, but it would have to do. She smiled radiantly, nodded at the orchestra leader and began the verse in a light clear alto.

As she sang a spirit of ironic humor slowly took possession of her—a desire to give them all a run for their money. And she did. She injected an East Side snarl into every word of slang; she ragged; she shimmied; she did a tickle-toe step she had learned once in an amateur musical comedy; and in a burst of inspiration finished up in an Al Jolson position, on her knees with her arms stretched out to her audience in syncopated appeal.

Then she rose, bowed and left the stage.

For an instant there was silence, the silence of a cold tomb; then perhaps half a dozen hands joined in a faint, perfunctory applause that in a second had died completely away.

"Heavens!" thought Myra. "Was it as bad as all that? Or did I shock 'em?"

Mr. Whitney, however, seemed delighted. He was waiting for her in the wings and seizing her hand shook it enthusiastically.

"Quite wonderful!" he chuckled. "You are a delightful little actress—and you'll be a valuable addition to our little plays. Would you like to give an encore?"

"No!" said Myra shortly, and turned away.

In a shadowy corner she waited until the crowd had filed out, with an angry unwillingness to face them immediately after their rejection of her effort.

When the ballroom was quite empty she walked slowly up the stairs, and there she came upon Knowlton and Mr. Whitney alone in the dark hall, evidently engaged in a heated argument.

They ceased when she appeared and looked toward her eagerly.

"Myra," said Mr. Whitney, "Knowlton wants to talk to you."

"Father," said Knowlton intensely, "I ask you—"

"Silence!" cried his father, his voice ascending testily. "You'll do your duty—now."

Knowleton cast one more appealing glance at him, but Mr. Whitney only shook his head excitedly and, turning, disappeared phantomlike up the stairs.

Knowleton stood silent a moment and finally with a look of dogged determination took her hand and led her toward a room that opened off the hall at the back. The yellow light fell through the door after them and she found herself in a dark wide chamber where she could just distinguish on the walls great square shapes which she took to be frames. Knowleton pressed a button, and immediately forty portraits sprang into life—old gallants from colonial days, ladies with floppity Gainsborough hats, fat women with ruffs and placid clasped hands.

She turned to Knowleton inquiringly, but he led her forward to a row of pictures on the side.

"Myra," he said slowly and painfully, "there's something I have to tell you. These"—he indicated the pictures with his hand—"are family portraits."

There were seven of them, three men and three women, all of them of the period just before the Civil War. The one in the middle, however, was hidden by crimson-velvet curtains.

"Ironic as it may seem," continued Knowleton steadily, "that frame contains a picture of my great-grandmother."

Reaching out, he pulled a little silken cord and the curtains parted, to expose a portrait of a lady dressed as a European but with the unmistakable features of a Chinese.

"My great-grandfather, you see, was an Australian tea importer. He met his future wife in Hong-Kong."

Myra's brain was whirling. She had a sudden vision of Mr. Whitney's yellowish face, peculiar eyebrows and tiny hands and feet—she remembered ghastly tales she had heard of reversions to type—of Chinese babies—and then with a final surge of horror she thought of that sudden hushed cry in the night. She gasped, her knees seemed to crumple up and she sank slowly to the floor.

In a second Knowleton's arms were round her.

"Dearest, dearest!" he cried. "I shouldn't have told you! I shouldn't have told you!"

As he said this Myra knew definitely and unmistakably that she could never marry him, and when she realized it she

cast him a wild pitiful look, and for the first time in her life
fainted dead away.

IV

When she next recovered full consciousness she was in bed.
She imagined a maid had undressed her, for on turning up the
reading lamp she saw that her clothes had been neatly put
away. For a minute she lay there, listening idly while the hall
clock struck two, and then her overwrought nerves jumped in
terror as she heard again that child's cry from the room next
door. The morning seemed suddenly infinitely far away. There
was some shadowy secret near her—her feverish imagination
pictured a Chinese child brought up there in the half dark.

In a quick panic she crept into a negligee and, throwing
open the door, slipped down the corridor toward Knowleton's
room. It was very dark in the other wing, but when she
pushed open his door she could see by the faint hall light that
his bed was empty and had not been slept in. Her terror increased. What could take him out at this hour of the night?
She started for Mrs. Whitney's room, but at the thought of the
dogs and her bare ankles she gave a little discouraged cry and
passed by the door.

Then she suddenly heard the sound of Knowleton's voice
issuing from a faint crack of light far down the corridor, and
with a glow of joy she fled toward it. When she was within
a foot of the door she found she could see through the
crack—and after one glance all thought of entering left her.

Before an open fire, his head bowed in an attitude of great
dejection, stood Knowleton, and in the corner, feet perched
on the table, sat Mr. Whitney in his shirt sleeves, very quiet
and calm, and pulling contentedly on a huge black pipe.
Seated on the table was a part of Mrs. Whitney—that is, Mrs.
Whitney without any hair. Out of the familiar great bust projected Mrs. Whitney's head, but she was bald; on her cheeks
was the faint stubble of a beard, and in her mouth was a large
black cigar, which she was puffing with obvious enjoyment.

"A thousand," groaned Knowleton as if in answer to a
question. "Say twenty-five hundred and you'll be nearer the
truth. I got a bill from the Graham Kennels to-day for those
poodle dogs. They're soaking me two hundred and saying
that they've got to have 'em back tomorrow."

"Well," said Mrs. Whitney in a low barytone voice, "send 'em back. We're through with 'em."

"That's a mere item," continued Knowleton glumly. "Including your salary, and Appleton's here, and that fellow who did the chauffeur, and seventy supes for two nights, and an orchestra—that's nearly twelve hundred, and then there's the rent on the costumes and that darn Chinese portrait and the bribes to the servants. Lord! There'll probably be bills for one thing or another coming in for the next month."

"Well, then," said Appleton, "for pity's sake pull yourself together and carry it through to the end. Take my word for it, that girl will be out of the house by twelve noon."

Knowleton sank into a chair and covered his face with his hands.

"Oh—"

"Brace up! It's all over. I thought for a minute there in the hall that you were going to balk at that Chinese business."

"It was the vaudeville that knocked the spots out of me," groaned Knowleton. "It was about the meanest trick ever pulled on any girl, and she was so darned game about it!"

"She had to be," said Mrs. Whitney cynically.

"Oh, Kelly, if you could have seen the girl look at me tonight just before she fainted in front of that picture. Lord, I believe she loves me! Oh, if you could have seen her!"

Outside Myra flushed crimson. She leaned closer to the door, biting her lip until she could taste the faintly bitter savor of blood.

"If there was anything I could do now," continued Knowleton—"anything in the world that would smooth it over I believe I'd do it."

Kelly crossed ponderously over, his bald shiny head ludicrous above his feminine negligee, and put his hand on Knowleton's shoulder.

"See here, my boy—your trouble is just nerves. Look at it this way: You undertook somep'n to get yourself out of an awful mess. It's a cinch the girl was after your money—now you've beat her at her own game an' saved yourself an unhappy marriage and your family a lot of suffering. Ain't that so, Appleton?"

"Absolutely!" said Appleton emphatically. "Go through with it."

"Well," said Knowleton with a dismal attempt to be righteous, "if she really loved me she wouldn't have let it all affect her this much. She's not marrying my family."

Appleton laughed.

"I thought we'd tried to make it pretty obvious that she is."

"Oh, shut up!" cried Knowleton miserably.

Myra saw Appleton wink at Kelly.

" 'At's right," he said; "she's shown she was after your money. Well, now then, there's no reason for not going through with it. See here. On one side you've proved she didn't love you and you're rid of her and free as air. She'll creep away and never say a word about it—and your family never the wiser. On the other side twenty-five hundred thrown to the bow-wows, miserable marriage, girl sure to hate you as soon as she finds out, and your family all broken up and probably disownin' you for marryin' her. One big mess, I'll tell the world."

"You're right," admitted Knowleton gloomily. "You're right, I suppose—but oh, the look in that girl's face! She's probably in there now lying awake, listening to the Chinese baby—"

Appleton rose and yawned.

"Well—" he began.

But Myra waited to hear no more. Pulling her silk kimono close about her she sped like lightning down the soft corridor, to dive headlong and breathless into her room.

"My heavens!" she cried, clenching her hands in the darkness. "My heavens!"

V

Just before dawn Myra drowsed into a jumbled dream that seemed to act on through interminable hours. She awoke about seven and lay listlessly with one blue-veined arm hanging over the side of the bed. She who had danced in the dawn at many proms was very tired.

A clock outside her door struck the hour, and with her nervous start something seemed to collapse within her—she turned over and began to weep furiously into her pillow, her tangled hair spreading like a dark aura round her head. To her, Myra Harper, had been done this cheap vulgar trick by a man she had thought shy and kind.

Lacking the courage to come to her and tell her the truth he had gone into the highways and hired men to frighten her.

Between her fevered broken sobs she tried in vain to comprehend the working of a mind which could have conceived this in all its subtlety. Her pride refused to let her think of it as a deliberate plan of Knowleton's. It was probably an idea fostered by this little actor Appleton or by the fat Kelly with his horrible poodles. But it was all unspeakable—unthinkable. It gave her an intense sense of shame.

But when she emerged from her room at eight o'clock and, disdaining breakfast, walked into the garden she was a very self-possessed young beauty, with dry cool eyes only faintly shadowed. The ground was firm and frosty with the promise of winter, and she found gray sky and dull air vaguely comforting and one with her mood. It was a day for thinking and she needed to think.

And then turning a corner suddenly she saw Knowleton seated on a stone bench, his head in his hands, in an attitude of profound dejection. He wore his clothes of the night before and it was quite evident that he had not been to bed.

He did not hear her until she was quite close to him, and then as a dry twig snapped under her heel he looked up wearily. She saw that the night had played havoc with him—his face was deathly pale and his eyes were pink and puffed and tired. He jumped up with a look that was very like dread.

"Good morning," said Myra quietly.

"Sit down," he began nervously. "Sit down; I want to talk to you! I've got to talk to you."

Myra nodded and taking a seat beside him on the bench clasped her knees with her hands and half closed her eyes.

"Myra, for heaven's sake have pity on me!"

She turned wondering eyes on him.

"What do you mean?"

He groaned.

"Myra, I've done a ghastly thing—to you, to me, to us. I haven't a word to say in favor of myself—I've been just rotten. I think it was a sort of madness that came over me."

"You'll have to give me a clew to what you're talking about."

"Myra—Myra"—like all large bodies his confession seemed difficult to imbue with momentum—"Myra—Mr. Whitney is not my father."

"You mean you were adopted?"

"No; I mean—Ludlow Whitney is my father, but this man you've met isn't Ludlow Whitney."

"I know," said Myra coolly. "He's Warren Appleton, the actor."

Knowleton leaped to his feet.

"How on earth—"

"Oh," lied Myra easily, "I recognized him the first night. I saw him five years ago in *The Swiss Grapefruit*."

At this Knowleton seemed to collapse utterly. He sank down limply on to the bench.

"You knew?"

"Of course! How could I help it? It simply made me wonder what it was all about."

With a great effort he tried to pull himself together.

"I'm going to tell you the whole story, Myra."

"I'm all ears."

"Well, it starts with my mother—my real one, not the woman with those idiotic dogs; she's an invalid and I'm her only child. Her one idea in life has always been for me to make a fitting match, and her idea of a fitting match centers round social position in England. Her greatest disappointment was that I wasn't a girl so I could marry a title; instead she wanted to drag me to England—marry me off to the sister of an earl or the daughter of a duke. Why, before she'd let me stay up here alone this fall she made me promise I wouldn't go to see any girl more than twice. And then I met you."

He paused for a second and continued earnestly: "You were the first girl in my life whom I ever thought of marrying. You intoxicated me, Myra. It was just as though you were making me love you by some invisible force."

"I was," murmured Myra.

"Well, that first intoxication lasted a week, and then one day a letter came from mother saying she was bringing home some wonderful English girl, Lady Helena Something-or-Other. And the same day a man told me that he'd heard I'd been caught by the most famous husband hunter in New York. Well, between these two things I went half crazy. I came into town to see you and call it off—got as far as the Biltmore entrance and didn't dare. I started wandering down Fifth Avenue like a wild man, and then I met Kelly. I told him the whole story—and within an hour we'd hatched up this ghastly plan. It was his plan—all the details. His histrionic instinct got the better of him and he had me thinking it was the kindest way out."

"Finish," commanded Myra crisply.

"Well, it went splendidly, we thought. Everything—the station meeting, the dinner scene, the scream in the night, the vaudeville—though I thought that was a little too much—until—until——Oh, Myra, when you fainted under that picture and I held you there in my arms, helpless as a baby, I knew I loved you. I was sorry then, Myra."

There was a long pause while she sat motionless, her hands still clasping her knees—then he burst out with a wild plea of passionate sincerity.

"Myra!" he cried. "If by any possible chance you can bring yourself to forgive and forget I'll marry you when you say, let my family go to the devil, and love you all my life."

For a long while she considered, and Knowleton rose and began pacing nervously up and down the aisle of bare bushes, his hands in his pockets, his tired eyes pathetic now, and full of dull appeal. And then she came to a decision.

"You're perfectly sure?" she asked calmly.

"Yes."

"Very well, I'll marry you to-day."

With her words the atmosphere cleared and his troubles seemed to fall from him like a ragged cloak. An Indian summer sun drifted out from behind the gray clouds and the dry bushes rustled gently in the breeze.

"It was a bad mistake," she continued, "but if you're sure you love me now, that's the main thing. We'll go to town this morning, get a license, and I'll call up my cousin, who's a minister in the First Presbyterian Church. We can go West to-night."

"Myra!" he cried jubilantly. "You're a marvel and I'm not fit to tie your shoe strings. I'm going to make up to you for this, darling girl."

And taking her supple body in his arms he covered her face with kisses.

The next two hours passed in a whirl. Myra went to the telephone and called her cousin, and then rushed upstairs to pack. When she came down a shining roadster was waiting miraculously in the drive and by ten o'clock they were bowling happily toward the city.

They stopped for a few minutes at the City Hall and again at the jeweler's, and then they were in the house of the Reverend Walter Gregory on Sixty-ninth Street, where a sanctimonious gentleman with twinkling eyes and a slight stutter received them cordially and urged them to a breakfast of bacon and eggs before the ceremony.

On the way to the station they stopped only long enough to wire Knowleton's father, and then they were sitting in their compartment on the Broadway Limited.

"Darn!" exclaimed Myra. "I forgot my bag. Left it at Cousin Walter's in the excitement."

"Never mind. We can get a whole new outfit in Chicago."

She glanced at her wrist watch.

"I've got time to telephone him to send it on."

She rose.

"Don't be long, dear."

She leaned down and kissed his forehead.

"You know I couldn't. Two minutes, honey."

Outside Myra ran swiftly along the platform and up the steel stairs to the great waiting room, where a man met her—a twinkly-eyed man with a slight stutter.

"How d-did it go, M-myra?"

"Fine! Oh, Walter, you were splendid! I almost wish you'd join the ministry so you could officiate when I do get married."

"Well—I r-rehearsed for half an hour after I g-got your telephone call."

"Wish we'd had more time. I'd have had him lease an apartment and buy furniture."

"H'm," chuckled Walter. "Wonder how far he'll go on his honeymoon."

"Oh, he'll think I'm on the train till he gets to Elizabeth." She shook her little fist at the great contour of the marble dome. "Oh, he's getting off too easy—far too easy!"

"I haven't f-figured out what the f-fellow did to you, M-myra."

"You never will, I hope."

They had reached the side drive and he hailed her a taxicab.

"You're an angel!" beamed Myra. "And I can't thank you enough."

"Well, any time I can be of use t-to you— By the way, what are you going to do with all the rings?"

Myra looked laughingly at her hand.

"That's the question," she said. "I may send them to Lady Helena Something-or-Other—and—well, I've always had a strong penchant for souvenirs. Tell the driver 'Biltmore,' Walter."

Babes in the Woods

I

She paused at the top of the staircase. The emotions of divers on spring-boards, leading ladies on opening nights, and lumpy, be-striped young men on the day of the Big Game, crowded through her. She felt as if she should have descended to a burst of drums or to a discordant blend of gems from "Thaïs" and "Carmen." She had never been so worried about her appearance, she had never been so satisfied with it. She had been sixteen years old for six months.

"Isabelle!" called Elaine, her cousin, from the doorway of the dressing-room.

"I'm ready." She caught a slight lump of nervousness in her throat.

"I've had to send back to the house for another pair of slippers—it'll be just a minute."

Isabelle started toward the dressing-room for a last peek at a mirror, but something decided her to stand there and gaze down the stairs. They curved tantalizingly and she could just catch a glimpse of two pairs of masculine feet in the hall below.

Pump shod in uniform black they gave no hint of identity, but eagerly she wondered if one pair were attached to Stephen Palms. This young man, as yet unmet, had taken up a considerable part of her day—the first day of her arrival.

Going up in a machine from the station Elaine had volunteered, amid a rain of questions and comment, revelation and exaggeration—

"You remember Stephen Palms; well he is simply mad to see you again. He's stayed over a day from college and he's coming tonight. He's heard *so* much about you—"

It had pleased her to know this. It put them on more equal terms, although she was accustomed to stage her own romances with or without a send-off.

But following her delighted tremble of anticipation came a sinking sensation which made her ask:

"How do you mean he's heard about me? What sort of things?"

Elaine smiled—she felt more or less in the capacity of a show-woman with her more exotic cousin.

"He knows you're good-looking and all that." She paused—"I guess he knows you've been kissed."

Isabelle had shuddered a bit under the fur robe. She was accustomed to be followed by this, but it never failed to arouse in her the same feeling of resentment; yet—in a strange town it was an advantage.

She was a "speed," was she? Well, let them find out! She wasn't quite old enough to be sorry nor nearly old enough to be glad.

Out of the window Isabelle watched the high-piled snow glide by in the frosty morning. It was ever so much colder here than in Baltimore, she had not remembered; the glass of the side door was iced and the windows were shirred with snow in the corners.

Her mind played still with one subject: Did *he* dress like that boy there who walked so calmly down what was evidently a bustling business street, in moccasins and winter-carnival costume? How very *western*! Of course he wasn't that way; he went to college, was a freshman or something.

Really she had no distinct idea of him. A two year back picture had not impressed her except by the big eyes, which he had probably grown up to by now.

However, in the last two weeks, when her Christmas visit to Elaine had been decided on, he had assumed the proportions of a worthy adversary. Children, the most astute of matchmakers, plot and plan quickly, and Elaine had cleverly played a correspondence sonata to Isabelle's excitable temperament. Isabelle was, and had been for some time, capable of very strong, if very transient emotions.

They drew up at a white stone building, set back from the snowy street. Mrs. Hollis greeted her warmly and her various younger cousins were produced from the corners where they skulked politely. Isabelle met them quite tactfully. At her best she allied all with whom she came in contact, except older girls and some women. All the impressions that she made were conscious. The half dozen girls she renewed acquaintance with that morning were all rather impressed—and as much by her direct personality as by her reputation.

Stephen Palms was an open subject of conversation. Evidently he was a bit light of love. He was neither popular nor unpopular. Every girl there seemed to have had an affair with him at some time or other, but no one volunteered any really useful information. He was going to "fall for her" . . .

Elaine had issued that statement to her young set and they were retailing it back to Elaine as fast as they set eyes on Isabelle. Isabelle resolved, that if necessary, she would force herself to like him—she owed it to Elaine—even though she were terribly disappointed. Elaine had painted him in such glowing colors—he was good-looking, had a "line" and was properly inconstant.

In fact, he summed up all the romance that her age and environment led her to desire. Were those his dancing shoes that "shimmied" tentatively around the soft rug below?

All impressions, and in fact all ideas, were terribly kaleidoscopic to Isabelle. She had that curious mixture of the social and artistic temperaments, found so often in two classes, society girls and actresses. Her education, or rather her sophistication, had been absorbed from the boys who had dangled from her favor, her tact was instinctive and her capacity for love affairs was limited only by the number of boys she met. Flirt smiled from her large, black-brown eyes and figured in her intense physical magnetism.

So she waited at the head of the stairs at the Country Club that evening while slippers were fetched. Just as she was getting impatient Elaine came out of the dressing-room beaming with her accustomed good nature and high spirits, and together they descended the broad stairs while the nervous searchlight of Isabelle's mind flashed on two ideas. She was glad she had high color tonight and she wondered if he danced well.

Downstairs, in the Club's great room, the girls she had met in the afternoon surrounded her for a moment, looking unbelievably changed by the soft yellow light; then she heard Elaine's voice repeating a cycle of names and she found herself bowing to a sextet of black and white and terribly stiff figures.

The name Palms figured somewhere, but she did not place him at first. A confused and very juvenile moment of awkward backings and bumpings, and all found themselves arranged talking to the persons they least desired to.

Isabelle maneuvered herself and Duncan Collard, a freshman from Harvard with whom she had once played hopscotch, to a seat on the stairs. A reference, supposedly humorous, to the past was all she needed.

What Isabelle could do socially with one idea was remarkable. First, she repeated it rapturously in an enthusiastic contralto with a trace of a Southern accent; then she held it off at a distance and smiled at it—her wonderful smile; then she delivered it in variations and played a sort of mental catch with it, all this in the nominal form of dialogue.

Duncan was fascinated and totally unconscious that this was being done, not for him, but for the eyes that glistened under the shining, carefully watered hair, a little to her left. As an actor even in the fullest flush of his own conscious magnetism gets a lasting impression of most of the people in the front row, so Isabelle sized up Stephen Palms. First, he was light, and from her feeling of disappointment, she knew that she had expected him to be dark and of pencil slenderness. For the rest, a faint flush and a straight romantic profile, the effect set off by a close-fitting dress suit and a silk ruffled shirt of the kind that women still delight in on men, but men were just beginning to get tired of.

Stephen was just quietly smiling.

"Don't *you* think so?" she said suddenly, turning to him innocent eyed.

He nodded and smiled—an expectant, waiting smile.

Then there was a stir and Elaine led the way over to their table.

Stephen struggled to her side and whispered:

"You're my dinner partner—Isabelle."

Isabelle gasped—this was rather right in line. But really she felt as if a good speech had been taken from the star and given to a minor character—she mustn't lose the leadership a bit. The dinner table glittered with laughter at the confusion of getting places and then curious eyes were turned on her, sitting near the head.

She was enjoying this immensely, and Duncan Collard was so engrossed with the added sparkle of her rising color that he forgot to pull out Elaine's chair and fell into a dim confusion. Stephen was on the other side, full of confidence and vanity, looking at her most consciously. He began directly and so did Duncan.

"I've heard a lot about you since you wore braids—"

"Wasn't it funny this afternoon—"

Both stopped.

Isabelle turned to Stephen shyly.

Her face was always enough answer for anyone, but she decided to speak.

"How—who from?"

"From everybody—for all the years since you've been away."

She blushed appropriately.

On her right, Duncan was hors-de-combat already although he hadn't quite realized it.

"I'll tell you what I remembered about you all these years," Stephen continued.

She leaned slightly toward him and looked modestly at the celery before her.

Duncan sighed—he knew Stephen and the situations that Stephen was born to handle. He turned to Elaine and asked her if she was going away to school next year.

II

Isabelle and Stephen were distinctly not innocent, nor were they otherwise. Moreover, amateur standing had very little value in the game they were beginning—they were each playing a part that they might play for years. They had both started with good looks and excitable temperaments, and the rest was the result of certain accessible popular novels, and dressing-room conversation culled from a slightly older set.

When Isabelle's eyes, wide and innocent, proclaimed the ingénue most, Stephen was proportionately less deceived. He waited for the mask to drop off, but at the same time he did not question her right to wear it.

She, on her part, was not impressed by his studied air of blasé sophistication. She had lived in a larger city and had slightly an advantage in range. But she accepted his pose. It was one of a dozen little conventions of this kind of affair. He was aware that he was getting this particular favor now because she had been coached. He knew that he stood for merely the best thing in sight, and that he would have to improve his opportunity before he lost his advantage.

So they proceeded, with an infinite guile that would have horrified the parents of both.

After the half dozen little dinners were over the dance began.

Everything went smoothly—boys cut in on Isabelle every few feet and then squabbled in the corners with: "You might let me get more than an *inch*!" and "She didn't like it either—she told me so next time I cut in."

It was true—she told everyone so, and gave every hand a parting pressure that said, "You know that your dances are *making* my evening."

But time passed, two hours of it, and the less subtle beaux had better learn to focus their pseudo-passionate glances elsewhere, for eleven o'clock found Isabelle and Stephen sitting on a leather lounge in a little den off the reading room. She was conscious that they were a handsome pair and seemed to belong distinctly on this leather lounge while lesser lights fluttered and chattered downstairs. Boys who passed the door looked in enviously—girls who passed only laughed and frowned, and grew wise within themselves.

They had now reached a very definite stage. They had traded ages and accounts of their lives since they had met last. She had listened to much that she had heard before. He was a freshman at college and was on his class hockey team. He had learned that some of the boys she went with in Baltimore were "terrible speeds" and came to parties intoxicated—most of them were twenty or so, and drove alluring Stutzes. A good half of them seemed to have flunked out of various boarding schools and colleges, but some of them bore sporting names that made him look at her admiringly.

As a matter of fact, Isabelle's closer acquaintance with the colleges was chiefly through older cousins. She had bowing acquaintances with a lot of young men who thought she was "a pretty kid" and "worth keeping an eye on." But Isabelle strung the names into a fabrication of gaiety that would have dazzled a Viennese nobleman. Such is the power of young contralto voices on leather sofas.

I have said that they had reached a very definite stage—nay more, a very critical stage. Stephen had stayed over a day to see her and his train left at twelve-eighteen that night. His trunk and suitcase awaited him at the station and his watch was already beginning to hang heavy in his pocket.

"Isabelle," he said suddenly. "I want to tell you something."

They had been talking lightly about "that funny look in her eyes," and on the relative attractions of dancing and sitting out, and Isabelle knew from the change in his manner exactly what was coming—indeed, she had been wondering how soon it would come.

Stephen reached above their heads and turned out the electric light, so they were in the dark except for the flow from the red lamps that fell through the door from the reading-room. Then he began:

"I don't know—I don't know whether or not you know what you—what I'm going to say. Lordy, Isabelle—this sounds like a line, but it isn't."

"I know," said Isabelle softly.

"We may never meet again like this—I have darned hard luck sometimes."

He was leaning away from her on the other arm of the lounge, but she could see his black eyes plainly in the dark.

"You'll see me again—silly." There was just the slightest emphasis on the last word—so that it became almost a term of endearment.

He continued a bit huskily:

"I've fallen for a lot of people—girls—and I guess you have, too—boys, I mean—but honestly you—" He broke off suddenly and leaned forward, chin on his hands, a favorite and studied gesture. "Oh, what's the use? You'll go your way and I suppose I'll go mine."

Silence for a moment. Isabelle was quite stirred—she wound her handkerchief into a tight ball and by the faint light that streamed over her, dropped it deliberately on the floor. Their hands touched for an instant, but neither spoke. Silences were becoming more frequent and more delicious. Outside another stray couple had come up and were experimenting on the piano in the next room. After the usual preliminary of "chopsticks," one of them started "Babes in the Woods" and a light tenor carried the words into the den—

> "Give me your hand,
> I'll understand,
> We're off to slumberland."

Isabelle hummed it softly and trembled as she felt Stephen's hand close over hers.

"Isabelle," he whispered, "you know I'm mad about you. You *do* give a darn about me?"

"Yes."

"How much do you care—do you like anyone better?"

"No." He could scarcely hear her, although he bent so near that he felt her breath against his cheek.

"Isabelle, I'm going back to college for six long months and why shouldn't we—if I could only just have one thing to remember you by—"

"Close the door."

Her voice had just stirred so that he half wondered whether she had spoken at all.

As he swung the door softly shut, the music seemed quivering just outside.

> "Moonlight is bright,
> Kiss me good night."

What a wonderful song, she thought—everything was wonderful tonight, most of all this romantic scene in the den with their hands clinging and the inevitable looming charmingly close.

The future vista of her life seemed an unending succession of scenes like this, under moonlight and pale starlight, and in the backs of warm limousines and in low, cosy roadsters stopped under sheltering trees—only the boy might change, and this one was so nice.

"Isabelle!"

His whisper blended in the music and they seemed to float nearer together.

Her breath came faster.

"Can't I kiss you, Isabelle?"

Lips half parted, she turned her head to him in the dark.

Suddenly the ring of voices, the sound of running footsteps surged toward them.

Like a flash Stephen reached up and turned on the light and when the door opened and three boys, the wrathy and dance-craving Duncan among them, rushed in, he was turning over the magazines on the table, while she sat without moving, serene and unembarrassed, and even greeted them with a welcoming smile. But her heart was beating wildly and she felt somehow as if she had been deprived.

It was evidently over. There was a clamor for a dance, there was a glance that passed between them, on his side despair, on hers regret, and then the evening went on, with the reassured beaux and the eternal cutting in.

At quarter to twelve Stephen shook hands with her gravely, in a small crowd assembled to wish him goodspeed.

For an instant he lost his poise and she felt slightly unnecessary, when a satirical voice from a concealed wit on the edge of the company cried:

"Take her outside, Stephen."

As he took her hand he pressed it a little and she returned the pressure as she had done to twenty hands that evening—that was all.

At two o'clock, back at Hollis', Elaine asked her if she and Stephen had had a "time" in the den. Isabelle turned to her quietly. In her eyes was the light of the idealist, the inviolate dreamer of Joan-like dreams.

"No!" she answered. "I don't do that sort of thing any more—he asked me to, but I said 'No.' "

As she crept into bed she wondered what he'd say in his special delivery tomorrow. He had such a good-looking mouth—would she ever—?

"Fourteen angels were watching o'er them," sang Elaine sleepily from the next room.

"Damn!" muttered Isabelle as she explored the cold sheets cautiously. "Damn!"

The Camel's Back

The restless, wearied eye of the tired magazine reader resting for a critical second on the above title will judge it to be merely metaphorical. Stories about the cup and the lip and the bad penny and the new broom rarely have anything to do with cups and lips and pennies and brooms. This story is the great exception. It has to do with an actual, material, visible and large-as-life camel's back.

Starting from the neck we will work tailward. Meet Mr. Perry Parkhurst, twenty-eight, lawyer, native of Toledo. Perry has nice teeth, a Harvard education, and parts his hair in the middle. You have met him before—in Cleveland, Portland, St. Paul, Indianapolis, Kansas City and elsewhere. Baker Brothers, New York, pause on their semi-annual trip through the West to clothe him; Montmorency & Co. dispatch a young man posthaste every three months to see that he has the correct number of little punctures on his shoes. He has a domestic roadster now, will have a French roadster if he lives long enough, and doubtless a Chinese one if it comes into fashion. He looks like the advertisement of the young man rubbing his sunset-colored chest with liniment, goes East every year to the Harvard reunion—does everything—smokes a little too much— Oh, you've seen him.

Meet his girl. Her name is Betty Medill, and she would take well in the movies. Her father gives her two hundred a month to dress on and she has tawny eyes and hair, and feather fans of three colors. Meet her father, Cyrus Medill. Though he is to all appearances flesh and blood he is, strange to say, commonly known in Toledo as the Aluminum Man. But when he sits in his club window with two or three Iron Men and the White Pine Man and the Brass Man they look very much as you and I do, only more so, if you know what I mean.

Meet the camel's back—or no—don't meet the camel's back yet. Meet the story.

During the Christmas holidays of 1919, the first real Christmas holidays since the war, there took place in Toledo, counting only the people with the italicized *the,* forty-one dinner parties, sixteen dances, six luncheons male and female, eleven luncheons female, twelve teas, four stag dinners, two weddings and thirteen bridge parties. It was the cumulative effect of all this that moved Perry Parkhurst on the twenty-ninth day of December to a desperate decision.

Betty Medill would marry him and she wouldn't marry him. She was having such a good time that she hated to take such a definite step. Meanwhile, their secret engagement had got so long that it seemed as if any day it might break off of its own weight. A little man named Warburton, who knew it all, persuaded Perry to superman her, to get a marriage license and go up to the Medill house and tell her she'd have to marry him at once or call it off forever. This is some stunt—but Perry tried it on December the twenty-ninth. He presented self, heart, license and ultimatum, and within five minutes they were in the midst of a violent quarrel, a burst of sporadic open fighting such as occurs near the end of all long wars and engagements. It brought about one of those ghastly lapses in which two people who are in love pull up sharp, look at each other coolly and think it's all been a mistake. Afterward they usually kiss wholesomely and assure the other person it was all their fault. Say it all was my fault! Say it was! I want to hear you say it!

But while reconciliation was trembling in the air, while each was, in a measure, stalling it off, so that they might the more voluptuously and sentimentally enjoy it when it came, they were permanently interrupted by a twenty-minute phone call for Betty from a garrulous aunt who lived in the country. At the end of eighteen minutes Perry Parkhurst, torn by pride and suspicion and urged on by injured dignity, put on his long fur coat, picked up his light brown soft hat and stalked out the door.

"It's all over," he muttered brokenly as he tried to jam his car into first. "It's all over—if I have to choke you for an hour, darn you!" This last to the car, which had been standing some time and was quite cold.

He drove downtown—that is, he got into a snow rut that led him downtown.

He sat slouched down very low in his seat, much too dispirited to care where he went. He was living over the next twenty years without Betty.

In front of the Clarendon Hotel he was hailed from the sidewalk by a bad man named Baily, who had big huge teeth and lived at the hotel and had never been in love.

"Perry," said the bad man softly when the roadster drew up beside him at the curb, "I've got six quarts of the doggonedest champagne you ever tasted. A third of it's yours, Perry, if you'll come upstairs and help Martin Macy and me drink it."

"Baily," said Perry tensely, "I'll drink your champagne. I'll drink every drop of it. I don't care if it kills me, I don't care if it's fifty-proof wood alcohol."

"Shut up, you nut!" said the bad man gently. "They don't put wood alcohol in champagne. This is the stuff that proves the world is more than six thousand years old. It's so ancient that the cork is petrified. You have to pull it with a stone drill."

"Take me upstairs," said Perry moodily. "If that cork sees my heart it'll fall out from pure mortification."

The room upstairs was full of those innocent hotel pictures of little girls eating apples and sitting in swings and talking to dogs. The other decorations were neckties and a pink man reading a pink paper devoted to ladies in pink tights.

"When you have to go into the highways and byways—" said the pink man, looking reproachfully at Baily and Perry.

"Hello, Martin Macy," said Perry shortly, "where's this stone-age champagne?"

"What's the rush? This isn't an operation, understand. This is a party."

Perry sat down dully and looked disapprovingly at all the neckties.

Baily leisurely opened the door of a wardrobe and brought out six wicked-looking bottles and three glasses.

"Take off that darn fur coat!" said Martin Macy to Perry. "Or maybe you'd like to have us open all the windows."

"Give me champagne," said Perry.

"Going to the Townsends' circus ball tonight?"

"Am not!"

" 'Vited?"

"Uh-huh."

"Why not go?"

"Oh, I'm sick of parties," exclaimed Perry. "I'm sick of 'em. I've been to so many that I'm sick of 'em."

"Maybe you're going to the Howard Tates' party?"

"No, I tell you; I'm sick of 'em."

"Well," said Macy consolingly, "the Tates' is just for college kids anyways."

"I tell you—"

"I thought you'd be going to one of 'em anyways. I see by the papers you haven't missed a one this Christmas."

"Hm," grunted Perry morosely.

He would never go to any more parties. Classical phrases played in his mind—that side of his life was closed, closed. Now when a man says "closed, closed" like that, you can be pretty sure that some woman has double-closed him, so to speak. Perry was also thinking that other classical thought, about how cowardly suicide is. A noble thought that one— warm and uplifting. Think of all the fine men we should lose if suicide were not so cowardly!

An hour later was six o'clock, and Perry had lost all resemblance to the young man in the liniment advertisement. He looked like a rough draft for a riotous cartoon. They were singing—an impromptu song of Baily's improvisation:

"One Lump Perry, the parlor snake,
    Famous through the city for the way he drinks his tea;
Plays with it, toys with it,
Makes no noise with it,
    Balanced on a napkin on his well-trained knee."

"Trouble is," said Perry, who had just banged his hair with Baily's comb and was tying an orange tie round it to get the effect of Julius Caesar, "that you fellas can't sing worth a damn. Soon's I leave th' air an' start singin' tenor you start singin' tenor too."

"'M a natural tenor," said Macy gravely. "Voice lacks cultivation, tha's all. Gotta natural voice, m'aunt used say. Naturally good singer."

"Singers, singers, all good singers," remarked Baily, who was at the telephone. "No, not the cabaret; I want night clerk. I mean refreshment clerk or some dog-gone clerk 'at's got food—food! I want—"

"Julius Caesar," announced Perry, turning round from the mirror. "Man of iron will and stern 'termination."

"Shut up!" yelled Baily. "Say, iss Mr. Baily. Sen' up enormous supper. Use y'own judgment. Right away."

He connected the receiver and the hook with some difficulty, and then with his lips closed and an air of solemn intensity in his eyes went to the lower drawer of his dresser and pulled it open.

"Lookit!" he commanded. In his hands he held a truncated garment of pink gingham.

"Pants," he explained gravely. "Lookit!" This was a pink blouse, a red tie and a Buster Brown collar.

"Lookit!" he repeated. "Costume for the Townsends' circus ball. I'm h'l' boy carries water for the elephants."

Perry was impressed in spite of himself.

"I'm going to be Julius Caesar," he announced after a moment of concentration.

"Thought you weren't going!" said Macy.

"Me? Sure. I'm goin'. Never miss a party. Good for the nerves—like celery."

"Caesar!" scoffed Baily. "Can't be Caesar! He's not about a circus. Caesar's Shakspere. Go as a clown."

Perry shook his head.

"Nope: Caesar."

"Caesar?"

"Sure. Chariot."

Light dawned on Baily.

"That's right. Good idea."

Perry looked round the room searchingly.

"You lend me a bathrobe and this tie," he said finally.

Baily considered.

"No good."

"Sure, tha's all I need. Caesar was a savage. They can't kick if I come as Caesar if he was a savage."

"No," said Baily, shaking his head slowly. "Get a costume over at a costumer's. Over at Nolak's."

"Closed up."

"Find out."

After a puzzling five minutes at the phone a small, weary voice managed to convince Perry that it was Mr. Nolak speaking, and that they would remain open until eight because of the Townsends' ball. Thus assured, Perry ate a great amount of filet mignon and drank his third of the last bottle of champagne. At eight-fifteen the man in the tall hat who stands in front of the Clarendon found him trying to start his roadster.

"Froze up," said Perry wisely. "The cold froze it. The cold air."

"Froze, eh?"

"Yes. Cold air froze it."

"Can't start it?"

"Nope. Let it stand here till summer. One those hot ole August days'll thaw it out awright."

"Goin' let it stand?"

"Sure. Let 'er stand. Take a hot thief to steal it. Gemme taxi."

The man in the tall hat summoned a taxi.

"Where to, mister?"

"Go to Nolak's—costume fella."

II

Mrs. Nolak was short and ineffectual looking, and on the cessation of the world war had belonged for a while to one of the new nationalities. Owing to the unsettled European conditions she had never since been quite sure what she was. The shop in which she and her husband performed their daily stint was dim and ghostly and peopled with suits of armor and Chinese mandarins and enormous papier-mâché birds suspended from the ceiling. In a vague background many rows of masks glared eyelessly at the visitor, and there were glass cases full of crowns and scepters and jewels and enormous stomachers and paints and powders and crape hair and face creams and wigs of all colors.

When Perry ambled into the shop Mrs. Nolak was folding up the last troubles of a strenuous day, so she thought, in a drawer full of pink silk stockings.

"Something for you?" she queried pessimistically.

"Want costume of Julius Hur, the charioteer."

Mrs. Nolak was sorry, but every stitch of charioteer had been rented long ago. Was it for the Townsends' circus ball?

It was.

"Sorry," she said, "but I don't think there's anything left that's really circus."

This was an obstacle.

"Hm," said Perry. An idea struck him suddenly. "If you've got a piece of canvas I could go's a tent."

"Sorry, but we haven't anything like that. A hardware store is where you'd have to go to. We have some very nice Confederate soldiers."

"No, no soldiers."

"And I have a very handsome king."

He shook his head.

"Several of the gentlemen," she continued hopefully, "are wearing stovepipe hats and swallow-tail coats and going as ringmasters—but we're all out of tall hats. I can let you have some crape hair for a mustache."

"Want somep'm 'stinctive."

"Something—let's see. Well, we have a lion's head, and a goose, and a camel—"

"Camel?" The idea seized Perry's imagination, gripped it fiercely.

"Yes, but it needs two people."

"Camel. That's an idea. Lemme see it."

The camel was produced from his resting place on a top shelf. At first glance he appeared to consist entirely of a very gaunt, cadaverous head and a sizable hump, but on being spread out he was found to possess a dark brown, unwholesome-looking body made of thick, cottony cloth.

"You see it takes two people," explained Mrs. Nolak, holding the camel up in frank admiration. "If you have a friend he could be part of it. You see there's sorta pants for two people. One pair is for the fella in front and the other pair for the fella in back. The fella in front does the lookin' out through these here eyes an' the fella in back he's just gotta stoop over an' folla the front fella round."

"Put it on," commanded Perry.

Obediently Mrs. Nolak put her tabby-cat face inside the camel's head and turned it from side to side ferociously.

Perry was fascinated.

"What noise does a camel make?"

"What?" asked Mrs. Nolak as her face emerged, somewhat smudgy. "Oh, what noise? Why, he sorta brays."

"Lemme see it in a mirror."

Before a wide mirror Perry tried on the head and turned from side to side appraisingly. In the dim light the effect was distinctly pleasing. The camel's face was a study in pessimism, decorated with numerous abrasions, and it must be admitted that his coat was in that state of general negligence peculiar to camels—in fact, he needed to be cleaned and pressed—but distinctive he certainly was. He was majestic. He would have attracted attention in any gathering if only by his melancholy cast of feature and the look of pensive hunger lurking round his shadowy eyes.

"You see you have to have two people," said Mrs. Nolak again.

Perry tentatively gathered up the body and legs and wrapped them about him, tying the hind legs as a girdle round his waist. The effect on the whole was bad. It was even irreverent—like one of those medieval pictures of a monk changed into a beast by the ministrations of Satan. At the very best the ensemble resembled a humpbacked cow sitting on her haunches among blankets.

"Don't look like anything at all," objected Perry gloomily.

"No," said Mrs. Nolak; "you see you got to have two people."

A solution flashed upon Perry.

"You got a date to-night?"

"Oh, I couldn't possibly—"

"Oh, come on," said Perry encouragingly. "Sure you can! Here! Be a good sport and climb into these hind legs."

With difficulty he located them and extended their yawning depths ingratiatingly. But Mrs. Nolak seemed loath. She backed perversely away.

"Oh, no—"

"C'm on! Why, you can be the front if you want to. Or we'll flip a coin."

"Oh, no—"

"Make it worth your while."

Mrs. Nolak set her lips firmly together.

"Now you just stop!" she said with no coyness implied. "None of the gentlemen ever acted up this way before. My husband—"

"You got a husband?" demanded Perry. "Where is he?"

"He's home."

"Wha's telephone number?"

After considerable parley he obtained the telephone number pertaining to the Nolak penates and got into communication with that small, weary voice he had heard once before that day. But Mr. Nolak, though taken off his guard and somewhat confused by Perry's brilliant flow of logic, stuck staunchly to his point. He refused firmly but with dignity to help out Mr. Parkhurst in the capacity of back part of a camel.

Having rung off, or rather having been rung off on, Perry sat down on a three-legged stool to think it over. He named over to himself those friends on whom he might call, and then his mind paused as Betty Medill's name hazily and sorrowfully occurred to him. He had a sentimental thought. He would ask her. Their love affair was over, but she could not refuse this last request. Surely it was not much to ask—to help him keep up his end of social obligation for one short night. And if she insisted she could be the front of the camel and he would go as the back. His magnanimity pleased him. His mind even turned to rosy-colored dreams of a tender reconciliation inside the camel—there hidden away from all the world.

"Now you'd better decide right off."

The bourgeois voice of Mrs. Nolak broke in upon his mellow fancies and roused him to action. He went to the phone and called up the Medill house. Miss Betty was out; had gone out to dinner.

Then, when all seemed lost, the camel's back wandered curiously into the store. He was a dilapidated individual with a cold in his head and a general trend about him of downwardness. His cap was pulled down low on his head, and his chin was pulled down low on his chest, his coat hung down to his shoes, he looked run-down, down at the heels, and—Salvation Army to the contrary—down and out. He said that he was the taxicab driver that the gentleman had hired at the Clarendon Hotel. He had been instructed to wait outside, but he had waited some time and a suspicion had grown upon him that the gentleman had gone out the back way with purpose to defraud him—gentlemen sometimes did—so he had come in. He sank down onto the three-legged stool.

"Wanta go to a party?" demanded Perry sternly.

"I gotta work," answered the taxi driver lugubriously. "I gotta keep my job."

"It's a very good party."

"'S a very good job."

"Come on!" urged Perry. "Be a good fella. See—it's pretty!" He held the camel up and the taxi driver looked at it cynically.

"Huh!"

Perry searched feverishly among the folds of the cloth.

"See!" he cried enthusiastically, holding up a selection of folds. "This is your part. You don't even have to talk. All you have to do is to walk—and sit down occasionally. You do all the sitting down. Think of it. I'm on my feet all the time and you can sit down some of the time. The only time I can sit down is when we're lying down, and you can sit down when—oh, any time. See?"

"What's 'at thing?" demanded the individual dubiously. "A shroud?"

"Not at all," said Perry hurriedly. "It's a camel."

"Huh?"

Then Perry mentioned a sum of money, and the conversation left the land of grunts and assumed a practical tinge. Perry and the taxi driver tried on the camel in front of the mirror.

"You can't see it," explained Perry, peering anxiously out through the eyeholes, "but honestly, ole man, you look sim'ly great! Honestly!"

A grunt from the bump acknowledged this somewhat dubious compliment.

"Honestly, you look great!" repeated Perry enthusiastically. "Move round a little."

The hind legs moved forward, giving the effect of a huge cat-camel hunching his back preparatory to a spring.

"No; move sideways."

The camel's hips went neatly out of joint; a hula dancer would have writhed in envy.

"Good, isn't it?" demanded Perry, turning to Mrs. Nolak for approval.

"It looks lovely," agreed Mrs. Nolak.

"We'll take it," said Perry.

The bundle was safely stowed under Perry's arm and they left the shop.

"Go to the party!" he commanded as he took his seat in the back.

"What party?"

"Fanzy-dress party."

"Where'bouts is it?"

This presented a new problem. Perry tried to remember, but the names of all those who had given parties during the holidays danced confusedly before his eyes. He could ask Mrs. Nolak, but on looking out the window he saw that the shop was dark. Mrs. Nolak had already faded out, a little black smudge far down the snowy street.

"Drive uptown," directed Perry with fine confidence. "If you see a party, stop. Otherwise I'll tell you when we get there."

He fell into a hazy daydream and his thoughts wandered again to Betty—he imagined vaguely that they had had a disagreement because she refused to go to the party as the back part of the camel. He was just slipping off into a chilly doze when he was wakened by the taxi driver opening the door and shaking him by the arm.

"Here we are, maybe."

Perry looked out sleepily. A striped awning led from the curb up to a spreading gray stone house, from inside which issued the low drummy whine of expensive jazz. He recognized the Howard Tate house.

"Sure," he said emphatically; " 'at's it! Tate's party to-night. Sure, everybody's goin'."

"Say," said the individual anxiously after another look at the awning, "you sure these people ain't gonna romp on me for comin' here?"

Perry drew himself up with dignity.

" 'F anybody says anything to you, just tell 'em you're part of my costume."

The visualization of himself as a thing rather than a person seemed to reassure the individual.

"All right," he said reluctantly.

Perry stepped out under the shelter of the awning and began unrolling the camel.

"Let's go," he commanded.

Several minutes later a melancholy, hungry-looking camel, emitting clouds of smoke from his mouth and from the tip of his noble hump, might have been seen crossing the threshold of the Howard Tate residence, passing a startled footman without so much as a snort, and heading directly for the main stairs that led up to the ballroom. The beast walked with a peculiar gait which varied between an uncertain lockstep and a stampede—but can best be described by the word "halting." The camel had a halting gait—and as he walked he alternately elongated and contracted like a gigantic concertina.

III

The Howard Tates are, as everyone who lives in Toledo knows, the most formidable people in town. Mrs. Howard Tate was a Chicago Todd before she became a Toledo Tate, and the family generally affect that conscious simplicity which has begun to be the earmark of American aristocracy. The Tates have reached the stage where they talk about pigs and farms and look at you icy-eyed if you are not amused. They have begun to prefer retainers rather than friends as dinner guests, spend a lot of money in a quiet way and, having lost all sense of competition, are in process of growing quite dull.

The dance this evening was for little Millicent Tate, and though there was a scattering of people of all ages present the dancers were mostly from school and college—the younger married crowd was at the Townsends' circus ball up at the Tallyho Club. Mrs. Tate was standing just inside the ballroom, following Millicent round with her eyes and beaming whenever she caught her eye. Beside her were two middle-aged sycophants who were saying what a perfectly exquisite child Millicent was. It was at this moment that Mrs. Tate was grasped firmly by the skirt and her youngest daughter, Emily, aged eleven, hurled herself with an "Oof!" into her mother's arms.

"Why, Emily, what's the trouble?"

"Mamma," said Emily, wild-eyed but voluble, "there's something out on the stairs."

"What?"

"There's a thing out on the stairs, mamma. I think it's a big dog, mamma, but it doesn't look like a dog."

"What do you mean, Emily?"

The sycophants waved their heads and hemmed sympathetically.

"Mamma, it looks like a—like a camel."

Mrs. Tate laughed.

"You saw a mean old shadow, dear, that's all."

"No, I didn't. No, it was some kind of thing, mamma—big. I was going downstairs to see if there were any more people and this dog or something, he was coming upstairs. Kinda funny, mamma, like he was lame. And then he saw me and gave a sort of growl and then he slipped at the top of the landing and I ran."

Mrs. Tate's laugh faded.

"The child must have seen something," she said.

The sycophants agreed that the child must have seen something—and suddenly all three women took an instinctive step away from the door as the sounds of muffled footsteps were audible just outside.

And then three startled gasps rang out as a dark brown form rounded the corner and they saw what was apparently a huge beast looking down at them hungrily.

"Oof!" cried Mrs. Tate.

"O-o-oh!" cried the ladies in a chorus.

The camel suddenly humped his back, and the gasps turned to shrieks.

"Oh—look!"

"What is it?"

The dancing stopped, but the dancers hurrying over got quite a different impression of the invader from that of the ladies by the door; in fact, the young people immediately suspected that it was a stunt, a hired entertainer come to amuse the party. The boys in long trousers looked at it rather disdainfully and sauntered over with their hands in their pockets, feeling that their intelligence was being insulted. But the girls ran over with much handclapping and many little shouts of glee.

"It's a camel!"

"Well, if he isn't the funniest!"

The camel stood there uncertainly, swaying slightly from side to side and seeming to take in the room in a careful, appraising glance; then as if he had come to an abrupt decision he turned and ambled swiftly out the door.

Mr. Howard Tate had just come out of his den on the lower floor and was standing chatting with a good-looking young man in the hall. Suddenly they heard the noise of shouting upstairs and almost immediately a succession of bumping sounds, followed by the precipitous appearance at the foot of the stairway of a large brown beast who seemed to be going somewhere in a great hurry.

"Now what the devil!" said Mr. Tate, starting.

The beast picked itself up with some dignity and affecting an air of extreme nonchalance, as if he had just remembered an important engagement, started at a mixed gait toward the front door. In fact, his front legs began casually to run.

"See here now," said Mr. Tate sternly. "Here! Grab it, Butterfield! Grab it!"

The young man enveloped the rear of the camel in a pair of brawny arms, and evidently realizing that further locomotion was quite impossible the front end submitted to capture and stood resignedly in a state of some agitation. By this time a flood of young people was pouring downstairs, and Mr. Tate, suspecting everything from an ingenious burglar to an escaped lunatic, gave crisp directions to the good-looking young man:

"Hold him! Lead him in here; we'll soon see."

The camel consented to be led into the den, and Mr. Tate, after locking the door, took a revolver from a table drawer and instructed the young man to take the thing's head off. Then he gasped and returned the revolver to its hiding place.

"Well, Perry Parkhurst!" he exclaimed in amazement.

"'M in the wrong pew," said Perry sheepishly. "Got the wrong party, Mr. Tate. Hope I didn't scare you."

"Well—you gave us a thrill, Perry." Realization dawned on him. "Why, of course; you're bound for the Townsends' circus ball."

"That's the general idea."

"Let me introduce Mr. Butterfield, Mr. Parkhurst. Parkhurst is our most famous young bachelor here." Then turning to Perry: "Butterfield's staying with us for a few days."

"I got a little mixed up," mumbled Perry. "I'm very sorry."

"Heavens, it's perfectly all right; most natural mistake in the world. I've got a clown costume and I'm going down there myself after a while. Silly idea for a man of my age." He turned to Butterfield. "Better change your mind and come down with us."

The good-looking young man demurred. He was going to bed.

"Have a drink, Perry?" suggested Mr. Tate.

"Thanks, I will."

"And, say," continued Tate quickly, "I'd forgotten all about your—friend here." He indicated the rear part of the camel. "I didn't mean to seem discourteous. Is it anyone I know? Bring him out."

"It's not a friend," explained Perry hurriedly. "I just rented him."

"Does he drink?"

"Do you?" demanded Perry, twisting himself tortuously round.

There was a faint sound of assent.

"Sure he does!" said Mr. Tate heartily. "A really efficient camel ought to be able to drink so it'd last him three days."

"Tell you, sir," said Perry anxiously, "he isn't exactly dressed up enough to come out. If you give me the bottle I can hand it back to him and he can take his inside."

From under the cloth was audible the enthusiastic smacking sound inspired by this suggestion. When a butler had appeared with bottles, glasses and siphon one of the bottles was handed back, and thereafter the silent partner could be heard imbibing long potations at frequent intervals.

Thus passed a peaceful hour. At ten o'clock Mr. Tate decided that they'd better be starting. He donned his clown's costume; Perry replaced the camel's head with a sigh; and side by side they progressed on foot the single block between the Tate house and the Tallyho Club.

The circus ball was in full swing. A great tent fly had been put up inside the ballroom and round the walls had been built rows of booths representing the various attractions of a circus side show, but these were now vacated and on the floor swarmed a shouting, laughing medley of youth and color—clowns, bearded ladies, acrobats, bareback riders, ringmasters, tattooed men and charioteers. The Townsends had determined to assure their party of success, so a great quantity of liquor had been surreptitiously brought over from their house in automobiles and it was flowing freely. A green ribbon ran along the wall completely round the ballroom, with pointing arrows alongside of it and signs which instructed the uninitiated to "Follow the green line!" The green line led down to the bar, where waited pure punch and wicked punch and plain dark-green bottles.

On the wall above the bar was another arrow, red and very wavy, and under it the slogan: "Now follow this!"

But even amid the luxury of costume and high spirits represented there the entrance of the camel created something of a stir, and Perry was immediately surrounded by a curious, laughing crowd who were anxious to penetrate the identity of this beast who stood by the wide doorway eying the dancers with his hungry, melancholy gaze.

And then Perry saw Betty. She was standing in front of a booth talking to a group of clowns, comic policemen and

ringmasters. She was dressed in the costume of an Egyptian
snake charmer, a costume carried out to the smallest detail.
Her tawny hair was braided and drawn through brass rings,
the effect crowned with a glittering Oriental tiara. Her fair
face was stained to a warm olive glow and on her bare arms
and the half moon of her back writhed painted serpents with
single eyes of venomous green. Her feet were in sandals and
her skirt was slit to the knees, so that when she walked one
caught a glimpse of other slim serpents painted just above her
bare ankles. Wound around her neck was a huge, glittering,
cotton-stuffed cobra, and her bracelets were in the form of
tiny garter snakes. Altogether a very charming and beautiful
costume—one that made the more nervous among the older
women shrink away from her when she passed, and the more
troublesome ones to make a great talk about "shouldn't be allowed" and "perfectly disgraceful."

But Perry, peering through the uncertain eyes of the camel,
saw only her face, radiant, animated and glowing with excitement, and her arms and shoulders, whose mobile, expressive
gestures made her always the outstanding figure in any gathering. He was fascinated and his fascination exercised a
strangely sobering effect on him. With a growing clarity the
events of the day came back—he had lost forever this shimmering princess in emerald green and black. Rage rose within
him, and with a half-formed intention of taking her away
from the crowd he started toward her—or rather he elongated
slightly, for he had neglected to issue the preparatory command necessary to locomotion.

But at this point fickle Kismet, who for a day had played
with him bitterly and sardonically, decided to reward him in
full for the amusement he had afforded her. Kismet turned the
tawny eyes of the snake charmer to the camel. Kismet led her
to lean toward the man beside her and say, "Who's that? That
camel?"

They all gazed.

"Darned if I know."

But a little man named Warburton, who knew it all, found
it necessary to hazard an opinion:

"It came in with Mr. Tate. I think it's probably Warren
Butterfield, the architect, who's visiting the Tates."

Something stirred in Betty Medill—that age-old interest of
the provincial girl in the visiting man.

"Oh," she said casually after a slight pause.

At the end of the next dance Betty and her partner finished up within a few feet of the camel. With the informal audacity that was the keynote of the evening she reached out and gently rubbed the camel's nose.

"Hello, old camel."

The camel stirred uneasily.

"You 'fraid of me?" said Betty, lifting her eyebrows in mock reproof. "Don't be. You see I'm a snake charmer, but I'm pretty good at camels too."

The camel bowed very low and the groups round laughed and made the obvious remark about the beauty and the beast.

Mrs. Townsend came bustling up.

"Well, Mr. Butterfield," she beamed, "I wouldn't have recognized you."

Perry bowed again and smiled gleefully behind his mask.

"And who is this with you?" she inquired.

"Oh," said Perry in a disguised voice, muffled by the thick cloth and quite unrecognizable, "he isn't a fellow, Mrs. Townsend. He's just part of my costume."

This seemed to get by, for Mrs. Townsend laughed and bustled away. Perry turned again to Betty.

"So," he thought, "this is how much she cares! On the very day of our final rupture she starts a flirtation with another man—an absolute stranger."

On an impulse he gave her a soft nudge with his shoulder and waved his head suggestively toward the hall, making it clear that he desired her to leave her partner and accompany him. Betty seemed quite willing.

"By-by, Bobby," she called laughingly to her partner. "This old camel's got me. Where are we going, Prince of Beasts?"

The noble animal made no rejoinder, but stalked gravely along in the direction of a secluded nook on the side stairs.

There Betty seated herself, and the camel, after some seconds of confusion which included gruff orders and sounds of a heated dispute going on in his interior, placed himself beside her—his hind legs stretching out uncomfortably across two steps.

"Well, camel," said Betty cheerfully, "how do you like our happy party?"

The camel indicated that he liked it by rolling his head ecstatically and executing a gleeful kick with his hoofs.

"This is the first time that I ever had a tête-à-tête with a

man's valet round"—she pointed to the hind legs—"or whatever that is."

"Oh," said Perry, "he's deaf and blind. Forget about him."

"That sure is some costume! But I should think you'd feel
rather handicapped—you can't very well shimmy, even if you
want to."

The camel hung his head lugubriously.

"I wish you'd say something," continued Betty sweetly.
"Say you like me, camel. Say you think I'm pretty. Say you'd
like to belong to a pretty snake charmer."

The camel would.

"Will you dance with me, camel?"

The camel would try.

Betty devoted half an hour to the camel. She devoted at
least half an hour to all visiting men. It was usually sufficient.
When she approached a new man the current débutantes were
accustomed to scatter right and left like a close column de-
ploying before a machine gun. And so to Perry Parkhurst was
awarded the unique privilege of seeing his love as others saw
her. He was flirted with violently!

IV

This paradise of frail foundation was broken into by the
sound of a general ingress to the ballroom; the cotillion was
beginning. Betty and the camel joined the crowd, her brown
hand resting lightly on his shoulder, defiantly symbolizing her
complete adoption of him.

When they entered, the couples were already seating themselves at tables round the walls, and Mrs. Townsend, resplendent as a super bareback rider with rather too rotund calves,
was standing in the center with the ringmaster who was in
charge of arrangements. At a signal to the band everyone rose
and began to dance.

"Isn't it just slick!" breathed Betty.

"You bet!" said the camel.

"Do you think you can possibly dance?"

Perry nodded enthusiastically. He felt suddenly exuberant.
After all, he was here incognito talking to his girl—he felt
like winking patronizingly at the world.

"I think it's the best idea," cried Betty, "to give a party like
this! I don't see how they ever thought of it. Come on, let's
dance!"

So Perry danced the cotillion. I say danced, but that is stretching the word far beyond the wildest dreams of the jazziest terpsichorean. He suffered his partner to put her hands on his helpless shoulders and pull him here and there gently over the floor while he hung his huge head docilely over her shoulder and made futile dummy motions with his feet. His hind legs danced in a manner all their own, chiefly by hopping first on one foot and then on the other. Never being sure whether dancing was going on or not, the hind legs played safe by going through a series of steps whenever the music started playing. So the spectacle was frequently presented of the front part of the camel standing at ease and the rear keeping up a constant energetic motion calculated to rouse a sympathetic perspiration in any soft-hearted observer.

He was frequently favored. He danced first with a tall lady covered with straw who announced jovially that she was a bale of hay and coyly begged him not to eat her.

"I'd like to; you're so sweet," said the camel gallantly.

Each time the ringmaster shouted his call of "Men up!" he lumbered ferociously for Betty with the cardboard wiener-wurst or the photograph of the bearded lady or whatever the favor chanced to be. Sometimes he reached her first, but usually his rushes were unsuccessful and resulted in intense interior arguments.

"For heaven's sake," Perry would snarl fiercely between his clenched teeth, "get a little pep! I could have gotten her that time if you'd picked your feet up!"

"Well, gimme a little warnin'!"

"I did, darn you!"

"I can't see a dog-gone thing in here."

"All you have to do is follow me. It's just like dragging a load of sand round to walk with you."

"Maybe you wanta try back here."

"You shut up! If these people found you in this room they'd give you the worst beating you ever had. They'd take your taxi license away from you!"

Perry surprised himself by the ease with which he made this monstrous threat, but it seemed to have a soporific influence on his companion, for he muttered an "aw gwan" and subsided into abashed silence.

The ringmaster mounted to the top of the piano and waved his hand for silence.

"Prizes!" he cried. "Gather round!"

"Yea! Prizes!"

Self-consciously the circle swayed forward. The rather pretty girl who had mustered the nerve to come as a bearded lady trembled with excitement, hoping to be rewarded for an evening's hideousness. The man who had spent the afternoon having tattoo marks painted on him by a sign painter skulked on the edge of the crowd, blushing furiously when anyone told him he was sure to get it.

"Lady and gent performers of the circus," announced the ringmaster jovially. "I am sure we will all agree that a good time has been had by all. We will now bestow honor where honor is due by bestowing the prizes. Mrs. Townsend has asked me to bestow the prizes. Now, fellow performers, the first prize is for that lady who has displayed this evening the most striking, becoming"—at this point the bearded lady sighed resignedly—"and original costume." Here the bale of hay pricked up her ears. "Now I am sure that the decision which has been decided upon will be unanimous with all here present. The first prize goes to Miss Betty Medill, the charming Egyptian snake charmer."

There was a great burst of applause, chiefly masculine, and Miss Betty Medill, blushing beautifully through her olive paint, was passed up to receive her award. With a tender glance the ringmaster handed down to her a huge bouquet of orchids.

"And now," he continued, looking round him, "the other prize is for that man who has the most amusing and original costume. This prize goes without dispute to a guest in our midst, a gentleman who is visiting here but whose stay we all hope will be long and merry—in short to the noble camel who has entertained us all by his hungry look and his brilliant dancing throughout the evening."

He ceased and there was a hearty burst of applause, for it was a popular choice. The prize, a huge box of cigars, was put aside for the camel, as he was anatomically unable to accept it in person.

"And now," continued the ringmaster, "we will wind up the cotillion with the marriage of Mirth to Folly!

"Form for the grand wedding march, the beautiful snake charmer and the noble camel in front!"

Betty skipped forward cheerily and wound an olive arm round the camel's neck. Behind them formed the procession of little boys, little girls, country jakes, policemen, fat ladies, thin men, sword swallowers, wild men of Borneo, armless wonders and charioteers, some of them well in their cups, all of them excited and happy and dazzled by the flow of light and color round them and by the familiar faces strangely unfamiliar under bizarre wigs and barbaric paint. The voluminous chords of the wedding march done in mad syncopation issued in a delirious blend from the saxophones and trombones—and the march began.

"Aren't you glad, camel?" demanded Betty sweetly as they stepped off. "Aren't you glad we're going to be married and you're going to belong to the nice snake charmer ever afterward?"

The camel's front legs pranced, expressing exceeding joy.

"Minister, minister! Where's the minister?" cried voices out of the revel. "Who's going to be the cler-gy-man?"

The head of Jumbo, rotund negro waiter at the Tallyho Club for many years, appeared rashly through a half-opened pantry door.

"Oh, Jumbo!"

"Get old Jumbo. He's the fella!"

"Come on, Jumbo. How 'bout marrying us a couple?"

"Yea!"

Jumbo despite his protestations was seized by four brawny clowns, stripped of his apron and escorted to a raised dais at the head of the ball. There his collar was removed and replaced back side forward to give him a sanctimonious effect. He stood there grinning from ear to ear, evidently not a little pleased, while the parade separated into two lines leaving an aisle for the bride and groom.

"Lawdy, man," chuckled Jumbo, "Ah got ole Bible 'n' ev'ythin', sho nuff."

He produced a battered Bible from a mysterious interior pocket.

"Yea! Old Jumbo's got a Bible!"

"Razor, too, I'll bet!"

"Marry 'em off, Jumbo!"

Together the snake charmer and the camel ascended the cheering aisle and stopped in front of Jumbo, who adopted a grave pontifical air.

"Where's your license, camel?"

"Make it legal, camel."

A man near by prodded Perry.

"Give him a piece of paper, camel. Anything'll do."

Perry fumbled confusedly in his pocket, found a folded paper and pushed it out through the camel's mouth. Holding it upside down Jumbo pretended to scan it earnestly.

"Dis yeah's a special camel's license," he said. "Get your ring ready, camel."

Inside the camel Perry turned round and addressed his worse half.

"Gimme a ring, for Pete's sake!"

"I ain't got none," protested a weary voice.

"You have. I saw it."

"I ain't goin' to take it offen my hand."

"If you don't I'll kill you."

There was a gasp and Perry felt a huge affair of rhinestone and brass inserted into his hand.

Again he was nudged from the outside.

"Speak up!"

"I do!" cried Perry quickly.

He heard Betty's responses given in a laughing debonair tone, and the sound of them even in this burlesque thrilled him.

If it was only real! he thought. If it only was!

Then he had pushed the rhinestone through a tear in the camel's coat and was slipping it on her finger, muttering ancient and historic words after Jumbo. He didn't want anyone to know about this ever. His one idea was to slip away without having to disclose his identity, for Mr. Tate had so far kept his secret well. A dignified young man, Perry—and this might injure his infant law practice.

"Kiss her, camel!"

"Embrace the bride!"

"Unmask, camel, and kiss her!"

Instinctively his heart beat high as Betty turned to him laughingly and began playfully to stroke the cardboard muzzle. He felt his self-control giving away, he longed to seize her in his arms and declare his identity and kiss those scarlet lips that smiled teasingly at him from only a foot away—when suddenly, the laughter and applause round them died away and a curious hush fell over the hall. Perry and Betty looked up in surprise. Jumbo had given vent to a huge "Hello!" in such a startled and amazed voice that all eyes were bent on him.

"Hello!" he said again. He had turned round the camel's

marriage license, which he had been holding upside down, produced spectacles and was studying it intently.

"Why," he exclaimed, and in the pervading silence his words were heard plainly by everyone in the room, "this yeah's a sho-nuff marriage permit."

"What?"

"Huh?"

"Say it again, Jumbo!"

"Sure you can read?"

Jumbo waved them to silence and Perry's blood burned to fire in his veins as he realized the break he had made.

"Yassuh!" repeated Jumbo. "This yeah's a sho-nuff license, and the pa'ties concerned one of 'em is dis yeah young lady, Miz Betty Medill, and th' other's Mistah Perry Pa'khurst!"

There was a general gasp, and a low rumble broke out as all eyes fell on the camel. Betty shrank away from him quickly, her tawny eyes giving out sparks of fury.

"Is you Mistah Pa'khurst, you camel?"

Perry made no answer. The crowd pressed up closer and stared at him as he stood frozen rigid with embarrassment, his cardboard face still hungry and sardonic, regarding the ominous Jumbo.

"You-all bettah speak up!" said Jumbo slowly, "this yeah's a mighty serous mattah. Outside mah duties at this club ah happens to be a sho-nuff minister in the Firs' Cullud Baptis' Church. It done look to me as though you-all is gone an' got married."

V

The scene that followed will go down forever in the annals of the Tallyho Club. Stout matrons fainted, strong men swore, wild-eyed débutantes babbled in lightning groups instantly formed and instantly dissolved, and a great buzz of chatter, virulent yet oddly subdued, hummed through the chaotic ballroom. Feverish youths swore they would kill Perry or Jumbo or themselves or someone and the Baptis' preacheh was besieged by a tempestuous covey of clamorous amateur lawyers, asking questions, making threats, demanding precedents, ordering the bonds annulled, and especially trying to ferret out any hint or suspicion of prearrangement in what had occurred.

In the corner Mrs. Townsend was crying softly on the

shoulder of Mr. Howard Tate, who was trying vainly to comfort her; they were exchanging "all my fault's" volubly and voluminously. Outside on a snow covered walk Mr. Cyrus Medill, the Aluminum Man, was being paced slowly up and down between two brawny charioteers giving vent now to a grunt, now to a string of unrepeatables, now to wild pleadings that they'd just let him get at Jumbo. He was facetiously attired for the evening as a wild man of Borneo, and the most exacting stage manager after one look at his face would have acknowledged that any improvement in casting the part would have been quite impossible.

Meanwhile the two principals held the real center of the stage. Betty Medill—or was it Betty Parkhurst?—weeping furiously, was surrounded by the plainer girls—the prettier ones were too busy talking about her to pay much attention to her—and over on the other side of the hall stood the camel, still intact except for his headpiece, which dangled pathetically on his chest. Perry was earnestly engaged in making protestations of his innocence to a ring of angry, puzzled men. Every few minutes just as he had apparently proved his case someone would mention the marriage certificate, and the inquisition would begin again.

A girl named Marion Cloud, considered the second best belle of Toledo, changed the gist of the situation by a remark she made to Betty.

"Well," she said maliciously, "it'll all blow over, dear. The courts will annul it without question."

Betty's tears dried miraculously in her eyes, her lips shut tightly together, and she flashed a withering glance at Marion. Then she rose and scattering her sympathizers right and left walked directly across the room to Perry, who also rose and stood looking at her in terror. Again silence crept down upon the room.

"Will you have the decency," she said "to grant me five minutes' conversation—or wasn't that included in your plans?"

He nodded, his mouth unable to form words.

Indicating coldly that he was to follow her she walked out into the hall with her chin uptilted and headed for the privacy of one of the little card rooms.

Perry started after her, but was brought to a jerky halt by the failure of his hind legs to function.

"You stay here!" he commanded savagely.

"I can't," whined a voice from the hump, "unless you get out first and let me get out."

Perry hesitated, but the curious crowd was unbearable, and unable any longer to tolerate eyes he muttered a command and with as much dignity as possible the camel moved carefully out on its four legs.

Betty was waiting for him.

"Well," she began furiously, "you see what you've done! You and that crazy license! I told you you shouldn't have gotten it! I told you!"

"My dear girl, I—"

"Don't dear-girl me! Save that for your real wife if you ever get one after this disgraceful performance."

"I—"

"And don't try to pretend it wasn't all arranged. You know you gave that colored waiter money! You know you did! Do you mean to say you didn't try to marry me?"

"No—I mean, yes—of course—"

"Yes, you'd better admit it! You tried it, and now what are you going to do? Do you know my father's nearly crazy? It'll serve you right if he tries to kill you. He'll take his gun and put some cold steel in you. O-o-oh! Even if this marr—this thing can be annulled it'll hang over me all the rest of my life!"

Perry could not resist quoting softly: " 'Oh, camel, wouldn't you like to belong to the pretty snake charmer for all your—' "

"Shut up!" cried Betty.

There was a pause.

"Betty," said Perry finally with a very faint hopefulness, "there's only one thing to do that will really get us out clear. That's for you to marry me."

"Marry you!"

"Yes. Really it's the only—"

"You shut up! I wouldn't marry you if—if—"

"I know. If I were the last man on earth. But if you care anything about your reputation—"

"Reputation!" she cried. "You're a nice one to think about my reputation *now*. Why didn't you think about my reputation before you hired that horrible Jumbo to—to—"

Perry tossed up his hands hopelessly.

"Very well. I'll do anything you want. Lord knows I renounce all claims!"

"But," said a new voice, "I don't."

Perry and Betty started, and she put her hand to her heart.

"For heaven's sake, what was that?"

"It's me," said the camel's back.

In a minute Perry had whipped off the camel's skin, and a lax, limp object, his clothes hanging on him damply, his hand clenched tightly on an almost empty bottle, stood defiantly before them.

"Oh," cried Betty, tears starting again to her eyes, "you brought that object in here to frighten me! You told me he was deaf—that awful person!"

The ex-camel's back sat down on a chair with a sigh of satisfaction.

"Don't talk 'at way about me, lady; I ain't no person. I'm your husband."

"Husband!"

The cry was wrung simultaneously from Betty and Perry.

"Why, sure. I'm as much your husband as that gink is. The smoke didn't marry you to the camel's front. He married you to the whole camel. Why, that's my ring you got on your finger!"

With a little cry she snatched the ring from her finger and flung it passionately at the floor.

"What's all this?" demanded Perry dazedly.

"Jes' that you better fix me an' fix me right. If you don't I'm a-gonna have the same claim you got to bein' married to her!"

"That's bigamy," said Perry, turning gravely to Betty.

Then came the supreme moment of Perry's early life, the ultimate chance on which he risked his fortunes. He rose and looked first at Betty, where she sat weakly, her face aghast at this new complication, and then at the individual who swayed from side to side on his chair, uncertainly yet menacingly.

"Very well," said Perry slowly to the individual, "you can have her. Betty, I'm going to prove to you that as far as I'm concerned our marriage was entirely accidental. I'm going to renounce utterly my rights to have you as my wife, and give you to—to the man whose ring you wear—your lawful husband."

There was a pause and four horror-stricken eyes were turned on him.

"Good-by, Betty," he said brokenly. "Don't forget me in

your new-found happiness. I'm going to leave for the Far West on the morning train. Think of me kindly, Betty."

With a last glance at them he turned on his heel and his head bowed on his chest as his hand touched the door knob.

"Good-by," he repeated. He turned the door knob.

But at these words a flying bundle of snakes and silk and tawny hair hurled itself at him.

"Oh, Perry, don't leave me! I can't face it alone! Perry, Perry, take me with you!"

Her tears rained down in a torrent and flowed damply on his neck. Calmly he folded his arms about her.

"I don't care," she cried tearfully. "I love you and if you can wake up a minister at this hour and have it done over again I'll go West with you."

Over her shoulder the front part of the camel looked at the back part of the camel and they exchanged a particularly subtle, esoteric sort of wink that only true camels can understand.

The Lees of Happiness

I

If you should look through the files of old magazines for the first years of the present century you would find, sandwiched in between the stories of Richard Harding Davis and Frank Norris and others long since dead, the work of one Jeffrey Curtain: a novel or two, and perhaps three or four dozen short stories. You could, if you were interested, follow them along until, say, 1908, when they suddenly disappeared.

When you had read them all you would have been quite sure that here were no masterpieces—here were passably good stories, a bit out of date now, but doubtless the sort that would then have whiled away a dreary half hour's wait in a dental office. The man who did them was of good intelligence surely, talented, glib, probably young. In the samples of his work you found there would have been nothing to stir you to more than a faint interest in the whims of life—no deep interior laughs, no sense of futility or hint of tragedy.

After reading them you would yawn and put the number back in the files and perhaps if you were in some library reading room you would decide that by way of variety you would look at a newspaper of the period and see whether the Japs had taken Port Arthur. But if by any chance the newspaper you had chosen was the right one and had crackled open at the theatrical page your eyes would have been arrested and held and for at least a minute you would have forgotten Port Arthur as quickly as you forgot Chateau Thierry. For you would, by this fortunate chance, be looking at the portrait of an exquisitely beautiful woman.

Those were the days of Florodora and of sextets, of pinched in waists and blown out sleeves, of almost bustles and absolute ballet skirts, but here, without doubt, disguised as she might be by the unaccustomed stiffness and old fashion of her costume, was a butterfly of butterflies. Here was the gayety of the period—the soft wine of eyes, the songs that flurried hearts, the toasts and the bouquets, the dances and the dinners. Here was a Venus of the hansom cab, the Gibson girl in her glorious prime. Here was . . .

. . . here was, you find by looking at the name beneath, one Roxanne Milbank, who had been chorus girl and understudy in "The Daisy Chain," but who, by reason of an excellent performance when the star was indisposed, gained a leading part.

You would look again—and wonder. Why you had never heard of her. Why did her name not linger in popular songs and vaudeville jokes and cigar bands and the memory of that gay old uncle of yours along with Lillian Russell and Stella Mayhew and Anna Held? Roxanne Milbank—where had she gone? What dark trap door had opened suddenly and swallowed her up? Was her name in the list of actresses married to English noblemen that you read in last Sunday's supplement? No doubt she was dead—poor beautiful young lady—and quite forgotten.

I am hoping too much. I am having you stumble on Jeffrey Curtain's stories and Roxanne Milbank's picture. It would be incredible that you would find a little newspaper item six months later—a single item two inches by four which informed the public of the marriage very quietly of Miss Roxanne Milbank, who had been on tour with "The Daisy Chain," to Mr. Jeffrey Curtain, the popular author. "Mrs. Curtain," it added dispassionately, "will retire from the stage."

It was a marriage of love. He was sufficiently spoiled to be irresistible; she was ingenuous enough to be quite charming. Like two floating logs they met in a head-on rush, caught inseparably, and sped along the stream together. Yet had Jeffrey Curtain kept at scrivening for two score years he could not have put a twist or quirk into one of his stories weirder than the twist and quirk that came into his own life. Had Roxanne Milbank played three dozen parts and filled five thousand houses she could never have had a role with more of happiness and despair of tragic intensity and divine irony than were in the rôle prepared for Roxanne Curtain.

For a year they lived in hotels, traveled to California, to Alaska, to Florida, to Mexico, loved and quarreled gently, and kissed and gloried in the golden triflings of his wit and her beauty—they were young and gravely passionate; they were companions inseparable; they yielded all and demanded all and then yielded again in ecstasies of unselfishness and pride. She loved the swift tones of his voice, his summer tan, his frantic, unfounded jealousy. He loved her dark radiance, the white irises of her eyes, and the warm, lustrous enthusiasm of her smile.

"Don't you like her?" he would demand rather excitedly and shyly. "Isn't she a wonder? Did you ever see—"

"Yes," they would answer grinning because they couldn't help themselves. "She's a wonder. You're lucky."

"You bet I am!" he would exclaim, his voice trembling. "You just bet I am!"

The year passed. They tired of hotels. They bought an old house and twenty acres near the town of Marlowe, half an hour from Chicago; bought a little car, and moved out riotously with a pioneering hallucination that would have confounded Balboa.

"Your room will be here!" they cried in turn.

—And then:

"And my room here!"

"And the nursery here when we have children."

"And we'll build a sleeping porch—O next year."

"O, won't it be good—good!"

They moved out in April. In July Jeffrey's closest friend, Harry Cromwell, came out to spend a week—they met him at the end of the long lawn and escorted him proudly and triumphantly to the house.

Harry was married also. His wife had had a baby some six months before and was still recuperating at her mother's in New York. Roxanne had gathered from Jeffrey that Harry's wife was not as attractive as Harry—Jeffrey had met her once and considered her—O, rather shallow. But Harry had been married nearly two years and was apparently happy, so Jeffrey guessed that she was probably all right, but—well, not congenial.

"I'm making biscuits," chattered Roxanne gravely. "Can your wife make biscuits? The cook is showing me how. I think every woman should know how to make biscuits. It sounds so utterly disarming. A woman who can make biscuits can surely do no—"

"You'll have to come out here and live," insisted Jeffrey. "Get a place out in the country like us, for you and Kitty."

"You don't know Kitty," protested Harry. "She's probably more civic than a sidewalk. She's got to have her theaters and vaudevilles."

"Bring her out," repeated Jeffrey. "We'll have a colony. There's a nice crowd of young people here already. We'll put the fresh air in her and— O, bring her out!"

They were at the porch steps now and Roxanne made a brisk graceful gesture toward a dilapidated structure on the right.

"The garage," she announced. "It will also be Jeffrey's writing studio within the month. Meanwhile dinner is at seven. Meanwhile to that I will mix a cocktail."

She vanished into the kitchen and the two men ascended the stairs—that is, they ascended half way, for at the first landing Jeffrey dropped his guest's suitcase and in a cross between a wild query and an anxious cry exclaimed:

"For God's sake, Harry, how do you like her? Isn't she a marvel?"

"We will go upstairs," answered his guest, "and we will shut the door."

Half an hour later as the two men were sitting together in the library uttering brave phrases over their cocktails Roxanne reissued from the kitchen, bearing before her a pan of biscuits. Jeffrey and Harry rose.

"They're beautiful, dear," said the husband eagerly.

"They may be said," corroborated Harry without a smile, "to be esthetically exquisite."

Roxanne beamed.

"Taste one. I couldn't bear to touch them before you'd seen them all and I can't bear to take them back until I find what they taste like."

"Like manna, darling."

Simultaneously the two men raised the biscuits to their lips, nibbled tentatively. Simultaneously they tried to casually change the subject. But Roxanne, undeceived, set down the pan and seized a biscuit feverishly. After a second her comment rang out with lugubrious finality.

"Absolutely bum!"

"Really—"

"Why, I didn't notice—"

Roxanne roared.

"O, I'm useless," she cried, laughing. "Turn me out, Jeffrey—I'm a parasite; I'm no good—"

Jeffrey's arm slipped around her.

"Darling, I'll eat your biscuits."

"They're beautiful anyway," insisted Roxanne.

"They're—they're decorative," suggested Harry.

Jeffrey took him up enthusiastically.

"That's the word. They're decorative; they're masterpieces. We'll use them."

He rushed to the kitchen and returned with a hammer and a handful of nails.

"We'll use them, by golly, Roxanne!" he cried. "We'll make a frieze out of them."

"Don't!" wailed Roxanne. "Our beautiful house."

"Never mind. We're going to have the library repapered in October. Don't you remember?"

"Well—"

Bang! The first biscuit was impaled to the wall where it quivered for a moment like a live thing.

Bang! Bang! Bang!

When Roxanne returned with a second round of cocktails the biscuits were in a perpendicular row, twelve of them, like a collection of primitive spear heads.

"Roxanne," exclaimed Jeffrey, "you're an artist! Cook?—nonsense! You shall illustrate my books!"

During dinner the twilight twined gently into dusk and later it was a starry dark outside filled and permeated with the frail gorgeousness of Roxanne's filmy white dress and the richness of her low laugh.

—Such a little girl she is, thought Harry, Not as old as Kitty.

He mentally compared the two. Kitty—nervous without being sensitive, temperamental without temperament, a woman who seemed to flit and never light—and Roxanne, who was as young as a spring night and as full of adolescent laughter.

—A good match for Jeffrey, he thought again. Two very young people, the sort who'll stay very young until they suddenly find themselves very old.

Harry thought these things between his constant thoughts about Kitty. He was depressed about Kitty. It seemed to him that she was well enough to come back to Chicago and bring his little son. He was thinking vaguely of Kitty when he said goodnight to his friend's wife and his friend at the foot of the stairs.

"You're our first real house guest," cried Roxanne after him. "Aren't you thrilled and proud?"

When he was out of sight around the stair corner she

turned to Jeffrey, who was standing beside her resting his hand on the end of the banister.

"Are you tired, my dearest?"

Jeffrey rubbed the center of his forehead with his fingers. "A little. How did you know?"

"O, how could I help knowing about you—about you?"

"It's a headache," he said moodily. "Splitting. I'll take some aspirin."

She reached over and snapped out the light and with his arm tight about her slender waist they walked up the stairs together.

II

Harry's week was a delight. They drove about the dreamy lanes rare with honeysuckle or idled day-long by the lake, swimming. In the evening Roxanne sitting inside played to them while the ashes whitened on the glowing ends of their cigars. Then came a telegram from Kitty saying that she wanted Harry to come for her, so Roxanne and Jeffrey were left alone in that privacy of which they never seemed to tire.

"Alone" thrilled them again. They wandered about the house feeling the presence of the other and reveling in it; they sat on the same side of the table like honeymooners; they were intensely absorbed in each other, intensely happy.

The town of Marlowe, though a comparatively old settlement, had only recently acquired a "society." Five or six years before, alarmed at the smoky swelling of Chicago, two or three young married couples, "bungalow people," had moved out; they had persuaded their friends that they had found a paradise, and the friends followed. The Jeffrey Curtains found an already formed but open armed set prepared to welcome them; the country club, ballroom, and golf links yawned for their dancing feet and facile mashies, and there were bridge parties, and poker parties, and parties where they drank beer, and parties where they drank nothing at all.

It was at a poker party that they found themselves a week after Harry's departure. There were two tables, and a good proportion of the young wives were smoking cigarets and shouting their bets and being very daringly mannish for those days.

Roxanne had left the game early and taken to perambulation; she wandered into the pantry and found herself some grape juice—beer gave her a headache—and then passed from table to table, looking over shoulders at the hands, keeping a tender eye on Jeffrey and being pleasantly unexcited and content. Jeffrey, with an expression of intense concentration, was raising a sturdy pile of chips of all colors, and Roxanne knew by the deepened wrinkle between his eyes that he was interested. She was glad—she liked to see him interested in small things.

She crossed over quietly and sat down on the arm of his chair.

She must have sat there five minutes, listening to the sharp intermittent comments of the men and the chatter of the women which rose from the table like soft smoke—and yet scarcely hearing either. Then quite innocently she reached out her hand, intending to place it on Jeffrey's shoulder—as it touched him he started of a sudden, gave a little grunt, and, sweeping back his arm furiously, caught her a glancing blow on her elbow.

There was a general gasp. Roxanne regained her balance, gave a little cry, and rose quickly to her feet. It had been the greatest shock of her life. This, from Jeffrey, the heart of kindness, of consideration—this instinctively brutal gesture.

The gasp became a silence. A dozen eyes were turned on Jeffrey, who looked up as though seeing Roxanne for the first time. An expression of bewilderment settled on his face.

"Why—Roxanne—" he said haltingly.

Into a dozen minds entered a quick suspicion, a rumor of scandal. Could it be that behind the scenes with this couple outwardly so well mated, so in love, there lurked some secret antipathy? What was this streak of fire across such a cloudless heaven!

"Jeffrey!"—Roxanne's voice was almost pleading—startled and horrified, she yet knew that it was a mistake. It never occurred to her to blame him or to resent it. Her word was a trembling supplication—"Tell me, Jeffrey," it said, "tell Roxanne, your own Roxanne."

"Why, Roxanne—" began Jeffrey again. The bewildered look changed to pain. He was clearly as startled as she. "I didn't intend that," he went on: "you startled me. You—I felt as if some one were attacking me. I—how—how idiotic!"

"Jeffrey!" Again the word was a prayer, incense offered up to a high God through some new and unfathomable darkness.

They were both on their feet, they were saying good-by,

faltering, apologizing, explaining. There was no attempt to pass it off easily. That way lay sacrilege. Jeffrey had not been feeling well, they said. He had become nervous. Back of both their minds was the unexplained horror of that blow—the marvel that there had been for an instant something between them—his anger and her fear—and now to both a sorrow, momentary, no doubt, but to be bridged at once, at once, while there was yet time. Was that swift water lashing under their feet—the fierce glint of some uncharted chasm?

Out in their car under the harvest moon he talked brokenly. It was just—incomprehensible to him, he said. He had been thinking of the poker game—absorbed—and the touch on his shoulder had seemed like an attack. An attack, that was it! He clung to that word, flung it up as a shield. He had hated what touched him. With the impact of his hand it had gone, that— nervousness. That was all he knew.

Both their eyes filled with tears and they whispered love there under the broad night as the serene streets of Marlowe sped by. Later, when they went to bed, they were quite calm. Jeffrey was to take a week off all work—was simply to loll, and sleep, and go on long walks until this nervousness left him. When they had decided this safety settled down upon Roxanne. The pillows underhead became soft and friendly; the bed on which they lay seemed wide, and white, and sturdy under the radiance that streamed in at the window.

Five days later, in the first cool of late afternoon, Jeffrey picked up an oak chair and sent it crashing through his own front window. Then he lay down on the couch like a little child, weeping piteously and begging to die. A blood clot the size of a marble had broken in his brain.

III

There is a sort of waking nightmare that sets in sometimes when one has missed a sleep or two, a feeling that comes with extreme fatigue and a new sun, that the quality of the life around has changed. It is a fully convinced, articulate conviction that somehow the existence one is then leading is a branch shoot of life and is related to life only as a moving picture or a mirror—that the people, and streets, and houses are only projections from a very dim and chaotic past. It was in such a state that Roxanne found herself during the first months of Jeffrey's illness. She slept only when she was ut-

terly exhausted; she awoke under a cloud. The long, sober
voiced consultations, the faint aura of medicine in the halls,
the sudden tiptoeing in a house that had echoed to many
cheerful footsteps, and, most of all, Jeffrey's white face amid
the pillows of the bed they had shared together—these things
subdued her and made her indelibly older. The doctors held
out hope, but that was all. A long rest, they said, a long rest
and quiet. So responsibility came to Roxanne. It was she now
who paid the bills, pored over his bank book, corresponded
with his publishers. She was in the kitchen constantly. She
learned from the nurse how to prepare his meals and after the
first month took complete charge of the sickroom. She had
had to let the nurse go for reasons of economy. One of the
two colored girls left at the same time. Roxanne had realized
that except for a very scanty invested capital they had been
living from short story to short story.

The most frequent visitor was Harry Cromwell. He had
been shocked and depressed by the news and though his wife
was now living with him in Chicago he found time to come
out for an hour or two several times a month. Roxanne found
his sympathy welcome—there was some quality of suffering
in the man, some inherent pitifulness that made her comfortable when he was near. Roxanne's nature had suddenly and
strangely deepened. She felt sometimes that with Jeffrey she
was losing her children also, those children that now most of
all she needed and should have had.

It was six months after Jeffrey's collapse and when the
nightmare had faded, leaving not the old world but a new
one, grayer and colder, that she went to see Harry's wife.
Finding herself in Chicago with an extra hour before train
time, she decided out of a mixture of curiosity and courtesy
to call.

As she stepped inside the door she had an immediate impression that the apartment was very like some place she had
seen before—and almost instantly she remembered a round-
the-corner bakery of her childhood, a bakery full of rows and
rows of pink frosted cakes—a stuffy pink, pink as a food,
pink triumphant, vulgar, and odious.

And this apartment was like that. It was pink. It smelled
pink!

Mrs. Cromwell, attired in a wrapper of pink and black,
opened the door. Her hair was yellow, heightened, Roxanne
imagined, by a dash of peroxide in the shampoo water every

two weeks. Her eyes were a thin waxen blue—she was pretty and a bit too consciously graceful. Her cordiality was strident and intimate, hostility melted so quickly to hospitality that it seemed they were both merely in the face and voice—never touching nor touched by the deep core of egotism beneath.

But to Roxanne these things were secondary; her eyes were caught and held in uncanny fascination by the wrapper. It was vilely unclean. From its lowest hem up four inches it was sheerly dirty with the blue dust of the floor; for the next three inches it was a gray—then it shaded off into its natural color, which was—pink. It was dirty at the sleeves, too, and at the collar—and when the woman turned to lead the way into the parlor Roxanne was sure that her neck was dirty.

A one sided rattle of conversation began. Mrs. Cromwell became explicit about her likes and dislikes, her head, her stomach, her teeth, her members, her apartment—avoiding with a sort of insolent meticulousness any inclusion of Roxanne with life, as if presuming that Roxanne, having been dealt a blow, wished life to be carefully skirted.

Roxanne smiled. That kimono! That neck.

After five minutes a little boy toddled into the parlor—a very dirty little boy clad in much used pink rompers. His face was smudgy—Roxanne wanted to take him into her lap and wipe his nose; other parts in the vicinity of his head needed attention, his tiny shoes were kicked out at the toes. Unspeakable!

"What a darling little boy!" exclaimed Roxanne, smiling radiantly. "Come her to me."

Mrs. Cromwell looked coldly at her son.

"He will get dirty. Look at that face!" She held her head on one side and regarded it critically.

"Isn't he *darling*," repeated Roxanne.

"Look at his rompers," frowned Mrs. Cromwell.

"He needs a change, don't you, George?"

George stared at her curiously. One could see that to his mind the word rompers connotated a garment extraneously smeared as this one.

"I tried to make him look respectable this morning," complained Mrs. Cromwell with the air of one whose patience has been sorely tried, "and I found he didn't have any more rompers—so rather than have him go round without any I put him back in those—and his face—"

"How many pairs has he?" Roxanne's voice was quite

pleasantly curious—"How many feather fans have you?" she
might have asked.

"O—" Mrs. Cromwell considered, wrinkling her pretty
brow. "Five, I think. Plenty, I know."

"You can get them for fifty cents a pair."

Mrs. Cromwell's eyes showed surprise—and the faintest
superiority. The price of rompers!

"Can you really? I had no idea. He ought to have plenty,
but I haven't had a minute all week to send the laundry
out." Then, as though dismissing the subject as utterly
irrelevant—"I must show you some things—"

They rose and Roxanne followed her past an open bathroom door whose garment littered floor showed indeed that
the laundry hadn't been sent out for some time, into another
room that was, so to speak, the quintessence of pinkness.
This was Mrs. Cromwell's room.

Here the hostess opened a closet door and displayed before
Roxanne's eyes an amazing collection of lingerie. There were
dozens of filmy marvels of lace and silk, all clean, unruffled,
seemingly not yet touched. On hangers beside them were two
brand new evening dresses.

"I have some beautiful things," said Mrs. Cromwell, "but
not much of a chance to wear them. Harry doesn't care much
about going out." Spite crept into her voice. "He's content to
let me play nursemaid and housekeeper all day and loving
wife in the evening."

Roxanne smiled again.

"You've got some very beautiful clothes here."

"Yes, I have. Let me show you—"

"Beautiful," repeated Roxanne, interrupting, "but I'll have
to run if I'm going to catch my train."

She felt that her hands were trembling. She wanted to put
them on this woman and shake her—shake her. She wanted
her locked up somewhere and set to scrubbing floors.

"Beautiful," she repeated, "and I just came in for a moment."

"Well, I'm sorry Harry isn't here."

They moved toward the door.

"—and, O," said Roxanne with an effort—yet still her
voice was gentle and her lips were smiling—"I think it's Argile's where you can get those rompers. Good-by."

"Argile's. I'll remember."

It was not until she had reached the station and bought her

ticket to Marlowe that Roxanne realized it was the first five minutes in six months that her mind had been off Jeffrey.

IV

A week later Harry appeared at Marlowe in person, arrived unexpectedly at 5 o'clock, and coming up the walk sank into a porch chair in a state of utter exhaustion. Roxanne herself had had a busy day and was quite worn out. The doctors were coming at five-thirty, bringing a celebrated nerve specialist from New York. She was excited and thoroughly depressed, but something in Harry's eyes as he greeted her made her sit down in a chair beside him.

"What's the matter, Harry?"

"Nothing, Roxanne," he denied. "I came to see how Jeff was doing. Don't you bother about me."

"Harry," insisted Roxanne, "there's something the matter."

"Nothing," he repeated. "How's Jeff?"

An anxious look darkened on her face.

"He's a little worse, Harry. Dr. Jewett has come on from New York. They thought he could tell me something definite. He's going to try and find whether this paralysis has anything to do with the original blood clot."

Harry rose uncertainly.

"O, I'm sorry," he said jerkily. "I didn't know you expected a consultation. I wouldn't have come. I thought I'd just rock on your porch for an hour——"

"Sit down," she commanded.

Harry hesitated.

"Sit down, Harry, dear boy." Her kindness flooded out now—enveloped him. "I know there's something the matter. You're white as a sheet. I'm going to get you a cool bottle of beer."

All at once he collapsed into his chair and covered his face with his hands.

"I can't make her happy," he cried passionately. "I've tried and I've tried. This morning we had some words about breakfast—I'd been getting my breakfast downtown—and—well, just after I went to the office she left the house, went east to her mother's with George and a suitcase full of lace underwear."

"Harry!"

"And I don't know——"

There was a crunch on the gravel, a car turning into the drive. Roxanne gave a little cry.

"It's Dr. Jewett," she said quickly.

"O, I'll—"

"You'll wait, won't you?" she interrupted abstractedly. He saw that his problem had already died on the troubled surface of her mind.

There was an embarrassing minute of vague elided introductions and then Harry followed the party inside and watched them disappear up the stairs. He went into the library and sat down on the big sofa.

For an hour he watched the sun creep down and hide itself in the folds of the chintz curtains. In the deep quiet a trapped wasp buzzing on the inside of the window pane assumed the proportions of a clamor. From time to time, another buzzing drifted down from upstairs, resembling several more larger wasps caught on larger window panes. He heard low footfalls, the clink of bottles, the clamor of pouring water.

What had he and Roxanne done that life should deal these crashing blows to them? Upstairs there was taking place a living inquest on the soul of his friend; he was sitting here in a quiet room listening to the plaint of a wasp, just as when he was a boy he had been compelled by a strict aunt to sit hourlong on a chair and atone for some misbehavior. But who had put him here? What ferocious aunt had leaned out of the sky to make him atone for—what?

About Kitty he felt a great hopelessness. She was too expensive—that was the word—expensive. Suddenly he hated her. He wanted to throw her down and kick at her—to tell her she was a cheat and a leech—that she was dirty. Moreover, she must give him back his boy.

He got up and began pacing up and down the room. Simultaneously he heard some one begin walking down the hallway upstairs in exact time with him. He found himself wondering if they would walk in time until the person reached the end of the hall.

Kitty had gone to her mother. God help her, what a mother to go to! He tried to imagine the meeting: the abused wife collapsing upon the mother's breast. He could not. That Kitty was capable of any deep grief was impossible. He had gradually grown to think of her as something unapproachable and callous. She would get a divorce, of course, and eventually she would marry again. He began to consider this. Whom would she marry? He laughed bitterly and then stopped; a picture had suddenly flashed to him—of Kitty's arms around some man whose face he could not see, of Kitty's lips pressed close to other lips in what was surely passion.

"God!" he cried aloud. "God! God! God!"

Then the pictures came thick and fast. The Kitty of this morning faded; the soiled kimono rolled up and disappeared; the pouts, and rages, and tears all were washed away. Again she was Kitty Carr—Kitty Carr with yellow hair and great baby eyes. Ah, she had loved him, she had loved him.

After a while he perceived that something was amiss with him, something that had nothing to do with Kitty or Jeff, something of a different genre. Amazingly it burst on him at last; he was hungry. Simple enough, that! He would go into the kitchen in a moment and ask the colored cook for a sandwich. After that he must hurry. He must go back to the city.

He paused at the wall, jerked at something round, and, fingering it absently, put it to his mouth and tasted it as a baby tastes a bright toy. His teeth closed on it—Ah!

She'd left that damn kimono, that dirty pink kimono. She might have had the decency to take it with her, he thought. It would hang in the house like the corpse of love. He would try to throw it away, but he would never be able to bring himself to move it. It would be like Kitty, soft and pliable, withal impervious. You couldn't move Kitty; you couldn't reach Kitty. There was nothing there to reach. He understood that perfectly and it seemed now that he had understood it all along.

He reached to the wall for another biscuit and with an effort pulled it out, nail and all. He carefully removed the nail from the centre, wondering idly if he had eaten the nail with the first biscuit. Preposterous! He would have remembered— it was a huge nail. He felt his stomach. He must be very hungry. He considered—he remembered now—yesterday he had had no dinner. It was the girl's day out and Kitty had lain in her room eating chocolate drops. She had said she felt "smothery" and couldn't bear having him near her. He had given George a bath and put him to bed and then laid down on the couch intending to rest a minute before getting his own dinner. There he had fallen asleep and awakened about eleven to find that there was nothing in the ice-box except a spoonful of potato salad. This he had eaten, together with some chocolate drops that he found on Kitty's bureau. This morning he had breakfasted hurriedly down town before going to the office. But at noon, beginning to worry about Kitty, he had decided to go home and take her out to lunch. After that there had been the note on his pillow. One suitcase was gone; also the pile of lingerie in the closet—and she had left instructions for sending her trunk.

He had never been so hungry, he thought.

At five o'clock, when the visiting nurse tiptoed downstairs, he was sitting on the sofa staring at the carpet.

"Mr. Cromwell?"

"Yes?"

"Oh, Mrs. Curtain won't be able to see you at dinner. She's not well. She told me to tell you that the cook will fix you something and that there's a spare bedroom."

"She's sick, you say?"

"She's lying down in her room. The consultation is just over."

"Did they—did they decide anything?"

"Yes," said the nurse softly. "Doctor Jewett says there's no hope. Mr. Curtain may live indefinitely, but he'll never see again or move again or think. He'll just breathe."

"Just breathe?"

"Yes."

For the first time the nurse noted that beside the writing desk she remembered to have seen a line of a dozen or so curious round objects she had vaguely imagined to be some exotic form of decoration; there was now only one. Where the others had been was a series of little nail holes.

Harry followed her glance dazedly and then rose to his feet.

"I don't believe I'll stay," he said, abstractedly taking out his watch; "I believe there's a train."

She nodded. Harry picked up his hat.

"Good-by," she said pleasantly.

"Good-by," he answered, as though talking to himself and, still abstractedly evidently moved by some invisible and involuntary forces, he paused on his way to the door and she saw him pluck the last object from the wall and drop it into his pocket.

Then he opened the screen door and, descending the porch steps, passed out of her sight.

V

After a while the coat of clean white paint on the Jeffrey Curtain house made a definite compromise with the suns of many Julys and showed its good faith by turning gray. It scaled— huge peelings of very brittle old paint leaned over backward like aged men practising grotesque gymnastics and finally dropped to a moldy death in the overgrown grass beneath. The paint on the front pillars became streaky; the white ball was knocked off the left hand doorpost; the green blinds darkened until they lost all pretense of color.

It began to be a house that was avoided—some church bought a lot diagonally opposite for a graveyard and this, combined with "the place where Mrs. Curtain stays with that living corpse," was enough to throw a ghostly aura over that quarter of the road. Not that she was left alone. Men and women came to see her, met her down town, where she went to do her marketing, brought her home in their cars—and came in for a moment to chat and to rest, so to speak, in the glamour that still played in her gently radiant smile. Men who did not know her no longer followed her with admiring glances in the street; a diaphanous veil had come down over her beauty, destroying its vividness, yet bringing neither wrinkles nor fat.

She acquired a character in the village—a group of little stories were told of her: how when the country was frozen over one winter so that no wagons nor automobiles could run, she taught herself to skate so that she could make quick time to the grocer and druggist, and not leave Jeffrey alone for long. It was said that every night since his paralysis she slept in a small bed beside his bed, holding his hand.

Jeffrey Curtain was spoken of as though he were already dead. As the years dropped by those who had known him died or moved away—there were but half a dozen of the old crowd who had drunk cocktails together, called each other's wives by their first names, and thought that Jeff was about the best hearted and wittiest and most talented fellow that Marlowe had ever known. Now, to the casual visitor, he was merely the reason that Mrs. Curtain excused herself sometimes and hurried upstairs; he was a groan or a sharp cry borne to the silent parlor on the heavy air of a Sunday afternoon.

He could not move; he was stone blind, dumb, and totally unconscious. All day he lay in his bed except for a shift to his wheelchair every morning while she straightened the room. His paralysis was creeping slowly toward his heart. At first— for the first year—Roxanne had received the faintest answering pressure sometimes when she held his hand—then it had gone, ceased one evening and never come back, and through two nights Roxanne lay wide eyed, staring into the dark and wondering what had gone, what fraction of his soul had taken flight, what last grain of comprehension those shattered broken nerves still carried to the brain.

After that hope died. Had it not been for her unceasing care the last spark would have gone long before. Every morning she shaved and bathed him, shifted him with her own hands from bed to chair and back to bed. She was in his room constantly, bearing medicine, straightening a pillow, talking to him almost as one talks to a nearly human dog, without hope of response or appreciation, but with the dim persuasion of habit, like a prayer when faith has gone.

Not a few people, one celebrated nerve specialist among them, gave her a plain impression that it was futile to exercise so much care, that if Jeffrey had been conscious he would have wished to die, that if his spirit were hovering in some wider air it would agree to no such sacrifice from her, it would fret only for the prison of its body to give it full release.

"But you see," she replied, shaking her head gently, "when I married Jeffrey it was—until I ceased to love him."

"But," was protested in effect, "you can't love that."

"I can love what it once was. What else is there?"

The specialist shrugged his shoulders and went away to say that Mrs. Curtain was a remarkable woman and just about as sweet as they come—but, he added, it was a pity—a terrible pity.

"She's so sweet—and so beautiful! There must be some man, or a dozen, just aching to take care of her. . . ."

Casually—there were. Here and there some one began in hope—and ended in worship, a reverential worship. There was no love in the woman except, strangely enough, for life, for the people in the world, from the casual tramp to whom she gave food she could ill afford to the butcher who sold her a cheap cut of steak across the meaty board. The other phase was sealed up somewhere in that expressionless mummy who lay with his face turned ever toward the light as mechanically as a compass needle and waited dumbly for the last wave to wash over his heart.

After eleven years he died in the middle of a May night, when the scent of the syringa hung upon the window sill and a breeze wafted in the shrillings of the frogs and cicadas outside. Roxanne awoke at two, and realized with a start she was alone in the house at last.

VI

After that she sat on her weather beaten porch through the afternoons of several months and gazing down across the fields that undulated in a slow descent to the white and green town thought what she might do with her life. She was thirty-six, handsome, strong, and free. The years had eaten up Jeffrey's insurance; she had reluctantly parted with the acres to right and left of her, and had even placed a small mortgage on the house.

With her husband's death had come a great physical restlessness. She missed having to care for him in the morning, her rush to town, and the brief and therefore accentuated neighborly meetings in the butcher's and grocer's; she missed the cooking for two, the preparation of delicate liquid food for him—one day consumed with energy, she went out and spaded up the whole garden, a thing that had not been done for years.

And she was alone at night in the room that had seen the glory of her marriage and then the pain. To meet Jeff again she went back in spirit to that wonderful year, that intense, passionate absorption and companionship, rather than looked forward to a problematical meeting hereafter; she awoke often to lie and wish for that presence beside her—inanimate yet breathing—still Jeff.

One afternoon six months after his death she was sitting on the porch, clad in a black dress which took away the faintest suggestion of plumpness from her figure. It was Indian summer—golden brown all about her; a hush broken by the sighing of leaves; over west a four o'clock sun dripping streaks of red and yellow over a flaming sky. Most of the birds had gone—only a sparrow that had built itself a nest on the cornice of a pillar kept up an intermittent cheeping varied by occasional fluttering sallies overhead. Roxanne moved her chair to where she could watch him and her mind idled drowsily on the bosom of the afternoon.

Harry Cromwell was coming out from Chicago to dinner. Since his divorce over eight years before he had been a fre-

quent visitor. They had had what amounted to a tradition between them: when he arrived they would go to look at Jeff;
Harry would sit down on the edge of the bed and in a hearty
voice ask:

"Well, Jeff, old man, how do you feel today?"

Roxanne, standing beside, would look intently at Jeff,
dreaming vaguely that some shadowy recognition of this
former friend might pass across that broken mind—but the
head, pale and carven as a statue, would only move slowly in
its sole gesture toward the light as if something behind the
blind eyes were groping, groping for another light long since
gone away.

These visits stretched over eight years—at Easter, Christmas, Thanksgiving, and on many a Sunday Harry had arrived,
paid his call on Jeff, and then talked for a long while with
Roxanne on the porch. He was devoted to her. To him she
was all good, the symbol of faith and hope. He made no pretense of hiding it—he made no attempt to deepen this rela-
tion. She was his best friend as the mass of flesh on the bed
there had been his best friend. She was peace, she was rest;
she was the past. Of his own tragedy she alone knew.

He had been out to Marlowe for the funeral, but since then
the firm he worked for had shifted him to the east and it was
only a business trip that had brought him to the vicinity of
Chicago. Roxanne had written him to come when he could—
she needed advice, sound business advice, so after a night in
the city he had gladly caught a train out.

They shook hands warmly and he helped her move two
rockers together.

"How's George," she demanded, her smile radiant as ever.

"He's fine, Roxanne. Seems to like school."

She nodded in agreement.

"Of course it was the only thing to do, to send him."

"Of course, but—"

"You miss him like anything, Harry?"

"Yes—I do miss him. He's a great boy."

He talked a lot about George. His life was bound up in the
boy now. Roxanne was interested. Harry must bring him out
on his next vacation. She had only seen him once in her
life—a little shaver in dirty rompers.

She left him with the newspaper while she prepared dinner—she had four chops tonight and some late vegetables
from her own garden. She put it all on and then called him,

and sitting down together they continued their talk about George.

"If I had a child—" she would say.

Afterward, Harry having given her what slender advice he could about investments, they walked through the garden, pausing here and there to recognize what had once been a cement bench, where the tennis court had lain.

"Do you remember—"

Then they were off on a flood of reminiscences: the day they had taken all the snapshots and Jeff had insisted on being photographed astride the calf; the day they had developed the idea of making the old barn a writing room for Jeff, and the sketch they had made, lying sprawled in the grass, their heads almost touching. There was to have been a covered lattice connecting the studio and the house so that Jeff could get there on wet days—the lattice had even been started as a result, but nothing remained except a broken triangular piece that still adhered to the house and resembled a battered chicken coop.

"And the mint juleps!"

"And Jeff's note book! Do you remember how we'd laugh, Harry, when we'd get it out of his pocket and read aloud a page of material. And how frantic he used to get?"

"Wild! He was such a kid about his writing."

They were both silent a moment and then Harry burst out again.

"We were to have a place out here, too. Do you remember? We were to buy the adjoining twenty acres. And what parties we four were to have!"

Again there was a pause, broken this time by a low question from Roxanne.

"Do you ever hear of her, Harry?"

The shadow of a frown deepened on his brow.

"Why—yes," he admitted slowly. "She's in Seattle. She's married again to a man named Horton, a sort of lumber king. He's a great deal older than she, I believe."

"And she's—behaving?"

"Yes—that is, I've heard so. She has everything, you see. Nothing much to do except dress up for this—fellow at dinner time."

"I see."

With an effort he changed the subject.

"Are you going to keep the house?"

"I think so," she said nodding. "I've lived here so long,

Harry, it'd seem terrible to move. I thought of trained nursing, but of course that'd mean leaving. I've about decided to be a boarding house lady."

"Live in one?"

"No. Keep one," she laughed. "Is there such an anatomy as a boarding house lady? Anyway I'd have a Negress and keep about eight people in the summer and two or three, if I can get them, in the winter. Of course I'll have to have the house repainted and gone over inside."

Harry considered.

"Roxanne, why—naturally you know best what you can do, but it does seem a shock, Roxanne. You came here as a bride."

"Perhaps," she said unsmilingly, "that's why I don't mind remaining here as a boarding house lady."

"I remember," he mused, his eyes twinkling, "a certain batch of biscuits."

"O, those biscuits," she laughed. "Still from all I heard about the way you devoured them they couldn't have been so bad. I was so low that day, yet somehow I laughed when the nurse told me about those biscuits."

"I noticed that the twelve nail holes are still in the library wall where Jeff drove them."

"Yes."

It was getting very dark now, a crispness settled in the air; a little gust of wind sent down a last spray of leaves. Roxanne shivered slightly.

"We'd better go in."

He looked at his watch.

"It's late. I must be leaving. I go east tomorrow."

"Must you?"

They lingered for a moment just below the stoop, watching a moon that seemed full of snow float out of the distance where the lake lay. Summer was gone and now Indian summer. The grass was cold and there was no mist and no dew. After he left she would go in and light the gas and he would go down the path, past the cemetery and on to the village. To these two life had come quickly and gone, leaving not bitterness but pity, not disillusion but only pain. There was already enough moonlight when they shook hands for each to see the gathered kindness in the other's eyes.

The Smilers

We all have that exasperated moment!

There are times when you almost tell the harmless old lady next door what you really think of her face—that it ought to be on a night-nurse in a house for the blind; when you'd like to ask the man you've been waiting ten minutes for if he isn't all over-heated from racing the postman down the block; when you nearly say to the waiter that if they deducted a cent from the bill for every degree the soup was below tepid the hotel would owe you half a dollar; when—and this is the infallible earmark of true exasperation—a smile affects you as an oil-baron's undershirt affects a cow's husband.

But the moment passes. Scars may remain on your dog or your collar or your telephone receiver, but your soul has slid gently back into its place between the lower edge of your heart and the upper edge of your stomach, and all is at peace.

But the imp who turns on the shower-bath of exasperation apparently made it so hot one time in Sylvester Stockton's early youth that he never dared dash in and turn it off—in consequence no first old man in an amateur production of a Victorian comedy was ever more pricked and prodded by the daily phenomena of life than was Sylvester at thirty.

Accusing eyes behind spectacles—suggestion of a stiff neck—this will have to do for his description, since he is not the hero of this story. He is the plot. He is the factor that makes it one story instead of three stories. He makes remarks at the beginning and end.

The late afternoon sun was loitering pleasantly along Fifth Avenue when Sylvester, who had just come out of that hideous public library where he had been consulting some ghastly book, told his impossible chauffeur (it is true that I am following his movements through his own spectacles) that he wouldn't need his stupid, incompetent services any longer. Swinging his cane (which he found too short) in his left hand (which he should have cut off long ago since it was constantly offending him), he began walking slowly down the Avenue.

When Sylvester walked at night he frequently glanced behind and on both sides to see if anyone was sneaking up on him. This had become a constant mannerism. For this reason he was unable to pretend that he didn't see Betty Tearle sitting in her machine in front of Tiffany's.

Back in his early twenties he had been in love with Betty Tearle. But he had depressed her. He had misanthropically dissected every meal, motor trip and musical comedy that they attended together, and on the few occasions when she had tried to be especially nice to him—from a mother's point of view he had been rather desirable—he had suspected hidden motives and fallen into a deeper gloom than ever. Then one day she told him that she would go mad if he ever again parked his pessimism in her sun-parlour.

And ever since then she had seemed to be smiling— uselessly, insultingly, charmingly smiling.

"Hello, Sylvo," she cried.

"Why—how do, Betty." He wished she wouldn't call him Sylvo—it sounded like a—like a darn monkey or something.

"How goes it?" she asked cheerfully. "Not very well, I suppose."

"Oh, yes," he answered stiffly. "I manage."

"Taking in the happy crowd?"

"Heavens, yes." He looked around him. "Betty, why are they happy? What are they smiling at? What do they find to smile at?"

Betty flashed at him a glance of radiant amusement.

"The women may smile because they have pretty teeth, Sylvo."

"You smile," continued Sylvester cynically, "because you're comfortably married and have two children. You imagine you're happy, so you suppose everyone else is."

Betty nodded.

"You may have hit it, Sylvo—" The chauffeur glanced around and she nodded at him. "Good-bye."

Sylvo watched with a pang of envy which turned suddenly to exasperation as he saw she had turned and smiled at him once more. Then her car was out of sight in the traffic, and with a voluminous sigh he galvanized his cane into life and continued his stroll.

At the next corner he stopped in at a cigar store and there he ran into Waldron Crosby. Back in the days when Sylvester had been a prize pigeon in the eyes of debutantes he had also been a game partridge from the point of view of promoters. Crosby, then a young bond salesman, had given him much safe and sane advice and saved him many dollars. Sylvester liked Crosby as much as he could like anyone. Most people did like Crosby.

"Hello, you old bag of 'nerves,' " cried Crosby genially, "come and have a big gloom-dispelling Corona."

Sylvester regarded the cases anxiously. He knew he wasn't going to like what he bought.

"Still out at Larchmont, Waldron?" he asked.

"Right-o."

"How's your wife?"

"Never better."

"Well," said Sylvester suspiciously, "you brokers always look as if you're smiling at something up your sleeve. It must be a hilarious profession."

Crosby considered.

"Well," he admitted, "it varies—like the moon and the price of soft drinks—but it has its moments."

"Waldron," said Sylvester earnestly, "you're a friend of mine—please do me the favour of not smiling when I leave you. It seems like a—like a mockery."

A broad grin suffused Crosby's countenance.

"Why, you crabbed old son-of-a-gun!"

But Sylvester with an irate grunt had turned on his heel and disappeared.

He strolled on. The sun finished its promenade and began calling in the few stray beams it had left among the westward streets. The Avenue darkened with black bees from the department stores; the traffic swelled in to an interlaced jam; the busses were packed four deep like platforms above the thick crowd; but Sylvester, to whom the daily shift and change of the city was a matter only of sordid monotony, walked on, taking only quick sideward glances through his frowning spectacles.

He reached his hotel and was elevated to his four-room suite on the twelfth floor.

"If I dine down-stairs," he thought, "the orchestra will play either 'Smile, Smile, Smile' or 'The Smiles That You Gave To Me.' But then if I go to the Club I'll meet all the cheerful people I know, and if I go somewhere else where there's no music, I won't get anything fit to eat."

He decided to have dinner in his rooms.

An hour later, after disparaging some broth, a squab and a salad, he tossed fifty cents to the room-waiter, and then held up his hand warningly.

"Just oblige me by not smiling when you say thanks?"

He was too late. The waiter had grinned.

"Now, will you please tell me," asked Sylvester peevishly, "what on earth you have to smile about?"

The waiter considered. Not being a reader of the magazines he was not sure what was characteristic of waiters, yet he supposed something characteristic was expected of him.

"Well, Mister," he answered, glancing at the ceiling with all the ingenuousness he could muster in his narrow, sallow countenance, "it's just something my face does when it sees four bits comin'."

Sylvester waved him away.

"Waiters are happy because they've never had anything better," he thought. "They haven't enough imagination to want anything."

At nine o'clock from sheer boredom he sought his expressionless bed.

II

As Sylvester left the cigar store, Waldron Crosby followed him out, and turning off Fifth Avenue down a cross street entered a brokerage office. A plump man with nervous hands rose and hailed him.

"Hello, Waldron."

"Hello, Potter—I just dropped in to hear the worst."

The plump man frowned.

"We've just got the news," he said.

"Well, what is it? Another drop?"

"Closed at seventy-eight. Sorry, old boy."

"Whew!"

"Hit pretty hard?"

"Cleaned out!"

The plump man shook his head, indicating that life was too much for him, and turned away.

Crosby sat there for a moment without moving. Then he

rose, walked into Potter's private office and picked up the phone.

"Gi'me Larchmont 838."

In a moment he had his connection.

"Mrs. Crosby there?"

A man's voice answered him.

"Yes; this you, Crosby? This is Doctor Shipman."

"Dr. Shipman?" Crosby's voice showed sudden anxiety.

"Yes—I've been trying to reach you all afternoon The situation's changed and we expect the child tonight."

"Tonight?"

"Yes. Everything's O. K. But you'd better come right out."

"I will. Good-bye."

He hung up the receiver and started out the door, but paused as an idea struck him. He returned, and this time called a Manhattan number.

"Hello, Donny, this is Crosby."

"Hello, there, old boy. You just caught me; I was going—"

"Say, Donny, I want a job right away, quick."

"For whom?"

"For me."

"Why, what's the—"

"Never mind. Tell you later. Got one for me?"

"Why, Waldron, there's not a blessed thing here except a clerkship. Perhaps next—"

"What salary goes with the clerkship?"

"Forty—say forty-five a week."

"I've got you. I start tomorrow."

"All right. But say, old man—"

"Sorry, Donny, but I've got to run."

Crosby hurried from the brokerage office with a wave and a smile at Potter. In the street he took out a handful of small change and after surveying it critically hailed a taxi.

"Grand Central—quick!" he told the driver.

III

At six o'clock Betty Tearle signed the letter, put it into an envelope and wrote her husband's name upon it. She went into his room and after a moment's hesitation set a black cushion on the bed and laid the white letter on it so that it could not fail to attract his attention when he came in. Then with a quick glance around the room she walked into the hall and upstairs to the nursery.

"Clare," she called softly.

"Oh, Mummy!" Clare left her doll's house and scurried to her mother.

"Where's Billy, Clare?"

Billy appeared eagerly from under the bed.

"Got anything for me?" he inquired politely.

His mother's laugh ended in a little catch and she caught both her children to her and kissed them passionately. She found that she was crying quietly and their flushed little faces seemed cool against the sudden fever racing through her blood.

"Take care of Clare—always—Billy darling—"

Billy was puzzled and rather awed.

"You're crying," he accused gravely.

"I know—I know I am—"

Clare gave a few tentative sniffles, hesitated, and then clung to her mother in a storm of weeping.

"I d-don't feel good, Mummy—I don't feel good."

Betty soothed her quietly.

"We won't cry any more, Clare dear—either of us."

But as she rose to leave the room her glance at Billy bore a mute appeal, too vain, she knew, to be registered on his childish consciousness.

Half an hour later as she carried her travelling bag to a taxi-cab at the door she raised her hand to her face in mute admission that a veil served no longer to hide her from the world.

"But I've chosen," she thought dully.

As the car turned the corner she wept again, resisting a temptation to give up and go back.

"Oh, my God!" she whispered. "What am I doing? What have I done? What have I done?"

IV

When Jerry, the sallow, narrow-faced waiter, left Sylvester's rooms he reported to the head-waiter, and then checked out for the day.

He took the subway south and alighting at Williams Street walked a few blocks and entered a billiard parlour.

An hour later he emerged with a cigarette drooping from

his bloodless lips, and stood on the sidewalk as if hesitating before making a decision. He set off eastward.

As he reached a certain corner his gait suddenly increased and then quite as suddenly slackened. He seemed to want to pass by, yet some magnetic attraction was apparently exerted on him, for with a sudden face-about he turned in at the door of a cheap restaurant—half-cabaret, half chop-suey parlour—where a miscellaneous assortment gathered nightly.

Jerry found his way to a table situated in the darkest and most obscure corner. Seating himself with a contempt for his surroundings that betokened familiarity rather than superiority he ordered a glass of claret.

The evening had begun. A fat woman at the piano was expelling the last jauntiness from a hackneyed foxtrot, and a lean, dispirited male was assisting her with lean, dispirited notes from a violin. The attention of the patrons was directed at a dancer wearing soiled stockings and done largely in peroxide and rouge who was about to step upon a small platform, meanwhile exchanging pleasantries with a fat, eager person at the table beside her who was trying to capture her hand.

Over in the corner Jerry watched the two by the platform and, as he gazed, the ceiling seemed to fade out, the walls growing into tall buildings and the platform becoming the top of a Fifth Avenue bus on a breezy spring night three years ago. The fat, eager person disappeared, the short skirt of the dancer rolled down and the rouge faded from her cheeks—and he was beside her again in an old delirious ride, with the lights blinking kindly at them from the tall buildings beside and the voices of the street merging into a pleasant somnolent murmur around them.

"Jerry," said the girl on top of the bus, "I've said that when you were gettin' seventy-five I'd take a chance with you. But, Jerry, I can't wait forever."

Jerry watched several street numbers sail by before he answered.

"I don't know what's the matter," he said helplessly, "they won't raise me. If I can locate a new job—"

"You better hurry, Jerry," said the girl; "I'm gettin' sick of just livin' along. If I can't get married I got a couple of chances to work in a cabaret—get on the stage maybe."

"You keep out of that," said Jerry quickly. "There ain't no need, if you just wait about another month or two."

"I can't wait forever, Jerry," repeated the girl. "I'm tired of stayin' poor alone."

"It won't be long," said Jerry clenching his free hand, "I can make it somewhere, if you'll just wait."

But the bus was fading out and the ceiling was taking shape and the murmur of the April streets was fading into the rasping whine of the violin—for that was all three years before and now he was sitting here.

The girl glanced up on the platform and exchanged a metallic impersonal smile with the dispirited violinist, and Jerry shrank farther back in his corner watching her with burning intensity.

"Your hands belong to anybody that wants them now," he cried silently and bitterly. "I wasn't man enough to keep you out of that—not man enough, by God, by God!"

But the girl by the door still toyed with the fat man's clutching fingers as she waited for her time to dance.

V

Sylvester Stockton tossed restlessly upon his bed. The room, big as it was, smothered him, and a breeze drifting in and bearing with it a rift of moon seemed laden only with the cares of the world he would have to face next day.

"They don't understand," he thought. "They don't see, as I do, the underlying misery of the whole damn thing. They're hollow optimists. They smile because they think they're always going to be happy.

"Oh, well," he mused drowsily. "I'll run up to Rye tomorrow and endure more smiles and more heat. That's all life is—just smiles and heat, smiles and heat."

The Offshore Pirate

I

This unlikely story begins on a sea that was a blue dream, as colorful as blue-silk stockings, and beneath a sky as blue as the irises of children's eyes. From the western half of the sky the sun was shying little golden disks at the sea—if you gazed intently enough you could see them skip from wave tip to wave tip until they joined a broad collar of golden coin that was collecting half a mile out and would eventually be a dazzling sunset. About half-way between the Florida shore and the golden collar a white steam-yacht, very young and graceful, was riding at anchor and under a blue-and-white awning aft a yellow-haired girl reclined in a wicker settee reading The Revolt of the Angels, by Anatole France.

She was about nineteen, slender and supple, with a spoiled alluring mouth and quick gray eyes full of a radiant curiosity. Her feet, stockingless, and adorned rather than clad in blue-satin slippers which swung nonchalantly from her toes, were perched on the arm of a settee adjoining the one she occupied. And as she read she intermittently regaled herself by a faint application to her tongue of a half-lemon that she held in her hand. The other half, sucked dry, lay on the deck at her feet and rocked very gently to and fro at the almost imperceptible motion of the tide.

The second half-lemon was well-nigh pulpless and the golden collar had grown astonishing in width, when suddenly the drowsy silence which enveloped the yacht was broken by the sound of heavy footsteps and an elderly man topped with orderly gray hair and clad in a white-flannel suit appeared at the head of the companionway. There he paused for a moment until his eyes became accustomed to the sun, and then seeing the girl under the awning he uttered a long even grunt of disapproval.

If he had intended thereby to obtain a rise of any sort he was doomed to disappointment. The girl calmly turned over two pages, turned back one, raised the lemon mechanically to tasting distance, and then very faintly but quite unmistakably yawned.

"Ardita!" said the gray-haired man sternly.

Ardita uttered a small sound indicating nothing.

"Ardita!" he repeated. "Ardita!"

Ardita raised the lemon languidly, allowing three words to slip out before it reached her tongue.

"Oh, shut up."

"Ardita!"

"What?"

"Will you listen to me—or will I have to get a servant to hold you while I talk to you?"

The lemon descended slowly and scornfully.

"Put it in writing."

"Will you have the decency to close that abominable book and discard that damn lemon for two minutes?"

"Oh, can't you lemme alone for a second?"

"Ardita, I have just received a telephone message from the shore—"

"Telephone?" She showed for the first time a faint interest.

"Yes, it was—"

"Do you mean to say," she interrupted wonderingly, " 'at they let you run a wire out here?"

"Yes, and just now—"

"Won't other boats bump into it?"

"No. It's run along the bottom. Five min—"

"Well, I'll be darned! Gosh! Science is golden or something—isn't it?"

"Will you let me say what I started to?"

"Shoot!"

"Well, it seems—well, I am up here—" He paused and swallowed several times distractedly. "Oh, yes. Young woman, Colonel Moreland has called up again to ask me to be sure to bring you in to dinner. His son Toby has come all the way from New York to meet you and he's invited several other young people. For the last time, will you—"

"No," said Ardita shortly, "I won't. I came along on this darn cruise with the one idea of going to Palm Beach, and you knew it, and I absolutely refuse to meet any darn old colonel or any darn young Toby or any darn old young people or to set foot in any other darn old town in this crazy state.

So you either take me to Palm Beach or else shut up and go away."

"Very well. This is the last straw. In your infatuation for this man—a man who is notorious for his excesses, a man your father would not have allowed to so much as mention your name—you have reflected the demi-monde rather than the circles in which you have presumably grown up. From now on—"

"I know," interrupted Ardita ironically, "from now on you go your way and I go mine. I've heard that story before. You know I'd like nothing better."

"From now on," he announced grandiloquently, "you are no niece of mine. I—"

"O-o-o-oh!" The cry was wrung from Ardita with the agony of a lost soul. "Will you stop boring me! Will you go 'way! Will you jump overboard and drown! Do you want me to throw this book at you!"

"If you dare do any—"

Smack! The Revolt of the Angels sailed through the air, missed its target by the length of a short nose, and bumped cheerfully down the companionway.

The gray-haired man made an instinctive step backward and then two cautious steps forward. Ardita jumped to her five feet four and stared at him defiantly, her gray eyes blazing.

"Keep off!"

"How dare you!" he cried.

"Because I darn please!"

"You've grown unbearable! Your disposition—"

"You've made me that way! No child ever has a bad disposition unless it's her family's fault! Whatever I am, you did it."

Muttering something under his breath her uncle turned and, walking forward, called in a loud voice for the launch. Then he returned to the awning, where Ardita had again seated herself and resumed her attention to the lemon.

"I am going ashore," he said slowly. "I will be out again at nine o'clock to-night. When I return we will start back to New York, where I shall turn you over to your aunt for the rest of your natural, or rather unnatural, life."

He paused and looked at her, and then all at once something in the utter childishness of her beauty seemed to puncture his anger like an inflated tire and render him helpless, uncertain, utterly fatuous.

"Ardita," he said not unkindly, "I'm no fool. I've been round. I know men. And, child, confirmed libertines don't reform until they're tired—and then they're not themselves—they're husks of themselves." He looked at her as if expecting agreement, but receiving no sight or sound of it he continued. "Perhaps the man loves you—that's possible. He's loved many women and he'll love many more. Less than a month ago, one month, Ardita, he was involved in a notorious affair with that red-haired woman, Mimi Merril; promised to give her the diamond bracelet that the Czar of Russia gave his mother. You know—you read the papers."

"Thrilling scandals by an anxious uncle," yawned Ardita. "Have it filmed. Wicked clubman making eyes at virtuous flapper. Virtuous flapper conclusively vamped by his lurid past. Plans to meet him at Palm Beach. Foiled by anxious uncle."

"Will you tell me why the devil you want to marry him?"

"I'm sure I couldn't say," said Ardita shortly. "Maybe because he's the only man I know, good or bad, who has an imagination and the courage of his convictions. Maybe it's to get away from the young fools that spend their vacuous hours pursuing me around the country. But as for the famous Russian bracelet, you can set your mind at rest on that score. He's going to give it to me at Palm Beach—if you'll show a little intelligence."

"How about the—red-haired woman?"

"He hasn't seen her for six months," she said angrily. "Don't you suppose I have enough pride to see to that? Don't you know by this time that I can do any darn thing with any darn man I want to?"

She put her chin in the air like the statue of France Aroused, and then spoiled the pose somewhat by raising the lemon for action.

"Is it the Russian bracelet that fascinates you?"

"No, I'm merely trying to give you the sort of argument that would appeal to your intelligence. And I wish you'd go 'way," she said, her temper rising again. "You know I never change my mind. You've been boring me for three days until I'm about to go crazy. I won't go ashore! Won't! Do you hear? Won't!"

"Very well," he said, "and you won't go to Palm Beach either. Of all the selfish, spoiled, uncontrolled, disagreeable, impossible girls I have—"

Splash! The half-lemon caught him in the neck. Simultaneously came a hail from over the side.

"The launch is ready, Mr. Farnam."

Too full of words and rage to speak, Mr. Farnam cast one utterly condemning glance at his niece and, turning, ran swiftly down the ladder.

II

Five o'clock rolled down from the sun and plumped soundlessly into the sea. The golden collar widened into a glittering island; and a faint breeze that had been playing with the edges of the awning and swaying one of the dangling blue clippers became suddenly freighted with song. It was a chorus of men in close harmony and in perfect rhythm to an accompanying sound of oars cleaving the blue waters. Ardita lifted her head and listened.

> "Carrots and peas,
> Beans on their knees,
> Pigs in the seas,
>   Lucky fellows!
> Blow us a breeze,
> Blow us a breeze,
> Blow us a breeze,
>   With your bellows."

Ardita's brow wrinkled in astonishment. Sitting very still she listened eagerly as the chorus took up a second verse.

> "Onions and beans,
> Marshalls and Deans,
> Goldbergs and Greens
>   And Costellos.
> Blow us a breeze,
> Blow us a breeze,
> Blow us a breeze,
>   With your bellows."

With an exclamation she tossed her book to the deck, where it sprawled at a straddle, and hurried to the rail. Fifty feet away a large rowboat was approaching containing seven men, six of them rowing and one standing up in the stern keeping time to their song with an orchestra leader's baton.

> "Oysters and rocks,
> Sawdust and socks,
> Who could make clocks
> Out of cellos?—"

The leader's eyes suddenly rested on Ardita, who was leaning over the rail spellbound with curiosity. He made a quick movement with his baton and the singing instantly ceased. She saw that he was the only white man in the boat—the six rowers were Negroes.

"Narcissus ahoy!" he called politely.

"What's the idea of all the discord?" demanded Ardita cheerfully. "Is this the varsity crew from the county nut farm?"

By this time the boat was scraping the side of the yacht and a great hulking Negro in the bow turned round and grasped the ladder. Thereupon the leader left his position in the stern and before Ardita had realized his intention he ran up the ladder and stood breathless before her on the deck.

"The women and children will be spared!" he said briskly. "All crying babies will be immediately drowned and all males put in double irons!"

Digging her hands excitedly down into the pockets of her dress Ardita stared at him, speechless with astonishment.

He was a young man with a scornful mouth and the bright blue eyes of a healthy baby set in a dark sensitive face. His hair was pitch black, damp and curly—the hair of a Grecian statue gone brunette. He was trimly built, trimly dressed, and graceful as an agile quarter-back.

"Well, I'll be a son of a gun!" she said dazedly.

They eyed each other coolly.

"Do you surrender the ship?"

"Is this an outburst of wit?" demanded Ardita. "Are you an idiot—or just being initiated to some fraternity?"

"I asked you if you surrendered the ship."

"I thought the country was dry," said Ardita disdainfully. "Have you been drinking finger-nail enamel? You better get off this yacht!"

"What?" The young man's voice expressed incredulity.

"Get off the yacht! You heard me!"

He looked at her for a moment as if considering what she had said.

"No," said his scornful mouth slowly, "no, I won't get off the yacht. You can get off if you wish."

Going to the rail he gave a curt command and immediately the crew of the rowboat scrambled up the ladder and ranged themselves in line before him, a coal-black and burly darky at one end and a miniature mulatto of four feet nine at the other. They seemed to be uniformly dressed in some sort of blue costume ornamented with dust, mud, and tatters; over the shoulder of each was slung a small, heavy-looking white sack, and under their arms they carried large black cases apparently containing musical instruments.

" 'Ten-*shun!*" commanded the young man, snapping his own heels together crisply. "Right *dress*! Front! Step out here, Babe!"

The smallest Negro took a quick step forward and saluted. "Yas-suh!"

"Take command, go down below, catch the crew and tie 'em up—all except the engineer. Bring him up to me. Oh, and pile those bags by the rail there."

"Yas-suh!"

Babe saluted again and wheeling about motioned for the five others to gather about him. Then after a short whispered consultation they all filed noiselessly down the companionway.

"Now," said the young man cheerfully to Ardita, who had witnessed this last scene in withering silence, "if you will swear on your honor as a flapper—which probably isn't worth much—that you'll keep that spoiled little mouth of yours tight shut for forty-eight hours, you can row yourself ashore in our rowboat."

"Otherwise what?"

"Otherwise you're going to sea in a ship."

With a little sigh as for a crisis well passed, the young man sank into the settee Ardita had lately vacated and stretched his arms lazily. The corners of his mouth relaxed appreciatively as he looked round at the rich striped awning, the polished brass, and the luxurious fittings of the deck. His eye fell on the book, and then on the exhausted lemon.

"Hm," he said, "Stonewall Jackson claimed that lemon-juice cleared his head. Your head feel pretty clear?"

Ardita disdained to answer.

"Because inside of five minutes you'll have to make a clear decision whether it's go or stay."

He picked up the book and opened it curiously.

"The Revolt of the Angels. Sounds pretty good. French, eh?" He stared at her with new interest. "You French?"

"No."

"What's your name?"

"Farnam."

"Farnam what?"

"Ardita Farnam."

"Well, Ardita, no use standing up there and chewing out the insides of your mouth. You ought to break those nervous habits while you're young. Come over here and sit down."

Ardita took a carved jade case from her pocket, extracted a cigarette and lit it with a conscious coolness, though she knew her hand was trembling a little; then she crossed over with her supple, swinging walk, and sitting down in the other settee blew a mouthful of smoke at the awning.

"You can't get me off this yacht," she said steadily, "and you haven't got very much sense if you think you'll get far with it. My uncle'll have wirelesses zigzagging all over this ocean by half past six."

"Hm."

She looked quickly at his face, caught anxiety stamped there plainly in the faintest depression of the mouth's corners.

"It's all the same to me," she said, shrugging her shoulders. "'Tisn't my yacht. I don't mind going for a coupla hours' cruise. I'll even lend you that book so you'll have something to read on the revenue boat that takes you up to Sing Sing."

He laughed scornfully.

"If that's advice you needn't bother. This is part of a plan arranged before I ever knew this yacht existed. If it hadn't been this one it'd have been the next one we passed anchored along the coast."

"Who are you?" demanded Ardita suddenly. "And what are you?"

"You've decided not to go ashore?"

"I never even faintly considered it."

"We're generally known," he said, "all seven of us, as Curtis Carlyle and his Six Black Buddies, late of the Winter Garden and the Midnight Frolic."

"You're singers?"

"We were until to-day. At present, due to those white bags you see there, we're fugitives from justice, and if the reward offered for our capture hasn't by this time reached twenty thousand dollars I miss my guess."

"What's in the bags?" asked Ardita curiously.

"Well," he said, "for the present we'll call it—mud—Florida mud."

III

Within ten minutes after Curtis Carlyle's interview with a very frightened engineer, the yacht Narcissus was under way, steaming south through a balmy tropical twilight. The little mulatto, Babe, who seemed to have Carlyle's implicit confidence, took full command of the situation. Mr. Farnam's valet and the chef, the only members of the crew on board except the engineer, having shown fight, were now reconsidering, strapped securely to their bunks below. Trombone Mose, the biggest Negro, was set busy with a can of paint obliterating the name Narcissus from the bow, and substituting the name Hula Hula, and the others congregated aft and became intently involved in a game of craps.

Having given orders for a meal to be prepared and served on deck at seven-thirty, Carlyle rejoined Ardita, and, sinking back into his settee, half closed his eyes and fell into a state of profound abstraction.

Ardita scrutinized him carefully—and classed him immediately as a romantic figure. He gave the effect of towering self-confidence erected on a slight foundation—just under the surface of each of his decisions she discerned a hesitancy that was in decided contrast to the arrogant curl of his lips.

"He's not like me," she thought. "There's a difference somewhere."

Being a supreme egotist Ardita frequently thought about herself; never having had her egotism disputed she did it entirely naturally and with no detraction from her unquestioned charm. Though she was nineteen she gave the effect of a high-spirited, precocious child, and in the present glow of her youth and beauty all the men and women she had known were but driftwood on the ripples of her temperament. She had met other egotists—in fact she found that selfish people bored her rather less than unselfish people—but as yet there had not been one she had not eventually defeated and brought to her feet.

But though she recognized an egotist in the settee next to her, she felt none of that usual shutting of doors in her mind which meant clearing ship for action; on the contrary her instinct told her that this man was somehow completely pregnable and quite defenseless. When Ardita defied convention—and of late it had been her chief amusement—it was from an intense desire to be herself, and she felt that this man, on the contrary, was preoccupied with his own defiance.

She was much more interested in him than she was in her own situation, which affected her as the prospect of a matinée might affect a ten-year-old child. She had implicit confidence in her ability to take care of herself under any and all circumstances.

The night deepened. A pale new moon smiled misty-eyed upon the sea, and as the shore faded dimly out and dark clouds were blown like leaves along the far horizon a great haze of moonshine suddenly bathed the yacht and spread an avenue of glittering mail in her swift path. From time to time there was the bright flare of a match as one of them lighted a cigarette, but except for the low undertone of the throbbing engines and the even wash of the waves about the stern, the yacht was quiet as a dream boat star-bound through the heavens. Round them flowed the smell of the night sea, bringing with it an infinite languor.

Carlyle broke the silence at last.

"Lucky girl," he sighed, "I've always wanted to be rich—and buy all this beauty."

Ardita yawned.

"I'd rather be you," she said frankly.

"You would—for about a day. But you do seem to possess a lot of nerve for a flapper."

"I wish you wouldn't call me that."

"Beg your pardon."

"As to nerve," she continued slowly, "it's my one redeeming feature. I'm not afraid of anything in heaven or earth."

"Hm, I am."

"To be afraid," said Ardita, "a person has either to be very great and strong—or else a coward. I'm neither." She paused for a moment, and eagerness crept into her tone. "But I want to talk about you. What on earth have you done—and how did you do it?"

"Why?" he demanded cynically. "Going to write a movie about me?"

"Go on," she urged. "Lie to me by the moonlight. Do a fabulous story."

A Negro appeared, switched on a string of small lights under the awning, and began setting the wicker table for supper. And while they ate cold sliced chicken, salad, artichokes, and strawberry jam from the plentiful larder below, Carlyle began to talk, hesitantly at first, but eagerly as he saw she was interested. Ardita scarcely touched her food as she watched his dark young face—handsome, ironic, faintly ineffectual.

He began life as a poor kid in a Tennessee town, he said, so poor that his people were the only white family in their street. He never remembered any white children—but there were inevitably a dozen pickaninnies streaming in his trail, passionate admirers whom he kept in tow by the vividness of his imagination and the amount of trouble he was always getting them in and out of. And it seemed that this association diverted a rather unusual musical gift into a strange channel.

There had been a colored woman named Belle Pope Calhoun who played the piano at parties given for white children—nice white children that would have passed Curtis Carlyle with a sniff. But the ragged little "poh white" used to sit beside her piano by the hour and try to get in an alto with one of those kazoos that boys hum through. Before he was thirteen he was picking up a living teasing ragtime out of a battered violin in little cafés round Nashville. Eight years later the ragtime craze hit the country, and he took six darkies on the Orpheum circuit. Five of them were boys he had grown up with; the other was the little mulatto, Babe Divine, who was a wharf nigger round New York, and long before that a plantation hand in Bermuda, until he stuck an eight-inch stiletto in his master's back. Almost before Carlyle realized his good fortune he was on Broadway, with offers of engagements on all sides, and more money than he had ever dreamed of.

It was about then that a change began in his whole attitude, a rather curious, embittering change. It was when he realized that he was spending the golden years of his life gibbering round a stage with a lot of black men. His act was good of its kind—three trombones, three saxophones, and Carlyle's flute—and it was his own peculiar sense of rhythm that made all the difference; but he began to grow strangely sensitive about it, began to hate the thought of appearing, dreaded it from day to day.

They were making money—each contract he signed called for more—but when he went to managers and told them that he wanted to separate from his sextet and go on as a regular pianist, they laughed at him and told him he was crazy—it would be an artistic suicide. He used to laugh afterward at the phrase "artistic suicide." They all used it.

Half a dozen times they played at private dances at three thousand dollars a night, and it seemed as if these crystallized all his distaste for his mode of livelihood. They took place in clubs and houses that he couldn't have gone into in the day-time. After all, he was merely playing the role of the eternal monkey, a sort of sublimated chorus man. He was sick of the very smell of the theatre, of powder and rouge and the chatter of the greenroom, and the patronizing approval of the boxes. He couldn't put his heart into it any more. The idea of a slow approach to the luxury of leisure drove him wild. He was, of course, progressing toward it, but, like a child, eating his ice-cream so slowly that he couldn't taste it at all.

He wanted to have a lot of money and time, and opportunity to read and play, and the sort of men and women round him that he could never have—the kind who, if they thought of him at all, would have considered him rather contemptible, in short he wanted all those things which he was beginning to lump under the general head of aristocracy, an aristocracy which it seemed almost any money could buy except money made as he was making it. He was twenty-five then, without family or education or any promise that he would succeed in a business career. He began speculating wildly, and within three weeks he had lost every cent he had saved.

Then the war came. He went to Plattsburg, and even there his profession followed him. A brigadier-general called him up to headquarters and told him he could serve the country better as a band leader—so he spent the war entertaining celebrities behind the line with a headquarters band. It was not so bad—except that when the infantry came limping back from the trenches he wanted to be one of them. The sweat and mud they wore seemed only one of those ineffable symbols of aristocracy that were forever eluding him.

"It was the private dances that did it. After I came back from the war the old routine started. We had an offer from a syndicate of Florida hotels. It was only a question of time then."

He broke off and Ardita looked at him expectantly, but he shook his head.

"No," he said, "I'm not going to tell you about it. I'm enjoying it too much, and I'm afraid I'd lose a little of that enjoyment if I shared it with any one else. I want to hang on to those few breathless, heroic moments when I stood out before them all and let them know I was more than a damn bobbing, squawking clown."

From up forward came suddenly the low sound of singing. The Negroes had gathered together on the deck and their voices rose together in a haunting melody that soared in poignant harmonics toward the moon. And Ardita listened in enchantment.

> "Oh down—
>   Oh down,
> Mammy wanna take me downa milky way,
> Oh down—
>   Oh down,
> Pappy say to-morra-a-a-ah!
> But mammy say to-day,
> Yes—mammy say to-day!"

Carlyle sighed and was silent for a moment, looking up at the gathered host of stars blinking like arclights in the warm sky. The Negroes' song had died away to a plaintive humming, and it seemed as if minute by minute the brightness and the great silence were increasing until he could almost hear the midnight toilet of the mermaids as they combed their silver dripping curls under the moon and gossiped to each other of the fine wrecks they lived in on the green opalescent avenues below.

"You see," said Carlyle softly, "this is the beauty I want. Beauty has to be astonishing, astounding—it's got to burst in on you like a dream, like the exquisite eyes of a girl."

He turned to her, but she was silent.

"You see, don't you, Anita—I mean, Ardita?"

Again she made no answer. She had been sound asleep for some time.

IV

In the dense sun-flooded noon of next day a spot in the sea before them resolved casually into a green-and-gray islet, apparently composed of a great granite cliff at its northern end which slanted south through a mile of vivid coppice and grass to a sandy beach melting lazily into the surf. When Ardita, reading in her favorite seat, came to the last page of The Revolt of the Angels, and, slamming the book shut, looked up and saw it, she gave a little cry of delight and called to Carlyle, who was standing moodily by the rail.

"Is this it? Is this where you're going?"

Carlyle shrugged his shoulders carelessly.

"You've got me." He raised his voice and called up to the acting skipper: "Oh, Babe, is this your island?"

The mulatto's miniature head appeared from round the corner of the deck-house.

"Yas-suh! This yeah's it."

Carlyle joined Ardita.

"Looks sort of sporting, doesn't it?"

"Yes," she agreed, "but it doesn't look big enough to be much of a hiding-place."

"You still putting your faith in those wirelesses your uncle was going to have zigzagging round?"

"No," said Ardita frankly. "I'm all for you. I'd really like to see you make a getaway."

He laughed.

"You're our Lady Luck. Guess we'll have to keep you with us as a mascot—for the present, anyway."

"You couldn't very well ask me to swim back," she said coolly. "If you do I'm going to start writing dime novels founded on that interminable history of your life you gave me last night."

He flushed and stiffened slightly.

"I'm very sorry I bored you."

"Oh, you didn't—until just at the end with some story about how furious you were because you couldn't dance with the ladies you played music for."

He rose angrily.

"You have got a darn mean little tongue."

"Excuse me," she said, melting into laughter, "but I'm not used to having men regale me with the story of their life ambitions—especially if they've lived such deathly platonic lives."

"Why? What do men usually regale you with?"

"Oh, they talk about me," she yawned. "They tell me I'm the spirit of youth and beauty."

"What do you tell them?"

"Oh, I agree quietly."

"Does every man you meet tell you he loves you?"

Ardita nodded.

"Why shouldn't he? All life is just a progression toward, and then a recession from, one phrase—'I love you.' "

Carlyle laughed and sat down.

"That's very true. That's—that's not bad. Did you make that up?"

"Yes—or rather I found it out. It doesn't mean anything especially. It's just clever."

"It's the sort of remark," he said gravely, "that's typical of your class."

"Oh," she interrupted impatiently, "don't start that lecture on aristocracy again! I distrust people who can be intense at this hour in the morning. It's a mild form of insanity—a sort of breakfast-food jag. Morning's the time to sleep, swim, and be careless."

Ten minutes later they had swung round in a wide circle as if to approach the island from the north.

"There's a trick somewhere," commented Ardita thoughtfully. "He can't mean just to anchor up against this cliff."

They were heading straight in now toward the solid rock, which must have been well over a hundred feet tall, and not until they were within fifty yards of it did Ardita see their objective. Then she clapped her hands in delight. There was a break in the cliff entirely hidden by a curious overlapping of rock, and through this break the yacht entered and very slowly traversed a narrow channel of crystal-clear water between high gray walls. Then they were riding at anchor in a miniature world of green and gold, a gilded bay smooth as glass and set round with tiny palms, the whole resembling the mirror lakes and twig trees that children set up in sand piles.

"Not so darned bad!" said Carlyle excitedly. "I guess that little coon knows his way round this corner of the Atlantic."

His exuberance was contagious, and Ardita became quite jubilant.

"It's an absolutely sure-fire hiding-place!"

"Lordy, yes! It's the sort of island you read about."

The rowboat was lowered into the golden lake and they pulled ashore.

"Come on," said Carlyle as they landed in the slushy sand, "we'll go exploring."

The fringe of palms was in turn ringed in by a round mile of flat, sandy country. They followed it south and brushing through a farther rim of tropical vegetation came out on a pearl-gray virgin beach where Ardita kicked off her brown golf shoes—she seemed to have permanently abandoned stockings—and went wading. Then they sauntered back to the yacht, where the indefatigable Babe had luncheon ready for them. He had posted a lookout on the high cliff to the north to watch the sea on both sides, though he doubted if the entrance to the cliff was generally known—he had never even seen a map on which the island was marked.

"What's its name," asked Ardita—"the island, I mean?"

"No name 'tall," chuckled Babe. "Reckin she jus' island, 'at's all."

In the late afternoon they sat with their backs against great boulders on the highest part of the cliff and Carlyle sketched for her his vague plans. He was sure they were hot after him by this time. The total proceeds of the coup he had pulled off, and concerning which he still refused to enlighten her, he estimated as just under a million dollars. He counted on lying up here several weeks and then setting off southward, keeping well outside the usual channels of travel, rounding the Horn and heading for Callao, in Peru. The details of coaling and provisioning he was leaving entirely to Babe, who, it seemed, had sailed these seas in every capacity from cabin-boy aboard a coffee trader to virtual first mate on a Brazilian pirate craft, whose skipper had long since been hung.

"If he'd been white he'd have been king of South America long ago," said Carlyle emphatically. "When it comes to intelligence he makes Booker T. Washington look like a moron. He's got the guile of every race and nationality whose blood is in his veins, and that's half a dozen or I'm a liar. He worships me because I'm the only man in the world who can play better ragtime than he can. We used to sit together on the wharfs down on the New York water-front, he with a bassoon and me with an oboe, and we'd blend minor keys in African harmonics a thousand years old until the rats would crawl up the posts and sit round groaning and squeaking like dogs will in front of a phonograph."

Ardita roared.

"How you can tell 'em!"

Carlyle grinned.

"I swear that's the gos—"

"What you going to do when you get to Callao?" she interrupted.

"Take ship for India. I want to be a rajah. I mean it. My idea is to go up into Afghanistan somewhere, buy up a palace and a reputation, and then after about five years appear in England with a foreign accent and a mysterious past. But India first. Do you know, they say that all the gold in the world drifts very gradually back to India. Something fascinating about that to me. And I want leisure to read—an immense amount."

"How about after that?"

"Then," he answered defiantly, "comes aristocracy. Laugh if you want to—but at least you'll have to admit that I know what I want—which I imagine is more than you do."

"On the contrary," contradicted Ardita, reaching in her pocket for her cigarette case, "when I met you I was in the midst of a great uproar of all my friends and relatives because I did know what I wanted."

"What was it?"

"A man."

He started.

"You mean you were engaged?"

"After a fashion. If you hadn't come aboard I had every intention of slipping ashore yesterday evening—how long ago it seems—and meeting him in Palm Beach. He's waiting there for me with a bracelet that once belonged to Catharine of Russia. Now don't mutter anything about aristocracy," she put in quickly. "I liked him simply because he had had an imagination and the utter courage of his convictions."

"But your family disapproved, eh?"

"What there is of it—only a silly uncle and a sillier aunt. It seems he got into some scandal with a red-haired woman named Mimi something—it was frightfully exaggerated, he said, and men don't lie to me—and anyway I didn't care what he'd done; it was the future that counted. And I'd see to that. When a man's in love with me he doesn't care for other amusements. I told him to drop her like a hot cake, and he did."

"I feel rather jealous," said Carlyle, frowning—and then he laughed. "I guess I'll just keep you along with us until we get to Callao. Then I'll lend you enough money to get back to the States. By that time you'll have had a chance to think that gentleman over a little more."

"Don't talk to me like that!" fired up Ardita. "I won't tolerate the parental attitude from anybody! Do you understand me?"

He chuckled and then stopped, rather abashed, as her cold anger seemed to fold him about and chill him.

"I'm sorry," he offered uncertainly.

"Oh, don't apologize! I can't stand men who say 'I'm sorry' in that manly, reserved tone. Just shut up!"

A pause ensued, a pause which Carlyle found rather awkward, but which Ardita seemed not to notice at all as she sat contentedly enjoying her cigarette and gazing out at the shining sea. After a minute she crawled out on the rock and lay with her face over the edge looking down. Carlyle, watching her, reflected how it seemed impossible for her to assume an ungraceful attitude.

"Oh, look!" she cried. "There's a lot of sort of ledges down there. Wide ones of all different heights."

He joined her and together they gazed down the dizzy height.

"We'll go swimming to-night!" she said excitedly. "By moon-light."

"Wouldn't you rather go in at the beach on the other end?"

"Not a chance. I like to dive. You can use my uncle's bathing suit, only it'll fit you like a gunny sack, because he's a very flabby man. I've got a one-piece affair that's shocked the natives all along the Atlantic coast from Biddeford Pool to St. Augustine."

"I suppose you're a shark."

"Yes, I'm pretty good. And I look cute too. A sculptor up at Rye last summer told me my calves were worth five hundred dollars."

There didn't seem to be any answer to this, so Carlyle was silent, permitting himself only a discreet interior smile.

V

When the night crept down in shadowy blue and silver, they threaded the shimmering channel in the rowboat and, tying it to a jutting rock, began climbing the cliff together. The first shelf was ten feet up, wide, and furnishing a natural diving platform. There they sat down in the bright moonlight and watched the faint incessant surge of the waters, almost stilled now as the tide set seaward.

"Are you happy?" he asked suddenly.

She nodded.

"Always happy near the sea. You know," she went on, "I've been thinking all day that you and I are somewhat alike. We're both rebels—only for different reasons. Two years ago, when I was just eighteen, and you were—"

"Twenty-five."

"—well, we were both conventional successes. I was an utterly devastating débutante and you were a prosperous musician just commissioned in the army—"

"Gentleman by act of Congress," he put in ironically.

"Well, at any rate, we both fitted. If our corners were not rubbed off they were at least pulled in. But deep in us both was something that made us require more for happiness. I didn't know what I wanted. I went from man to man, restless, impatient, month by month getting less acquiescent and more dissatisfied. I used to sit sometimes chewing at the insides of my mouth and thinking I was going crazy—I had a frightful sense of transiency. I wanted things now—now—now! Here I was—beautiful—I am, aren't I?"

"Yes," agreed Carlyle tentatively.

Ardita rose suddenly.

"Wait a second. I want to try this delightful-looking sea."

She walked to the end of the ledge and shot out over the sea, doubling up in mid-air and then straightening out and entering the water straight as a blade in a perfect jack-knife dive.

In a minute her voice floated up to him.

"You see, I used to read all day and most of the night. I began to resent society—"

"Come on up here," he interrupted. "What on earth are you doing?"

"Just floating round on my back. I'll be up in a minute. Let me tell you. The only thing I enjoyed was shocking people;

wearing something quite impossible and quite charming to a
fancy-dress party, going round with the fastest men in New
York, and getting into some of the most hellish scrapes imag-
inable."

The sounds of splashing mingled with her words, and then
he heard her hurried breathing as she began climbing up the
side of the ledge.

"Go on in!' she called.

Obediently he rose and dived. When he emerged, dripping,
and made the climb, he found that she was no longer on the
ledge, but after a frightened second he heard her light laughter from another shelf ten feet up. There he joined her and
they both sat quietly for a moment, their arms clasped round
their knees, panting a little from the climb.

"The family were wild," she said suddenly. "They tried to
marry me off. And then when I'd begun to feel that after all
life was scarcely worth living I found something"—her eyes
went skyward exultantly—"I found something!"

Carlyle waited and her words came with a rush.

"Courage—just that; courage as a rule of life, and something to cling to always. I began to build up this enormous
faith in myself. I began to see that in all my idols in the past
some manifestation of courage had unconsciously been the
thing that attracted me. I began separating courage from the
other things of life. All sorts of courage—the beaten, bloody
prize-fighter coming up for more—I used to make men take
me to prize-fights; the déclassé woman sailing through a nest
of cats and looking at them as if they were mud under her
feet; the liking what you like always; the utter disregard for
other people's opinions—just to live as I liked always and to
die in my own way—Did you bring up the cigarettes?"

He handed one over and held a match for her silently.

"Still," Ardita continued, "the men kept gathering—old
men and young men, my mental and physical inferiors, most
of them, but all intensely desiring to have me—to own this
rather magnificent proud tradition I'd built up round me. Do
you see?"

"Sort of. You never were beaten and you never apolo-
gized."

"Never!"

She sprang to the edge, poised for a moment like a cruci-
fied figure against the sky; then describing a dark parabola,

plunked without a slash between two silver ripples twenty feet below.

Her voice floated up to him again.

"And courage to me meant ploughing through that dull gray mist that comes down on life—not only overriding people and circumstances but overriding the bleakness of living. A sort of insistence on the value of life and the worth of transient things."

She was climbing up now, and at her last words her head, with the damp yellow hair slicked symmetrically back, appeared on his level.

"All very well," objected Carlyle. "You can call it courage, but your courage is really built, after all, on a pride of birth. You were bred to that defiant attitude. On my gray days even courage is one of the things that's gray and lifeless."

She was sitting near the edge, hugging her knees and gazing abstractedly at the white moon; he was farther back, crammed like a grotesque god into a niche in the rock.

"I don't want to sound like Pollyanna," she began, "but you haven't grasped me yet. My courage is faith—faith in the eternal resilience of me—that joy'll come back, and hope and spontaneity. And I feel that till it does I've got to keep my lips shut and my chin high, and my eyes wide—not necessarily any silly smiling. Oh, I've been through hell without a whine quite often—and the female hell is deadlier than the male."

"But supposing," suggested Carlyle, "that before joy and hope and all that came back the curtain was drawn on you for good?"

Ardita rose, and going to the wall climbed with some difficulty to the next ledge, another ten or fifteen feet above.

"Why," she called back, "then I'd have won!"

He edged out till he could see her.

"Better not dive from there! You'll break your back," he said quickly.

She laughed.

"Not I!"

Slowly she spread her arms and stood there swan-like, radiating a pride in her young perfection that lit a warm glow in Carlyle's heart.

"We're going through the black air with our arms wide," she called, "and our feet straight out behind like a dolphin's tail, and we're going to think we'll never hit the silver down there till suddenly it'll be all warm round us and full of little kissing, caressing waves."

Then she was in the air, and Carlyle involuntarily held his breath. He had not realized that the dive was nearly forty feet. It seemed an eternity before he heard the swift compact sound as she reached the sea.

And it was with his glad sigh of relief when her light watery laughter curled up the side of the cliff and into his anxious ears that he knew he loved her.

VI

Time, having no axe to grind, showered down upon them three days of afternoons. When the sun cleared the port-hole of Ardita's cabin an hour after dawn she rose cheerily, donned her bathing-suit, and went up on deck. The Negroes would leave their work when they saw her, and crowd, chuckling and chattering, to the rail as she floated, an agile minnow, on and under the surface of the clear water. Again in the cool of the afternoon she would swim—and loll and smoke with Carlyle upon the cliff; or else they would lie on their sides in the sands of the southern beach, talking little, but watching the day fade colorfully and tragically into the infinite languor of a tropical evening.

And with the long, sunny hours Ardita's idea of the episode as incidental, madcap, a sprig of romance in a desert of reality, gradually left her. She dreaded the time when he would strike off southward; she dreaded all the eventualities that presented themselves to her; thoughts were suddenly troublesome and decisions odious. Had prayers found place in the pagan rituals of her soul she would have asked of life only to be unmolested for a while, lazily acquiescent to the ready, naïve flow of Carlyle's ideas, his vivid boyish imagination, and the vein of monomania that seemed to run crosswise through his temperament and colored his every action.

But this is not a story of two on an island, nor concerned primarily with love bred of isolation. It is merely the presentation of two personalities, and its idyllic setting among the palms of the Gulf Stream is quite incidental. Most of us are content to exist and breed and fight for the right to do both, and the dominant idea, the foredoomed attempt to control one's destiny, is reserved for the fortunate or unfortunate few.

To me the interesting thing about Ardita is the courage that will tarnish with her beauty and youth.

"Take me with you," she said late one night as they sat lazily in the grass under the shadowy spreading palms. The Negroes had brought ashore their musical instruments, and the sound of weird ragtime was drifting softly over on the warm breath of the night. "I'd love to reappear in ten years as a fabulously wealthy high-caste Indian lady," she continued.

Carlyle looked at her quickly.

"You can, you know."

She laughed.

"Is it a proposal of marriage? Extra! Ardita Farnam becomes pirate's bride. Society girl kidnapped by ragtime bank robber."

"It wasn't a bank."

"What was it? Why won't you tell me?"

"I don't want to break down your illusions."

"My dear man, I have no illusions about you."

"I mean your illusions about yourself."

She looked up in surprise.

"About myself! What on earth have I got to do with whatever stray felonies you've committed?"

"That remains to be seen."

She reached over and patted his hand.

"Dear Mr. Curtis Carlyle," she said softly, "are you in love with me?"

"As if it mattered."

"But it does—because I think I'm in love with you."

He looked at her ironically.

"Thus swelling your January total to half a dozen," he suggested. "Suppose I call your bluff and ask you to come to India with me?"

"Shall I?"

He shrugged his shoulders.

"We can get married in Callao."

"What sort of life can you offer me? I don't mean that unkindly, but seriously; what would become of me if the people who want that twenty-thousand-dollar reward ever catch up with you?"

"I thought you weren't afraid."

"I never am—but I won't throw my life away just to show one man I'm not."

"I wish you'd been poor. Just a little poor girl dreaming over a fence in a warm cow country."

"Wouldn't it have been nice?"

"I'd have enjoyed astonishing you—watching your eyes open on things. If you only wanted things! Don't you see?"

"I know—like girls who stare into the windows of jewelry-stores."

"Yes—and want the big oblong watch that's platinum and has diamonds all round the edge. Only you'd decide it was too expensive and choose one of white gold for a hundred dollars. Then I'd say: 'Expensive? I should say not!' And we'd go into the store and pretty soon the platinum one would be gleaming on your wrist."

"That sounds so nice and vulgar—and fun, doesn't it?" murmured Ardita.

"Doesn't it? Can't you see us travelling round and spending money right and left, and being worshipped by bell-boys and waiters? Oh, blessed are the simple rich, for they inherit the earth!"

"I honestly wish we were that way."

"I love you, Ardita," he said gently.

Her face lost its childish look for a moment and became oddly grave.

"I love to be with you," she said, "more than with any man I've ever met. And I like your looks and your dark old hair, and the way you go over the side of the rail when we come ashore. In fact, Curtis Carlyle, I like all the things you do when you're perfectly natural. I think you've got nerve, and you know how I feel about that. Sometimes when you're around I've been tempted to kiss you suddenly and tell you that you were just an idealistic boy with a lot of caste non-sense in his head. Perhaps if I were just a little bit older and a little more bored I'd go with you. As it is, I think I'll go back and marry—that other man."

Over across the silver lake the figures of the Negroes writhed and squirmed in the moonlight, like acrobats who, hav-ing been too long inactive, must go through their tricks from sheer surplus energy. In single file they marched, weaving in concentric circles, now with their heads thrown back, now bent over their instruments like piping fauns. And from trombone and saxophone ceaselessly whined a blended melody, some-times riotous and jubilant, sometimes haunting and plaintive as a death-dance from the Congo's heart.

"Let's dance!" cried Ardita. "I can't sit still with that perfect jazz going on."

Taking her hand he led her out into a broad stretch of hard sandy soil that the moon flooded with great splendor. They floated out like drifting moths under the rich hazy light, and as the fantastic symphony wept and exulted and wavered and despaired, Ardita's last sense of reality dropped away, and she abandoned her imagination to the dreamy summer scents of tropical flowers and the infinite starry spaces overhead, feeling that if she opened her eyes it would be to find herself dancing with a ghost in a land created by her own fancy.

"This is what I should call an exclusive private dance," he whispered.

"I feel quite mad—but delightfully mad!"

"We're enchanted. The shades of unnumbered generations of cannibals are watching us from high up on the side of the cliff there."

"And I'll bet the cannibal women are saying that we dance too close, and that it was immodest of me to come without my nose-ring."

They both laughed softly—and then their laughter died as over across the lake they heard the trombone stop in the middle of a bar, and the saxophones give a startled moan and fade out.

"What's the matter?" called Carlyle.

After a moment's silence they made out the dark figure of a man rounding the silver lake at a run. As he came closer they saw it was Babe in a state of unusual excitement. He drew up before them and gasped out his news in a breath.

"Ship stan'in' off sho' 'bout half a mile, suh. Mose, he uz on watch, he say look's if she's done ancho'd."

"A ship—what kind of a ship?" demanded Carlyle anxiously.

Dismay was in his voice, and Ardita's heart gave a sudden wrench as she saw his whole face suddenly droop.

"He say he don't know, suh."

"Are they landing a boat?"

"No, suh."

"We'll go up," said Carlyle.

They ascended the hill in silence, Ardita's hand still resting in Carlyle's as it had when they finished dancing. She felt it clinch nervously from time to time as though he were unaware of the contact, but though he hurt her she made no attempt to remove it. It seemed an hour's climb before they reached the top and crept cautiously across the silhouetted plateau to the edge of the cliff. After one short look Carlyle involuntarily gave a little cry. It was a revenue boat with six-inch guns mounted fore and aft.

"They know!" he said with a short intake of breath. "They know! They picked up the trail somewhere."

"Are you sure they know about the channel? They may be only standing by to take a look at the island in the morning. From where they are they couldn't see the opening in the cliff."

"They could with field-glasses," he said hopelessly. He looked at his wrist-watch. "It's nearly two now. They won't do anything until dawn, that's certain. Of course there's always the faint possibility that they're waiting for some other ship to join; or for a coaler."

"I suppose we may as well stay right here."

The hours passed and they lay there side by side, very silently, their chins in their hands like dreaming children. In back of them squatted the Negroes, patient, resigned, acquiescent, announcing now and then with sonorous snores that not even the presence of danger could subdue their unconquerable African craving for sleep.

Just before five o'clock Babe approached Carlyle. There were half a dozen rifles aboard the Narcissus he said. Had it been decided to offer no resistance? A pretty good fight might be made, he thought, if they worked out some plan.

Carlyle laughed and shook his head.

"That isn't a Spic army out there, Babe. That's a revenue boat. It'd be like a bow and arrow trying to fight a machine-gun. If you want to bury those bags somewhere and take a chance on recovering them later, go on and do it. But it won't work—they'd dig this island over from one end to the other. It's a lost battle all round, Babe."

Babe inclined his head silently and turned away, and Carlyle's voice was husky as he turned to Ardita.

"There's the best friend I ever had. He'd die for me, and be proud to, if I'd let him."

"You've given up?"

"I've no choice. Of course there's always one way out—the sure way—but that can wait. I wouldn't miss my trial for anything—it'll be an interesting experiment in notoriety.

'Miss Farnam testifies that the pirate's attitude to her was at all times that of a gentleman.' "

"Don't!" she said. "I'm awfully sorry."

When the color faded from the sky and lustreless blue changed to leaden gray a commotion was visible on the ship's deck, and they made out a group of officers clad in white duck, gathered near the rail. They had field-glasses in their hands and were attentively examining the islet.

"It's all up," said Carlyle grimly.

"Damn!" whispered Ardita. She felt tears gathering in her eyes.

"We'll go back to the yacht," he said. "I prefer that to being hunted out up here like a 'possum."

Leaving the plateau they descended the hill, and reaching the lake were rowed out to the yacht by the silent Negroes. Then, pale and weary, they sank into the settees and waited.

Half an hour later, in the dim gray light, the nose of the revenue boat appeared in the channel and stopped, evidently fearing that the bay might be too shallow. From the peaceful look of the yacht, the man and the girl in the settees, and the Negroes lounging curiously against the rail, they evidently judged that there would be no resistance, for two boats were lowered casually over the side, one containing an officer and six bluejackets, and the other, four rowers and, in the stern, two gray-haired men in yachting flannels. Ardita and Carlyle stood up, and half unconsciously started toward each other. Then he paused and putting his hand suddenly into his pocket he pulled out a round, glittering object and held it out to her.

"What is it?" she asked wonderingly.

"I'm not positive, but I think from the Russian inscription inside that it's your promised bracelet."

"Where—where on earth—"

"It came out of one of those bags. You see, Curtis Carlyle and his Six Black Buddies, in the middle of their performance in the tea-room of the hotel at Palm Beach, suddenly changed their instruments for automatics and held up the crowd. I took this bracelet from a pretty, overrouged woman with red hair."

Ardita frowned and then smiled.

"So that's what you did! You *have* got nerve!"

He bowed.

"A well-known bourgeois quality," he said.

And then dawn slanted dynamically across the deck and flung the shadows reeling into gray corners. The dew rose and turned to golden mist, thin as a dream, enveloping them until they seemed gossamer relics of the late night, infinitely transient and already fading. For a moment sea and sky were breathless, and dawn held a pink hand over the young mouth of life—then from out in the lake came the complaint of a rowboat and the swish of oars.

Suddenly against the golden furnace low in the east their two graceful figures melted into one, and he was kissing her spoiled young mouth.

"It's a sort of glory," he murmured after a second.

She smiled up at him.

"Happy, are you?"

Her sigh was a benediction—an ecstatic surety that she was youth and beauty now as much as she would ever know. For another instant life was radiant and time a phantom and their strength eternal—then there was a bumping, scraping sound as the rowboat scraped alongside.

Up the ladder scrambled the two gray-haired men, the officer and two of the sailors with their hands on their revolvers. Mr. Farnam folded his arms and stood looking at his niece.

"So," he said, nodding his head slowly.

With a sigh her arms unwound from Carlyle's neck, and her eyes, transfigured and far away, fell upon the boarding party. Her uncle saw her upper lip slowly swell into that arrogant pout he knew so well.

"So," he repeated savagely. "So this is your idea of—of romance. A runaway affair, with a high-seas pirate."

Ardita glanced at him carelessly.

"What an old fool you are!" she said quietly.

"Is that the best you can say for yourself?"

"No," she said, as if considering. "No, there's something else. There's that well-known phrase with which I have ended most of our conversations for the past few years—'Shut up!' "

And with that she turned, included the two old men, the officer, and the two sailors in a curt glance of contempt, and walked proudly down the companionway.

But had she waited an instant longer she would have heard a sound from her uncle quite unfamiliar in most of their interviews. He gave vent to a whole-hearted amused chuckle, in which the second old man joined.

The latter turned briskly to Carlyle, who had been regarding this scene with an air of cryptic amusement.

"Well, Toby," he said genially, "you incurable, harebrained, romantic chaser of rainbows, did you find that she was the person you wanted?"

Carlyle smiled confidently.

"Why—naturally," he said. "I've been perfectly sure ever since I first heard tell of her wild career. That's why I had Babe send up the rocket last night."

"I'm glad you did," said Colonel Moreland gravely. "We've been keeping pretty close to you in case you should have trouble with those six strange niggers. And we hoped we'd find you two in some such compromising position," he sighed. "Well, set a crank to catch a crank!"

"Your father and I sat up all night hoping for the best—or perhaps it's the worst. Lord knows you're welcome to her, my boy. She's run me crazy. Did you give her the Russian bracelet my detective got from that Mimi woman?"

Carlyle nodded.

"Sh!" he said. "She's coming on deck."

Ardita appeared at the head of the companionway and gave a quick involuntary glance at Carlyle's wrists. A puzzled look passed across her face. Back aft the Negroes had begun to sing, and the cool lake, fresh with dawn, echoed serenely to their low voices.

"Ardita," said Carlyle unsteadily.

She swayed a step toward him.

"Ardita," he repeated breathlessly, "I've got to tell you the—the truth. It was all a plant, Ardita. My name isn't Carlyle. It's Moreland, Toby Moreland. The story was invented, Ardita, invented out of thin Florida air."

She stared at him, bewildered amazement, disbelief, and anger flowing in quick waves across her face. The three men held their breaths. Moreland, Senior, took a step toward her; Mr. Farnam's mouth dropped a little open as he waited, panic-stricken, for the expected crash.

But it did not come. Ardita's face became suddenly radiant, and with a little laugh she went swiftly to young Moreland and looked up at him without a trace of wrath in her gray eyes.

"Will you swear," she said quietly, "that it was entirely a product of your own brain?"

"I swear," said young Moreland eagerly.

She drew his head down and kissed him gently.

"What an imagination!" she said softly and almost enviously. "I want you to lie to me just as sweetly as you know how for the rest of my life."

The Negroes' voices floated drowsily back, mingled in an air that she had heard them sing before.

> "Time is a thief;
> Gladness and grief
> Cling to the leaf
> As it yellows—"

"What was in the bags?" she asked softly.

"Florida mud," he answered. "That was one of the two true things I told you."

"Perhaps I can guess the other one," she said; and reaching up on her tiptoes she kissed him softly in the illustration.

The Ice Palace

I

The sunlight dripped over the house like golden paint over an art jar, and the freckling shadows here and there only intensified the rigor of the bath of light. The Butterworth and Larkin houses flanking were intrenched behind great stodgy trees; only the Happer house took the full sun, and all day long faced the dusty road-street with a tolerant kindly patience. This was the city of Tarleton in southernmost Georgia, September afternoon.

Up in her bedroom window Sally Carrol Happer rested her nineteen-year-old chin on a fifty-two-year-old sill and watched Clark Darrow's ancient Ford turn the corner. The car was hot—being partly metallic it retained all the heat it absorbed or evolved—and Clark Darrow sitting bolt upright at the wheel wore a pained, strained expression as though he considered himself a spare part, and rather likely to break. He laboriously crossed two dust ruts, the wheels squeaking indignantly at the encounter, and then with a terrifying expression he gave the steering-gear a final wrench and deposited self and car approximately in front of the Happer steps. There was a plaintive heaving sound, a death-rattle, followed by a short silence; and then the air was rent by a startling whistle.

Sally Carrol gazed down sleepily. She started to yawn, but finding this quite impossible unless she raised her chin from the windowsill, changed her mind and continued silently to regard the car, whose owner sat brilliantly if perfunctorily at attention as he waited for an answer to his signal. After a moment the whistle once more split the dusty air.

"Good mawnin'."

With difficulty Clark twisted his tall body round and bent a distorted glance on the window.

" 'Tain't mawnin', Sally Carrol."

"Isn't it, sure enough?"

"What you doin'?"

"Eatin' 'n apple."

"Come on go swimmin'—want to?"

"Reckon so."

"How 'bout hurrin' up?"

"Sure enough."

Sally Carrol sighed voluminously and raised herself with profound inertia from the floor, where she had been occupied in alternately destroying parts of a green apple and painting paper dolls for her younger sister. She approached a mirror, regarded her expression with a pleased and pleasant languor, dabbed two spots of rouge on her lips and a grain of powder on her nose, and covered her bobbed corn-colored hair with a rose-littered sunbonnet. Then she kicked over the painting water, said, "Oh, damn!"—but let it lay—and left the room.

"How you, Clark?" she inquired a minute later as she slipped nimbly over the side of the car.

"Mighty fine, Sally Carrol."

"Where we go swimmin'?"

"Out to Walley's Pool. Told Marylyn we'd call by an' get her an' Joe Ewing."

Clark was dark and lean, and when on foot was rather inclined to stoop. His eyes were ominous and his expression somewhat petulant except when startlingly illuminated by one of his frequent smiles. Clark had "a income"—just enough to keep himself in ease and his car in gasolene—and he had spent the two years since he graduated from Georgia Tech in dozing round the lazy streets of his home town, discussing how he could best invest his capital for an immediate fortune.

Hanging round he found not at all difficult; a crowd of little girls had grown up beautifully, the amazing Sally Carrol foremost among them; and they enjoyed being swum with and danced with and made love to in the flower-filled summery evenings—and they all liked Clark immensely. When feminine company palled there were half a dozen other youths who were always just about to do something, and meanwhile were quite willing to join him in a few holes of golf, or a game of billiards, or the consumption of a quart of "hard yella licker." Every once in a while one of these contemporaries made a farewell round of calls before going up to New York or Philadelphia or Pittsburgh to go into business, but mostly they just stayed round in this languid paradise of dreamy skies and firefly evenings and noisy niggery street fairs—and especially of gracious, soft-voiced girls, who were brought up on memories instead of money.

The Ford having been excited into a sort of restless, resentful life, Clark and Sally Carrol rolled and rattled down Valley Avenue into Jefferson Street, where the dust road became a pavement; along opiate Millicent Place, where there were half a dozen prosperous, substantial mansions; and on into the down-town section. Driving was perilous here, for it was shopping time; the population idled casually across the streets and a drove of low-moaning oxen were being urged along in front of a placid street-car; even the shops seemed only yawning their doors and blinking their windows in the sunshine before retiring into a state of utter and finite coma.

"Sally Carrol," said Clark suddenly, "it a fact that you're engaged?"

She looked at him quickly.

"Where'd you hear that?"

"Sure enough, you engaged?"

" 'At's a nice question!"

"Girl told me you were engaged to a Yankee you met up in Asheville last summer."

Sally Carrol sighed.

"Never saw such an old town for rumors."

"Don't marry a Yankee, Sally Carrol. We need you round here."

Sally Carrol was silent a moment.

"Clark," she demanded suddenly, "who on earth shall I marry?"

"I offer my services."

"Honey, you couldn't support a wife," she answered cheerfully. "Anyway, I know you too well to fall in love with you."

" 'At doesn't mean you ought to marry a Yankee," he persisted.

"S'pose I love him?"

He shook his head.

"You couldn't. He'd be a lot different from us, every way."

He broke off as he halted the car in front of a rambling, dilapidated house. Marylyn Wade and Joe Ewing appeared in the doorway.

" 'Lo, Sally Carrol."

"Hi!"

"How you-all?"

"Sally Carrol," demanded Marylyn as they started off again, "you engaged?"

"Lawdy, where'd all this start? Can't I look at a man 'thout everybody in town engagin' me to him?"

Clark stared straight in front of him at a bolt on the clattering wind-shield.

"Sally Carrol," he said with a curious intensity, "don't you like us?"

"What?"

"Us down here?"

"Why, Clark, you know I do. I adore all you boys."

"Then why you gettin' engaged to a Yankee?"

"Clark, I don't know. I'm not sure what I'll do, but—well, I want to go places and see people. I want my mind to grow. I want to live where things happen on a big scale."

"What you mean?"

"Oh, Clark, I love you, and I love Joe here, and Ben Arrot, and you-all, but you'll—you'll—"

"We'll all be failures?"

"Yes. I don't mean only money failures, but just sort of—of ineffectual and sad, and—oh, how can I tell you?"

"You mean because we stay here in Tarleton?"

"Yes, Clark; and because you like it and never want to change things or think or go ahead."

He nodded and she reached over and pressed his hand.

"Clark," she said softly, "I wouldn't change you for the world. You're sweet the way you are. The things that'll make you fail I'll love always—the living in the past, the lazy days and nights you have, and all your carelessness and generosity."

"But you're goin' away?"

"Yes—because I couldn't ever marry you. You've a place in my heart no one else could have, but tied down here I'd get restless. I'd feel I was—wastin' myself. There's two sides to me, you see. There's the sleepy old side you love; an' there's a sort of energy—the feelin' that makes me do wild things. That's the part of me that may be useful somewhere, that'll last when I'm not beautiful any more."

She broke off with characteristic suddenness and sighed, "Oh, sweet cooky!" as her mood changed.

Half closing her eyes and tipping back her head till it rested on the seat-back she let the savory breeze fan her eyes and ripple the fluffy curls of her bobbed hair. They were in the country now, hurrying between tangled growths of bright-green coppice and grass and tall trees that sent sprays of foliage to hang a cool welcome over the road. Here and there they passed a battered negro cabin, its oldest white-haired inhabitant smoking a corncob pipe beside the door, and half a dozen scantily clothed pickaninnies parading tattered dolls on the wild-grown grass in front. Farther out were lazy cotton-fields, where even the workers seemed intangible shadows lent by the sun to the earth, not for toil, but to while away some age-old tradition in the golden September fields. And round the drowsy picturesqueness, over the trees and shacks and muddy rivers, flowed the heat, never hostile, only comforting, like a great warm nourishing bosom for the infant earth.

"Sally Carrol, we're here!"

"Poor chile's soun' asleep."

"Honey, you dead at last outa sheer laziness?"

"Water, Sally Carrol! Cool water waitin' for you!"

Her eyes opened sleepily.

"Hi!" she murmured, smiling.

II

In November Harry Bellamy, tall, broad, and brisk, came down from his Northern city to spend four days. His intention was to settle a matter that had been hanging fire since he and Sally Carrol had met in Asheville, North Carolina, in mid-summer. The settlement took only a quiet afternoon and an evening in front of a glowing open fire, for Harry Bellamy had everything she wanted; and, besides, she loved him—loved him with that side of her she kept especially for loving. Sally Carrol had several rather clearly defined sides.

On his last afternoon they walked, and she found their steps tending half-unconsciously toward one of her favorite haunts, the cemetery. When it came in sight, gray-white and golden-green under the cheerful late sun, she paused, irresolute, by the iron gate.

"Are you mournful by nature, Harry?" she asked with a faint smile.

"Mournful? Not I."

"Then let's go in here. It depresses some folks, but I like it."

They passed through the gateway and followed a path that

led through a wavy valley of graves—dusty-gray and mouldly for the fifties; quaintly carved with flowers, and jars for the seventies; ornate and hideous for the nineties, with fat marble cherubs lying in sodden sleep on stone pillows, and great impossible growths of nameless granite flowers. Occasionally they saw a kneeling figure with tributary flowers, but over most of the graves lay silence and withered leaves with only the fragrance that their own shadowy memories could waken in living minds.

They reached the top of a hill where they were fronted by a tall, round head-stone, freckled with dark spots of damp and half grown over with vines.

"Margery Lee," she read, "1844–1873. Wasn't she nice? She died when she was twenty-nine. Dear Margery Lee," she added softly. "Can't you see her, Harry?"

"Yes, Sally Carrol."

He felt a little hand insert itself into his.

"She was dark, I think; and she always wore her hair with a ribbon in it, and gorgeous hoopskirts of Alice blue and old rose."

"Yes."

"Oh, she was sweet, Harry! And she was the sort of girl born to stand on a wide, pillared porch and welcome folks in. I think perhaps a lot of men went away to war meanin' to come back to her; but maybe none of 'em ever did."

He stooped down close to the stone, hunting for any record of marriage.

"There's nothing here to show."

"Of course not. How could there be anything there better than just 'Margery Lee,' and that eloquent date?"

She drew close to him and an unexpected lump came into his throat as her yellow hair brushed his cheek.

"You see how she was, don't you, Harry?"

"I see," he agreed gently. "I see through your precious eyes. You're beautiful now, so I know she must have been."

Silent and close they stood, and he could feel her shoulders trembling a little. An ambling breeze swept up the hill and stirred the brim of her floppidy hat.

"Let's go down there!"

She was pointing to a flat stretch on the other side of the hill where along the green turf were a thousand grayish-white crosses stretching in endless, ordered rows like the stacked arms of a battalion.

"Those are the Confederate dead," said Sally Carrol simply.

They walked along and read the inscriptions, always only a name and a date, sometimes quite indecipherable.

"The last row is the saddest—see, 'way over there. Every cross has just a date on it, and the word 'Unknown.' "

She looked at him and her eyes brimmed with tears.

"I can't tell you how real it is to me, darling—if you don't know."

"How you feel about it is beautiful to me."

"No, no, it's not me, it's them—that old time that I've tried to have live in me. These were just men, unimportant evidently or they wouldn't have been 'unknown'; but they died for the most beautiful thing in the world—the dead South. You see," she continued, her voice still husky, her eyes glistening with tears, "people have these dreams they fasten onto things, and I've always grown up with that dream. It was so easy because it was all dead and there weren't any disillusions comin' to me. I've tried in a way to live up to those past standards of noblesse oblige—there's just the last remnants of it, you know, like the roses of an old garden dying all around us—streaks of strange courtliness and chivalry in some of these boys an' stories I used to hear from a Confederate soldier who lived next door, and a few old darkies. Oh, Harry, there was something, there was something! I couldn't ever make you understand, but it was there."

"I understand," he assured her again quietly.

Sally Carrol smiled and dried her eyes on the tip of a handkerchief protruding from his breast pocket.

"You don't feel depressed, do you, lover? Even when I cry I'm happy here, and I get a sort of strength from it."

Hand in hand they turned and walked slowly away. Finding soft grass she drew him down to a seat beside her with their backs against the remnants of a low broken wall.

"Wish those three old women would clear out," he complained. "I want to kiss you, Sally Carrol."

"Me, too."

They waited impatiently for the three bent figures to move off, and then she kissed him until the sky seemed to fade out and all her smiles and tears to vanish in an ecstasy of eternal seconds.

Afterward they walked slowly back together, while on the

corners twilight played at somnolent black-and-white check-ers with the end of day.

"You'll be up about mid-January," he said, "and you've got to stay a month at least. It'll be slick. There's a winter carnival on, and if you've never really seen snow it'll be like fairy-land to you. There'll be skating and skiing and tobog-ganing and sleigh-riding, and all sorts of torchlight parades on snow-shoes. They haven't had one for years, so they're going to make it a knock-out."

"Will I be cold, Harry?" she asked suddenly.

"You certainly won't. You may freeze your nose, but you won't be shivery cold. It's hard and dry, you know."

"I guess I'm a summer child. I don't like any cold I've ever seen."

She broke off, and they were both silent for a minute.

"Sally Carrol," he said very slowly, "what do you say to—March?"

"I say I love you."

"March?"

"March, Harry."

III

All night in the Pullman it was very cold. She rang for the porter to ask for another blanket, and when he couldn't give her one she tried vainly, by squeezing down into the bottom of her berth and doubling back the bedclothes, to snatch a few hours' sleep. She wanted to look her best in the morning.

She rose at six and sliding uncomfortably into her clothes stumbled up to the diner for a cup of coffee. The snow had filtered into the vestibules and covered the floor with a slip-pery coating. It was intriguing, this cold, it crept in every-where. Her breath was quite visible and she blew into the air with a naïve enjoyment. Seated in the diner she stared out the window at white hills and valleys and scattered pines whose every branch was a green platter for a cold feast of snow. Sometimes a solitary farmhouse would fly by, ugly and bleak and lone on the white waste; and with each one she had an instant of chill compassion for the souls shut in there waiting for spring.

As she left the diner and swayed back into the Pullman she experienced a surging rush of energy and wondered if she was feeling the bracing air of which Harry had spoken. This was the North, the North—her land now!

> "Then, blow, ye winds, heigho!
> A-roving I will go,"

she chanted exultantly to herself.

"What's 'at?" inquired the porter politely.

"I said: 'Brush me off.' "

The long wires of the telegraph-poles doubled; two tracks ran up beside the train—three—four; came a succession of white-roofed houses, a glimpse of a trolley-car with frosted windows, streets—more streets—the city.

She stood for a dazed moment in the frosty station before she saw three fur-bundled figures descending upon her.

"There she is!"

"Oh, Sally Carol!"

Sally Carol dropped her bag.

"Hi!"

A faintly familiar icy-cold face kissed her, and then she was in a group of faces all apparently emitting great clouds of heavy smoke; she was shaking hands. There were Gordon, a short, eager man of thirty who looked like an amateur knocked-about model for Harry, and his wife, Myra, a listless lady with flaxen hair under a fur automobile cap. Almost immediately Sally Carol thought of her as vaguely Scandinavian. A cheerful chauffeur adopted her bag, and amid ricochets of half-phrases, exclamations, and perfunctory listless "my dears" from Myra, they swept each other from the station.

Then they were in a sedan bound through a crooked succession of snowy streets where dozens of little boys were hitching sleds behind grocery wagons and automobiles.

"Oh," cried Sally Carol, "I want to do that! Can we, Harry?"

"That's for kids. But we might—"

"It looks like such a circus!" she said regretfully.

Home was a rambling frame house set on a white lap of snow, and there she met a big, gray-haired man of whom she approved, and a lady who was like an egg, and who kissed her—these were Harry's parents. There was a breathless, indescribable hour crammed full of half-sentences, hot water, bacon and eggs and confusion; and after that she was alone with Harry in the library, asking him if she dared smoke.

It was a large room with a Madonna over the fireplace and rows upon rows of books in covers of light gold and dark gold and shiny red. All the chairs had little lace squares where one's head should rest, the couch was just comfortable, the books looked as if they had been read—some—and Sally Carrol had an instantaneous vision of the battered old library at home, with her father's huge medical books, and the oil-paintings of her three great-uncles, and the old couch that had been mended up for forty-five years and was still luxurious to dream in. This room struck her as being neither attractive nor particularly otherwise. It was simply a room with a lot of fairly expensive things in it that all looked about fifteen years old.

"What do you think of it up here?" demanded Harry eagerly. "Does it surprise you? Is it what you expected, I mean?"

"You are, Harry," she said quietly, and reached out her arms to him.

But after a brief kiss he seemed anxious to extort enthusiasm from her.

"The town, I mean. Do you like it? Can you feel the pep in the air?"

"Oh, Harry," she laughed, "you'll have to give me time. You can't just fling questions at me."

She puffed at her cigarette with a sigh of contentment.

"One thing I want to ask you," he began rather apologetically "You Southerners put quite an emphasis on family, and all that—not that it isn't quite all right, but you'll find it a little different here. I mean—you'll notice a lot of things that'll seem to you sort of vulgar display at first, Sally Carrol; but just remember that this is a three-generation town. Everybody has a father, and about half of us have grandfathers. Back of that we don't go."

"Of course," she murmured.

"Our grandfathers, you see, founded the place, and a lot of them had to take some pretty queer jobs while they were doing the founding. For instance, there's one woman who at present is about the social model for the town; well, her father was the first public ash man—things like that."

"Why," said Sally Carrol, puzzled, "did you s'pose I was goin' to make remarks about people?"

"Not at all," interrupted Harry, "and I'm not apologizing for any one either. It's just that—well, a Southern girl came up here last summer and said some unfortunate things, and—oh, I just thought I'd tell you."

Sally Carrol felt suddenly indignant—as though she had been unjustly spanked—but Harry evidently considered the subject closed, for he went on with a great surge of enthusiasm.

"It's carnival time, you know. First in ten years. And there's an ice palace they're building now that's the first they've had since eighty-five. Built out of blocks of the clearest ice they could find—on a tremendous scale."

She rose and walking to the window pushed aside the heavy Turkish portières and looked out.

"Oh!" she cried suddenly. "There's two little boys makin' a snow man! Harry, do you reckon I can go out an' help 'em?"

"You dream! Come here and kiss me."

She left the window rather reluctantly.

"I don't guess this is a very kissable climate, is it? I mean, it makes you so you don't want to sit round, doesn't it?"

"We're not going to. I've got a vacation for the first week you're here, and there's a dinner-dance to-night."

"Oh, Harry," she confessed, subsiding in a heap, half in his lap, half in the pillows, "I sure do feel confused. I haven't got an idea whether I'll like it or not, an' I don't know what people expect, or anythin'. You'll have to tell me, honey."

"I'll tell you," he said softly, "if you'll just tell me you're glad to be here."

"Glad—just awful glad!" she whispered, insinuating herself into his arms in her own peculiar way. "Where you are is home for me, Harry."

And as she said this she had the feeling for almost the first time in her life that she was acting a part.

That night, amid the gleaming candles of a dinner-party, where the men seemed to do most of the talking while the girls sat in a haughty and expensive aloofness, even Harry's presence on her left failed to make her feel at home.

"They're a good-looking crowd, don't you think?" he demanded. "Just look round. There's Spud Hubbard, tackle at Princeton last year, and Junie Morton—he and the red-haired fellow next to him were both Yale hockey captains; Junie was in my class. Why, the best athletes in the world come from

these states round here. This is a man's country, I tell you.
Look at John J. Fishburn!"

"Who's he?" asked Sally Carrol innocently.

"Don't you know?"

"I've heard the name."

"Greatest wheat man in the Northwest, and one of the
greatest financiers in the country."

She turned suddenly to a voice on her right.

"I guess they forgot to introduce us. My name's Roger
Patton."

"My name is Sally Carrol Happer," she said graciously.

"Yes, I know. Harry told me you were coming."

"You a relative?"

"No, I'm a professor."

"Oh," she laughed.

"At the university. You're from the South, aren't you?"

"Yes; Tarleton, Georgia."

She liked him immediately—a reddish-brown mustache
under watery blue eyes that had something in them that these
other eyes lacked, some quality of appreciation. They exchanged stray sentences through dinner, and she made up her
mind to see him again.

After coffee she was introduced to numerous good-looking
young men who danced with conscious precision and seemed
to take it for granted that she wanted to talk about nothing
except Harry.

"Heavens," she thought, "they talk as if my being engaged
made me older than they are—as if I'd tell their mothers on
them!"

In the South an engaged girl, even a young married
woman, expected the same amount of half-affectionate badinage and flattery that would be accorded a débutante, but
here all that seemed banned. One young man, after getting
well started on the subject of Sally Carrol's eyes, and how
they had allured him ever since she entered the room, went
into a violent confusion when he found she was visiting the
Bellamys—was Harry's fiancée. He seemed to feel as though
he had made some risqué and inexcusable blunder, became
immediately formal, and left her at the first opportunity.

She was rather glad when Roger Patton cut in on her and
suggested that they sit out a while.

"Well," he inquired, blinking cheerily, "how's Carmen
from the South?"

"Mighty fine. How's—how's Dangerous Dan McGrew? Sorry, but he's the only Northerner I know much about."

He seemed to enjoy that.

"Of course," he confessed, "as a professor of literature I'm not supposed to have read Dangerous Dan McGrew."

"Are you a native?"

"No, I'm a Philadelphian. Imported from Harvard to teach French. But I've been here ten years."

"Nine years, three hundred an' sixty-four days longer than me."

"Like it here?"

"Uh-huh. Sure do!"

"Really?"

"Well, why not? Don't I look as if I were havin' a good time?"

"I saw you look out the window a minute ago—and shiver."

"Just my imagination," laughed Sally Carrol. "I'm used to havin' everythin' quiet outside, an' sometimes I look out an' see a flurry of snow, an' it's just as if somethin' dead was movin'."

He nodded appreciatively.

"Ever been North before?"

"Spent two Julys in Asheville, North Carolina."

"Nice-looking crowd, aren't they?" suggested Patton, indicating the swirling floor.

Sally Carrol started. This had been Harry's remark.

"Sure are! They're—canine."

"What?"

She flushed.

"I'm sorry; that sounded worse than I meant it. You see, I always think of people as feline or canine, irrespective of sex."

"Which are you?"

"I'm feline. So are you. So are most Southern men an' most of these girls here."

"What's Harry?"

"Harry's canine distinctly. All the men I've met to-night seem to be canine."

"What does 'canine' imply? A certain conscious masculinity as opposed to subtlety?"

"Reckon so. I never analyzed it—only I just look at people

an' say 'canine' or 'feline' right off. It's right absurd, I guess."

"Not at all. I'm interested. I used to have a theory about these people. I think they're freezing up."

"What?"

"I think they're growing like Swedes—Ibsenesque, you know. Very gradually getting gloomy and melancholy. It's these long winters. Ever read any Ibsen?"

She shook her head.

"Well, you find in his characters, a certain brooding rigidity. They're righteous, narrow, and cheerless, without infinite possibilities for great sorrow or joy."

"Without smiles or tears?"

"Exactly. That's my theory. You see there are thousands of Swedes up here. They come, I imagine, because the climate is very much like their own, and there's been a gradual mingling. There're probably not half a dozen here to-night, but— we've had four Swedish governors. Am I boring you?"

"I'm mighty interested."

"Your future sister-in-law is half Swedish. Personally I like her, but my theory is that Swedes react rather badly on us as a whole. Scandinavians, you know, have the largest suicide rate in the world."

"Why do you live here if it's so depressing?"

"Oh, it doesn't get me. I'm pretty well cloistered, and I suppose books mean more than people to me anyway."

"But writers all speak about the South being tragic. You know—Spanish señoritas, black hair and daggers an' haunting music."

He shook his head.

"No, the Northern races are the tragic races—they don't indulge in the cheering luxury of tears."

Sally Carrol thought of her graveyard. She supposed that that was vaguely what she had meant when she said it didn't depress her.

"The Italians are about the gayest people in the world—but it's a dull subject," he broke off. "Anyway, I want to tell you you're marrying a pretty fine man."

Sally Carrol was moved by an impulse of confidence.

"I know. I'm the sort of person who wants to be taken care of after a certain point, and I feel sure I will be."

"Shall we dance? You know," he continued as they rose, "it's encouraging to find a girl who knows what she's marrying for. Nine-tenths of them think of it as a sort of walking into a moving-picture sunset."

She laughed, and liked him immensely.

Two hours later on the way home she nestled near Harry in the back seat.

"Oh, Harry," she whispered, "it's so co-old!"

"But it's warm in here, darling girl."

"But outside it's cold; and oh, that howling wind!"

She buried her face deep in his fur coat and trembled involuntarily as his cold lips kissed the tip of her ear.

IV

The first week of her visit passed in a whirl. She had her promised toboggan-ride at the back of an automobile through a chill January twilight. Swathed in furs she put in a morning tobogganing on the country-club hill; even tried skiing, to sail through the air for a glorious moment and then land in a tangled laughing bundle on a soft snowdrift. She liked all the winter sports, except an afternoon spent snow-shoeing over a glaring plain under pale yellow sunshine, but she soon realized that these things were for children—that she was being humored and that the enjoyment round her was only a reflection of her own.

At first the Bellamy family puzzled her. The men were reliable and she liked them; to Mr. Bellamy especially, with his iron-gray hair and energetic dignity, she took an immediate fancy, once she found that he was born in Kentucky; this made of him a link between the old life and the new. But toward the women she felt a definite hostility. Myra, her future sister-in-law, seemed the essence of spiritless conventionality. Her conversation was so utterly devoid of personality that Sally Carrol, who came from a country where a certain amount of charm and assurance could be taken for granted in the women, was inclined to despise her.

"If those women aren't beautiful," she thought, "they're nothing. They just fade out when you look at them. They're glorified domestics. Men are the centre of every mixed group."

Lastly there was Mrs. Bellamy, whom Sally Carrol detested. The first day's impression of an egg had been confirmed—an egg with a cracked, veiny voice and such an ungracious dumpiness of carriage that Sally Carrol felt that if she once fell she would surely scramble. In addition, Mrs. Bellamy seemed to typify the town in being innately hostile to strangers. She called Sally Carrol "Sally," and could not be persuaded that the double name was anything more than a tedious, ridiculous nickname. To Sally Carrol this shortening of her name was like presenting her to the public half clothed. She loved "Sally Carrol"; she loathed "Sally." She knew also that Harry's mother disapproved of her bobbed hair; and she had never dared smoke down-stairs after that first day when Mrs. Bellamy had come into the library sniffing violently.

Of all the men she met she preferred Roger Patton, who was a frequent visitor at the house. He never again alluded to the Ibsenesque tendency of the populace, but when he came in one day and found her curled upon the sofa bent over "Peer Gynt," he laughed and told her to forget what he'd said—that it was all rot.

And then one afternoon in her second week she and Harry hovered on the edge of a dangerously steep quarrel. She considered that he precipitated it entirely, though the Serbia in the case was an unknown man who had not had his trousers pressed.

They had been walking homeward between mounds of high-piled snow and under a sun which Sally Carrol scarcely recognized. They passed a little girl done up in gray wool until she resembled a small Teddy bear, and Sally Carrol could not resist a gasp of maternal appreciation.

"Look! Harry!"

"What?"

"That little girl—did you see her face?"

"Yes, why?"

"It was red as a little strawberry. Oh, she was cute!"

"Why, your own face is almost as red as that already! Everybody's healthy here. We're out in the cold as soon as we're old enough to walk. Wonderful climate!"

She looked at him and had to agree. He was mighty healthy-looking; so was his brother. And she had noticed the new red in her own cheeks that very morning.

Suddenly their glances were caught and held, and they stared for a moment at the street-corner ahead of them. A man was standing there, his knees bent, his eyes gazing upward with a tense expression as though he were about to make a leap toward the chilly sky. And then they both exploded into a shout of laughter, for coming closer they dis-

covered it had been a ludicrous momentary illusion produced
by the extreme bagginess of the man's trousers.

"Reckon that's one on us," she laughed.

"He must be a Southerner, judging by those trousers," suggested Harry mischievously.

"Why, Harry!"

Her surprised look must have irritated him.

"Those damn Southerners!"

Sally Carrol's eyes flashed.

"Don't call 'em that!"

"I'm sorry, dear," said Harry, malignantly apologetic, "but
you know what I think of them. They're sort of—sort of
degenerates—not at all like the old Southerners. They've
lived so long down there with all the colored people that
they've gotten lazy and shiftless."

"Hush your mouth, Harry!" she cried angrily. "They're
not! They may be lazy—anybody would be in that climate—
but they're my best friends, an' I don't want to hear 'em crit-
icised in any such sweepin' way. Some of 'em are the finest
men in the world."

"Oh, I know. They're all right when they come North to
college, but of all the hangdog, ill-dressed, slovenly lot I ever
saw, a bunch of small-town Southerners are the worst!"

Sally Carrol was clenching her gloved hands and biting her
lip furiously.

"Why," continued Harry, "there was one in my class at
New Haven, and we all thought that at last we'd found the
true type of Southern aristocrat, but it turned out that he
wasn't an aristocrat at all—just the son of a Northern carpet-
bagger who owned about all the cotton round Mobile."

"A Southerner wouldn't talk the way you're talking now,"
she said evenly.

"They haven't the energy!"

"Or the somethin' else."

"I'm sorry, Sally Carrol, but I've heard you say yourself
that you'd never marry—"

"That's quite different. I told you I wouldn't want to tie my
life to any of the boys that are round Tarleton now, but I
never made any sweepin' generalities."

They walked along in silence.

"I probably spread it on a bit thick, Sally Carrol. I'm
sorry."

She nodded but made no answer. Five minutes later as they stood in the hallway she suddenly threw her arms round him.

"Oh, Harry," she cried, her eyes brimming with tears, "let's get married next week. I'm afraid of having fusses like that. I'm afraid, Harry. It wouldn't be that way if we were married."

But Harry, being in the wrong, was still irritated.

"That'd be idiotic. We decided on March."

The tears in Sally Carrol's eyes faded; her expression hardened slightly.

"Very well—I suppose I shouldn't have said that."

Harry melted.

"Dear little nut!" he cried. "Come and kiss me and let's forget."

That very night at the end of a vaudeville performance the orchestra played "Dixie," and Sally Carrol felt something stronger and more enduring than her tears and smiles of the day brim up inside her. She leaned forward gripping the arms of her chair until her face grew crimson.

"Sort of get you, dear?" whispered Harry.

But she did not hear him. To the spirited throb of the violins and the inspiring beat of the kettledrums her own old ghosts were marching by and on into the darkness, and as fifes whistled and sighed in the low encore they seemed so nearly out of sight that she could have waved good-by.

> "Away, Away,
>   Away down South in Dixie!
> Away, Away,
>   Away down South in Dixie!"

V

It was a particularly cold night. A sudden thaw had nearly cleared the streets the day before, but now they were traversed again with a powdery wraith of loose snow that travelled in wavy lines before the feet of the wind, and filled the lower air with a fine-particled mist. There was no sky—only a dark, ominous tent that draped in the tops of the streets and was in reality a vast approaching army of snowflakes—while over it all, chilling away the comfort from the brown-and-green glow of lighted windows and muffling the steady trot of the horse pulling their sleigh, interminably washed the north wind. It was a dismal town after all, she thought—dismal.

Sometimes at night it had seemed to her as though no one lived here—they had all gone long ago—leaving lighted houses to be covered in time by tombing heaps of sleet. Oh, if there should be snow on her grave! To be beneath great piles of it all winter long, where even her headstone would be a light shadow against light shadows. Her grave—a grave that should be flower-strewn and washed with sun and rain.

She thought again of those isolated country houses that her train had passed, and of the life there the long winter through—the ceaseless glare through the windows, the crust forming on the soft drifts of snow, finally the slow, cheerless melting, and the harsh spring of which Roger patton had told her. Her spring—to lose it forever—with its lilacs and the lazy sweetness it stirred in her heart. She was laying away that spring—afterward she would lay away that sweetness.

With a gradual insistence the storm broke. Sally Carrol felt a film of flakes melt quickly on her eyelashes, and Harry reached over a furry arm and drew down her complicated flannel cap. Then the small flakes came in skirmish-line, and the horse bent his neck patiently as a transparency of white momentarily appeared on his coat.

"Oh, he's cold, Harry," she said quickly.

"Who? The horse? Oh, no, he isn't. He likes it!"

After another ten minutes they turned a corner and came in sight of their destination. On a tall hill, outlined in vivid glaring green against the wintry sky, stood the ice palace. It was three stories in the air, with battlements and embrasures and narrow icicled windows, and the innumerable electric lights inside made a gorgeous transparency of the great central hall. Sally Carrol clutched Harry's hand under the fur robe.

"It's beautiful!" he cried excitedly. "My golly, it's beautiful, isn't it! They haven't had one here since eighty-five!"

Somehow the notion of there not having been one since eighty-five oppressed her. Ice was a ghost, and this mansion of it was surely peopled by those shades of the eighties, with pale faces and blurred snow-filled hair.

"Come on, dear," said Harry.

She followed him out of the sleigh and waited while he hitched the horse. A party of four—Gordon, Myra, Roger Patton, and another girl—drew up beside them with a mighty jingle of bells. There was quite a crowd already, bundled in fur or sheepskin, shouting and calling to each other as they moved through the snow, which was now so thick that people could scarcely be distinguished a few yards away.

"It's a hundred and seventy feet tall," Harry was saying to a muffled figure beside him as they trudged toward the entrance, "covers six thousand square yards."

She caught snatches of conversation: "One main hall"—"walls twenty to forty inches thick"—"and the ice cave has almost a mile of—"—"this Canuck who built it—"

They found their way inside, and dazed by the magic of the great crystal walls Sally Carrol found herself repeating over and over two lines from "Kubla Khan":

> "It was a miracle of rare device,
> A sunny pleasure-dome with caves of ice!"

In the great glittering cavern with the dark shut out she took a seat on a wooden bench, and the evening's oppression lifted. Harry was right—it was beautiful; and her gaze travelled the smooth surface of the walls, the blocks for which had been selected for their purity and clearness to obtain this opalescent, translucent effect.

"Look! Here we go—oh, boy!" cried Harry.

A band in a far corner struck up "Hail, Hail, the Gang's All Here!" which echoed over to them in wild muddled acoustics, and then the lights suddenly went out; silence seemed to flow down the icy sides and sweep over them. Sally Carrol could still see her white breath in the darkness, and a dim row of pale faces over on the other side.

The music eased to a sighing complaint, and from outside drifted in the full-throated resonant chant of the marching clubs. It grew louder like some pæan of a viking tribe traversing an ancient wild; it swelled—they were coming nearer; then a row of torches appeared, and another and another, and keeping time with their moccasined feet a long column of gray-mackinawed figures swept in, snowshoes slung at their shoulders, torches soaring and flickering as their voices rose along the great walls.

The gray column ended and another followed, the light streaming luridly this time over red toboggan caps and flaming crimson mackinaws, and as they entered they took up the refrain; then came a long platoon of blue and white, of green, of white, of brown and yellow.

"Those white ones are the Wacouta Club," whispered Harry eagerly. "Those are the men you've met round at dances."

The volume of the voices grew; the great cavern was a phantasmagoria of torches waving in great banks of fire, of colors and the rhythm of soft-leather steps. The leading column turned and halted, platoon deployed in front of platoon until the whole procession made a solid flag of flame, and then from thousands of voices burst a mighty shout that filled the air like a crash of thunder, and sent the torches wavering. It was magnificent, it was tremendous! To Sally Carrol it was the North offering sacrifice on some mighty altar to the gray pagan God of Snow. As the shout died the band struck up again and there came more singing, and then long reverberating cheers by each club. She sat very quiet, listening while the staccato cries rent the stillness; and then she started, for there was a volley of explosion, and great clouds of smoke went up here and there through the cavern—the flash-light photographers at work—and the council was over. With the band at their head the clubs formed in column once more, took up their chant, and began to march out.

"Come on!" shouted Harry. "We want to see the labyrinths down-stairs before they turn the lights off!"

They all rose and started toward the chute—Harry and Sally Carrol in the lead, her little mitten buried in his big fur gantlet. At the bottom of the chute was a long empty room of ice, with the ceiling so low that they had to stoop—and their hands were parted. Before she realized what he intended Harry had darted down one of the half-dozen glittering passages that opened into the room and was only a vague receding blot against the green shimmer.

"Harry!" she called.

"Come on!" he cried back.

She looked round the empty chamber; the rest of the party had evidently decided to go home, were already outside somewhere in the blundering snow. She hesitated and then darted in after Harry.

"Harry!" she shouted.

She had reached a turning-point thirty feet down; she heard a faint muffled answer far to the left, and with a touch of panic fled toward it. She passed another turning, two more yawning alleys.

"Harry!"

No answer. She started to run straight forward, and then turned like lightning and sped back the way she had come, enveloped in a sudden icy terror.

She reached a turn—was it here?—took the left and came to what should have been the outlet into the long, low room, but it was only another glittering passage with darkness at the end. She called again, but the walls gave back a flat, lifeless echo with no reverberations. Retracing her steps she turned another corner, this time following a wide passage. It was like the green lane between the parted waters of the Red Sea, like a damp vault connecting empty tombs.

She slipped a little now as she walked, for ice had formed on the bottom of her overshoes; she had to run her gloves along the half-slippery, half-sticky walls to keep her balance.

"Harry!"

Still no answer. The sound she made bounced mockingly down to the end of the passage.

Then on an instant the lights went out, and she was in complete darkness. She gave a small, frightened cry, and sank down into a cold little heap on the ice. She felt her left knee do something as she fell, but she scarcely noticed it as some deep terror far greater than any fear of being lost settled upon her. She was alone with this presence that came out of the North, the dreary loneliness that rose from ice-bound whalers in the Arctic seas, from smokeless, trackless wastes where were strewn the whitened bones of adventure. It was an icy breath of death; it was rolling down low across the land to clutch at her.

With a furious, despairing energy she rose again and started blindly down the darkness. She must get out. She might be lost in here for days, freeze to death and lie embedded in the ice like corpses she had read of, kept perfectly preserved until the melting of a glacier. Harry probably thought she had left with the others—he had gone by now; no one would know until late next day. She reached pitifully for the wall. Forty inches thick, they had said—forty inches thick!

"Oh!"

On both sides of her along the walls she felt things creeping, damp souls that haunted this palace, this town, this North.

"Oh, send somebody—send somebody!" she cried aloud.

Clark Darrow—he would understand; or Joe Ewing; she couldn't be left here to wander forever—to be frozen, heart, body, and soul. This her—this Sally Carrol! Why, she was a happy thing. She was a happy little girl. She liked warmth and summer and Dixie. These things were foreign—foreign.

"You're not crying," something said aloud. "You'll never cry any more. Your tears would just freeze; all tears freeze up here!"

She sprawled full length on the ice.

"Oh, God!" she faltered.

A long single file of minutes went by, and with a great weariness she felt her eyes closing. Then some one seemed to sit down near her and take her face in warm, soft hands. She looked up gratefully.

"Why, it's Margery Lee," she crooned softly to herself. "I knew you'd come." It really was Margery Lee, and she was just as Sally Carrol had known she would be, with a young, white brow, and wide, welcoming eyes, and a hoop-skirt of some soft material that was quite comforting to rest on.

"Margery Lee."

It was getting darker now and darker—all those tombstones ought to be repainted, sure enough, only that would spoil 'em, of course. Still, you ought to be able to see 'em.

Then after a succession of moments that went fast and then slow, but seemed to be ultimately resolving themselves into a multitude of blurred rays converging toward a pale-yellow sun, she heard a great cracking noise break her new-found stillness.

It was the sun, it was a light; a torch, and a torch beyond that, and another one, and voices; a face took flesh below the torch, heavy arms raised her, and she felt something on her cheek—it felt wet. Some one had seized her and was rubbing her face with snow. How ridiculous—with snow!

"Sally Carrol! Sally Carrol!"

It was Dangerous Dan McGrew; and two other faces she didn't know.

"Child, child! We've been looking for you two hours! Harry's half-crazy!"

Things came rushing back into place—the singing, the torches, the great shout of the marching clubs. She squirmed in Patton's arms and gave a long, low cry.

"Oh, I want to get out of here! I'm going back home. Take me home"—her voice rose to a scream that sent a chill to Harry's heart as he came racing down the next passage—

"to-morrow!" she cried with delirious, unrestrained passion—
"To-morrow! To-morrow! To-morrow!"

VI

The wealth of golden sunlight poured a quite enervating yet
oddly comforting heat over the house where day long it faced
the dusty stretch of road. Two birds were making a great
to-do in a cool spot found among the branches of a tree next
door, and down the street a colored woman was announcing
herself melodiously as a purveyor of strawberries. It was
April afternoon.

Sally Carrol Happer, resting her chin on her arm, and her
arm on an old window-seat, gazed sleepily down over the
spangled dust whence the heat waves were rising for the first
time this spring. She was watching a very ancient Ford turn
a perilous corner and rattle and groan to a jolting stop at the
end of the walk. She made no sound, and in a minute a strident familiar whistle rent the air. Sally Carrol smiled and
blinked.

"Good mawnin'."

A head appeared tortuously from under the cartop below.

"'Tain't mawnin', Sally Carrol."

"Sure enough!" she said in affected surprise. "I guess
maybe not."

"What you doin'?"

"Eatin' green peach. 'Spect to die any minute."

Clark twisted himself a last impossible notch to get a view
of her face.

"Water's warm as a kettla steam, Sally Carrol. Wanta go
swimmin'?"

"Hate to move," sighed Sally Carrol lazily, "but I reckon
so."

Head and Shoulders

I

In 1915 Horace Tarbox was thirteen years old. In that year he took the examinations for entrance to Princeton University and received the Grade A—excellent—in Caesar, Cicero, Vergil, Xenophon, Homer, Algebra, Plane Geometry, Solid Geometry, and Chemistry.

Two years later, while George M. Cohan was composing "Over There," Horace was leading the sophomore class by several lengths and digging out theses on "The Syllogism as an Obsolete Scholastic Form," and during the battle of Château-Thierry he was sitting at his desk deciding whether or not to wait until his seventeenth birthday before beginning his series of essays on "The Pragmatic Bias of the New Realists."

After a while some newsboy told him that the war was over, and he was glad, because it meant that Peat Brothers, publishers, would get out their new edition of "Spinoza's Improvement of the Understanding." Wars were all very well in their way, made young men self-reliant or something, but Horace felt that he could never forgive the President for allowing a brass band to play under his window on the night of the false armistice, causing him to leave three important sentences out of his thesis on "German Idealism."

The next year he went up to Yale to take his degree as Master of Arts.

He was seventeen then, tall and slender, with near-sighted gray eyes and an air of keeping himself utterly detached from the mere words he let drop.

"I never feel as though I'm talking to him," expostulated Professor Dillinger to a sympathetic colleague. "He makes me feel as though I were talking to his representative. I always expect him to say: 'Well, I'll ask myself and find out.' "

And then, just as nonchalantly as though Horace Tarbox had been Mr. Beef the butcher or Mr. Hat the haberdasher, life reached in, seized him, handled him, stretched him, and unrolled him like a piece of Irish lace on a Saturday-afternoon bargain-counter.

To move in the literary fashion I should say that this was all because when way back in colonial days the hardy pioneers had come to a bald place in Connecticut and asked of each other, "Now, what shall we build here?" the hardiest one among 'em had answered: "Let's build a town where theatrical managers can try out musical comedies!" How afterward they founded Yale College there, to try the musical comedies on, is a story every one knows. At any rate one December, "Home James" opened at the Shubert, and all the students encored Marcia Meadow, who sang a song about the Blundering Blimp in the first act and did a shaky, shivery, celebrated dance in the last.

Marcia was nineteen. She didn't have wings, but audiences agreed generally that she didn't need them. She was a blonde by natural pigment, and she wore no paint on the streets at high noon. Outside of that she was no better than most women.

It was Charlie Moon who promised her five thousand Pall Malls if she would pay a call on Horace Tarbox, prodigy extraordinary. Charlie was a senior in Sheffield, and he and Horace were first cousins. They liked and pitied each other.

Horace had been particularly busy that night. The failure of the Frenchman Laurier to appreciate the significance of the new realists was preying on his mind. In fact, his only reaction to a low, clearcut rap at his study was to make him speculate as to whether any rap would have actual existence without an ear there to hear it. He fancied he was verging more and more toward pragmatism. But at that moment, though he did not know it, he was verging with astounding rapidity toward something quite different.

The rap sounded—three seconds leaked by—the rap sounded.

"Come in," muttered Horace automatically.

He heard the door open and then close, but, bent over his book in the big armchair before the fire, he did not look up.

"Leave it on the bed in the other room," he said absently.

"Leave what on the bed in the other room?"

Marcia Meadow had to talk her songs, but her speaking voice was like byplay on a harp.

"The laundry."

"I can't."

Horace stirred impatiently in his chair.

"Why can't you?"

"Why, because I haven't got it."

"Hm!" he replied testily. "Suppose you go back and get it."

Across the fire from Horace was another easychair. He was accustomed to change to it in the course of an evening by way of exercise and variety. One chair he called Berkeley, the other he called Hume. He suddenly heard a sound as of a rustling, diaphanous form sinking into Hume. He glanced up.

"Well," said Marcia with the sweet smile she used in Act Two ("Oh, so the Duke liked my dancing!"), "Well, Omar Khayyam, here I am beside you singing in the wilderness."

Horace stared at her dazedly. The momentary suspicion came to him that she existed there only as a phantom of his imagination. Women didn't come into men's rooms and sink into men's Humes. Women brought laundry and took your seat in the street-car and married you later on when you were old enough to know fetters.

This woman had clearly materialized out of Hume. The very froth of her brown gauzy dress was an emanation from Hume's leather arm there! If he looked long enough he would see Hume right through her and then he would be alone again in the room. He passed his fist across his eyes. He really must take up those trapeze exercises again.

"For Pete's sake, don't look so critical!" objected the emanation pleasantly. "I feel as if you were going to wish me away with that patent dome of yours. And then there wouldn't be anything left of me except my shadow in your eyes."

Horace coughed. Coughing was one of his two gestures. When he talked you forgot he had a body at all. It was like hearing a phonograph record by a singer who had been dead a long time.

"What do you want?" he asked.

"I want them letters," whined Marcia melodramatically— "them letters of mine you bought from my grandsire in 1881."

Horace considered.

"I haven't got your letters," he said evenly. "I am only seventeen years old. My father was not born until March 3, 1879. You evidently have me confused with some one else."

"You're only seventeen?" repeated Marcia suspiciously.

"Only seventeen."

"I knew a girl," said Marcia reminiscently, "who went on the ten-twenty-thirty when she was sixteen. She was so stuck on herself that she could never say 'sixteen' without putting the 'only' before it. We got to calling her 'Only Jessie.' And she's just where she was when she started—only worse. 'Only' is a bad habit, Omar—it sounds like an alibi."

"My name is not Omar."

"I know," agreed Marcia, nodding—"your name's Horace. I just call you Omar because you remind me of a smoked cigarette."

"And I haven't your letters. I doubt if I've ever met your grandfather. In fact, I think it very improbable that you yourself were alive in 1881."

Marcia stared at him in wonder.

"Me—1881? Why sure! I was second-line stuff when the Florodora Sextette was still in the convent. I was the original nurse to Mrs. Sol Smith's Juliette. Why, Omar, I was a canteen singer during the War of 1812."

Horace's mind made a sudden successful leap, and he grinned.

"Did Charlie Moon put you up to this?"

Marcia regarded him inscrutably.

"Who's Charlie Moon?"

"Small—wide nostrils—big ears."

She grew several inches and sniffed.

"I'm not in the habit of noticing my friends' nostrils."

"Then it was Charlie?"

Marcia bit her lip—and then yawned.

"Oh, let's change the subject, Omar. I'll pull a snore in this chair in a minute."

"Yes," replied Horace gravely, "Hume has often been considered soporific."

"Who's your friend—and will he die?"

Then of a sudden Horace Tarbox rose slenderly and began to pace the room with his hands in his pockets. This was his other gesture.

"I don't care for this," he said, as if he were talking to himself—"at all. Not that I mind your being here—I don't. You're quite a pretty little thing, but I don't like Charlie Moon's sending you up here. Am I a laboratory experiment on which the janitors as well as the chemists can make experiments? Is my intellectual development humorous in any way? Do I look like the pictures of the little Boston boy in the comic magazines? Has that callow ass, Moon, with his eternal tales about his week in Paris, any right to—"

"No," interrupted Marcia emphatically. "And you're a sweet boy. Come here and kiss me."

Horace stopped quickly in front of her.

"Why do you want me to kiss you?" he asked intently. "Do you just go round kissing people?"

"Why, yes," admitted Marcia, unruffled. " 'At's all life is. Just going round kissing people."

"Well," replied Horace emphatically. "I must say your ideas are horribly garbled! In the first place life isn't just that, and in the second place I won't kiss you. It might get to be a habit and I can't get rid of habits. This year I've got in the habit of lolling in bed until seven-thirty."

Marcia nodded understandingly.

"Do you ever have any fun?" she asked.

"What do you mean by fun?"

"See here," said Marcia sternly, "I like you, Omar, but I wish you'd talk as if you had a line on what you were saying. You sound as if you were gargling a lot of words in your mouth and lost a bet every time you spilled a few. I asked you if you ever had any fun."

Horace shook his head.

"Later, perhaps," he answered. "You see I'm a plan. I'm an experiment. I don't say that I don't get tired of it sometimes—I do. Yet—oh, I can't explain! But what you and Charlie Moon call fun wouldn't be fun to me."

"Please explain."

Horace stared at her, started to speak and then, changing his mind, resumed his walk. After an unsuccessful attempt to determine whether or not he was looking at her Marcia smiled at him.

"Please explain."

Horace turned.

"If I do, will you promise to tell Charlie Moon that I wasn't in?"

"Uh-uh."

"Very well, then. Here's my history: I was a 'why' child. I wanted to see the wheels go round. My father was a young economics professor at Princeton. He brought me up on the system of answering every question I asked him to the best of his ability. My response to that gave him the idea of making an experiment in precocity. To aid in the massacre I had ear trouble—seven operations between the ages of nine and twelve. Of course this kept me apart from other boys and made me ripe for forcing. Anyway, while my generation was laboring through Uncle Remus I was honestly enjoying Catullus in the original.

"I passed off my college examinations when I was thirteen because I couldn't help it. My chief associates were professors, and I took a tremendous pride in knowing that I had a fine intelligence, for though I was unusually gifted I was not abnormal in other ways. When I was sixteen I got tired of being a freak; I decided that some one had made a bad mistake. Still as I'd gone that far I concluded to finish it up by taking my degree of Master of Arts. My chief interest in life is the study of modern philosophy. I am a realist of the School of Anton Laurier—with Bergsonian trimmings—and I'll be eighteen years old in two months. That's all."

"Whew!" exclaimed Marcia. "That's enough! You do a neat job with the parts of speech."

"Satisfied?"

"No, you haven't kissed me."

"It's not in my programme," demurred Horace. "Understand that I don't pretend to be above physical things. They have their place, but—"

"Oh, don't be so darned reasonable!"

"I can't help it."

"I hate these slot-machine people."

"I assure you I—" began Horace.

"Oh, shut up!"

"My own rationality—"

"I didn't say anything about your nationality. You're an Amuricun, ar'n't you?"

"Yes."

"Well, that's O.K. with me. I got a notion I want to see you do something that isn't in your highbrow programme. I want to see if a what-ch-call-em with Brazilian trimmings—that thing you said you were—can be a little human."

Horace shook his head again.

"I won't kiss you."

"My life is blighted," muttered Marcia tragically. "I'm a beaten woman. I'll go through life without ever having a kiss with Brazilian trimmings." She sighed. "Anyways, Omar, will you come and see my show?"

"What show?"

"I'm a wicked actress from 'Home James'!"

"Light opera?"

"Yes—at a stretch. One of the characters is a Brazilian rice-planter. That might interest you."

"I saw 'The Bohemian Girl' once," reflected Horace aloud. "I enjoyed it—to some extent."

"Then you'll come?"

"Well, I'm—I'm—"

"Oh, I know—you've got to run down to Brazil for the weekend."

"Not at all. I'd be delighted to come."

Marcia clapped her hands.

"Goodyforyou! I'll mail you a ticket—Thursday night?"

"Why, I—"

"Good! Thursday night it is."

She stood up and walking close to him laid both hands on his shoulders.

"I like you, Omar. I'm sorry I tried to kid you. I thought you'd be sort of frozen, but you're a nice boy."

He eyed her sardonically.

"I'm several thousand generations older than you are."

"You carry your age well."

They shook hands gravely.

"My name's Marcia Meadow," she said emphatically. "'Member it—Marcia Meadow. And I won't tell Charlie Moon you were in."

An instant later, as she was skimming down the last flight of stairs three at a time, she heard a voice call over the upper banister: "Oh, say—"

She stopped and looked up—made out a vague form leaning over.

"Oh, say!" called the prodigy again. "Can you hear me?"

"Here's your connection, Omar."

"I hope I haven't given you the impression that I consider kissing intrinsically irrational."

"Impression? Why, you didn't even give me the kiss—Never fret—so long."

Two doors near her opened curiously at the sound of a feminine voice. A tentative cough sounded from above. Gathering her skirts, Marcia dived wildly down the last flight and was swallowed up in the murky Connecticut air outside.

Up-stairs Horace paced the floor of his study. From time to time he glanced toward Berkeley waiting there in suave dark-red respectability, an open book lying suggestively on his cushions. And then he found that his circuit of the floor was bringing him each time nearer to Hume. There was something about Hume that was strangely and inexpressibly different. The diaphanous form still seemed hovering near, and had Horace sat there he would have felt as if he were sitting on a lady's lap. And though Horace couldn't have named the quality of difference, there was such a quality—quite intangible to the speculative mind, but real, nevertheless. Hume was radiating something that in all the two hundred years of his influence he had never radiated before.

Hume was radiating attar of roses.

II

On Thursday night Horace Tarbox sat in an aisle seat in the fifth row and witnessed "Home James." Oddly enough he found that he was enjoying himself. The cynical students near him were annoyed at his audible appreciation of time-honored jokes in the Hammerstein tradition. But Horace was waiting with anxiety for Marcia Meadow singing her song about a Jazz-bound Blundering Blimp. When she did appear, radiant under a floppity flower-faced hat, a warm glow settled over him, and when the song was over he did not join in the storm of applause. He felt somewhat numb.

In the intermission after the second act an usher materialized beside him, demanded to know if he were Mr. Tarbox, and then handed him a note written in a round adolescent hand. Horace read it in some confusion, while the usher lingered with withering patience in the aisle.

DEAR OMAR: After the show I always grow an awful hunger. If you want to satisfy it for me in the Taft Grill just communicate your answer to the big-timber guide that brought this and oblige.

Your friend,

MARCIA MEADOW.

"Tell her"—he coughed—"tell her that it will be quite all right. I'll meet her in front of the theatre."

The big-timber guide smiled arrogantly.

"I giss she meant for you to come round' t' the stage door."

"Where—where is it?"

"Ou'side. Tunayulef. Down ee alley."

"What?"

"Ou'side. Turn to y' left! Down ee alley!"

The arrogant person withdrew. A freshman behind Horace snickered.

Then half an hour later, sitting in the Taft Grill opposite the hair that was yellow by natural pigment, the prodigy was saying an odd thing.

"Do you have to do that dance in the last act?" he was asking earnestly—"I mean, would they dismiss you if you refused to do it?"

Marcia grinned.

"It's fun to do it. I like to do it."

And then Horace came out with a *faux pas*.

"I should think you'd detest it," he remarked succinctly. "The people behind me were making remarks about your bosom."

Marcia blushed fiery red.

"I can't help that," she said quickly. "The dance to me is only a sort of acrobatic stunt. Lord, it's hard enough to do! I rub liniment into my shoulders for an hour every night."

"Do you have—fun while you're on the stage?"

"Uh-huh—sure! I got in the habit of having people look at me, Omar, and I like it."

"Hm!" Horace sank into a brownish study.

"How's the Brazilian trimmings?"

"Hm!" repeated Horace, and then after a pause: "Where does the play go from here?"

"New York."

"For how long?"

"All depends. Winter—maybe."

"Oh!"

"Coming up to lay eyes on me, Omar, or aren't you int'rested? Not as nice here, is it, as it was up in your room? I wish we was there now."

"I feel idiotic in this place," confessed Horace, looking around him nervously.

"Too bad! We got along pretty well."

At this he looked suddenly so melancholy that she changed her tone, and reaching over patted his hand.

"Ever take an actress out to supper before?"

"No," said Horace miserably, "and I never will again. I don't know why I came to-night. Here under all these lights and with all these people laughing and chattering I feel completely out of my sphere. I don't know what to talk to you about."

"We'll talk about me. We talked about you last time."

"Very well."

"Well, my name really is Meadow, but my first name isn't Marcia—it's Veronica. I'm nineteen. Question—how did the girl make her leap to the footlights? Answer—she was born in Passaic, New Jersey, and up to a year ago she got the right to breathe by pushing Nabiscoes in Marcel's tea-room in Trenton. She started going with a guy named Robbins, a singer in the Trent House cabaret, and he got her to try a song and dance with him one evening. In a month we were filling the supper-room every night. Then we went to New York with meet-my-friend letters thick as a pile of napkins.

"In two days we'd landed a job at Divinerries', and I learned to shimmy from a kid at the Palais Royal. We stayed at Divinerries' six months until one night Peter Boyce Wendell, the columnist, ate his milk-toast there. Next morning a poem about Marvellous Marcia came out in his newspaper, and within two days I had three vaudeville offers and a chance at the Midnight Frolic. I wrote Wendell a thank-you letter, and he printed it in his column—said that the style was like Carlyle's, only more rugged, and that I ought to quit dancing and do North American literature. This got me a coupla more vaudeville offers and a chance as an ingénue in a regular show. I took it—and here I am, Omar."

When she finished they sat for a moment in silence, she draping the last skeins of a Welsh rabbit on her fork and waiting for him to speak.

"Let's get out of here," he said suddenly.

Marcia's eyes hardened.

"What's the idea? Am I making you sick?"

"No, but I don't like it here. I don't like to be sitting here with you."

Without another word Marcia signalled for the waiter.

"What's the check?" she demanded briskly. "My part—the rabbit and the ginger ale."

Horace watched blankly as the waiter figured it.

"See here," he began, "I intend to pay for yours too. You're my guest."

With a half-sigh Marcia rose from the table and walked from the room. Horace, his face a document in bewilderment, laid a bill down and followed her out, up the stairs and into the lobby. He overtook her in front of the elevator and they faced each other.

"See here," he repeated, "you're my guest. Have I said something to offend you?"

After an instant of wonder Marcia's eyes softened.

"You're a rude fella," she said slowly. "Don't you know you're rude?"

"I can't help it," said Horace with a directness she found quite disarming. "You know I like you."

"You said you didn't like being with me."

"I didn't like it."

"Why not?"

Fire blazed suddenly from the gray forests of his eyes.

"Because I didn't. I've formed the habit of liking you. I've been thinking of nothing much else for two days."

"Well, if you—"

"Wait a minute," he interrupted. "I've got something to say. It's this: in six weeks I'll be eighteen years old. When I'm eighteen years old I'm coming up to New York to see you. Is there some place in New York where we can go and not have a lot of people in the room?"

"Sure!" smiled Marcia. "You can come up to my 'partment. Sleep on the couch, if you want to."

"I can't sleep on couches," he said shortly. "But I want to talk to you."

"Why, sure," repeated Marcia—"in my 'partment."

In his excitement Horace put his hands in his pockets.

"All right—just so I can see you alone. I want to talk to you as we talked up in my room."

"Honey boy," cried Marcia, laughing, "is it that you want to kiss me?"

"Yes," Horace almost shouted. "I'll kiss you if you want me to."

The elevator man was looking at them reproachfully. Marcia edged toward the grated door.

"I'll drop you a post-card," she said.

Horace's eyes were quite wild.

"Send me a post-card! I'll come up any time after January first. I'll be eighteen then."

And as she stepped into the elevator he coughed enigmatically, yet with a vague challenge, at the ceiling, and walked quickly away.

III

He was there again. She saw him when she took her first glance at the restless Manhattan audience—down in the front row with his head bent a bit forward and his gray eyes fixed on her. And she knew that to him they were alone together in a world where the high-rouged row of ballet faces and the massed whines of the violins were as imperceivable as powder on a marble Venus. An instinctive defiance rose within her.

"Silly boy!" she said to herself hurriedly, and she didn't take her encore.

"What do they expect for a hundred a week—perpetual motion?" she grumbled to herself in the wings.

"What's the trouble, Marcia?"

"Guy I don't like down in front."

During the last act, as she waited for specialty, she had an odd attack of stage fright. She had never sent Horace the promised post-card. Last night she had pretended not to see him—had hurried from the theatre immediately after her dance to pass a sleepless night in her apartment, thinking—as she had so often in the last month—of his pale, rather intent face, his slim, boyish figure, the merciless, unworldly abstraction that made him charming to her.

And now that he had come she felt vaguely sorry—as though an unwonted responsibility was being forced on her.

"Infant prodigy!" she said aloud.

"What?" demanded the Negro comedian standing beside her.

"Nothing—just talking about myself."

On the stage she felt better. This was her dance—and she always felt that the way she did it wasn't suggestive any more than to some men every pretty girl is suggestive. She made it a stunt.

"Uptown, downtown, jelly on a spoon,
After sundown shiver by the moon."

He was not watching her now. She saw that clearly. He was looking very deliberately at a castle on the back drop, wearing that expression he had worn in the Taft Grill. A wave of exasperation swept over her—he was criticising her.

"That's the vibration that thr-ills me,
Funny how affection fi-lls me,
Uptown, downtown—"

Unconquerable revulsion seized her. She was suddenly and horribly conscious of her audience as she had never been since her first appearance. Was that a leer on a pallid face in the front row, a droop of disgust on one young girl's mouth? These shoulders of hers—these shoulders shaking—were they hers? Were they real? Surely shoulders weren't made for this!

"Then—you'll see at a glance
I'll need some funeral ushers with St. Vitus dance
At the end of the world I'll—"

The bassoon and two cellos crashed into a final chord. She paused and poised a moment on her toes with every muscle tense, her young face looking out dully at the audience in what one young girl afterward called "such a curious, puzzled look," and then without bowing rushed from the stage. Into the dressing-room she sped, kicked out of one dress and into another, and caught a taxi outside.

Her apartment was very warm—small, it was, with a row of professional pictures and sets of Kipling and O. Henry which she had bought once from a blue-eyed agent and read occasionally. And there were several chairs which matched, but were none of them comfortable, and a pink-shaded lamp with blackbirds painted on it and an atmosphere of rather stifled pink throughout. There were nice things in it—nice things unrelentingly hostile to each other, offsprings of a vicarious, impatient taste acting in stray moments. The worst was typified by a great picture framed in oak bark of Passaic as seen from the Erie Railroad—altogether a frantic, oddly extravagant, oddly penurious attempt to make a cheerful room. Marcia knew it was a failure.

Into this room came the prodigy and took her two hands awkwardly.

"I followed you this time," he said.

"Oh!"

"I want you to marry me," he said.

Her arms went out to him. She kissed his mouth with a sort of passionate wholesomeness.

"There!"

"I love you," he said.

She kissed him again and then with a little sigh flung herself into an armchair and half lay there, shaken with absurd laughter.

"Why, you infant prodigy!" she cried.

"Very well, call me that if you want to. I once told you that I was ten thousand years older than you—I am."

She laughed again.

"I don't like to be disapproved of."

"No one's ever going to disapprove of you again."

"Omar," she asked, "why do you want to marry me?"

The prodigy rose and put his hands in his pockets.

"Because I love you, Marcia Meadow."

And then she stopped calling him Omar.

"Dear boy," she said, "you know I sort of love you. There's something about you—I can't tell what—that just puts my heart through the wringer every time I'm round you. But, honey—" She paused.

"But what?"

"But lots of things. But you're only just eighteen, and I'm nearly twenty."

"Nonsense!" he interrupted. "Put it this way—that I'm in my nineteenth year and you're nineteen. That makes us pretty close—without counting that other ten thousand years I mentioned."

Marcia laughed.

"But there are some more 'buts.' Your people—"

"My people!" exclaimed the prodigy ferociously. "My people tried to make a monstrosity out of me." His face grew quite crimson at the enormity of what he was going to say. "My people can go way back and sit down!"

"My heavens!" cried Marcia in alarm. "All that? On tacks, I suppose."

"Tacks—yes," he agreed wildly—"on anything. The more

I think of how they allowed me to become a little dried-up mummy—"

"What makes you think you're that?" asked Marcia quietly—"me?"

"Yes. Every person I've met on the streets since I met you has made me jealous because they knew what love was before I did. I used to call it the 'sex impulse.' Heavens!"

"There's more 'buts,' " said Marcia.

"What are they?"

"How could we live?"

"I'll make a living."

"You're in college."

"Do you think I care anything about taking a Master of Arts degree?"

"You want to be Master of Me, hey?"

"Yes! What? I mean, no!"

Marcia laughed, and crossing swiftly over sat in his lap. He put his arm round her wildly and implanted the vestige of a kiss somewhere near her neck.

"There's something white about you," mused Marcia, "but it doesn't sound very logical."

"Oh, don't be so darned reasonable!"

"I can't help it," said Marcia.

"I hate these slot-machine people!"

"But we—"

"Oh, shut up!"

And as Marcia couldn't talk through her ears she had to.

IV

Horace and Marcia were married early in February. The sensation in academic circles both at Yale and Princeton was tremendous. Horace Tarbox, who at fourteen had been played up in the Sunday magazine sections of metropolitan newspapers, was throwing over his career, his chance of being a world authority on American philosophy, by marrying a chorus girl— they made Marcia a chorus girl. But like all modern stories it was a four-and-a-half-day wonder.

They took a flat in Harlem. After two weeks' search, during which his idea of the value of academic knowledge faded unmercifully, Horace took a position as clerk with a South American export company—some one had told him that exporting was the coming thing. Marcia was to stay in her show for a few months—anyway until he got on his feet. He was getting a hundred and twenty-five to start with, and though of course they told him it was only a question of months until he would be earning double that, Marcia refused even to consider giving up the hundred and fifty a week that she was getting at the time.

"We'll call ourselves Head and Shoulders, dear," she said softly, "and the shoulders'll have to keep shaking a little longer until the old head gets started."

"I hate it," he objected gloomily.

"Well," she replied emphatically, "your salary wouldn't keep us in a tenement. Don't think I want to be public—I don't. I want to be yours. But I'd be a half-wit to sit in one room and count the sunflowers on the wall-paper while I waited for you. When you pull down three hundred a month I'll quit."

And much as it hurt his pride, Horace had to admit that hers was the wiser course.

March mellowed into April. May read a gorgeous riot act to the parks and waters of Manhattan, and they were very happy. Horace, who had no habits whatsoever—he had never had time to form any—proved the most adaptable of husbands, and as Marcia entirely lacked opinions on the subjects that engrossed him there were very few joltings and bumpings. Their minds moved in different spheres, Marcia acted as practical factotum, and Horace lived either in his old world of abstract ideas or in a sort of triumphantly earthy worship and adoration of his wife. She was a continual source of astonishment to him—the freshness and originality of her mind, her dynamic, clear-headed energy, and her unfailing good humor.

And Marcia's co-workers in the nine-o'clock show, whither she had transferred her talents, were impressed with her tremendous pride in her husband's mental powers. Horace they knew only as a very slim, tight-lipped, and immature-looking young man, who waited every night to take her home.

"Horace," said Marcia one evening when she met him as usual at eleven, "you looked like a ghost standing there against the street lights. You losing weight?"

He shook his head vaguely.

"I don't know. They raised me to a hundred and thirty-five dollars to-day, and—"

"I don't care," said Marcia severely. "You're killing yourself working at night. You read those big books on economy—"

"Economics," corrected Horace.

"Well, you read 'em every night long after I'm asleep. And you're getting all stooped over like you were before we were married."

"But, Marcia, I've got to—"

"No, you haven't, dear. I guess I'm running this shop for the present, and I won't let my fella ruin his health and eyes. You got to get some exercise."

"I do. Every morning I—"

"Oh, I know! But those dumb-bells of yours wouldn't give a consumptive two degrees of fever. I mean real exercise. You've got to join a gymnasium. 'Member you told me you were such a trick gymnast once that they tried to get you out for the team in college and they couldn't because you had a standing date with Herb Spencer?"

"I used to enjoy it," mused Horace, "but it would take up too much time now."

"All right," said Marcia. "I'll make a bargain with you. You join a gym and I'll read one of those books from the brown row of 'em."

" 'Pepys' Diary'? Why, that ought to be enjoyable. He's very light."

"Not for me—he isn't. It'll be like digesting plate glass. But you been telling me how much it'd broaden my lookout. Well, you go to a gym three nights a week and I'll take one big dose of Sammy."

Horace hesitated.

"Well—"

"Come on, now! You do some giant swings for me and I'll chase some culture for you."

So Horace finally consented, and all through a baking summer he spent three and sometimes four evenings a week experimenting on the trapeze in Skipper's Gymnasium. And in August he admitted to Marcia that it made him capable of more mental work during the day.

"Mens sana in corpore sano," he said.

"Don't believe in it," replied Marcia. "I tried one of those patent medicines once and they're all bunk. You stick to gymnastics."

One night in early September, while he was going through one of his contortions on the rings in the nearly deserted room, he was addressed by a meditative fat man whom he had noticed watching him for several nights.

"Say, lad, do that stunt you were doin' last night."

Horace grinned at him from his perch.

"I invented it," he said. "I got the idea from the fourth proposition of Euclid."

"What circus he with?"

"He's dead."

"Well, he must of broke his neck doin' that stunt. I set here last night thinkin' sure you was goin' to break yours."

"Like this!" said Horace, and swinging onto the trapeze he did his stunt.

"Don't it kill your neck an' shoulder muscles?"

"It did at first, but inside of a week I wrote the *quod erat demonstrandum* on it."

"Hm!"

Horace swung idly on the trapeze.

"Ever think of takin' it up professionally?" asked the fat man.

"Not I."

"Good money in it if you're willin' to do stunts like 'at an' can get away with it."

"Here's another," chirped Horace eagerly, and the fat man's mouth dropped suddenly agape as he watched this pink-jerseyed Prometheus again defy the gods and Isaac Newton.

The night following this encounter Horace got home from work to find a rather pale Marcia stretched out on the sofa waiting for him.

"I fainted twice to-day," she began without preliminaries.

"What?"

"Yep. You see baby's due in four months now. Doctor says I ought to have quit dancing two weeks ago."

Horace sat down and thought it over.

"I'm glad, of course," he said pensively—"I mean glad that we're going to have a baby. But this means a lot of expense."

"I've got two hundred and fifty in the bank," said Marcia hopefully, "and two weeks' pay coming."

Horace computed quickly.

"Including my salary, that'll give us nearly fourteen hundred for the next six months."

Marcia looked blue.

"That all? Course I can get a job singing somewhere this month. And I can go to work again in March."

"Of course nothing!" said Horace gruffly. "You'll stay right here. Let's see now—there'll be doctor's bills and a nurse, besides the maid. We've got to have some more money."

"Well," said Marcia wearily. "I don't know where it's coming from. It's up to the old head now. Shoulders is out of business."

Horace rose and pulled on his coat.

"Where are you going?"

"I've got an idea," he answered. "I'll be right back."

Ten minutes later, as he headed down the street toward Skipper's Gymnasium, he felt a placid wonder, quite unmixed with humor, at what he was going to do. How he would have gaped at himself a year before! How every one would have gaped! But when you opened your door at the rap of life you let in many things.

The gymnasium was brightly lit, and when his eyes became accustomed to the glare he found the meditative fat man seated on a pile of canvas mats smoking a big cigar.

"Say," began Horace directly, "were you in earnest last night when you said I could make money on my trapeze stunts?"

"Why, yes," said the fat man in surprise.

"Well, I've been thinking it over, and I believe I'd like to try it. I could work at night and on Saturday afternoons—and regularly if the pay is high enough."

The fat man looked at his watch.

"Well," he said. "Charlie Paulson's the man to see. He'll book you inside of four days, once he sees you work out. He won't be in now, but I'll get hold of him for to-morrow night."

The fat man was as good as his word. Charlie Paulson arrived next night and put in a wondrous hour watching the prodigy swoop through the air in amazing parabolas, and on the night following he brought two large men with him who looked as though they had been born smoking black cigars and talking about money in low, passionate voices. Then on the succeeding Saturday Horace Tarbox's torso made its first professional appearance in a gymnastic exhibition at the Coleman Street Gardens. But though the audience numbered nearly five thousand people, Horace felt no nervousness.

From his childhood he had read papers to audiences—learned that trick of detaching himself.

"Marcia," he said cheerfully later that same night, "I think we're out of the woods. Paulson thinks he can get me an opening at the Hippodrome, and that means an all-winter engagement. The Hippodrome, you know, is a big—"

"Yes, I believe I've heard of it," interrupted Marcia, "but I want to know about this stunt you're doing. It isn't any spectacular suicide, is it?"

"It's nothing," said Horace quietly. "But if you can think of any nicer way of a man killing himself than taking a risk for you, why that's the way I want to die."

Marcia reached up and wound both arms tightly round his neck.

"Kiss me," she whispered, "and call me 'dear heart.' I love to hear you say 'dear heart.' And bring me a book to read tomorrow. No more Sam Pepys, but something trick and trashy. I've been wild for something to do all day. I felt like writing letters, but I didn't have anybody to write to."

"Write to me," said Horace. "I'll read them."

"I wish I could," breathed Marcia. "If I knew words enough I could write you the longest love-letter in the world—and never get tired."

But after two more months Marcia grew very tired indeed, and for a row of nights it was a very anxious, weary-looking young athlete who walked out before the Hippodrome crowd. Then there were two days when his place was taken by a young man who wore pale blue instead of white, and got very little applause. But after the two days Horace appeared again, and those who sat close to the stage remarked an expression of beatific happiness on that young acrobat's face, even when he was twisting breathlessly in the air in the middle of his amazing and original shoulder swing. After that performance he laughed at the elevator man and dashed up the stairs to the flat five steps at a time—and then tiptoed very carefully into a quiet room.

"Marcia," he whispered.

"Hello!" She smiled up at him wanly. "Horace, there's something I want you to do. Look in my top bureau drawer and you'll find a big stack of paper. It's a book—sort of—Horace. I wrote it down in these last three months while I've been laid up. I wish you'd take it to that Peter Boyce Wendell who put my letter in his paper. He could tell you whether it'd

be a good book. I wrote it just the way I talk, just the way
I wrote that letter to him. It's just a story about a lot of things
that happened to me. Will you take it to him, Horace?"

"Yes, darling."

He leaned over the bed until his head was beside her on
the pillow, and began stroking back her yellow hair.

"Dearest Marcia," he said softly.

"No," she murmured, "call me what I told you to call me."

"Dear heart," he whispered passionately—"dearest, dearest
heart."

"What'll we call her?"

They rested a minute in happy, drowsy content, while Horace considered.

"We'll call her Marcia Hume Tarbox," he said at length.

"Why the Hume?"

"Because he's the fellow who first introduced us."

"That so?" she murmured, sleepily surprised. "I thought
his name was Moon."

Her eyes closed, and after a moment the slow, lengthening
surge of the bedclothes over her breast showed that she was
asleep.

Horace tiptoed over to the bureau and opening the top
drawer found a heap of closely scrawled, lead-smeared pages.
He looked at the first sheet:

SANDRA PEPYS, SYNCOPATED
By Marcia Tarbox

He smiled. So Samuel Pepys had made an impression on
her after all. He turned a page and began to read. His smile
deepened—he read on. Half an hour passed and he became
aware that Marcia had waked and was watching him from the
bed.

"Honey," came in a whisper.

"What, Marcia?"

"Do you like it?"

Horace coughed.

"I seem to be reading on. It's bright."

"Take it to Peter Boyce Wendell. Tell him you got the
highest marks in Princeton once and that you ought to know
when a book's good. Tell him this one's a world beater."

"All right, Marcia," said Horace gently.

Her eyes closed again and Horace crossing over kissed her

forehead—stood there for a moment with a look of tender pity. Then he left the room.

All that night the sprawly writing on the pages, the constant mistakes in spelling and grammar, and the weird punctuation danced before his eyes. He woke several times in the night, each time full of a welling chaotic sympathy for this desire of Marcia's soul to express itself in words. To him there was something infinitely pathetic about it, and for the first time in months he began to turn over in his mind his own half-forgotten dreams.

He had meant to write a series of books, to popularize the new realism as Schopenhauer had popularized pessimism and William James pragmatism.

But life hadn't come that way. Life took hold of people and forced them into flying rings. He laughed to think of that rap at his door, and the diaphanous shadow in Hume, Marcia's threatened kiss.

"And it's still me," he said aloud in wonder as he lay awake in the darkness. "I'm the man who sat in Berkeley with temerity to wonder if that rap would have had actual existence had my ear not been there to hear it. I'm still that man. I could be electrocuted for the crimes he committed.

"Poor gauzy souls trying to express ourselves in something tangible. Marcia with her written book; I with my unwritten ones. Trying to choose our mediums and then taking what we get—and being glad."

V

"Sandra Pepys, Syncopated," with an introduction by Peter Boyce Wendell, the columnist, appeared serially in *Jordan's Magazine,* and came out in book form in March. From its first published instalment it attracted attention far and wide. A trite enough subject—a girl from a small New Jersey town coming to New York to go on the stage—treated simply, with a peculiar vividness of phrasing and a haunting undertone of sadness in the very inadequacy of its vocabulary, it made an irresistible appeal.

Peter Boyce Wendell, who happened at that time to be advocating the enrichment of the American language by the immediate adoption of expressive vernacular words, stood as its sponsor and thundered his indorsement over the placid bromides of the conventional reviewers.

Marcia received three hundred dollars an instalment for the serial publication, which came at an opportune time, for though Horace's monthly salary at the Hippodrome was now more than Marcia's had ever been, young Marcia was emitting shrill cries which they interpreted as a demand for country air. So early April found them installed in a bungalow in Westchester County, with a place for a lawn, a place for a garage, and a place for everything, including a sound-proof impregnable study, in which Marcia faithfully promised Mr. Jordan she would shut herself up when her daughter's demands began to be abated, and compose immortally illiterate literature.

"It's not half bad," thought Horace one night as he was on his way from the station to his house. He was considering several prospects that had opened up, a four months' vaudeville offer in five figures, a chance to go back to Princeton in charge of all gymnasium work. Odd! He had once intended to go back there in charge of all philosophic work, and now he had not even been stirred by the arrival in New York of Anton Laurier, his old idol.

The gravel crunched raucously under his heel. He saw the lights of his sitting-room gleaming and noticed a big car standing in the drive. Probably Mr. Jordan again, come to persuade Marcia to settle down to work.

She had heard the sound of his approach and her form was silhouetted against the lighted door as she came out to meet him.

"There's some Frenchman here," she whispered nervously. "I can't pronounce his name, but he sounds awful deep. You'll have to jaw with him."

"What Frenchman?"

"You can't prove it by me. He drove up an hour ago with Mr. Jordan and said he wanted to meet Sandra Pepys, and all that sort of thing."

Two men rose from chairs as they went inside.

"Hello, Tarbox," said Jordan. "I've just been bringing together two celebrities. I've brought M'sieur Laurier out with me. M'sieur Laurier, let me present Mr. Tarbox, Mrs. Tarbox's husband."

"Not Anton Laurier!" exclaimed Horace.

"But, yes. I must come. I have to come. I have read the book of Madame, and I have been charmed"—he fumbled in his pocket—"ah, I have read of you too. In this newspaper which I read to-day it has your name."

He finally produced a clipping from a magazine.

"Read it!" he said eagerly. "It has about you too."

Horace's eyes skipped down the page.

"A distinct contribution to American dialect literature," it said. "No attempt at literary tone; the book derives its very quality from this fact, as did 'Huckleberry Finn.' "

Horace's eyes caught a passage lower down; he became suddenly aghast—read on hurriedly:

"Marcia Tarbox's connection with the stage is not only as a spectator but as the wife of a performer. She was married last year to Horace Tarbox, who every evening delights the children at the Hippodrome with his wondrous flying-ring performance. It is said that the young couple have dubbed themselves Head and Shoulders, refering doubtless to the fact that Mrs. Tarbox supplies the literary and mental qualities, while the supple and agile shoulders of her husband contribute their share to the family fortunes.

"Mrs. Tarbox seems to merit that much-abused title— 'prodigy.' Only twenty—"

Horace stopped reading, and with a very odd expression in his eyes gazed intently at Anton Laurier.

"I want to advise you—" he began hoarsely.

"What?"

"About raps. Don't answer them! Let them alone—have a padded door."

The Cut-Glass Bowl

I

There was a rough stone age and a smooth stone age and a bronze age, and many years afterward a cut-glass age. In the cut-glass age, when young ladies had persuaded young men with long, curly mustaches to marry them, they sat down several months afterward and wrote thank-you notes for all sorts of cut-glass presents—punchbowls, finger-bowls, dinner-glasses, wine-glasses, ice-cream dishes, bonbon dishes, decanters, and vases—for, though cut glass was nothing new in the nineties, it was then especially busy reflecting the dazzling light of fashion from the Back Bay to the fastnesses of the Middle West.

After the wedding the punch-bowls were arranged on the side-board with the big bowl in the centre; the glasses were set up in the china-closet; the candlesticks were put at both ends of things—and then the struggle for existence began. The bonbon dish lost its little handle and became a pin-tray upstairs; a promenading cat knocked the little bowl off the sideboard, and the hired girl chipped the middle-sized one with the sugar-dish; then the wine-glasses succumbed to leg fractures, and even the dinner-glasses disappeared one by one like the ten little niggers, the last one ending up, scarred and maimed, as a tooth-brush holder among other shabby genteels on the bathroom shelf. But by the time all this had happened the cut-glass age was over, anyway.

It was well past its first glory on the day the curious Mrs. Roger Fairboalt came to see the beautiful Mrs. Harold Piper.

"My *dear*," said the curious Mrs. Roger Fairboalt, "I *love* your house. I think it's *quite* artistic."

"I'm *so* glad," said the beautiful Mrs. Harold Piper, lights appearing in her young, dark eyes; "and you *must* come often. I'm almost *always* alone in the afternoon."

Mrs. Fairboalt would have liked to remark that she didn't believe this at all and couldn't see how she'd expected to—it

was all over town that Mr. Freddy Gedney had been dropping
in on Mrs. Piper five afternoons a week for the past six
months. Mrs. Fairboalt was at that ripe age where she dis-
trusted all beautiful women—

"I love the dining-room *most*," she said, "all that *marvellous* china, and that *huge* cut-glass bowl."

Mrs. Piper laughed, so prettily that Mrs. Fairboalt's lingering
reservations about the Freddy Gedney story quite vanished.

"Oh, that big bowl!" Mrs. Piper's mouth forming the
words was a vivid rose petal. "There's a story about that
bowl—"

"Oh—"

"You remember young Carleton Canby? Well, he was very
attentive at one time, and the night I told him I was going to
marry Harold, seven years ago, in ninety-two, he drew himself way up and said: 'Evylyn, I'm going to give a present
that's as hard as you are and as beautiful and as empty and
as easy to see through.' He frightened me a little—his eyes
were so black. I thought he was going to deed me a haunted
house or something that would explode when you opened it.
That bowl came, and of course it's beautiful. Its diameter or
circumference or something is two and a half feet—or perhaps it's three and a half. Anyway, the sideboard is really too
small for it; it sticks way out."

"My *dear,* wasn't that *odd*! And he left town about then,
didn't he?" Mrs. Fairboalt was scribbling italicized notes on
her memory—"hard, beautiful, empty, and easy to see
through."

"Yes, he went West—or South—or somewhere," answered
Mrs. Piper, radiating that divine vagueness that helps to lift
beauty out of time.

Mrs. Fairboalt drew on her gloves, approving the effect of
largeness given by the open sweep from the spacious music-
room through the library, disclosing a part of the dining-room
beyond. It was really the nicest smaller house in town, and
Mrs. Piper had talked of moving to a larger one on
Devereaux Avenue. Harold Piper must be *coining* money.

As she turned into the sidewalk under the gathering autumn dusk she assumed that disapproving, faintly unpleasant
expression that almost all successful women of forty wear on
the street.

If *I* were Harold Piper, she thought, I'd spend a *little* less time on business and a *little* more time at home. Some *friend* should speak to him.

But if Mrs. Fairboalt had considered it a successful afternoon she would have named it a triumph had she waited two minutes longer. For while she was still a black receding figure a hundred yards down the street, a very good-looking distraught young man turned up the walk to the Piper house. Mrs. Piper answered the door-bell herself, and with a rather dismayed expression led him quickly into the library.

"I had to see you," he began wildly; "your note played the devil with me. Did Harold frighten you into this?"

She shook her head.

"I'm through, Fred," she said slowly, and her lips had never looked to him so much like tearings from a rose. "He came home last night sick with it. Jessie Piper's sense of duty was too much for her, so she went down to his office and told him. He was hurt and—oh, I can't help seeing it his way, Fred. He says we've been club gossip all summer and he didn't know it, and now he understands snatches of conversation he's caught and veiled hints people have dropped about me. He's mighty angry, Fred, and he loves me and I love him—rather."

Gedney nodded slowly and half closed his eyes.

"Yes," he said, "yes, my trouble's like yours. I can see other people's points of view too plainly." His gray eyes met her dark ones frankly. "The blessed thing's over. My God, Evylyn, I've been sitting down at the office all day looking at the outside of your letter, and looking at it and looking at it—"

"You've got to go, Fred," she said steadily, and the slight emphasis of hurry in her voice was a new thrust for him. "I gave him my word of honor I wouldn't see you. I know just how far I can go with Harold, and being here with you this evening is one of the things I can't do."

They were still standing, and as she spoke she made a little movement toward the door. Gedney looked at her miserably, trying, here at the end, to treasure up a last picture of her— and then suddenly both of them were stiffened into marble at the sound of steps on the walk outside. Instantly her arm reached out grasping the lapel of his coat—half urged, half swung him through the big door into the dark dining-room.

"I'll make him go up-stairs," she whispered close to his

ear. "Don't move till you hear him on the stairs. Then go out the front way."

Then he was alone listening as she greeted her husband in the hall.

Harold Piper was thirty-six, nine years older than his wife. He was handsome—with marginal notes: these being eyes that were too close together, and a certain woodenness when his face was in repose. His attitude toward this Gedney matter was typical of all his attitudes. He had told Evylyn that he considered the subject closed and would never reproach her nor allude to it in any form; and he told himself that this was rather a big way of looking at it—that she was not a little impressed. Yet, like all men who are preoccupied with their own broadness, he was exceptionally narrow.

He greeted Evylyn with emphasized cordiality this evening.

"You'll have to hurry and dress, Harold," she said eagerly. "We're going to the Bronsons."

He nodded.

"It doesn't take me long to dress, dear," and, his words trailing off, he walked on into the library. Evylyn's heart clattered loudly.

"Harold—" she began, with a little catch in her voice, and followed him in. He was lighting a cigarette. "You'll have to hurry, Harold," she finished, standing in the doorway.

"Why?" he asked, a trifle impatiently. "You're not dressed yourself yet, Evie."

He stretched out in a Morris chair and unfolded a newspaper. With a sinking sensation Evylyn saw that this meant at least ten minutes—and Gedney was standing breathless in the next room. Supposing Harold decided that before he went upstairs he wanted a drink from the decanter on the sideboard. Then it occurred to her to forestall this contingency by bringing him the decanter and a glass. She dreaded calling his attention to the dining-room in any way, but she couldn't risk the other chance.

But at the same moment Harold rose and, throwing his paper down, came toward her.

"Evie, dear," he said, bending and putting his arms about her, "I hope you're not thinking about last night—" She moved close to him, trembling. "I know," he continued, "it was just an imprudent friendship on your part. We all make mistakes."

Evylyn hardly heard him. She was wondering if by sheer clinging to him she could draw him out and up the stairs. She thought of playing sick, asking to be carried up—unfortunately, she knew he would lay her on the couch and bring her whiskey.

Suddenly her nervous tension moved up a last impossible notch. She had heard a very faint but quite unmistakable creak from the floor of the dining-room. Fred was trying to get out the back way.

Then her heart took a flying leap as a hollow ringing note like a gong echoed and re-echoed through the house. Gedney's arm had struck the big cut-glass bowl.

"What's that!" cried Harold. "Who's there?"

She clung to him but he broke away, and the room seemed to crash about her ears. She heard the pantry-door swing open, a scuffle, the rattle of a tin pan, and in wild despair she rushed into the kitchen and pulled up the gas. Her husband's arm slowly unwound from Gedney's neck, and he stood there very still, first in amazement, then with pain dawning in his face.

"My golly!" he said in bewilderment, and then repeated: "My *golly*!"

He turned as if to jump again at Gedney, stopped, his muscles visibly relaxed, and he gave a bitter little laugh.

"You people—you people—" Evylyn's arms were around him and her eyes were pleading with him frantically, but he pushed her away and sank dazed into a kitchen chair, his face like procelain. "You've been doing things to me, Evylyn. Why, you little devil! You little *devil*!"

She had never felt so sorry for him; she had never loved him so much.

"It wasn't her fault," said Gedney rather humbly. "I just came." But Piper shook his head, and his expression when he stared up was as if some physical accident had jarred his mind into a temporary inability to function. His eyes, grown suddenly pitiful, struck a deep, unsounded chord in Evylyn—and simultaneously a furious anger surged in her. She felt her eyelids burning; she stamped her foot violently; her hands scurried nervously over the table as if searching for a weapon, and then she flung herself wildly at Gedney.

"Get out!" she screamed, dark eyes blazing, little fists beating helplessly on his outstretched arm. "You did this! Get out of here—get out—get *out*! Get *out*!"

II

Concerning Mrs. Harold Piper at thirty-five, opinion was divided—women said she was still handsome; men said she was pretty no longer. And this was probably because the qualities in her beauty that women had feared and men had followed had vanished. Her eyes were still as large and as dark and as sad, but the mystery had departed; their sadness was no longer eternal, only human, and she had developed a habit, when she was startled or annoyed, of twitching her brows together and blinking several times. Her mouth also had lost: the red had receded and the faint down-turning of its corners when she smiled, that had added to the sadness of the eyes and been vaguely mocking and beautiful, was quite gone. When she smiled now the corners of her lips turned up. Back in the days when she revelled in her own beauty Evylyn had enjoyed that smile of hers—she had accentuated it. When she stopped accentuating it, it faded out and the last of her mystery with it.

Evylyn had ceased accentuating her smile within a month after the Freddy Gedney affair. Externally things had gone on very much as they had before. But in those few minutes during which she had discovered how much she loved her husband, Evylyn had realized how indelibly she had hurt him. For a month she struggled against aching silences, wild reproaches and accusations—she pled with him, made quiet, pitiful little love to him, and he laughed at her bitterly—and then she, too, slipped gradually into silence and a shadowy, unpenetrable barrier dropped between them. The surge of love that had risen in her she lavished on Donald, her little boy, realizing him almost wonderingly as a part of her life.

The next year a piling up of mutual interests and responsibilities and some stray flicker from the past brought husband and wife together again—but after a rather pathetic flood of passion Evylyn realized that her great opportunity was gone. There simply wasn't anything left. She might have been youth and love for both—but that time of silence had slowly dried up the springs of affection and her own desire to drink again of them was dead.

She began for the first time to seek women friends, to prefer books she had read before, to sew a little where she could watch her two children to whom she was devoted. She worried about little things—if she saw crumbs on the dinner-table

her mind drifted off the conversation: she was receding gradually into middle age.

Her thirty-fifth birthday had been an exceptionally busy
one, for they were entertaining on short notice that night, and
as she stood in her bedroom window in the late afternoon she
discovered that she was quite tired. Ten years before she
would have lain down and slept, but now she had a feeling
that things needed watching: maids were cleaning down-
stairs, bric-a-brac was all over the floor, and there were sure
to be grocery-men that had to be talked to imperatively—and
then there was a letter to write Donald, who was fourteen and
in his first year away at school.

She had nearly decided to lie down, nevertheless, when she
heard a sudden familiar signal from little Julie down-stairs.
She compressed her lips, her brows twitched together, and
she blinked.

"Julie!" she called.

"Ah-h-h-ow!" prolonged Julie plaintively. Then the voice
of Hilda, the second maid, floated up the stairs.

"She cut herself a little, Mis' Piper."

Evylyn flew to her sewing-basket, rummaged until she
found a torn handkerchief, and hurried down-stairs. In a moment Julie was crying in her arms as she searched for the cut,
faint, disparaging evidences of which appeared on Julie's
dress!

"My *thu*-mb!" explained Julie. "Oh-h-h-h, t'urts."

"It was the bowl here, the he one," said Hilda apologetically. "It was waitin' on the floor while I polished the sideboard, and Julie come along an' went to foolin' with it. She
yust scratch herself."

Evylyn frowned heavily at Hilda, and twisting Julie deci-
sively in her lap, began tearing strips off the handkerchief.

"Now—let's see it, dear."

Julie held it up and Evylyn pounced.

"There!"

Julie surveyed her swatched thumb doubtfully. She crooked
it; it waggled. A pleased, interested look appeared in her tear-
stained face. She sniffled and waggled it again.

"You *precious*!" cried Evylyn and kissed her, but before
she left the room she levelled another frown at Hilda. Careless! Servants all that way nowadays. If she could get a good
Irishwoman—but you couldn't any more—and these
Swedes—

At five o'clock Harold arrived and, coming up to her room, threatened in a suspiciously jovial tone to kiss her thirty-five times for her birthday. Evylyn resisted.

"You've been drinking," she said shortly, and then added qualitatively, "a little. You know I loathe the smell of it."

"Evie," he said, after a pause, seating himself in a chair by the window, "I can tell you something now. I guess you've known things haven't been going quite right down-town."

She was standing at the window combing her hair, but at these words she turned and looked at him.

"How do you mean? You've always said there was room for more than one wholesale hardware house in town." Her voice expressed some alarm.

"There *was*," said Harold significantly, "but this Clarence Ahearn is a smart man."

"I was surprised when you said he was coming to dinner."

"Evie," he went on, with another slap at his knee, "after January first 'The Clarence Ahearn Company' becomes 'The Ahearn, Piper Company'—and 'Piper Brothers' as a company ceases to exist."

Evylyn was startled. The sound of his name in second place was somehow hostile to her; still he appeared jubilant.

"I don't understand, Harold."

"Well, Evie, Ahearn had been fooling around with Marx. If those two had combined we'd have been the little fellow, struggling along, picking up smaller orders, hanging back on risks. It's a question of capital, Evie, and 'Ahearn and Marx' would have had the business just like 'Ahearn and Piper' is going to now." He paused and coughed and a little cloud of whiskey floated up to her nostrils. "Tell you the truth, Evie, I've suspected that Ahearn's wife had something to do with it. Ambitious little lady, I'm told. Guess she knew the Marxes couldn't help her much here."

"Is she—common?" asked Evie.

"Never met her, I'm sure—but I don't doubt it. Clarence Ahearn's name's been up at the Country Club five months—no action taken." He waved his hand disparagingly. "Ahearn and I had lunch together to-day and just about clinched it, so I thought it'd be nice to have him and his wife up to-night—just have nine, mostly family. After all, it's a big thing for me, and of course we'll have to see something of them, Evie."

"Yes," said Evie thoughtfully, "I suppose we will."

Evylyn was not disturbed over the social end of it—but the idea of "Piper Brothers" becoming "The Ahearn, Piper Company" startled her. It seemed like going down in the world.

Half an hour later, as she began to dress for dinner, she heard his voice from down-stairs.

"Oh, Evie, come down!"

She went out into the hall and called over the banister: "What is it?"

"I want you to help me make some of that punch before dinner."

Hurriedly rehooking her dress, she descended the stairs and found him grouping the essentials on the dining-room table. She went to the sideboard and, lifting one of the bowls, carried it over.

"Oh, no," he protested, "let's use the big one. There'll be Ahearn and his wife and you and I and Milton, that's five, and Tom and Jessie, that's seven, and your sister and Joe Ambler, that's nine. You don't know how quick that stuff goes when *you* make it."

"We'll use this bowl," she insisted. "It'll hold plenty. You know how Tom is."

Tom Lowrie, husband to Jessie, Harold's first cousin, was rather inclined to finish anything in a liquid way that he began.

Harold shook his head.

"Don't be foolish. That one holds only about three quarts and there's nine of us, and the servants'll want some—and it isn't very strong punch. It's so much more cheerful to have a lot, Evie; we don't have to drink all of it."

"I say the small one."

Again he shook his head obstinately.

"No; be reasonable."

"I *am* reasonable," she said shortly. "I don't want any drunken men in the house."

"Who said you did?"

"Then use the small bowl."

"Now, Evie—"

He grasped the smaller bowl to lift it back. Instantly her hands were on it, holding it down. There was a momentary struggle, and then, with a little exasperated grunt, he raised his side, slipped it from her fingers, and carried it to the sideboard.

She looked at him and tried to make her expression contemptuous, but he only laughed. Acknowledging her defeat but disclaiming all future interest in the punch, she left the room.

III

At seven-thirty, her cheeks glowing and her high-piled hair gleaming with a suspicion of brilliantine, Evylyn descended the stairs. Mrs. Ahearn, a little woman concealing a slight nervousness under red hair and an extreme Empire gown, greeted her volubly. Evylyn disliked her on the spot, but the husband she rather approved of. He had keen blue eyes and a natural gift of pleasing people that might have made him, socially, had he not so obviously committed the blunder of marrying too early in his career.

"I'm glad to know Piper's wife," he said simply. "It looks as though your husband and I are going to see a lot of each other in the future."

She bowed, smiled graciously, and turned to greet the others: Milton Piper, Harold's quiet, unassertive younger brother; the two Lowries, Jessie and Tom; Irene, her own unmarried sister; and finally Joe Ambler, a confirmed bachelor and Irene's perennial beau.

Harold led the way into dinner.

"We're having a punch evening," he announced jovially— Evylyn saw that he had already sampled his concoction—"so there won't be any cocktails except the punch. It's m' wife's greatest achievement, Mrs. Ahearn; she'll give you the recipe if you want it; but owing to a slight"—he caught his wife's eye and paused—"to a slight indisposition, I'm responsible for this batch. Here's how!"

All through dinner there was punch, and Evylyn, noticing that Ahearn and Milton Piper and all the women were shaking their heads negatively at the maid, knew she had been right about the bowl; it was still half full. She resolved to caution Harold directly afterward, but when the women left the table Mrs. Ahearn cornered her, and she found herself talking cities and dressmakers with a polite show of interest.

"We've moved around, a lot," chattered Mrs. Ahearn, her red hair nodding violently. "Oh, yes, we've never stayed so long in a town before—but I do hope we're here for good. I like it here; don't you?"

"Well, you see, I've always lived here, so, naturally—"

"Oh, that's true," said Mrs. Ahearn and laughed. "Clarence always used to tell me he had to have a wife he could come home to and say: 'Well, we're going to Chicago to-morrow to live, so pack up.' I got so I never expected to live *anywhere*." She laughed her little laugh again; Evylyn suspected that it was her society laugh.

"Your husband is a very able man, I imagine."

"Oh, yes," Mrs. Ahearn assured her eagerly. "He's brainy, Clarence is. Ideas and enthusiasm, you know. Finds out what he wants and then goes and gets it."

Evylyn nodded. She was wondering if the men were still drinking punch back in the dining-room. Mrs. Ahearn's history kept unfolding jerkily, but Evylyn had ceased to listen. The first odor of massed cigars began to drift in. It wasn't really a large house, she reflected; on an evening like this the library sometimes grew blue with smoke, and next day one had to leave the windows open for hours to air the heavy staleness out of the curtains. Perhaps this partnership might . . . she began to speculate on a new house . . .

Mrs. Ahearn's voice drifted in on her:

"I really would like the recipe if you have it written down somewhere—"

Then there was a sound of chairs in the dining-room and the men strolled in. Evylyn saw at once that her worst fears were realized. Harold's face was flushed and his words ran together at the ends of sentences, while Tom Lowrie lurched when he walked and narrowly missed Irene's lap when he tried to sink onto the couch beside her. He sat there blinking dazedly at the company. Evylyn found herself blinking back at him, but she saw no humor in it. Joe Ambler was smiling contentedly and puffing on his cigar. Only Ahearn and Milton Piper seemed unaffected.

"It's a pretty fine town, Ahearn," said Ambler, "you'll find that."

"I've found it so," said Ahearn pleasantly.

"You find it more, Ahearn," said Harold, nodding emphatically, "'f I've an'thin' do 'th it."

He soared into a eulogy of the city, and Evylyn wondered uncomfortably if it bored every one as it bored her. Apparently not. They were all listening attentively. Evylyn broke in at the first gap.

"Where've you been living, Mr. Ahearn?" she asked interestedly. Then she remembered that Mrs. Ahearn had told her,

but it didn't matter. Harold mustn't talk so much. He was
such an *ass* when he'd been drinking. But he plopped directly
back in.

"Tell me, Ahearn. Firs' you wanna get a house up here on
the hill. Get Stearne house or Ridgeway house. Wanna have
it so people say: 'There's Ahearn house.' Solid, you know,
tha's effec' it gives."

Evylyn flushed. This didn't sound right at all. Still Ahearn
didn't seem to notice anything amiss, only nodded gravely.

"Have you been looking—" But her words trailed off un-
heard as Harold's voice boomed on.

"Get house—tha's start. Then you get know people. Snobbish town first toward outsider, but not long—not after know
you. People like you"—he indicated Ahearn and his wife
with a sweeping gesture—"all right. Cordial as an'thin' once
get by first barrer-barbarrer—" He swallowed, and then said
"barrier," repeated it masterfully.

Evylyn looked appealingly at her brother-in-law, but before
he could intercede a thick mumble had come crowding out of
Tom Lowrie, hindered by the dead cigar which he gripped
firmly with his teeth.

"Huma uma ho huma ahdy um—"

"What?" demanded Harold earnestly.

Resignedly and with difficulty Tom removed the cigar—
that is, he removed part of it, and then blew the remainder
with a *whut* sound across the room, where it landed liquidly
and limply in Mrs. Ahearn's lap.

"Beg pardon," he mumbled, and rose with the vague intention of going after it. Milton's hand on his coat collapsed him
in time, and Mrs. Ahearn not ungracefully flounced the tobacco from her skirt to the floor, never once looking at it.

"I was sayin'," continued Tom thickly, " 'fore 'at
happened"—he waved his hand apologetically toward Mrs.
Ahearn—"I was sayin' I heard all truth that Country Club
matter."

Milton leaned and whispered something to him.

"Lemme 'lone," he said petulantly, "know what I'm doin'.
'At's what they came for."

Evylyn sat there in a panic, trying to make her mouth form
words. She saw her sister's sardonic expression and Mrs.
Ahearn's face turning a vivid red. Ahearn was looking down
at his watch-chain, fingering it.

"I heard who's been keepin' y' out, an' he's not a bit

better'n you. I can fix whole damn thing up. Would've before, but I didn't know you. Harol' tol' me you felt bad about the thing—"

Milton Piper rose suddenly and awkwardly to his feet. In a second every one was standing tensely and Milton was saying something very hurriedly about having to go early, and the Ahearns were listening with eager intentness. Then Mrs. Ahearn swallowed and turned with a forced smile toward Jessie. Evylyn saw Tom lurch forward and put his hand on Ahearn's shoulder—and suddenly she was listening to a new, anxious voice at her elbow, and, turning, found Hilda, the second maid.

"Please, Mis' Piper, I tank Yulie got her hand poisoned. It's all swole up and her cheeks is hot and she's moanin' an' groanin'—"

"Julie is?" Evylyn asked sharply. The party suddenly receded. She turned quickly, sought with her eyes for Mrs. Ahearn, slipped toward her.

"If you'll excuse me, Mrs.—" She had momentarily forgotten the name, but she went right on: "My little girl's been taken sick. I'll be down when I can." She turned and ran quickly up the stairs, retaining a confused picture of rays of cigar smoke and a loud discussion in the centre of the room that seemed to be developing into an argument.

Switching on the light in the nursery, she found Julie tossing feverishly and giving out odd little cries. She put her hand against the cheeks. They were burning. With an exclamation she followed the arm down under the cover until she found the hand. Hilda was right. The whole thumb was swollen to the wrist and in the centre was a little inflamed sore. Blood-poisoning! her mind cried in terror. The bandage had come off the cut and she'd gotten something in it. She'd cut it at three o'clock—it was now nearly eleven. Eight hours. Blood-poisoning couldn't possibly develop so soon. She rushed to the 'phone.

Doctor Martin across the street was out. Doctor Foulke, their family physician, didn't answer. She racked her brains and in desperation called her throat specialist, and bit her lip furiously while he looked up the numbers of two physicians. During that interminable moment she thought she heard loud voices down-stairs—but she seemed to be in another world now. After fifteen minutes she located a physician who sounded angry and sulky at being called out of bed. She ran back to the nursery and, looking at the hand, found it was somewhat more swollen.

"Oh, God!" she cried, and kneeling beside the bed began smoothing back Julie's hair over and over. With a vague idea of getting some hot water, she rose and started toward the door, but the lace of her dress caught in the bed-rail and she fell forward on her hands and knees. She struggled up and jerked frantically at the lace. The bed moved and Julie groaned. Then more quietly but with suddenly fumbling fingers she found the pleat in front, tore the whole pannier completely off, and rushed from the room.

Out in the hall she heard a single loud, insistent voice, but as she reached the head of the stairs it ceased and an outer door banged.

The music-room came into view. Only Harold and Milton were there, the former leaning against a chair, his face very pale, his collar open, and his mouth moving loosely.

"What's the matter?"

Milton looked at her anxiously.

"There was a little trouble—"

Then Harold saw her and, straightening up with an effort, began to speak.

"'Sult m'own cousin m'own house. God damn common nouveau rish. 'Sult m'own cousin—"

"Tom had trouble with Ahearn and Harold interfered," said Milton.

"My Lord, Milton," cried Evylyn, "couldn't you have done something?"

"I tried; I—"

"Julie's sick," she interrupted; "she's poisoned herself. Get him to bed if you can."

Harold looked up.

"Julie sick?"

Paying no attention, Evylyn brushed by through the dining-room, catching sight, with a burst of horror, of the big punch-bowl still on the table, the liquid from melted ice in its bottom. She heard steps on the front stairs—it was Milton helping Harold up—and then a mumble: "Why, Julie's a'righ'."

"Don't let him go into the nursery!" she shouted.

The hours blurred into a nightmare. The doctor arrived just before midnight and within a half-hour had lanced the wound. He left at two after giving her the addresses of two nurses to call up and promising to return at half past six. It was blood-poisoning.

At four, leaving Hilda by the bedside, she went to her room, and slipping with a shudder out of her evening dress, kicked it into a corner. She put on a house dress and returned to the nursery while Hilda went to make coffee.

Not until noon could she bring herself to look into Harold's room, but when she did it was to find him awake and staring very miserably at the ceiling. He turned blood-shot hollow eyes upon her. For a minute she hated him, couldn't speak. A husky voice came from the bed.

"What time is it?"

"Noon."

"I made a damn fool—"

"It doesn't matter," she said sharply. "Julie's got blood-poisoning. They may"—she choked over the words—"they think she'll have to lose her hand."

"What?"

"She cut herself on that—that bowl."

"Last night?"

"Oh, what does it matter?" she cried. "She's got blood-poisoning. Can't you hear?"

He looked at her bewildered—sat half-way up in bed.

"I'll get dressed," he said.

Her anger subsided and a great wave of weariness and pity for him rolled over her. After all, it was his trouble, too.

"Yes," she answered listlessly, "I suppose you'd better."

IV

If Evylyn's beauty had hesitated in her early thirties it came to an abrupt decision just afterward and completely left her. A tentative outlay of wrinkles on her face suddenly deepened and flesh collected rapidly on her legs and hips and arms. Her mannerism of drawing her brows together had become an expression—it was habitual when she was reading or speaking and even while she slept. She was forty-six.

As in most families whose fortunes have gone down rather than up, she and Harold had drifted into a colorless antagonism. In repose they looked at each other with the toleration they might have felt for broken old chairs; Evylyn worried a little when he was sick and did her best to be cheerful under the wearying depression of living with a disappointed man.

Family bridge was over for the evening and she sighed with relief. She had made more mistakes than usual this evening and she didn't care. Irene shouldn't have made that remark about the infantry being particularly dangerous. There had been no letter for three weeks now, and, while this was nothing out of the ordinary, it never failed to make her nervous; naturally she hadn't known how many clubs were out.

Harold had gone up-stairs, so she stepped out on the porch for a breath of fresh air. There was a bright glamour of moonlight diffusing on the sidewalks and lawns, and with a little half yawn, half laugh, she remembered one long moonlight affair of her youth. It was astonishing to think that life had once been the sum of her current love-affairs. It was now the sum of her current problems.

There was the problem of Julie—Julie was thirteen, and lately she was growing more and more sensitive about her deformity and preferred to stay always in her room reading. A few years before she had been frightened at the idea of going to school, and Evylyn could not bring herself to send her, so she grew up in her mother's shadow, a pitiful little figure with the artificial hand that she made no attempt to use but kept forlornly in her pocket. Lately she had been taking lessons in using it because Evylyn had feared she would cease to lift the arm altogether, but after the lessons, unless she made a move with it in listless obedience to her mother, the little hand would creep back to the pocket of her dress. For a while her dresses were made without pockets, but Julie had moped around the house so miserably at a loss all one month that Evylyn weakened and never tried the experiment again.

The problem of Donald had been different from the start. She had attempted vainly to keep him near her as she had tried to teach Julie to lean less on her—lately the problem of Donald had been snatched out of her hands; his division had been abroad for three months.

She yawned again—life was a thing for youth. What a happy youth she must have had! She remembered her pony, Bijou, and the trip to Europe with her mother when she was eighteen—

"Very, very complicated," she said aloud and severely to the moon, and, stepping inside, was about to close the door when she heard a noise in the library and started.

It was Martha, the middle-aged servant: they kept only one now.

"Why, Martha!" she said in surprise.

Martha turned quickly.

"Oh, I thought you was up-stairs. I was jist—"

"Is anything the matter?"

Martha hesitated.

"No; I—" She stood there fidgeting. "It was a letter, Mrs. Piper, that I put somewhere."

"A letter? Your own letter?" asked Evelyn, switching on the light.

"No, it was to you. 'Twas this afternoon, Mrs. Piper, in the last mail. The postman give it to me and then the back door-bell rang. I had it in my hand, so I must have stuck it somewhere. I thought I'd just slip in now and find it."

"What sort of a letter? From Mr. Donald?"

"No, it was an advertisement, maybe, or a business letter. It was a long, narrow one, I remember."

They began a search through the music-room, looking on trays and mantelpieces, and then through the library, feeling on the tops of rows of books. Martha paused in despair.

"I can't think where. I went straight to the kitchen. The dining-room, maybe." She started hopefully for the dining-room, but turned suddenly at the sound of a gasp behind her. Evylyn had sat down heavily in a Morris chair, her brows drawn very close together, eyes blinking furiously.

"Are you sick?"

For a minute there was no answer. Evylyn sat there very still and Martha could see the very quick rise and fall of her bosom.

"Are you sick?" she repeated.

"No," said Evylyn slowly, "but I know where the letter is. Go 'way, Martha. I know."

Wonderingly, Martha withdrew, and still Evylyn sat there, only the muscles around her eyes moving—contracting and relaxing and contracting again. She knew now where the letter was—she knew as well as if she had put it there herself. And she felt instinctively and unquestionably what the letter was. It was long and narrow like an advertisement, but up in the corner in large letters it said "War Department" and, in smaller letters below, "Official Business." She knew it lay there in the big bowl with her name in ink on the outside and her soul's death within.

Rising uncertainly, she walked toward the dining-room,

feeling her way along the bookcases and through the doorway. After a moment she found the light and switched it on.

There was the bowl, reflecting the electric light in crimson squares edged with black and yellow squares edged with blue, ponderous and glittering, grotesquely and triumphantly ominous. She took a step forward and paused again; another step and she would see over the top and into the inside—another step and she would see an edge of white—another step—her hands fell on the rough, cold surface—

In a moment she was tearing it open, fumbling with an obstinate fold, holding it before her while the typewritten page glared out and struck at her. Then it fluttered like a bird to the floor. The house that had seemed whirring, buzzing a moment since, was suddenly very quiet; a breath of air crept in through the open front door carrying the noise of a passing motor; she heard faint sounds from up-stairs and then a grinding racket in the pipe behind the bookcases—her husband turning off a water-tap—

And in that instant it was as if this were not, after all, Donald's hour except in so far as he was a marker in the insidious contest that had gone on in sudden surges and long, listless interludes between Evylyn and this cold, malignant thing of beauty, a gift of enmity from a man whose face she had long since forgotten. With its massive, brooding passivity it lay there in the centre of her house as it had lain for years, throwing out the ice-like beams of a thousand eyes, perverse glitterings merging each into each, never aging, never changing.

Evylyn sat down on the edge of the table and stared at it fascinated. It seemed to be smiling now, a very cruel smile, as if to say:

"You see, this time I didn't have to hurt you directly. I didn't bother. You know it was I who took your son away. You know how cold I am and how hard and how beautiful, because once you were just as cold and hard and beautiful."

The bowl seemed suddenly to turn itself over and then to distend and swell until it became a great canopy that glittered and trembled over the room, over the house, and, as the walls melted slowly into mist, Evylyn saw that it was still moving out, out and far away from her, shutting off far horizons and suns and moons and stars except as inky blots seen faintly through it. And under it walked all the people, and the light that came through to them was refracted and twisted until shadow seemed light and light seemed shadow—until the whole panorama of the world became changed and distorted under the twinkling heaven of the bowl.

Then there came a far-away, booming voice like a low, clear bell. It came from the centre of the bowl and down the great sides to the ground and then bounced toward her eagerly.

"You see, I am fate," it shouted, "and stronger than your puny plans; and I am how-things-turn-out and I am different from your little dreams, and I am the flight of time and the end of beauty and unfulfilled desire; all the accidents and imperceptions and the little minutes that shape the crucial hours are mine. I am the exception that proves no rules, the limits of your control, the condiment in the dish of life."

The booming sound stopped; the echoes rolled away over the wide land to the edge of the bowl that bounded the world and up the great sides and back to the centre where they hummed for a moment and died. Then the great walls began slowly to bear down upon her, growing smaller and smaller, coming closer and closer as if to crush her; and as she clinched her hands and waited for the swift bruise of the cold glass, the bowl gave a sudden wrench and turned over—and lay there on the sideboard, shining and inscrutable, reflecting in a hundred prisms myriad, many-colored glints and gleams and crossings and interlacings of light.

The cold wind blew in again through the front door, and with a desperate, frantic energy Evylyn stretched both her arms around the bowl. She must be quick—she must be strong. She tightened her arms until they ached, tauted the thin strips of muscle under her soft flesh, and with a mighty effort raised it and held it. She felt the wind blow cold on her back where her dress had come apart from the strain of her effort, and as she felt it she turned toward it and staggered under the great weight out through the library and on toward the front door. She must be quick—she must be strong. The blood in her arms throbbed dully and her knees kept giving way under her, but the feel of the cool glass was good.

Out the front door she tottered and over to the stone steps, and there, summoning every fibre of her soul and body for a last effort, swung herself half around—for a second, as she tried to loose her hold, her numb fingers clung to the rough surface, and in that second she slipped and, losing balance, toppled forward with a despairing cry, her arms still around the bowl . . . down . . .

Over the way lights went on; far down the block the crash was heard, and pedestrians rushed up wonderingly; up-stairs a tired man awoke from the edge of sleep and a little girl whimpered in a haunted doze. And all over the moonlit side-walk around the still, black form, hundreds of prisms and cubes and splinters of glass reflected the light in little gleams of blue, and black edged with yellow, and yellow, and crimson edged with black.

Bernice Bobs Her Hair

I

After dark one Saturday night one could stand on the first tee of the golf-course and see the country-club windows as a yellow expanse over a very black and wavy ocean. The waves of this ocean, so to speak, were the heads of many curious caddies, a few of the more ingenious chauffeurs, the golf professional's deaf sister—and there were usually several stray, diffident waves who might have rolled inside had they so desired. This was the gallery.

The balcony was inside. It consisted of the circle of wicker chairs that lined the wall of the combination clubroom and ballroom. At these Saturday-night dances it was largely feminine; a great babble of middle-aged ladies with sharp eyes and icy hearts behind lorgnettes and large bosoms. The main function of the balcony was critical. It occasionally showed grudging admiration, but never approval, for it is well known among ladies over thirty-five that when the younger set dance in the summer-time it is with the very worst intentions in the world, and if they are not bombarded with stony eyes, stray couples will dance weird barbaric interludes in the corners, and the more popular, more dangerous girls will sometimes be kissed in the parked limousines of unsuspecting dowagers.

But, after all, this critical circle is not close enough to the stage to see the actors' faces and catch the subtler byplay. It can only frown and lean, ask questions and make satisfactory deductions from its set of postulates, such as the one which states that every young man with a large income leads the life of a hunted partridge. It never really appreciates the drama of the shifting, semicruel world of adolescence. No; boxes, orchestra-circle, principals, and chorus are represented by the medley of faces and voices that sway to the plaintive African rhythm of Dyer's dance orchestra.

From sixteen-year-old Otis Ormonde, who has two more years at Hill School, to G. Reese Stoddard, over whose bureau at home hangs a Harvard law diploma; from little Madeleine Hogue, whose hair still feels strange and uncomfortable on top of her head, to Bessie MacRae, who has been the life of the party a little too long—more than ten years—the medley is not only the centre of the stage but contains the only people capable of getting an unobstructed view of it.

With a flourish and a bang the music stops. The couples exchange artificial, effortless smiles, facetiously repeat "*la-de-dad-da* dum-*dum*," and then the clatter of young feminine voices soars over the burst of clapping.

A few disappointed stags caught in midfloor as they had been about to cut in subsided listlessly back to the walls, because this was not like the riotous Christmas dances—these summer hops were considered just pleasantly warm and exciting, where even the younger marrieds rose and performed ancient waltzes and terrifying fox trots to the tolerant amusement of their younger brothers and sisters.

Warren McIntyre, who casually attended Yale, being one of the unfortunate stags, felt in his dinner-coat pocket for a cigarette and strolled out into the wide, semidark veranda, where couples were scattered at tables, filling the lantern-hung night with vague words and hazy laughter. He nodded here and there at the less absorbed and as he passed each couple some half-forgotten fragment of a story played in his mind, for it was not a large city and every one was Who's Who to every one else's past. There, for example, were Jim Strain and Ethel Demorest, who had been privately engaged for three years. Every one knew that as soon as Jim managed to hold a job for more than two months she would marry him. Yet how bored they both looked, and how wearily Ethel regarded Jim sometimes, as if she wondered why she had trained the vines of her affection on such a wind-shaken poplar.

Warren was nineteen and rather pitying with those of his friends who had gone East to college. But, like most boys, he bragged tremendously about the girls of his city when he was away from it. There was Genevieve Ormonde, who regularly made the rounds of dances, house-parties, and football games at Princeton, Yale, Williams, and Cornell; there was black-eyed Roberta Dillon, who was quite as famous to her own generation as Hiram Johnson or Ty Cobb; and, of course, there was Marjorie Harvey, who besides having a fairylike face and a dazzling, bewildering tongue was already justly celebrated for having turned five cart-wheels in succession during the last pump-and-slipper dance at New Haven.

Warren, who had grown up across the street from Marjorie, had long been "crazy about her." Sometimes she seemed to reciprocate his feeling with a faint gratitude, but she had tried him by her infallible test and informed him gravely that she did not love him. Her test was that when she was away from him she forgot him and had affairs with other boys. Warren found this discouraging, especially as Marjorie had been making little trips all summer, and for the first two or three days after each arrival home he saw great heaps of mail on the Harveys' hall table addressed to her in various masculine handwritings. To make matters worse, all during the month of August she had been visited by her cousin Bernice from Eau Claire, and it seemed impossible to see her alone. It was always necessary to hunt round and find some one to take care of Bernice. As August waned this was becoming more and more difficult.

Much as Warren worshipped Marjorie, he had to admit that Cousin Bernice was sorta dopeless. She was pretty, with dark hair and high color, but she was no fun on a party. Every Saturday night he danced a long arduous duty dance with her to please Marjorie, but he had never been anything but bored in her company.

"Warren"—a soft voice at his elbow broke in upon his thoughts, and he turned to see Marjorie, flushed and radiant as usual. She laid a hand on his shoulder and a glow settled almost imperceptibly over him.

"Warren," she whispered, "do something for me—dance with Bernice. She's been stuck with little Otis Ormonde for almost an hour."

Warren's glow faded.

"Why—sure," he answered half-heartedly.

"You don't mind, do you? I'll see that you don't get stuck."

" 'Sall right."

Marjorie smiled—that smile that was thanks enough.

"You're an angel, and I'm obliged loads."

With a sigh the angel glanced round the veranda, but Bernice and Otis were not in sight. He wandered back inside, and there in front of the women's dressing-room he found Otis in the center of a group of young men who were convulsed with laughter. Otis was brandishing a piece of timber he had picked up, and discoursing volubly.

"She's gone in to fix her hair," he announced wildly. "I'm waiting to dance another hour with her."

Their laughter was renewed.

"Why don't some of you cut in?" cried Otis resentfully. "She likes more variety."

"Why, Otis," suggested a friend, "you've just barely got used to her."

"Why the two-by-four, Otis?" inquired Warren, smiling.

"The two-by-four? Oh, this? This is a club. When she comes out I'll hit her on the head and knock her in again."

Warren collapsed on a settee and howled with glee.

"Never mind, Otis," he articulated finally. "I'm relieving you this time."

Otis simulated a sudden fainting attack and handed the stick to Warren.

"If you need it, old man," he said hoarsely.

No matter how beautiful or brilliant a girl may be, the reputation of not being frequently cut in on makes her position at a dance unfortunate. Perhaps boys prefer her company to that of the butterflies with whom they dance a dozen times an evening, but youth in this jazz-nourished generation is temperamentally restless, and the idea of fox-trotting more than one full fox trot with the same girl is distasteful, not to say odious. When it comes to several dances and the intermissions between she can be quite sure that a young man, once relieved, will never tread on her wayward toes again.

Warren danced the next full dance with Bernice, and finally, thankful for the intermission, he led her to a table on the veranda. There was a moment's silence while she did unimpressive things with her fan.

"It's hotter here than in Eau Claire," she said.

Warren stifled a sigh and nodded. It might be for all he knew or cared. He wondered idly whether she was a poor conversationalist because she got no attention or got no attention because she was a poor conversationalist.

"You going to be here much longer?" he asked, and then turned rather red. She might suspect his reasons for asking.

"Another week," she answered, and stared at him as if to lunge at his next remark when it left his lips.

Warren fidgeted. Then with a sudden charitable impulse he

decided to try part of his line on her. He turned and looked at her eyes.

"You've got an awfully kissable mouth," he began quietly.

This was a remark that he sometimes made to girls at college proms when they were talking in just such half-dark as this. Bernice distinctly jumped. She turned an ungraceful red and became clumsy with her fan. No one had ever made such a remark to her before.

"Fresh!"—the word had slipped out before she realized it, and she bit her lip. Too late she decided to be amused, and offered him a flustered smile.

Warren was annoyed. Though not accustomed to have that remark taken seriously, still it usually provoked a laugh or a paragraph of sentimental banter. And he hated to be called fresh, except in a joking way. His charitable impulse died and he switched the topic.

"Jim Strain and Ethel Demorest sitting out as usual," he commented.

This was more in Bernice's line, but a faint regret mingled with her relief as the subject changed. Men did not talk to her about kissable mouths, but she knew that they talked in some such way to other girls.

"Oh, yes," she said, and laughed. "I hear they've been mooning round for years without a red penny. Isn't it silly?"

Warren's disgust increased. Jim Strain was a close friend of his brother's, and anyway he considered it bad form to sneer at people for not having money. But Bernice had had no intention of sneering. She was merely nervous.

II

When Marjorie and Bernice reached home at half after midnight they said good night at the top of the stairs. Though cousins, they were not intimates. As a matter of fact Marjorie had no female intimates—she considered girls stupid. Bernice on the contrary all through this parent-arranged visit had rather longed to exchange those confidences flavored with giggles and tears that she considered an indispensable factor in all feminine intercourse. But in this respect she found Marjorie rather cold; felt somehow the same difficulty in talking to her that she had in talking to men. Marjorie never giggled, was never frightened, seldom embarrassed, and in fact had very few of the qualities which Bernice considered appropriately and blessedly feminine.

As Bernice busied herself with toothbrush and paste this night she wondered for the hundredth time why she never had any attention when she was away from home. That her family were the wealthiest in Eau Claire, that her mother entertained tremendously, gave little dinners for her daughter before all dances and bought her a car of her own to drive round in, never occurred to her as factors in her home-town social success. Like most girls she had been brought up on the warm milk prepared by Annie Fellows Johnston and on novels in which the female was beloved because of certain mysterious womanly qualities, always mentioned but never displayed.

Bernice felt a vague pain that she was not at present engaged in being popular. She did not know that had it not been for Marjorie's campaigning she would have danced the entire evening with one man; but she knew that even in Eau Claire other girls with less position and less pulchritude were given a much bigger rush. She attributed this to something subtly unscrupulous in those girls. It had never worried her, and if it had her mother would have assured her that the other girls cheapened themselves and that men really respected girls like Bernice.

She turned out the light in her bathroom, and on an impulse decided to go in and chat for a moment with her aunt Josephine, whose light was still on. Her soft slippers bore her noiselessly down the carpeted hall, but hearing voices inside she stopped near the partly opened door. Then she caught her own name, and without any definite intention of eavesdropping lingered—and the thread of the conversation going on inside pierced her consciousness sharply as if it had been drawn through with a needle.

"She's absolutely hopeless!" It was Marjorie's voice. "Oh, I know what you're going to say! So many people have told you how pretty and sweet she is, and how she can cook! What of it? She has a bum time. Men don't like her."

"What's a little cheap popularity?"

Mrs. Harvey sounded annoyed.

"It's everything when you're eighteen," said Marjorie emphatically. "I've done my best. I've been polite and I've made men dance with her, but they just won't stand being bored. When I think of that gorgeous coloring wasted on such a ninny, and think what Martha Carey could do with it—oh!"

"There's no courtesy these days."

Mrs. Harvey's voice implied that modern situations were too much for her. When she was a girl all young ladies who belonged to nice families had glorious times.

"Well," said Marjorie, "no girl can permanently bolster up a lame-duck visitor, because these days it's every girl for herself. I've even tried to drop her hints about clothes and things, and she's been furious—given me the funniest looks. She's sensitive enough to know she's not getting away with much, but I'll bet she consoles herself by thinking that she's very virtuous and that I'm too gay and fickle and will come to a bad end. All unpopular girls think that way. Sour grapes! Sarah Hopkins refers to Genevieve and Roberta and me as gardenia girls! I'll bet she'd give ten years of her life and her European education to be a gardenia girl and have three or four men in love with her and be cut in on every few feet at dances."

"It seems to me," interrupted Mrs. Harvey rather wearily, "that you ought to be able to do something for Bernice. I know she's not very vivacious."

Marjorie groaned.

"Vivacious! Good grief! I've never heard her say anything to a boy except that it's hot or the floor's crowded or that she's going to school in New York next year. Sometimes she asks them what kind of car they have and tells them the kind she has. Thrilling!"

There was a short silence, and then Mrs. Harvey took up her refrain: "All I know is that other girls not half so sweet and attractive get partners. Martha Carey, for instance, is stout and loud, and her mother is distinctly common. Roberta Dillon is so thin this year that she looks as though Arizona were the place for her. She's dancing herself to death."

"But, mother," objected Marjorie impatiently, "Martha is cheerful and awfully witty and an awfully slick girl, and Roberta's a marvellous dancer. She's been popular for ages!"

Mrs. Harvey yawned.

"I think it's that crazy Indian blood in Bernice," continued Marjorie. "Maybe she's a reversion to type. Indian women all just sat round and never said anything."

"Go to bed, you silly child," laughed Mrs. Harvey. "I wouldn't have told you that if I'd thought you were going to remember it. And I think most of your ideas are perfectly idiotic," she finished sleepily.

There was another silence, while Marjorie considered whether or not convincing her mother was worth the trouble. People over forty can seldom be permanently convinced of anything. At eighteen our convictions are hills from which we look; at forty-five they are caves in which we hide.

Having decided this, Marjorie said good night. When she came out into the hall it was quite empty.

III

While Marjorie was breakfasting late next day Bernice came into the room with a rather formal good morning, sat down opposite, stared intently over and slightly moistened her lips.

"What's on your mind?" inquired Marjorie, rather puzzled.

Bernice paused before she threw her hand-grenade.

"I heard what you said about me to your mother last night."

Marjorie was startled, but she showed only a faintly heightened color and her voice was quite even when she spoke.

"Where were you?"

"In the hall. I didn't mean to listen—at first."

After an involuntary look of contempt Marjorie dropped her eyes and became very interested in balancing a stray corn-flake on her finger.

"I guess I'd better go back to Eau Claire—if I'm such a nuisance." Bernice's lower lip was trembling violently and she continued on a wavering note: "I've tried to be nice, and—and I've been first neglected and then insulted. No one ever visited me and got such treatment."

Marjorie was silent.

"But I'm in the way, I see. I'm a drag on you. Your friends don't like me." She paused, and then remembered another one of her grievances. "Of course I was furious last week when you tried to hint to me that that dress was unbecoming. Don't you think I know how to dress myself?"

"No," murmured Marjorie less than half-aloud.

"What?"

"I didn't hint anything," said Marjorie succinctly. "I said, as I remember, that it was better to wear a becoming dress three times straight than to alternate it with two frights."

"Do you think that was a very nice thing to say?"

"I wasn't trying to be nice." Then after a pause: "When do you want to go?"

Bernice drew in her breath sharply.

"Oh!" It was a little half-cry.

Marjorie looked up in surprise.

"Didn't you say you were going?"

"Yes, but—"

"Oh, you were only bluffing!"

They stared at each other across the breakfast-table for a moment. Misty waves were passing before Bernice's eyes, while Marjorie's face wore that rather hard expression that she used when slightly intoxicated undergraduates were making love to her.

"So you were bluffing," she repeated as if it were what she might have expected.

Bernice admitted it by bursting into tears. Marjorie's eyes showed boredom.

"You're my cousin," sobbed Bernice. "I'm v-v-visiting you. I was to stay a month, and if I go home my mother will know and she'll wah-wonder—"

Marjorie waited until the shower of broken words collapsed into little sniffles.

"I'll give you my month's allowance," she said coldly, "and you can spend this last week anywhere you want. There's a very nice hotel—"

Bernice's sobs rose to a flute note, and rising of a sudden she fled from the room.

An hour later, while Marjorie was in the library absorbed in composing one of those non-committal, marvellously elusive letters that only a young girl can write, Bernice reappeared, very red-eyed and consciously calm. She cast no glance at Marjorie but took a book at random from the shelf and sat down as if to read. Marjorie seemed absorbed in her letter and continued writing. When the clock showed noon Bernice closed her book with a snap.

"I suppose I'd better get my railroad ticket."

This was not the beginning of the speech she had rehearsed up-stairs, but as Marjorie was not getting her cues—wasn't urging her to be reasonable, it's all a mistake—it was the best opening she could muster.

"Just wait till I finish this letter," said Marjorie without looking round. "I want to get it off in the next mail."

After another minute, during which her pen scratched busily, she turned round and relaxed with an air of "at your service." Again Bernice had to speak.

"Do you want me to go home?"

"Well," said Marjorie, considering. "I suppose if you're not having a good time you'd better go. No use being miserable."

"Don't you think common kindness—"

"Oh, please don't quote 'Little Women'!" cried Marjorie impatiently, "That's out of style."

"You think so?"

"Heavens, yes! What modern girl could live like those inane females?"

"They were the models for our mothers."

Marjorie laughed.

"Yes, they were—not! Besides, our mothers were all very well in their way, but they know very little about their daughters' problems."

Bernice drew herself up.

"Please don't talk about my mother."

Marjorie laughed.

"I don't think I mentioned her."

Bernice felt that she was being led away from her subject.

"Do you think you've treated me very well?"

"I've done my best. You're rather hard material to work with."

The lids of Bernice's eyes reddened.

"I think you're hard and selfish, and you haven't a feminine quality in you."

"Oh, my Lord!" cried Marjorie in desperation. "You little nut! Girls like you are responsible for all the tiresome colorless marriages; all those ghastly inefficiencies that pass as feminine qualities. What a blow it must be when a man with imagination marries the beautiful bundle of clothes that he's been building ideals around, and finds that she's just a weak, whining, cowardly mass of affectations!"

Bernice's mouth had slipped half open.

"The womanly woman!" continued Marjorie. "Her whole early life is occupied in whining criticisms of girls like me who really do have a good time."

Bernice's jaw descended farther as Marjorie's voice rose.

"There's some excuse for an ugly girl whining. If I'd been irretrievably ugly I'd never have forgiven my parents for bringing me into the world. But you're starting life without any handicap—" Marjorie's little fist clenched. "If you expect me to weep with you you'll be disappointed. Go or stay, just as you like." And picking up her letters she left the room.

Bernice claimed a headache and failed to appear at luncheon. They had a matinée date for the afternoon, but the headache persisting, Marjorie made explanation to a not very downcast boy. But when she returned late in the afternoon she found Bernice with a strangely set face waiting for her in her bedroom.

"I've decided," began Bernice without preliminaries, "that maybe you're right about things—possibly not. But if you'll tell me why your friends aren't—aren't interested in me I'll see if I can do what you want me to."

Marjorie was at the mirror shaking down her hair.

"Do you mean it?"

"Yes."

"Without reservations? Will you do exactly what I say?"

"Well, I—"

"Well nothing! Will you do exactly as I say?"

"If they're sensible things."

"They're not! You're no case for sensible things."

"Are you going to make—to recommend—"

"Yes, everything. If I tell you to take boxing-lessons you'll have to do it. Write home and tell your mother you're going to stay another two weeks."

"If you'll tell me—"

"All right—I'll just give you a few examples now. First, you have no ease of manner. Why? Because you're never sure about your personal appearance. When a girl feels that she's perfectly groomed and dressed she can forget that part of her. That's charm. The more parts of yourself you can afford to forget the more charm you have."

"Don't I look all right?"

"No; for instance, you never take care of your eyebrows. They're black and lustrous, but by leaving them straggly they're a blemish. They'd be beautiful if you'd take care of them in one-tenth the time you take doing nothing. You're going to brush them so that they'll grow straight."

Bernice raised the brows in question.

"Do you mean to say that men notice eyebrows?"

"Yes—subconsciously. And when you go home you ought to have your teeth straightened a little. It's almost imperceptible, still—"

"But I thought," interrupted Bernice in bewilderment, "that you despised little dainty feminine things like that."

"I hate dainty minds," answered Marjorie. "But a girl has to be dainty in person. If she looks like a million dollars she can talk about Russia, ping-pong, or the League of Nations and get away with it."

"What else?"

"Oh, I'm just beginning! There's your dancing."

"Don't I dance all right?"

"No, you don't—you lean on a man; yes, you do—ever so slightly. I noticed it when we were dancing together yesterday. And you dance standing up straight instead of bending over a little. Probably some old lady on the side-line once told you that you looked so dignified that way. But except with a very small girl it's much harder on the man, and he's the one that counts."

"Go on." Bernice's brain was reeling.

"Well, you've got to learn to be nice to men who are sad birds. You look as if you'd been insulted whenever you're thrown with any except the most popular boys. Why, Bernice, I'm cut in on every few feet—and who does most of it? Why, those very sad birds. No girl can afford to neglect them. They're the big part of any crowd. Young boys too shy to talk are the very best conversational practice. Clumsy boys are the best dancing practice. If you can follow them and yet look graceful you can follow a baby tank across a barb-wire sky-scraper."

Bernice sighed profoundly, but Marjorie was not through.

"If you go to a dance and really amuse, say, three sad birds that dance with you; if you talk so well to them that they forget they're stuck with you, you've done something. They'll come back next time, and gradually so many sad birds will dance with you that the attractive boys will see there's no danger of being stuck—then they'll dance with you."

"Yes," agreed Bernice faintly. "I think I begin to see."

"And finally," concluded Marjorie, "poise and charm will just come. You'll wake up some morning knowing you've attained it, and men will know it too."

Bernice rose.

"It's been awfully kind of you—but nobody's ever talked to me like this before, and I feel sort of startled."

Marjorie made no answer but gazed pensively at her own image in the mirror.

"You're a peach to help me," continued Bernice.

Still Marjorie did not answer, and Bernice thought she had seemed too grateful.

"I know you don't like sentiment," she said timidly.

Marjorie turned to her quickly.

"Oh, I wasn't thinking about that. I was considering whether we hadn't better bob your hair."

Bernice collapsed backward upon the bed.

IV

On the following Wednesday evening there was a dinner-dance at the country club. When the guests strolled in Bernice found her place-card with a slight feeling of irritation. Though at her right sat G. Reece Stoddard, a most desirable and distinguished young bachelor, the all-important left held only Charley Paulson. Charley lacked height, beauty, and social shrewdness, and in her new enlightenment Bernice decided that his only qualification to be her partner was that he had never been stuck with her. But this feeling of irritation left with the last of the soup-plates, and Marjorie's specific instruction came to her. Swallowing her pride she turned to Charley Paulson and plunged.

"Do you think I ought to bob my hair, Mr. Charley Paulson?"

Charley looked up in surprise.

"Why?"

"Because I'm considering it. It's such a sure and easy way of attracting attention."

Charley smiled pleasantly. He could not know this had been rehearsed. He replied that he didn't know much about bobbed hair. But Bernice was there to tell him.

"I want to be a society vampire, you see," she announced coolly, and went on to inform him that bobbed hair was the necessary prelude. She added that she wanted to ask his advice, because she had heard he was so critical about girls.

Charley, who knew as much about the psychology of women as he did of the mental states of Buddhist contempla-tives, felt vaguely flattered.

"So I've decided," she continued, her voice rising slightly, "that early next week I'm going down to the Sevier Hotel barber-shop, sit in the first chair, and get my hair bobbed." She faltered, noticing that the people near her had paused in their conversation and were listening; but after a confused second Marjorie's coaching told, and she finished her paragraph to the vicinity at large. "Of course I'm charging admission, but if you'll all come down and encourage me I'll issue passes for the inside seats."

There was a ripple of appreciative laughter, and under cover of it G. Reece Stoddard leaned over quickly and said close to her ear: "I'll take a box right now."

She met his eyes and smiled as if he had said something surpassingly brilliant.

"Do you believe in bobbed hair?" asked G. Reece in the same undertone.

"I think it's unmoral," affirmed Bernice gravely. "But, of course, you've either got to amuse people or feed 'em or shock 'em." Marjorie had culled this from Oscar Wilde. It was greeted with a ripple of laughter from the men and a series of quick, intent looks from the girls. And then as though she had said nothing of wit or moment Bernice turned again to Charley and spoke confidentially in his ear.

"I want to ask you your opinion of several people. I imagine you're a wonderful judge of character."

Charley thrilled faintly—paid her a subtle compliment by overturning her water.

Two hours later, while Warren McIntyre was standing passively in the stag line abstractedly watching the dancers and wondering whither and with whom Marjorie had disappeared, an unrelated perception began to creep slowly upon him—a perception that Bernice, cousin to Marjorie, had been cut in on several times in the past five minutes. He closed his eyes, opened them and looked again. Several minutes back she had been dancing with a visiting boy, a matter easily accounted for; a visiting boy would know no better. But now she was dancing with some one else, and there was Charley Paulson headed for her with enthusiastic determination in his eye. Funny—Charley seldom danced with more than three girls an evening.

Warren was distinctly surprised when—the exchange having been effected—the man relieved proved to be none other than G. Reece Stoddard himself. And G. Reece seemed not at all jubilant at being relieved. Next time Bernice danced near, Warren regarded her intently. Yes, she was pretty, distinctly pretty; and to-night her face seemed really vivacious. She had that look that no woman, however histrionically proficient, can successfully counterfeit—she looked as if she were having a good time. He liked the way she had her hair arranged, wondered if it was brilliantine that made it glisten so. And that dress was becoming—a dark red that set off her shadowy eyes and high coloring. He remembered that he had thought her pretty when she first came to town, before he had realized that she was dull. Too bad she was dull—dull girls unbearable—certainly pretty though.

His thoughts zigzagged back to Marjorie. This disappearance would be like other disappearances. When she reappeared he would demand where she had been—would be told emphatically that it was none of his business. What a pity she was so sure of him! She basked in the knowledge that no other girl in town interested him; she defied him to fall in love with Genevieve or Roberta.

Warren sighed. The way to Marjorie's affections was a labyrinth indeed. He looked up. Bernice was again dancing with the visiting boy. Half unconsciously he took a step out from the stag line in her direction, and hesitated. Then he said to himself that it was charity. He walked toward her—collided suddenly with G. Reece Stoddard.

"Pardon me," said Warren.

But G. Reece had not stopped to apologize. He had again cut in on Bernice.

That night at one o'clock Marjorie, with one hand on the electric-light switch in the hall, turned to take a last look at Bernice's sparkling eyes.

"So it worked?"

"Oh, Marjorie, yes!" cried Bernice.

"I saw you were having a gay time."

"I did! The only trouble was that about midnight I ran short of talk. I had to repeat myself—with different men of course. I hope they won't compare notes."

"Men don't," said Marjorie, yawning, "and it wouldn't matter if they did—they'd think you were even trickier."

She snapped out the light, and as they started up the stairs Bernice grasped the banister thankfully. For the first time in her life she had been danced tired.

"You see," said Marjorie at the top of the stairs, "one man sees another man cut in and he thinks there must be something there. Well, we'll fix up some new stuff to-morrow. Good night."

"Good night."

As Bernice took down her hair she passed the evening before her in review. She had followed instructions exactly. Even when Charley Paulson cut in for the eighth time she had simulated delight and had apparently been both interested and flattered. She had not talked about the weather or Eau Claire or automobiles or her school, but had confined her conversation to me, you, and us.

But a few minutes before she fell asleep a rebellious thought was churning drowsily in her brain—after all, it was she who had done it. Marjorie, to be sure, had given her her conversation, but then Marjorie got much of her conversation out of things she read. Bernice had bought the red dress, though she had never valued it highly before Marjorie dug it out of her trunk—and her own voice had said the words, her own lips had smiled, her own feet had danced. Marjorie nice girl—vain, though—nice evening—nice boys—like Warren—Warren—Warren—what's-his-name—Warren—

She fell asleep.

V

To Bernice the next week was a revelation. With the feeling that people really enjoyed looking at her and listening to her came the foundation of self-confidence. Of course there were numerous mistakes at first. She did not know, for instance, that Draycott Deyo was studying for the ministry; she was unaware that he had cut in on her because he thought she was a quiet, reserved girl. Had she known these things she would not have treated him to the line which began "Hello, Shell Shock!" and continued with the bathtub story—"It takes a frightful lot of energy to fix my hair in the summer—there's so much of it—so I always fix it first and powder my face and put on my hat; then I get into the bathtub, and dress afterward. Don't you think that's the best plan?"

Though Draycott Deyo was in the throes of difficulties concerning baptism by immersion and might possibly have seen a connection, it must be admitted that he did not. He considered feminine bathing an immoral subject, and gave her some of his ideas on the depravity of modern society.

But to offset that unfortunate occurrence Bernice had several signal successes to her credit. Little Otis Ormonde pleaded off from a trip East and elected instead to follow her with a puppylike devotion, to the amusement of his crowd

and to the irritation of G. Reece Stoddard, several of whose
afternoon calls Otis completely ruined by the disgusting ten-
derness of the glances he bent on Bernice. He even told her
the story of the two-by-four and the dressing-room to show
her how frightfully mistaken he and every one else had been
in their first judgment of her. Bernice laughed off that incident with a slight sinking sensation.

Of all Bernice's conversation perhaps the best known and
most universally approved was the line about the bobbing of
her hair.

"Oh, Bernice, when you goin' to get the hair bobbed?"

"Day after to-morrow maybe," she would reply, laughing.
"Will you come and see me? Because I'm counting on you,
you know."

"Will we? You know! But you better hurry up."

Bernice, whose tonsorial intentions were strictly dishonor-
able, would laugh again.

"Pretty soon now. You'd be surprised."

But perhaps the most significant symbol of her success was
the gray car of the hypercritical Warren McIntyre, parked
daily in front of the Harvey house. At first the parlor-maid
was distinctly startled when he asked for Bernice instead of
Marjorie; after a week of it she told the cook that Miss
Bernice had gotta holda Miss Marjorie's best fella.

And Miss Bernice had. Perhaps it began with Warren's desire to rouse jealousy in Marjorie; perhaps it was the familiar
though unrecognized strain of Marjorie in Bernice's conversation; perhaps it was both of these and something of sincere
attraction besides. But somehow the collective mind of the
younger set knew within a week that Marjorie's most reliable
beau had made an amazing face-about and was giving an in-
disputable rush to Marjorie's guest. The question of the moment was how Marjorie would take it. Warren called Bernice
on the 'phone twice a day, sent her notes, and they were frequently seen together in his roadster, obviously engrossed in
one of those tense, significant conversations as to whether or
not he was sincere.

Marjorie on being twitted only laughed. She said she was
mighty glad that Warren had at last found some one who appreciated him. So the younger set laughed, too, and guessed
that Marjorie didn't care and let it go at that.

One afternoon, when there were only three days left of her
visit, Bernice was waiting in the hall for Warren, with whom

she was going to a bridge party. She was in rather a blissful mood, and when Marjorie—also bound for the party— appeared beside her and began casually to adjust her hat in the mirror, Bernice was utterly unprepared for anything in the nature of a clash. Marjorie did her work very coldly and succinctly in three sentences.

"You may as well get Warren out of your head," she said coldly.

"What?" Bernice was utterly astounded.

"You may as well stop making a fool of yourself over Warren McIntyre. He doesn't care a snap of his fingers about you."

For a tense moment they regarded each other—Marjorie scornful, aloof; Bernice astounded, half-angry, half-afraid. Then two cars drove up in front of the house and there was a riotous honking. Both of them gasped faintly, turned, and side by side hurried out.

All through the bridge party Bernice strove in vain to master a rising uneasiness. She had offended Marjorie, the sphinx of sphinxes. With the most wholesome and innocent intentions in the world she had stolen Marjorie's property. She felt suddenly and horribly guilty. After the bridge game, when they sat in an informal circle and the conversation became general, the storm gradually broke. Little Otis Ormonde inadvertently precipitated it.

"When you going back to kindergarten, Otis?" some one had asked.

"Me? Day Bernice gets her hair bobbed."

"Then your education's over," said Marjorie quickly. "That's only a bluff of hers. I should think you'd have realized."

"That a fact?" demanded Otis, giving Bernice a reproachful glance.

Bernice's ears burned as she tried to think up an effectual comeback. In the face of this direct attack her imagination was paralyzed.

"There's a lot of bluffs in the world," continued Marjorie quite pleasantly. "I should think you'd be young enough to know that, Otis."

"Well," said Otis, "maybe so. But gee! With a line like Bernice's—"

"Really?" yawned Marjorie. "What's her latest bon mot?"

No one seemed to know. In fact, Bernice, having trifled with her muse's beau, had said nothing memorable of late.

"Was that really all a line?" asked Roberta curiously.

Bernice hesitated. She felt that wit in some form was demanded of her, but under her cousin's suddenly frigid eyes she was completely incapacitated.

"I don't know," she stalled.

"Splush!" said Marjorie. "Admit it!"

Bernice saw that Warren's eyes had left a ukulele he had been tinkering with and were fixed on her questioningly.

"Oh, I don't know!" she repeated steadily. Her cheeks were glowing.

"Splush!" remarked Marjorie again.

"Come through, Bernice," urged Otis. "Tell her where to get off."

Bernice looked round again—she seemed unable to get away from Warren's eyes.

"I like bobbed hair," she said hurriedly, as if he had asked her a question, "and I intend to bob mine."

"When?" demanded Marjorie.

"Any time."

"No time like the present," suggested Roberta.

Otis jumped to his feet.

"Good stuff!" he cried. "We'll have a summer bobbing party. Sevier Hotel barber-shop, I think you said."

In an instant all were on their feet. Bernice's heart throbbed violently.

"What?" she gasped.

Out of the group came Marjorie's voice, very clear and contemptuous.

"Don't worry—she'll back out!"

"Come on, Bernice!" cried Otis, starting toward the door.

Four eyes—Warren's and Marjorie's—stared at her, challenged her, defied her. For another second she wavered wildly.

"All right," she said swiftly, "I don't care if I do."

An eternity of minutes later, riding down-town through the late afternoon beside Warren, the others following in Roberta's car close behind, Bernice had all the sensations of Marie Antoinette bound for the guillotine in a tumbrel. Vaguely she wondered why she did not cry out that it was all a mistake. It was all she could do to keep from clutching her hair with both hands to protect it from the suddenly hostile world. Yet she did neither. Even the thought of her mother was no deterrent now. This was the test supreme of her sportsmanship, her right to walk unchallenged in the starry heaven of popular girls.

Warren was moodily silent, and when they came to the hotel he drew up at the curb and nodded to Bernice to precede him out. Roberta's car emptied a laughing crowd into the shop, which presented two bold plate-glass windows to the street.

Bernice stood on the curb and looked at the sign, Sevier Barber-Shop. It was a guillotine indeed, and the hangman was the first barber, who, attired in a white coat and smoking a cigarette, leaned nonchalantly against the first chair. He must have heard of her; he must have been waiting all week, smoking eternal cigarettes beside that portentous, too-often-mentioned first chair. Would they blindfold her? No, but they would tie a white cloth round her neck lest any of her blood—nonsense—hair—should get on her clothes.

"All right, Bernice," said Warren quickly.

With her chin in the air she crossed the sidewalk, pushed open the swinging screen-door, and giving not a glance to the uproarious, riotous row that occupied the waiting bench, went up to the first barber.

"I want you to bob my hair."

The first barber's mouth slid somewhat open. His cigarette dropped to the floor.

"Huh?"

"My hair—bob it!"

Refusing further preliminaries, Bernice took her seat on high. A man in the chair next to her turned on his side and gave her a glance, half lather, half amazement. One barber started and spoiled little Willy Schuneman's monthly haircut. Mr. O'Reilly in the last chair grunted and swore musically in ancient Gaelic as a razor bit into his cheek. Two bootblacks became wide-eyed and rushed for her feet. No, Bernice didn't care for a shine.

Outside a passer-by stopped and stared; a couple joined him; half a dozen small boys' noses sprang into life, flattened against the glass; and snatches of conversation borne on the summer breeze drifted in through the screen-door.

"Lookada long hair on a kid!"

"Where'd yuh get 'at stuff? 'At's a bearded lady he just finished shavin'."

But Bernice saw nothing, heard nothing. Her only living

sense told her that this man in the white coat had removed one tortoise-shell comb and then another; that his fingers were fumbling clumsily with unfamiliar hairpins; that this hair, this wonderful hair of hers, was going—she would never again feel its long voluptuous pull as it hung in a dark-brown glory down her back. For a second she was near breaking down, and then the picture before her swam mechanically into her vision—Marjorie's mouth curling in a faint ironic smile as if to say: "Give up and get down! You tried to buck me and I called your bluff. You see you haven't got a prayer."

And some last energy rose up in Bernice, for she clenched her hands under the white cloth, and there was a curious narrowing of her eyes that Marjorie remarked on to some one long afterward.

Twenty minutes later the barber swung her round to face the mirror, and she flinched at the full extent of the damage that had been wrought. Her hair was not curly, and now it lay in lank lifeless blocks on both sides of her suddenly pale face. It was ugly as sin—she had known it would be ugly as sin. Her face's chief charm had been a Madonna-like simplicity. Now that was gone and she was—well, frightfully mediocre—not stagy; only ridiculous, like a Greenwich Villager who had left her spectacles at home.

As she climbed down from the chair she tried to smile—failed miserably. She saw two of the girls exchange glances; noticed Marjorie's mouth curved in attenuated mockery—and that Warren's eyes were suddenly very cold.

"You see"—her words fell into an awkward pause—"I've done it."

"Yes, you've—done it," admitted Warren.

"Do you like it?"

There was a half-hearted "Sure" from two or three voices, another awkward pause, and then Marjorie turned swiftly and with serpentlike intensity to Warren.

"Would you mind running me down to the cleaners?" she asked. "I've simply got to get a dress there before supper. Roberta's driving right home and she can take the others."

Warren stared abstractedly at some infinite speck out the window. Then for an instant his eyes rested coldly on Bernice before they turned to Marjorie.

"Be glad to," he said slowly.

VI

Bernice did not fully realize the outrageous trap that had been set for her until she met her aunt's amazed glance just before dinner.

"Why, Bernice!"

"I've bobbed it, Aunt Josephine."

"Why, child!"

"Do you like it?"

"Why, Ber-nice!"

"I suppose I've shocked you."

"No, but what'll Mrs. Deyo think to-morrow night? Bernice, you should have waited until after the Deyos' dance—you should have waited if you wanted to do that."

"It was sudden, Aunt Josephine. Anyway, why does it matter to Mrs. Deyo particularly?"

"Why, child," cried Mrs. Harvey, "in her paper on 'The Foibles of the Younger Generation' that she read at the last meeting of the Thursday Club she devoted fifteen minutes to bobbed hair. It's her pet abomination. And the dance is for you and Marjorie!"

"I'm sorry."

"Oh, Bernice, what'll your mother say? She'll think I let you do it."

"I'm sorry."

Dinner was an agony. She had made a hasty attempt with a curling-iron, and burned her finger and much hair. She could see that her aunt was both worried and grieved, and her uncle kept saying, "Well, I'll be darned!" over and over in a hurt and faintly hostile tone. And Marjorie sat very quietly, intrenched behind a faint smile, a faintly mocking smile.

Somehow she got through the evening. Three boys called; Marjorie disappeared with one of them, and Bernice made a listless unsuccessful attempt to entertain the two others— sighed thankfully as she climbed the stairs to her room at half past ten. What a day!

When she had undressed for the night the door opened and Marjorie came in.

"Bernice," she said, "I'm awfully sorry about the Deyo dance. I'll give you my word of honor I'd forgotten all about it."

" 'Sall right," said Bernice shortly. Standing before the mirror she passed her comb slowly through her short hair.

"I'll take you down-town to-morrow," continued Marjorie, "and the hairdresser'll fix it so you'll look slick. I didn't imagine you'd go through with it. I'm really mighty sorry."

"Oh, 'sall right!"

"Still it's your last night, so I suppose it won't matter much."

Then Bernice winced as Marjorie tossed her own hair over her shoulders and began to twist it slowly into two long blond braids until in her cream-colored negligée she looked like a delicate painting of some Saxon princess. Fascinated, Bernice watched the braids grow. Heavy and luxurious they were, moving under the supple fingers like restive snakes— and to Bernice remained this relic and the curling-iron and a to-morrow full of eyes. She could see G. Reece Stoddard, who liked her, assuming his Harvard manner and telling his dinner partner that Bernice shouldn't have been allowed to go to the movies so much; she could see Draycott Deyo exchanging glances with his mother and then being conscientiously charitable to her. But then perhaps by to-morrow Mrs. Deyo would have heard the news; would send round an icy little note requesting that she fail to appear—and behind her back they would all laugh and know that Marjorie had made a fool of her; that her chance at beauty had been sacrificed to the jealous whim of a selfish girl. She sat down suddenly before the mirror, biting the inside of her cheek.

"I like it," she said with an effort. "I think it'll be becoming."

Marjorie smiled.

"It looks all right. For heaven's sake, don't let it worry you!"

"I won't."

"Good night, Bernice."

But as the door closed something snapped within Bernice. She sprang dynamically to her feet, clenching her hands, then swiftly and noiselessly crossed over to her bed and from underneath it dragged out her suitcase. Into it she tossed toilet articles and a change of clothing. Then she turned to her trunk and quickly dumped in two drawerfuls of lingerie and summer dresses. She moved quietly, but with deadly efficiency, and in three-quarters of an hour her trunk was locked and strapped and she was fully dressed in a becoming new travelling suit that Marjorie had helped her pick out.

Sitting down at her desk she wrote a short note to Mrs.

Harvey, in which she briefly outlined her reasons for going. She sealed it, addressed it, and laid it on her pillow. She glanced at her watch. The train left at one, and she knew that if she walked down to the Marborough Hotel two blocks away she could easily get a taxicab.

Suddenly she drew in her breath sharply and an expression flashed into her eyes that a practised character reader might have connected vaguely with the set look she had worn in the barber's chair—somehow a development of it. It was quite a new look for Bernice—and it carried consequences.

She went stealthily to the bureau, picked up an article that lay there, and turning out all the lights stood quietly until her eyes became accustomed to the darkness. Softly she pushed open the door to Marjorie's room. She heard the quiet, even breathing of an untroubled conscience asleep.

She was by the bedside now, very deliberate and calm. She acted swiftly. Bending over she found one of the braids of Marjorie's hair, followed it up with her hand to the point nearest the head, and then holding it a little slack so that the sleeper would feel no pull, she reached down with the shears and severed it. With the pigtail in her hand she held her breath. Marjorie had muttered something in her sleep. Bernice deftly amputated the other braid, paused for an instant, and then flitted swiftly and silently back to her own room.

Down-stairs she opened the big front door, closed it carefully behind her, and feeling oddly happy and exuberant stepped off the porch into the moonlight, swinging her heavy grip like a shopping-bag. After a minute's brisk walk she discovered that her left hand still held the two blond braids. She laughed unexpectedly—had to shut her mouth hard to keep from emitting an absolute peal. She was passing Warren's house now, and on the impulse she set down her baggage, and swinging the braids like pieces of rope flung them at the wooden porch, where they landed with a slight thud. She laughed again, no longer restraining herself.

"Huh!" she giggled wildly. "Scalp the selfish thing!"

Then picking up her suitcase she set off at a half-run down the moonlit street.

Benediction

The Baltimore Station was hot and crowded, so Lois was forced to stand by the telegraph desk for interminable, sticky seconds while a clerk with big front teeth counted and recounted a large lady's day message, to determine whether it contained the innocuous forty-nine words or the fatal fifty-one.

Lois, waiting, decided she wasn't quite sure of the address, so she took the letter out of her bag and ran over it again.

> Darling: *it began*— I understand and I'm happier than life ever meant me to be. If I could give you the things you've always been in tune with—but I can't, Lois; we can't marry and we can't lose each other and let all this glorious love end in nothing.
>
> Until your letter came, dear, I'd been sitting here in the half dark thinking and thinking where I could go and ever forget you; abroad, perhaps, to drift through Italy or Spain and dream away the pain of having lost you where the crumbling ruins of older, mellower civilizations would mirror only the desolation of my heart—and then your letter came.
>
> Sweetest, bravest girl, if you'll wire me I'll meet you in Wilmington—till then I'll be here just waiting and hoping for every long dream of you to come true.
>
> HOWARD.

She had read the letter so many times that she knew it word by word, yet it still startled her. In it she found many faint reflections of the man who wrote it—the mingled sweetness and sadness in his dark eyes, the furtive, restless excitement she felt sometimes when he talked to her, his dreamy sensuousness that lulled her mind to sleep. Lois was nineteen and very romantic and curious and courageous.

The large lady and the clerk having compromised on fifty

words, Lois took a blank and wrote her telegram. And there
were no overtones to the finality of her decision.

It's just destiny—she thought—it's just the way things
work out in this damn world. If cowardice is all that's been
holding me back there won't be any more holding back. So
we'll just let things take their course, and never be sorry.

The clerk scanned her telegram:

> ARRIVED BALTIMORE TODAY SPEND DAY WITH MY BROTHER
> MEET ME WILMINGTON THREE P.M. WEDNESDAY LOVE
> LOIS

"Fifty-four cents," said the clerk admiringly.

And never be sorry—thought Lois—and never be sorry—

II

Trees filtering light onto dappled grass. Trees like tall, languid ladies with feather fans coquetting airily with the ugly
roof of the monastery. Trees like butlers, bending courteously
over placid walks and paths. Trees, trees over the hills on either side and scattering out in clumps and lines and woods all
through eastern Maryland, delicate lace on the hems of many
yellow fields, dark opaque backgrounds for flowered bushes
or wild climbing gardens.

Some of the trees were very gay and young, but the monastery trees were older than the monastery which, by true mo-
nastic standards, wasn't very old at all. And, as a matter of
fact, it wasn't technically called a monastery, but only a seminary; nevertheless it shall be a monastery here despite its
Victorian architecture or its Edward VII additions, or even its
Woodrow Wilsonian, patented, last-a-century roofing.

Out behind was the farm where half a dozen lay brothers
were sweating lustily as they moved with deadly efficiency
around the vegetable-gardens. To the left, behind a row of
elms, was an informal baseball diamond where three novices
were being batted out by a fourth, amid great chasings and
puffings and blowings. And in front, as a great mellow bell
boomed the half-hour, a swarm of black, human leaves were
blown over the checker-board of paths under the courteous
trees.

Some of these black leaves were very old with cheeks fur-
rowed like the first ripples of a splashed pool. Then there was

a scattering of middle-aged leaves whose forms when viewed in profile in their revealing gowns were beginning to be faintly unsymmetrical. These carried thick volumes of Thomas Aquinas and Henry James and Cardinal Mercier and Immanuel Kant and many bulging notebooks filled with lecture data.

But most numerous were the young leaves; blond boys of nineteen with very stern, conscientious expressions; men in the late twenties with a keen self-assurance from having taught out in the world for five years—several hundreds of them, from city and town and country in Maryland and Pennsylvania and Virginia and West Virginia and Delaware.

There were many Americans and some Irish and some tough Irish and a few French, and several Italians and Poles, and they walked informally arm in arm with each other in twos and threes or in long rows, almost universally distinguished by the straight mouth and the considerable chin—for this was the Society of Jesus, founded in Spain five hundred years before by a tough-minded soldier who trained men to hold a breach or a salon, preach a sermon or write a treaty, and do it and not argue . . .

Lois got out of a bus into the sunshine down by the outer gate. She was nineteen with yellow hair and eyes that people were tactful enough not to call green. When men of talent saw her in a streetcar they often furtively produced little stub-pencils and backs of envelopes and tried to sum up that profile or the thing that the eyebrows did to her eyes. Later they looked at their results and usually tore them up with wondering sighs.

Though Lois was very jauntily attired in an expensively appropriate traveling affair, she did not linger to pat out the dust which covered her clothes, but started up the central walk with curious glances at either side. Her face was very eager and expectant, yet she hadn't at all that glorified expression that girls wear when they arrive for a Senior Prom at Princeton or New Haven; still, as there were no senior proms here, perhaps it didn't matter.

She was wondering what he would look like, whether she'd possibly know him from his picture. In the picture, which hung over her mother's bureau at home, he seemed very young and hollow-cheeked and rather pitiful, with only a well-developed mouth and an ill-fitting probationer's gown to show that he had already made a momentous decision about his life. Of course he had been only nineteen then and now he was thirty-six—didn't look like that at all; in recent snap-shots he was much broader and his hair had grown a little thin—but the impression of her brother she had always retained was that of the big picture. And so she had always been a little sorry for him. What a life for a man! Seventeen years of preparation and he wasn't even a priest yet—wouldn't be for another year.

Lois had an idea that this was all going to be rather solemn if she let it be. But she was going to give her very best imitation of undiluted sunshine, the imitation she could give even when her head was splitting or when her mother had a nervous breakdown or when she was particularly romantic and curious and courageous. This brother of hers undoubtedly needed cheering up, and he was going to be cheered up, whether he liked it or not.

As she drew near the great, homely front door she saw a man break suddenly away from a group and, pulling up the skirts of his gown, run toward her. He was smiling, she noticed, and he looked very big and—and reliable. She stopped and waited, knew that her heart was beating unusually fast.

"Lois!" he cried, and in a second she was in his arms. She was suddenly trembling.

"Lois!" he cried again, "why, this is wonderful! I can't tell you, Lois, how *much* I've looked forward to this. Why, Lois, you're beautiful!"

Lois gasped.

His voice, though restrained, was vibrant with energy and that odd sort of enveloping personality she had thought that she only of the family possessed.

"I'm mighty glad, too—Kieth."

She flushed, but not unhappily, at this first use of his name.

"Lois—Lois—Lois," he repeated in wonder. "Child, we'll go in here a minute, because I want you to meet the rector, and then we'll walk around. I have a thousand things to talk to you about."

His voice became graver. "How's mother?"

She looked at him for a moment and then said something that she had not intended to say at all, the very sort of thing she had resolved to avoid.

"Oh, Kieth—she's—she's getting worse all the time, every way."

He nodded slowly as if he understood.

"Nervous, well—you can tell me about that later. Now—"

She was in a small study with a large desk, saying something to a little, jovial, white-haired priest who retained her hand for some seconds.

"So this is Lois!"

He said it as if he had heard of her for years.

He entreated her to sit down.

Two other priests arrived enthusiastically and shook hands with her and addressed her as "Kieth's little sister," which she found she didn't mind a bit.

How assured they seemed; she had expected a certain shyness, reserve at least. There were several jokes unintelligible to her, which seemed to delight every one, and the little Father Rector referred to the trio of them as "dim old monks," which she appreciated, because of course they weren't monks at all. She had a lightning impression that they were especially fond of Kieth—the Father Rector had called him "Kieth" and one of the others had kept a hand on his shoulder all through the conversation. Then she was shaking hands again and promising to come back a little later for some ice-cream, and smiling and smiling and being rather absurdly happy . . . she told herself that it was because Kieth was so delighted in showing her off.

Then she and Kieth were strolling along a path, arm in arm, and he was informing her what an absolute jewel the Father Rector was.

"Lois," he broke off suddenly. "I want to tell you before we go any farther how much it means to me to have you come up here. I think it was—mighty sweet of you. I know what a gay time you've been having."

Lois gasped. She was not prepared for this. At first when she had conceived the plan of taking the hot journey down to Baltimore, staying the night with a friend and then coming out to see her brother, she had felt rather consciously virtuous, hoped he wouldn't be priggish or resentful about her not having come before—but walking here with him under the trees seemed such a little thing, and surprisingly a happy thing.

"Why, Kieth," she said quickly, "you know I couldn't have waited a day longer. I saw you when I was five, but of course I didn't remember, and how could I have gone on without practically ever having seen my only brother?"

"It was mighty sweet of you, Lois," he repeated.

Lois blushed—he *did* have personality.

"I want you to tell me all about yourself," he said after a pause. "Of course I have a general idea what you and mother did in Europe those fourteen years, and then we were all so worried, Lois, when you had pneumonia and couldn't come down with mother—let's see, that was two years ago—and then, well, I've seen your name in the papers, but it's all been so unsatisfactory. I haven't known you, Lois."

She found herself analyzing his personality as she analyzed the personality of every man she met. She wondered if the effect of—of intimacy that he gave was bred by his constant repetition of her name. He said it as if he loved the word, as if it had an inherent meaning to him.

"Then you were at school," he continued.

"Yes, at Farmington. Mother wanted me to go to a convent—but I didn't want to."

She cast a side glance at him to see if he would resent this. But he only nodded slowly.

"Had enough convents abroad, eh?"

"Yes—and Kieth, convents are different there anyway. Here even in the nicest ones there are so many *common* girls."

He nodded again.

"Yes," he agreed, "I suppose there are, and I know how you feel about it. It grated on me here, at first, Lois, though I wouldn't say that to any one but you; we're rather sensitive, you and I, to things like this."

"You mean the men here?"

"Yes, some of them of course were fine, the sort of men I'd always been thrown with, but there were others; a man named Regan, for instance—I hated the fellow, and now he's about the best friend I have. A wonderful character, Lois; you'll meet him later. Sort of man you'd like to have with you in a fight."

Lois was thinking that Kieth was the sort of man she'd like to have with *her* in a fight.

"How did you—how did you first happen to do it?" she asked, rather shyly, "to come here, I mean. Of course mother told me the story about the Pullman car."

"Oh, that—" He looked rather annoyed.

"Tell me that. I'd like to hear you tell it."

"Oh, it's nothing, except what you probably know. It was evening and I'd been riding all day and thinking about—

about a hundred things, Lois, and then suddenly I had a sense that some one was sitting across from me, felt that he'd been there for some time, and had a vague idea that he was another traveller. All at once he leaned over toward me and I heard a voice say: 'I want you to be a priest, that's what I want.' Well, I jumped up and cried out, 'Oh, my God, not that!'— made an idiot of myself before about twenty people; you see there wasn't any one sitting there at all. A week after that I went to the Jesuit College in Philadelphia and crawled up the last flight of stairs to the rector's office on my hands and knees."

There was another silence and Lois saw that her brother's eyes wore a far-away look, that he was staring unseeingly out over the sunny fields. She was stirred by the modulations of his voice and the sudden silence that seemed to flow about him when he finished speaking.

She noticed now that his eyes were of the same fibre as hers, with the green left out, and that his mouth was much gentler, really, than in the picture—or was it that the face had grown up to it lately? He was getting a little bald just on top of his head. She wondered if that was from wearing a hat so much. It seemed awful for a man to grow bald and no one to care about it.

"Were you—pious when you were young, Kieth?" she asked. "You know what I mean. Were you religious? If you don't mind these personal questions."

"Yes," he said with his eyes still far away—and she felt that his intense abstraction was as much a part of his personality as his attention. "Yes, I suppose I was, when I was— sober."

Lois thrilled slightly.

"Did you drink?"

He nodded.

"I was on the way to making a bad hash of things." He smiled and, turning his gray eyes on her, changed the subject.

"Child, tell me about mother. I know it's been awfully hard for you there, lately. I know you've had to sacrifice a lot and put up with a great deal, and I want you to know how fine of you I think it is. I feel, Lois, that you're sort of taking the place of both of us there."

Lois thought quickly how little she had sacrificed; how lately she had constantly avoided her nervous, half-invalid mother.

"Youth shouldn't be sacrificed to age, Kieth," she said steadily.

"I know," he sighed, "and you oughtn't to have the weight on your shoulders, child. I wish I were there to help you."

She saw how quickly he had turned her remark and instantly she knew what this quality was that he gave off. He was *sweet*. Her thoughts went off on a side-track and then she broke the silence with an odd remark.

"Sweetness is hard," she said suddenly.

"What?"

"Nothing," she denied in confusion. "I didn't mean to speak aloud. I was thinking of something—of a conversation with a man named Freddy Kebble."

"Maury Kebble's brother?"

"Yes," she said, rather surprised to think of him having known Maury Kebble. Still there was nothing strange about it. "Well, he and I were talking about sweetness a few weeks ago. Oh, I don't know—I said that a man named Howard— that a man I knew was sweet, and he didn't agree with me, and we began talking about what sweetness in a man was. He kept telling me I meant a sort of soppy softness, but I knew I didn't—yet I didn't know exactly how to put it. I see now. I meant just the opposite. I suppose real sweetness is a sort of hardness—and strength."

Kieth nodded.

"I see what you mean. I've known old priests who had it."

"I'm talking about young men," she said, rather defiantly.

"Oh!"

They had reached the now deserted baseball diamond and, pointing her to a wooden bench, he sprawled full length on the grass.

"Are these *young* men happy here, Kieth?"

"Don't they look happy, Lois?"

"I suppose so, but those *young* ones, those two we just passed—have they—are they—"

"Are they signed up?" he laughed. "No, but they will be next month."

"Permanently?"

"Yes—unless they break down mentally or physically. Of course in a discipline like ours a lot drop out."

"But those *boys*. Are they giving up fine chances outside— like you did?"

He nodded.

"Some of them."

"But, Kieth, they don't know what they're doing. They haven't had any experience of what they're missing."

"No, I suppose not."

"It doesn't seem fair. Life has just sort of scared them at first. Do they all come in so *young*?"

"No, some of them have knocked around, led pretty wild lives—Regan, for instance."

"I should think that sort would be better," she said meditatively, "men that had *seen* life."

"No," said Kieth earnestly, "I'm not sure that knocking about gives a man the sort of experience he can communicate to others. Some of the broadest men I've known have been absolutely rigid about themselves. And reformed libertines are a notoriously intolerant class. Don't you think so, Lois?"

She nodded, still meditative, and he continued:

"It seems to me that when one weak person goes to another, it isn't help they want; it's a sort of companionship in guilt, Lois. After you were born, when mother began to get nervous she used to go and weep with a certain Mrs. Comstock. Lord, it used to make me shiver. She said it comforted her, poor old mother. No, I don't think that to help others you've got to show yourself at all. Real help comes from a stronger person whom you respect. And their sympathy is all the bigger because it's impersonal."

"But people want human sympathy," objected Lois. "They want to feel the other person's been tempted."

"Lois, in their hearts they want to feel that the other person's been weak. That's what they mean by human.

"Here in this old monkery, Lois," he continued with a smile, "they try to get all that self-pity and pride in our own wills out of us right at the first. They put us to scrubbing floors—and other things. It's like that idea of saving your life by losing it. You see we sort of feel that the less human a man is, in your sense of human, the better servant he can be to humanity. We carry it out to the end, too. When one of us dies his family can't even have him then. He's buried here under a plain wooden cross with a thousand others."

His tone changed suddenly and he looked at her with a great brightness in his gray eyes.

"But way back in a man's heart there are some things he can't get rid of—and one of them is that I'm awfully in love with my little sister."

With a sudden impulse she knelt beside him in the grass and, leaning over, kissed his forehead.

"You're hard, Kieth," she said, "and I love you for it—and you're sweet."

III

Back in the reception-room Lois met a half-dozen more of Kieth's particular friends; there was a young man named Jarvis, rather pale and delicate-looking, who, she knew, must be a grandson of old Mrs. Jarvis at home, and she mentally compared this ascetic with a brace of his riotous uncles.

And there was Regan with a scarred face and piercing intent eyes that followed her about the room and often rested on Kieth with something very like worship. She knew then what Kieth had meant about "a good man to have with you in a fight."

He's the missionary type—she thought vaguely—China or something.

"I want Kieth's sister to show us what the shimmy is," demanded one young man with a broad grin.

Lois laughed.

"I'm afraid the Father Rector would send me shimmying out the gate. Besides, I'm not an expert."

"I'm sure it wouldn't be best for Jimmy's soul anyway," said Kieth solemnly. "He's inclined to brood about things like shimmys. They were just starting to do the—maxixe, wasn't it, Jimmy?—when he became monk, and it haunted him his whole first year. You'd see him when he was peeling potatoes, putting his arm around the bucket and making irreligious motions with his feet."

There was a general laugh in which Lois joined.

"An old lady who comes here to Mass sent Kieth this ice-cream," whispered Jarvis under cover of the laugh, "because she'd heard you were coming. It's pretty good, isn't it?"

There were tears trembling in Lois' eyes.

IV

Then half an hour later over in the chapel things suddenly went all wrong. It was several years since Lois had been at Benediction and at first she was thrilled by the gleaming monstrance with its central spot of white, the air rich and heavy with incense, and the sun shining through the stained-glass window of St. Francis Xavier overhead and falling in warm red tracery on the cassock of the man in front of her, but at the first notes of the *"O Salutaris Hostia"* a heavy weight seemed to descend upon her soul. Kieth was on her right and young Jarvis on her left, and she stole uneasy glances at both of them.

What's the matter with me? she thought impatiently.

She looked again. Was there a certain coldness in both their profiles that she had not noticed before—a pallor about the mouth and a curious set expression in their eyes? She shivered slightly: they were like dead men.

She felt her soul recede suddenly from Kieth's. This was her brother—this, this unnatural person. She caught herself in the act of a little laugh.

"What is the matter with me?"

She passed her hand over her eyes and the weight increased. The incense sickened her and a stray, ragged note from one of the tenors in the choir grated on her ear like the shriek of a slate-pencil. She fidgeted, and raising her hand to her hair touched her forehead, found moisture on it.

"It's hot in here, hot as the deuce."

Again she repressed a faint laugh, and then in an instant the weight upon her heart suddenly diffused into cold fear. . . . It was that candle on the altar. It was all wrong—wrong. Why didn't somebody see it? There was something *in* it. There was something coming out of it, taking form and shape above it.

She tried to fight down her rising panic, told herself it was the wick. If the wick wasn't straight, candles did something—but they didn't do this! With incalculable rapidity a force was gathering within her, a tremendous, assimilative force, drawing from every sense, every corner of her brain, and as it surged up inside her she felt an enormous, terrified repulsion. She drew her arms in close to her sides, away from Kieth and Jarvis.

Something in that candle . . . she was leaning forward—in another moment she felt she would go forward toward it—didn't any one see it? . . . anyone?

"Ugh!"

She felt a space beside her and something told her that Jarvis had gasped and sat down very suddenly . . . then she was kneeling and as the flaming monstrance slowly left the altar in the hands of the priest, she heard a great rushing noise in her ears—the crash of the bells was like hammer-blows ... and then in a moment that seemed eternal a great torrent rolled over her heart—there was a shouting there and a lashing as of waves ...

... She was calling, felt herself calling for Kieth, her lips mouthing the words that would not come:

"Kieth! Oh, my God! *Kieth!*"

Suddenly she became aware of a new presence, something external, in front of her, consummated and expressed in warm red tracery. Then she knew. It was the window of St. Francis Xavier. Her mind gripped at it, clung to it finally, and she felt herself calling again endlessly, impotently—Kieth—Kieth!

Then out of a great stillness came a voice:

"Blessed be God."

With a gradual rumble sounded the response rolling heavily through the chapel:

"Blessed be God."

The words sang instantly in her heart; the incense lay mystically and sweetly peaceful upon the air, and *the candle on the altar went out*.

"Blessed be His Holy Name."

"Blessed be His Holy Name."

Every thing blurred into a swinging mist. With a sound half-gasp, half-cry she rocked on her feet and reeled backward into Kieth's suddenly outstretched arms.

V

"Lie still, child."

She closed her eyes again. She was on the grass outside, pillowed on Kieth's arm, and Regan was dabbing her head with a cold towel.

"I'm all right," she said quietly.

"I know, but just lie still a minute longer. It was too hot in there. Jarvis felt it, too."

She laughed as Regan again touched her gingerly with the towel.

"I'm all right," she repeated.

But though a warm peace was filling her mind and heart she felt oddly broken and chastened, as if some one had held her stripped soul up and laughed.

VI

Half an hour later she walked leaning on Kieth's arm down the long central path toward the gate.

"It's been such a short afternoon," he sighed, "and I'm so sorry you were sick, Lois."

"Kieth, I'm feeling fine now, really; I wish you wouldn't worry."

"Poor old child. I didn't realize that Benediction'd be a long service for you after your hot trip out here and all."

She laughed cheerfully.

"I guess the truth is I'm not much used to Benediction. Mass is the limit of my religious exertions."

She paused and then continued quickly:

"I don't want to shock you, Kieth, but I can't tell you how—how *inconvenient* being a Catholic is. It really doesn't seem to apply any more. As far as morals go, some of the wildest boys I know are Catholics. And the brightest boys—I mean the ones who think and read a lot, don't seem to believe in much of anything any more."

"Tell me about it. The bus won't be here for another half-hour."

They sat down on a bench by the path.

"For instance, Gerald Carter, he's published a novel. He absolutely roars when people mention immortality. And then Howa—well, another man I've known well, lately, who was Phi Beta Kappa at Harvard, says that no intelligent person can believe in Supernatural Christianity. He says Christ was a great socialist, though. Am I shocking you?"

She broke off suddenly.

Kieth smiled.

"You can't shock a monk. He's a professional shock-absorber."

"Well," she continued, "that's about all. It seems so—so *narrow*. Church schools, for instance. There's more freedom about things that Catholic people can't see—like birth control."

Kieth winced, almost imperceptibly, but Lois saw it.

"Oh," she said quickly, "everybody talks about everything now."

"It's probably better that way."

"Oh, yes, much better. Well, that's all, Kieth. I just wanted to tell you why I'm a little—lukewarm, at present."

"I'm not shocked, Lois. I understand better than you think. We all go through those times. But I know it'll come out all right, child. There's that gift of faith that we have, you and I, that'll carry us past the bad spots."

He rose as he spoke and they started again down the path.

"I want you to pray for me sometimes, Lois. I think your prayers would be about what I need. Because we've come very close in these few hours, I think."

Her eyes were suddenly shining.

"Oh, we have, we have!" she cried. "I feel closer to you now than to any one in the world."

He stopped suddenly and indicated the side of the path.

"We might—just a minute—"

It was a pietà, a life-size statue of the Blessed Virgin set within a semicircle of rocks.

Feeling a little self-conscious she dropped on her knees beside him and made an unsuccessful attempt at prayer.

She was only half through when he rose. He took her arm again.

"I wanted to thank Her for letting us have this day together," he said simply.

Lois felt a sudden lump in her throat and she wanted to say something that would tell him how much it had meant to her, too. But she found no words.

"I'll always remember this," he continued, his voice trembling a little—"this summer day with you. It's been just what I expected. You're just what I expected, Lois."

"I'm awfully glad, Kieth."

"You see, when you were little they kept sending me snapshots of you, first as a baby and then as a child in socks playing on the beach with a pail and shovel, and then suddenly as a wistful little girl with wondering, pure eyes—and I used to build dreams about you. A man has to have something living to cling to. I think, Lois, it was your little white soul I tried to keep near me—even when life was at its loudest and every intellectual idea of God seemed the sheerest mockery, and desire and love and a million things came up to me and said: 'Look here at me! See, I'm Life. You're turning your back on it!' All the way through that shadow, Lois, I could always see your baby soul flitting on ahead of me, very frail and clear and wonderful."

Lois was crying softly. They had reached the gate and she rested her elbow on it and dabbed furiously at her eyes.

"And then later, child, when you were sick I knelt all one night and asked God to spare you for me—for I knew then that I wanted more; He had taught me to want more. I wanted to know you moved and breathed in the same world with me. I saw you growing up, that white innocence of yours changing to a flame and burning to give light to other weaker souls. And then I wanted some day to take your children on my knee and hear them call the crabbed old monk Uncle Kieth."

He seemed to be laughing now as he talked.

"Oh, Lois, Lois, I was asking God for more then. I wanted the letters you'd write me and the place I'd have at your table. I wanted an awful lot, Lois, dear."

"You've got me, Kieth," she sobbed, "you know it, say you know it. Oh, I'm acting like a baby but I didn't think you'd be this way, and I—oh, Kieth—Kieth—"

He took her hand and patted it softly.

"Here's the bus. You'll come again, won't you?"

She put her hands on his cheeks, and drawing his head down, pressed her tear-wet face against his.

"Oh, Kieth, brother, some day I'll tell you something—"

He helped her in, saw her take down her handkerchief and smile bravely at him, as the driver flicked his whip and the bus rolled off. Then a thick cloud of dust rose around it and she was gone.

For a few minutes he stood there on the road, his hand on the gate-post, his lips half parted in a smile.

"Lois," he said aloud in a sort of wonder, "Lois, Lois."

Later, some probationers passing noticed him kneeling before the pietà, and coming back after a time found him still there. And he was there until twilight came down and the courteous trees grew garrulous overhead and the crickets took up their burden of song in the dusky grass.

VII

The first clerk in the telegraph booth in the Baltimore Station whistled through his buck teeth at the second clerk.

"S'matter?"

"See that girl—no, the pretty one with the big black dots on her veil. Too late—she's gone. You missed somep'n."

"What about her?"

"Nothing. 'Cept she's damn good-looking. Came in here yesterday and sent a wire to some guy to meet her somewhere. Then a minute ago she came in with a telegram all written out and was standin' there goin' to give it to me when she changed her mind or somep'n and all of a sudden tore it up."

"Hm."

The first clerk came around the counter and picking up the two pieces of paper from the floor put them together idly. The second clerk read them over his shoulder and subconsciously counted the words as he read. There were just thirteen.

THIS IS IN THE WAY OF A PERMANENT GOODBYE. I SHOULD SUGGEST ITALY.

LOIS.

"Tore it up, eh?" said the second clerk.

Dalyrimple Goes Wrong

I

In the millennium an educational genius will write a book to be given to every young man on the date of his disillusion. This work will have the flavor of Montaigne's essays and Samuel Butler's notebooks—and a little of Tolstoi and Marcus Aurelius. It will be neither cheerful nor pleasant but will contain numerous passages of striking humor. Since first-class minds never believe anything very strongly until they've experienced it, its value will be purely relative . . . all people over thirty will refer to it as "depressing."

This prelude belongs to the story of a young man who lived, as you and I do, before the book.

II

The generation which numbered Bryan Dalyrimple drifted out of adolescence to a mighty fanfare of trumpets. Bryan played the star in an affair which included a Lewis gun and a nine-day romp behind the retreating German lines, so luck triumphant or sentiment rampant awarded him a row of medals and on his arrival in the States he was told that he was second in importance only to General Pershing and Sergeant York. This was a lot of fun. The governor of his State, a stray congressman, and a citizens' committee gave him enormous smiles and "By God, Sirs," on the dock at Hoboken; there were newspaper reporters and photographers who said "would you mind" and "if you could just"; and back in his home town there were old ladies, the rims of whose eyes grew red as they talked to him, and girls who hadn't remembered him so well since his father's business went blah! in nineteen-twelve.

But when the shouting died he realized that for a month he had been the house guest of the mayor, that he had only four-teen dollars in the world, and that "the name that will live forever in the annals and legends of this State" was already living there very quietly and obscurely.

One morning he lay late in bed and just outside his door he heard the up-stairs maid talking to the cook. The up-stairs maid said that Mrs. Hawkins, the mayor's wife, had been trying for a week to hint Dalyrimple out of the house. He left at eleven o'clock in intolerable confusion, asking that his trunk be sent to Mrs. Beebe's boarding-house.

Dalyrimple was twenty-three and he had never worked. His father had given him two years at the State University and passed away about the time of his son's nine-day romp, leaving behind him some mid-Victorian furniture and a thin packet of folded papers that turned out to be grocery bills. Young Dalyrimple had very keen gray eyes, a mind that delighted the army psychological examiners, a trick of having read it—whatever it was—some time before, and a cool hand in a hot situation. But these things did not save him a final unresigned sigh when he realized that he had to go to work—right away.

It was early afternoon when he walked into the office of Theron G. Macy, who owned the largest wholesale grocery house in town. Plump, prosperous, wearing a pleasant but quite unhumorous smile, Theron G. Macy greeted him warmly.

"Well—how do, Bryan? What's on your mind?"

To Dalyrimple, straining with his admission, his own words, when they came, sounded like an Arab beggar's whine for alms.

"Why—this question of a job." ("This question of a job" seemed somehow more clothed than just "a job.")

"A job?" An almost imperceptible breeze blew across Mr. Macy's expression.

"You see, Mr. Macy," continued Dalyrimple, "I feel I'm wasting time. I want to get started at something. I had several chances about a month ago but they all seem to have—gone—"

"Let's see," interrupted Mr. Macy. "What were they?"

"Well, just at the first the governor said something about a vacancy on his staff. I was sort of counting on that for a while, but I hear he's given it to Allen Gregg, you know, son of G. P. Gregg. He sort of forgot what he said to me—just talking, I guess."

"You ought to push those things."

"Then there was that engineering expedition, but they decided they'd have to have a man who knew hydraulics, so they couldn't use me unless I paid my own way."

"You had just a year at the university?"

"Two. But I didn't take any science or mathematics. Well, the day the battalion paraded, Mr. Peter Jordan said something about a vacancy in his store. I went around there to-day and I found he meant a sort of floor-walker—and then you said something one day"—he paused and waited for the older man to take him up, but noting only a minute wince continued—"about a position, so I thought I'd come and see you."

"There was a position," confessed Mr. Macy reluctantly, "but since then we've filled it." He cleared his throat again. "You've waited quite a while."

"Yes, I suppose I did. Everybody told me there was no hurry—and I'd had these various offers."

Mr. Macy delivered a paragraph on present-day opportunities which Dalyrimple's mind completely skipped.

"Have you had any business experience?"

"I worked on a ranch two summers as a rider."

"Oh, well," Mr. Macy disparaged this neatly, and then continued: "What do you think you're worth?"

"I don't know."

"Well, Bryan, I tell you, I'm willing to strain a point and give you a chance."

Dalyrimple nodded.

"Your salary won't be much. You'll start by learning the stock. Then you'll come in the office for a while. Then you'll go on the road. When could you begin?"

"How about to-morrow?"

"All right. Report to Mr. Hanson in the stock-room. He'll start you off."

He continued to regard Dalyrimple steadily until the latter, realizing that the interview was over, rose awkwardly.

"Well, Mr. Macy, I'm certainly much obliged."

"That's all right. Glad to help you, Bryan."

After an irresolute moment, Dalyrimple found himself in the hall. His forehead was covered with perspiration, and the room had not been hot.

"Why the devil did I thank the son of a gun?" he muttered.

III

Next morning Mr. Hanson informed him coldly of the necessity of punching the time-clock at seven every morning, and delivered him for instruction into the hands of a fellow workers, one Charley Moore.

Charley was twenty-six, with that faint musk of weakness hanging about him that is often mistaken for the scent of evil. It took no psychological examiner to decide that he had drifted into indulgence and laziness as casually as he had drifted into life, and was to drift out. He was pale and his clothes stank of smoke; he enjoyed burlesque shows, billiards, and Robert Service, and was always looking back upon his last intrigue or forward to his next one. In his youth his taste had run to loud ties, but now it seemed to have faded, like his vitality, and was expressed in pale-lilac four-in-hands and indeterminate gray collars. Charley was listlessly struggling that losing struggle against mental, moral, and physical anaemia that takes place ceaselessly on the lower fringe of the middle classes.

The first morning he stretched himself on a row of cereal cartons and carefully went over the limitations of the Theron G. Macy Company.

"It's a piker organization. My Gosh! Lookit what they give me. I'm quittin' in a coupla months. Hell! Me stay with this bunch!"

The Charley Moores are always going to change jobs next month. They do, once or twice in their careers, after which they sit around comparing their last job with the present one, to the infinite disparagement of the latter.

"What do you get?" asked Dalyrimple curiously.

"Me? I get sixty." This rather defiantly.

"Did you start at sixty."

"Me? No, I started at thirty-five. He told me he'd put me on the road after I learned the stock. That's what he tells 'em all!"

"How long've you been here?" asked Dalyrimple with a sinking sensation.

"Me? Four years. My last year, too, you bet your boots."

Dalyrimple rather resented the presence of the store detective as he resented the time-clock, and he came into contact with him almost immediately through the rule against smoking. This rule was a thorn in his side. He was accustomed to

his three or four cigarettes in a morning, and after three days
without it he followed Charley Moore by a circuitous route
up a flight of back stairs to a little balcony where they in-
dulged in peace. But this was not for long. One day in his
second week the detective met him in a nook of the stairs, on
his descent, and told him sternly that next time he'd be reported to Mr. Macy. Dalyrimple felt like an errant schoolboy.

Unpleasant facts came to his knowledge. There were
'cave-dwellers" in the basement who had worked there for
ten or fifteen years at sixty dollars a month, rolling barrels
and carrying boxes through damp, cement-walled corridors,
lost in that echoing half-darkness between seven and five-
thirty and, like himself, compelled several times a month to
work until nine at night.

At the end of a month he stood in line and received forty
dollars. He pawned a cigarette-case and a pair of field-glasses
and managed to live—to eat, sleep, and smoke. It was, however, a narrow scrape; as the ways and means of economy
were a closed book to him and the second month brought no
increase, he voiced his alarm.

"If you've got a drag with old Macy, maybe he'll raise
you," was Charley's disheartening reply. "But he didn't raise
me till I'd been here nearly two years."

"I've got to live," said Dalyrimple simply. "I could get
more pay as a laborer on the railroad but, Golly, I want to
feel I'm where there's a chance to get ahead."

Charles shook his head sceptically and Mr. Macy's answer
next day was equally unsatisfactory.

Dalyrimple had gone to the office just before closing time.

"Mr. Macy, I'd like to speak to you."

"Why—yes." The unhumorous smile appeared. The voice
was faintly resentful.

"I want to speak to you in regard to more salary."

Mr. Macy nodded.

"Well," he said doubtfully, "I don't know exactly what
you're doing. I'll speak to Mr. Hanson."

He knew exactly what Dalyrimple was doing, and
Dalyrimple knew he knew.

"I'm in the stock-room—and, sir, while I'm here I'd like to
ask you how much longer I'll have to stay there."

"Why—I'm not sure exactly. Of course it takes some time
to learn the stock."

"You told me two months when I started."

"Yes. Well, I'll speak to Mr. Hanson."

Dalyrimple paused, irresolute.

"Thank you, sir."

Two days later he again appeared in the office with the result of a count that had been asked for by Mr. Hesse, the
bookkeeper. Mr. Hesse was engaged and Dalyrimple, waiting,
began idly fingering a ledger on the stenographer's desk.

Half unconsciously he turned a page—he caught sight of
his name—it was a salary list:

Dalyrimple
Demming
Donahoe
Everett

His eyes stopped—

Everett $60

So Tom Everett, Macy's weak-chinned nephew, had started
at sixty—and in three weeks he had been out of the packing-
room and into the office.

So that was it! He was to sit and see man after man pushed
over him: sons, cousins, sons of friends, irrespective of their ca-
pabilities, while *he* was cast for a pawn, with "going on the
road" dangled before his eyes—put off with the stock remark:
"I'll see; I'll look into it." At forty, perhaps, he would be a
bookkeeper like old Hesse, tired, listless Hesse with dull routine
for his stint and a dull background of boarding-house conversation.

This was a moment when a genii should have pressed into
his hand the book for disillusioned young men. But the book
has not been written.

A great protest swelling into revolt surged up in him. Ideas
half forgotten, chaotically perceived and assimilated, filled his
mind. Get on—that was the rule of life—and that was all. How
he did it, didn't matter—but to be Hesse or Charley Moore.

"I won't!" he cried aloud.

The bookkeeper and the stenographers looked up in surprise.

"What?"

For a second Dalyrimple stared—then walked up to the desk.

"Here's that data," he said brusquely. "I can't wait any longer."

Mr. Hesse's face expressed surprise.

It didn't matter what he did—just so he got out of this rut. In a dream he stepped from the elevator into the stock-room, and walking to an unused aisle, sat down on a box, covering his face with his hands.

His brain was whirring with the frightful jar of discovering a platitude for himself.

"I've got to get out of this," he said aloud and then repeated, "I've got to get out"—and he didn't mean only out of Macy's wholesale house.

When he left at five-thirty it was pouring rain, but he struck off in the opposite direction from his boarding-house, feeling, in the first cool moisture that oozed soggily through his old suit, an odd exultation and freshness. He wanted a world that was like walking through rain, even though he could not see far ahead of him, but fate had put him in the world of Mr. Macy's fetid storerooms and corridors. At first merely the overwhelming need of change took him, then half-plans began to formulate in his imagination.

"I'll go East—to a big city—meet people—bigger people—people who'll help me. Interesting work somewhere. My God, there *must* be."

With sickening truth it occurred to him that his facility for meeting people was limited. Of all places it was here in his own own that he should be known, was known—famous—before the waters of oblivion had rolled over him.

You had to cut corners, that was all. Pull—relationship—wealthy marriages—

For several miles the continued reiteration of this preoccupied him and then he perceived that the rain had become thicker and more opaque in the heavy gray of twilight and that the houses were falling away. The district of full blocks, then of big houses, then of scattering little ones, passed and great sweeps of misty country opened out on both sides. It was hard walking here. The sidewalk had given place to a dirt road, streaked with furious brown rivulets that splashed and squashed around his shoes.

Cutting corners—the words began to fall apart, forming curious phrasings—little illuminated pieces of themselves. They resolved into sentences, each of which had a strangely familiar ring.

Cutting corners meant rejecting the old childhood principles that success came from faithfulness to duty, that evil was necessarily punished or virtue necessarily rewarded—that honest poverty was happier than corrupt riches.

It meant being hard.

This phrase appealed to him and he repeated it over and over. It had to do somehow with Mr. Macy and Charley Moore—the attitudes, the methods of each of them.

He stopped and felt his clothes. He was drenched to the skin. He looked about him and, selecting a place in the fence where a tree sheltered it, perched himself there.

In my credulous years—he thought—they told me that evil was a sort of dirty hue, just as definite as a soiled collar, but it seems to me that evil is only a manner of hard luck, or heredity-and-environment, or "being found out." It hides in the vacillations of dubs like Charley Moore as certainly as it does in the intolerance of Macy, and if it ever gets much more tangible it becomes merely an arbitrary label to paste on the unpleasant things in other people's lives.

In fact—he concluded—it isn't worth worrying over what's evil and what isn't. Good and evil aren't any standard to me—and they can be a devil of a bad hindrance when I want something. When I want something bad enough, common sense tells me to go and take it—and not get caught.

And then suddenly Dalyrimple knew what he wanted first. He wanted fifteen dollars to pay his overdue board bill.

With a furious energy he jumped from the fence, whipped off his coat, and from its black lining cut with his knife a piece about five inches square. He made two holes near its edge and then fixed it on his face, pulling his hat down to hold it in place. It flapped grotesquely and then dampened and clung to his forehead and cheeks.

Now ... The twilight had merged to dripping dusk ... black as pitch. He began to walk quickly back toward town, not waiting to remove the mask but watching the road with difficulty through the jagged eye-holes. He was not conscious of any nervousness ... the only tension was caused by a desire to do the thing as soon as possible.

He reached the first sidewalk, continued on until he saw a hedge far from any lamp-post, and turned in behind it. Within a minute he heard several series of footsteps—he waited—it was a woman and he held his breath until she passed ... and then a man, a laborer. The next passer, he felt, would be what

he wanted . . . the laborer's footfalls died far up the drenched
street . . . other steps grew near, grew suddenly louder.

Dalyrimple braced himself.

"Put up your hands!"

The man stopped, uttered an absurd little grunt, and thrust
pudgy arms skyward.

Dalyrimple went through the waistcoat.

"Now, you shrimp," he said, setting his hand suggestively
to his own hip pocket, "you run, and stamp—loud! If I hear
your feet stop I'll put a shot after you!"

Then he stood there in sudden uncontrollable laughter as
audibly frightened footsteps scurried away into the night.

After a moment he thrust the roll of bills into his pocket,
snatched off his mask, and running quickly across the street,
darted down an alley.

IV

Yet, however Dalyrimple justified himself intellectually, he
had many bad moments in the weeks immediately following
his decision. The tremendous pressure of sentiment and inherited tradition kept raising riot with his attitude. He felt morally lonely.

The noon after his first venture he ate in a little lunch-room
with Charley Moore and, watching him unspread the paper,
waited for a remark about the hold-up of the day before. But either the hold-up was not mentioned or Charley wasn't interested.
He turned listlessly to the sporting sheet, read Doctor Crane's
crop of seasoned bromides, took in an editorial on ambition with
his mouth slightly ajar, and then skipped to Mutt and Jeff.

Poor Charley—with his faint aura of evil and his mind that
refused to focus, playing a lifeless solitaire with cast-off mis-
chief.

Yet Charley belonged on the other side of the fence. In him
could be stirred up all the flamings and denunciations of righteousness; he would weep at a stage heroine's lost virtue, he
could become lofty and contemptuous at the idea of dishonor.

On my side, thought Dalyrimple, there aren't any resting-
places; a man who's a strong criminal is after the weak crim-
inals as well, so it's all guerilla warfare over here.

What will it all do to me? he thought, with a persistent
wariness. Will it take the color out of life with the honor?
Will it scatter my courage and dull my mind?—despiritualize

me completely—does it mean eventual barrenness, eventual remorse, failure?

With a great surge of anger, he would fling his mind upon the barrier—and stand there with the flashing bayonet of his pride. Other men who broke the laws of justice and charity lied to all the world. He at any rate would not lie to himself. He was more than Byronic now: not the spiritual rebel, Don Juan; not the philosophical rebel, Faust; but a new psychological rebel of his own century—defying the sentimental a priori forms of his own mind—

Happiness was what he wanted—a slowly rising scale of gratifications of the normal appetites—and he had a strong conviction that the materials, if not the inspiration of happiness, could be bought with money.

V

The night came that drew him out upon his second venture, and as he walked the dark street he felt in himself a great resemblance to a cat—a certain supple, swinging litheness. His muscles were rippling smoothly and sleekly under his spare, healthy flesh—he had an absurd desire to bound along the street, to run dodging among trees, to turn "cart-wheels" over soft grass.

It was not crisp, but in the air lay a faint suggestion of acerbity, inspirational rather than chilling.

"The moon is down—I have not heard the clock!"

He laughed in delight at the line which an early memory had endowed with a hushed, awesome beauty.

He passed a man, and then another a quarter of a mile afterward.

He was on Philmore Street now and it was very dark. He blessed the city council for not having put in new lamp-posts as a recent budget had recommended. Here was the red-brick Sterner residence which marked the beginning of the avenue; here was the Jordon house, the Eisenhaurs', the Dents', the Markhams', the Frasers'; the Hawkins, where he had been a guest; the Willoughbys', the Everetts', colonial and ornate; the little cottage where lived the Watts old maids between the imposing fronts of the Macy's' and the Kruptstadts'; the Craigs'—

Ah . . . *there*! He paused, wavered violently—far up the street was a blot, a man walking, possibly a policeman. After an eternal second he found himself following the vague, ragged shadow of a lamp-post across a lawn, running bent very low. Then he was standing tense, without breath or need of it, in the shadow of his limestone prey.

Interminably he listened—a mile off a cat howled, a hundred yards away another took up the hymn in a demoniacal snarl, and he felt his heart dip and swoop, acting as shock-absorber for his mind. There were other sounds; the faintest fragment of song far away; strident, gossiping laughter from a back porch diagonally across the alley; and crickets, crickets singing in the patched, patterned, moonlit grass of the yard. Within the house there seemed to lie an ominous silence. He was glad he did not know who lived here.

His slight shiver hardened to steel; the steel softened and his nerves became pliable as leather; gripping his hands he gratefully found them supple, and taking out knife and pliers he went to work on the screen.

So sure was he that he was unobserved that, from the dining-room where in a minute he found himself, he leaned out and carefully pulled the screen up into position, balancing it so it would neither fall by chance nor be a serious obstacle to a sudden exit.

Then he put the open knife in his coat pocket, took out his pocket-flash, and tiptoed around the room.

There was nothing here he could use—the dining-room had never been included in his plans, for the town was too small to permit disposing of silver.

As a matter of fact his plans were of the vaguest. He had found that with a mind like his, lucrative in intelligence, intuition, and lightning decision, it was best to have but the skeleton of a campaign. The machine-gun episode had taught him that. And he was afraid that a method preconceived would give him two points of view in a crisis—and two points of view meant wavering.

He stumbled slightly on a chair, held his breath, listened, went on, found the hall, found the stairs, started up; the seventh stair creaked at his step, the ninth, the fourteenth. He was counting them automatically. At the third creak he paused again for over a minute—and in that minute he felt more alone than he had ever felt before. Between the lines on patrol, even when alone, he had had behind him the moral support of half a billion people; now he was alone, pitted against that same moral pressure—a bandit. He had never felt this fear, yet he had never felt this exultation.

The stairs came to an end, a doorway approached; he went in

and listened to regular breathing. His feet were economical of steps and his body swayed sometimes at stretching as he felt over the bureau, pocketing all articles which held promise—he could not have enumerated them ten seconds afterward. He felt on a chair for possible trousers, found soft garments, women's lingerie. The corners of his mouth smiled mechanically.

Another room . . . the same breathing, enlivened by one ghastly snort that sent his heart again on its tour of his breast. Round object—watch; chain; roll of bills; stick-pins; two rings—he remembered that he had got rings from the other bureau. He started out, winced as a faint glow flashed in front of him, facing him. God!—it was the glow of his own wrist-watch on his outstretched arm.

Down the stairs. He skipped two creaking steps but found another. He was all right now, practically safe; as he neared the bottom he felt a slight boredom. He reached the dining-room—considered the silver—again decided against it.

Back in his room at the boarding-house he examined the additions to his personal property:

Sixty-five dollars in bills.

A platinum ring with three medium diamonds, worth, probably, about seven hundred dollars. Diamonds were going up.

A cheap gold-plated ring with the initials O. S. and the date inside—'03—probably a class-ring from school. Worth a few dollars. Unsalable.

A red-cloth case containing a set of false teeth.

A silver watch.

A gold chain worth more than the watch.

An empty ring-box.

A little ivory Chinese god—probably a desk ornament.

A dollar and sixty-two cents in small change.

He put the money under his pillow and the other things in the toe of an infantry boot, stuffing a stocking in on top of them. Then for two hours his mind raced like a high-power engine here and there through his life, past and future, through fear and laughter. With a vague, inopportune wish that he were married, he fell into a deep sleep about half past five.

VI

Though the newspaper account of the burglary failed to mention the false teeth, they worried him considerably. The picture of a human waking in the cool dawn and groping for them in vain, of a soft, toothless breakfast, of a strange, hollow, lisping voice calling the police station, of weary, dispirited visits to the dentist, roused a great fatherly pity in him.

Trying to ascertain whether they belonged to a man or a woman, he took them carefully out of the case and held them up near his mouth. He moved his own jaws experimentally; he measured with his fingers; but he failed to decide: they might belong either to a large-mouthed woman or a small-mouthed man.

On a warm impulse he wrapped them in brown paper from the bottom of his army trunk, and printed FALSE TEETH on the package in clumsy pencil letters. Then, the next night, he walked down Philmore Street, and shied the package onto the lawn so that it would be near the door. Next day the paper announced that the police had a clew—they knew that the burglar was in town. However, they didn't mention what the clew was.

VII

At the end of a month "Burglar Bill of the Silver District" was the nurse-girl's standby for frightening children. Five burglaries were attributed to him, but though Dalyrimple had only committed three, he considered that majority had it and appropriated the title to himself. He had once been seen—"a large bloated creature with the meanest face you ever laid eyes on." Mrs. Henry Coleman, awaking at two o'clock at the beam of an electric torch flashed in her eye, could not have been expected to recognize Bryan Dalyrimple at whom she had waved flags last Fourth of July, and whom she had described as "not at all the daredevil type, do you think?"

When Dalyrimple kept his imagination at white heat he managed to glorify his own attitude, his emancipation from petty scruples and remorses—but let him once allow his thought to rove unarmored, great unexpected horrors and depressions would overtake him. Then for reassurance he had to go back to think out the whole thing over again. He found that it was on the whole better to give up considering himself as a rebel. It was more consoling to think of everyone else as a fool.

His attitude toward Mr. Macy underwent a change. He no longer felt a dim animosity and inferiority in his presence. As his fourth month in the store ended he found himself regarding his employer in a manner that was almost fraternal. He had a vague but very assured conviction that Mr. Macy's innermost soul would have abetted and approved. He no longer worried about his future. He had the intention of accumulating several thousand dollars and then clearing out—going east, back to France, down to South America. Half a dozen times in the last two months he had been about to stop work, but a fear of attracting attention to his being in funds prevented him. So he worked on, no longer in listlessness, but with contemptuous amusement.

VIII

Then with astounding suddenness something happened that changed his plans and put an end to his burglaries.

Mr. Macy sent for him one afternoon and with a great show of jovial mystery asked him if he had an engagement that night. If he hadn't, would he please call on Mr. Alfred J. Fraser at eight o'clock. Dalyrimple's wonder was mingled with uncertainty. He debated with himself whether it were not his cue to take the first train out of town. But an hour's consideration decided him that his fears were unfounded and at eight o'clock he arrived at the big Fraser house in Philmore Avenue.

Mr. Fraser was commonly supposed to be the biggest political influence in the city. His brother was Senator Fraser, his son-in-law was Congressman Demming, and his influence, though not wielded in such a way as to make him an objectionable boss, was strong nevertheless.

He had a great, huge face, deep-set eyes, and a barn-door of an upper lip, the melange approaching a worthy climax in a long professional jaw.

During his conversation with Dalyrimple his expression kept starting toward a smile, reached a cheerful optimism, and then receded back to imperturbability.

"How do you do, sir?" he said, holding out his hand. "Sit down. I suppose you're wondering why I wanted you. Sit down."

Dalyrimple sat down.

"Mr. Dalyrimple, how old are you?"

"I'm twenty-three."

"You're young. But that doesn't mean you're foolish. Mr. Dalyrimple, what I've got to say won't take long. I'm going to make you a proposition. To begin at the beginning, I've been watching you ever since last Fourth of July when you made that speech in response to the loving-cup."

Dalyrimple murmured disparagingly, but Fraser waved him to silence.

"It was a speech I've remembered. It was a brainy speech, straight from the shoulder, and it got to everybody in that crowd. I know. I've watched crowds for years." He cleared his throat, as if tempted to digress on his knowledge of crowds— then continued. "But, Mr. Dalyrimple, I've seen too many young men who promised brilliantly go to pieces, fail through want of steadiness, too many high-power ideas, and not enough willingness to work. So I waited. I wanted to see what you'd do. I wanted to see if you'd go to work, and if you'd stick to what you started."

Dalyrimple felt a glow settle over him.

"So," continued Fraser, "when Theron Macy told me you'd started down at his place, I kept watching you, and I followed your record through him. The first month I was afraid for a while. He told me you were getting restless, too good for your job, hinting around for a raise—"

Dalyrimple started.

"—But he said after that you evidently made up your mind to shut up and stick to it. That's the stuff I like in a young man! That's the stuff that wins out. And don't think I don't understand. I know how much harder it was for you, after all that silly flattery a lot of old women had been giving you. I know what a fight it must have been—"

Dalyrimple's face was burning brightly. He felt young and strangely ingenuous.

"Dalyrimple, you've got brains and you've got the stuff in you—and that's what I want. I'm going to put you into the State Senate."

"The *what*?"

"The State Senate. We want a young man who has got brains, but is solid and not a loafer. And when I say State Senate I don't stop there. We're up against it here, Dalyrimple. We've got to get some young men into politics— you know the old blood that's been running on the party ticket year in and year out."

Dalyrimple licked his lips.

"You'll run me for the State Senate?"

"I'll *put* you in the State Senate?" Mr. Fraser's expression had now reached the point nearest a smile and Dalyrimple in a happy frivolity felt himself urging it mentally on—but it stopped, locked, and slid from him. The barn-door and the jaw were separated by a line straight as a nail. Dalyrimple remembered with an effort that it was a mouth, and talked to it.

"But I'm through," he said. "My notoriety's dead. People are fed up with me."

"Those things," answered Mr. Fraser, "are mechanical. Linotype is a resuscitator of reputations. Wait till you see the *Herald,* beginning next week—that is if you're with us—that is," and his voice hardened slightly, "if you haven't got too many ideas yourself about how things ought to be run."

"No," said Dalyrimple, looking him frankly in the eyes. "You'll have to give me a lot of advice at first."

"Very well. I'll take care of your reputation then. Just keep yourself on the right side of the fence."

Dalyrimple started at this repetition of a phrase he had thought of so much lately. There was a sudden ring of the door-bell.

"That's Macy now," observed Fraser, rising. "I'll go let him in. The servants have gone to bed."

He left Dalyrimple there in a dream. The world was opening up suddenly—The State Senate, the United States Senate—so life was this after all—cutting corners—cutting corners—common sense, that was the rule. No more foolish risks now unless necessity called—but it was being hard that counted—Never to let remorse or self-reproach lose him a night's sleep—let his life be a sword of courage—there was no payment—all that was drivel—drivel. He sprang to his feet with clenched hands in a sort of triumph.

"Well, Bryan," said Mr. Macy stepping through the portières. The two older men smiled their half-smiles at him.

"Well, Bryan," said Mr. Macy again.

Dalyrimple smiled also.

"How do, Mr. Macy?"

He wondered if some telepathy between them had made this new appreciation possible—some invisible realization. . . .

Mr. Macy held out his hand.

"I'm glad we're to be associated in this scheme—I've been for you all along—especially lately. I'm glad we're to be on the same side of the fence."

"I want to thank you, sir," said Dalyrimple simply. He felt a whimsical moisture gathering back of his eyes.

The Four Fists

I

At the present time no one I know has the slightest desire to hit Samuel Meredith; possibly this is because a man over fifty is liable to be rather severely cracked at the impact of a hostile fist, but, for my part, I am inclined to think that all his hitable qualities have quite vanished. But it is certain that at various times in his life hitable qualities were in his face, as surely as kissable qualities have ever lurked in a girl's lips.

I'm sure everyone has met a man like that, been casually introduced, even made a friend of him, yet felt he was the sort who aroused passionate dislike—expressed by some in the involuntary clenching of fists, and in others by mutterings about "takin' a poke" and "landin' a swift smash in ee eye." In the juxtaposition of Samuel Meredith's features this quality was so strong that it influenced his entire life.

What was it? Not the shape, certainly, for he was a pleasant-looking man from earliest youth: broad-browed, with gray eyes that were frank and friendly. Yet I've heard him tell a room full of reporters angling for a "success" story that he'd be ashamed to tell them the truth, that they wouldn't believe it, that it wasn't one story but four, that the public would not want to read about a man who had been walloped into prominence.

It all started at Phillips Andover Academy when he was fourteen. He had been brought up on a diet of caviar and bell-boys' legs in half the capitals of Europe, and it was pure luck that his mother had nervous prostration and had to delegate his education to less tender, less biassed hands.

At Andover he was given a roommate named Gilly Hood. Gilly was thirteen, undersized, and rather the school pet. From the September day when Mr. Meredith's valet stowed Samuel's clothing in the best bureau and asked, on departing, "hif there was hanything helse, Master Samuel?" Gilly cried out that the faculty had played him false. He felt like an irate frog in whose bowl has been put a goldfish.

"Good gosh!" he complained to his sympathetic contemporaries, "he's a damn stuck-up Willie. He said, 'Are the crowd here gentlemen?' and I said, 'No, they're boys,' and he said age didn't matter, and I said, 'Who said it did?' Let him get fresh with me, the ole pieface!"

For three weeks Gilly endured in silence young Samuel's comments on the clothes and habits of Gilly's personal friends, endured French phrases in conversation, endured a hundred half-feminine meannesses that show what a nervous mother can do to a boy, if she keeps close enough to him—then a storm broke in the aquarium.

Samuel was out. A crowd had gathered to hear Gilly be wrathful about his roommate's latest sins.

"He said, 'Oh, I don't like the windows open at night,' he said, 'except only a little bit,' " complained Gilly.

"Don't let him boss you."

"Boss me? You bet he won't. I open those windows, I guess, but the darn fool won't take turns shuttin' 'em in the morning."

"Make him, Gilly, why don't you?"

"I'm going to." Gilly nodded his head in fierce agreement. "Don't you worry. He needn't think I'm any ole butler."

"Le's see you make him."

At this point the darn fool entered in person and included the crowd in one of his irritating smiles. Two boys said, " 'Lo, Mer'dith"; the others gave him a chilly glance and went on talking to Gilly. But Samuel seemed unsatisfied.

"Would you mind not sitting on my bed?" he suggested politely to two of Gilly's particulars who were perched very much at ease.

"Huh?"

"My bed. Can't you understand English?"

This was adding insult to injury. There were several comments on the bed's sanitary condition and the evidence within it of animal life.

"S'matter with your old bed?" demanded Gilly truculently.

"The bed's all right, but—"

Gilly interrupted this sentence by rising and walking up to Samuel. He paused several inches away and eyed him fiercely.

"You an' your crazy ole bed," he began. "You an' your crazy—"

"Go to it, Gilly," murmured some one.

"Show the darn fool—"

Samuel returned the gaze coolly.

"Well," he said finally, "it's my bed—"

He got no further, for Gilly hauled off and hit him succinctly in the nose.

"Yea! Gilly!"

"Show the big bully!"

"Just let him touch you—he'll see!"

The group closed in on them and for the first time in his life Samuel realized the insuperable inconvenience of being passionately detested. He gazed around helplessly at the glowering, violently hostile faces. He towered a head taller than his roommate, so if he hit back he'd be called a bully and have half a dozen more fights on his hands within five minutes; yet if he didn't he was a coward. For a moment he stood there facing Gilly's blazing eyes, and then, with a sudden choking sound, he forced his way through the ring and rushed from the room.

The month following bracketed the thirty most miserable days of his life. Every waking moment he was under the lashing tongues of his contemporaries; his habits and mannerisms became butts for intolerable witticisms and, of course, the sensitiveness of adolescence was a further thorn. He considered that he was a natural pariah; that the unpopularity at school would follow him through life. When he went home for the Christmas holidays he was so despondent that his father sent him to a nerve specialist. When he returned to Andover he arranged to arrive late so that he could be alone in the bus during the drive from station to school.

Of course when he had learned to keep his mouth shut every one promptly forgot all about him. The next autumn, with his realization that consideration for others was the discreet attitude, he made good use of the clean start given him by the shortness of boyhood memory. By the beginning of his senior year Samuel Meredith was one of the best-liked boys of his class—and no one was any stronger for him than his first friend and constant companion, Gilly Hood.

II

Samuel became the sort of college student who in the early nineties drove tandems and coaches and tallyhos between Princeton and Yale and New York City to show that they appreciated the social importance of football games. He believed passionately in good form—his choosing of gloves, his tying of ties, his holding of reins were imitated by impressionable freshmen. Outside of his own set he was considered rather a snob, but as his set was *the* set, it never worried him. He played football in the autumn, drank high-balls in the winter, and rowed in the spring. Samuel despised all those who were merely sportsmen without being gentlemen, or merely gentlemen without being sportsmen.

He lived in New York and often brought home several of his friends for the week-end. Those were the days of the horse-car and in case of a crush it was, of course, the proper thing for any one of Samuel's set to rise and deliver his seat to a standing lady with a formal bow. One night in Samuel's junior year he boarded a car with two of his intimates. There were three vacant seats. When Samuel sat down he noticed a heavy-eyed laboring man sitting next to him who smelt objectionably of garlic, sagged slightly against Samuel and, spreading a little as a tired man will, took up quite too much room.

The car had gone several blocks when it stopped for a quartet of young girls, and, of course, the three men of the world sprang to their feet and proffered their sets with due observance of form. Unfortunately, the laborer, being unacquainted with the code of neckties and tallyhos, failed to follow their example, and one young lady was left at an embarrassed stance. Fourteen eyes glared reproachfully at the barbarian; seven lips curled slightly; but the object of scorn stared stolidly into the foreground in sturdy unconsciousness of his despicable conduct. Samuel was the most violently affected. He was humiliated that any male should so conduct himself. He spoke aloud.

"There's a lady standing," he said sternly.

That should have been quite enough, but the object of scorn only looked up blankly. The standing girl tittered and exchanged nervous glances with her companions. But Samuel was aroused.

"There's a lady standing," he repeated, rather raspingly. The man seemed to comprehend.

"I pay my fare," he said quietly.

Samuel turned red and his hands clenched, but the conductor was looking their way, so at a warning nod from his friends he subsided into sullen gloom.

They reached their destination and left the car, but so did the laborer, who followed them, swinging his little pail. Seeing his chance, Samuel no longer resisted his aristocratic inclination. He turned around and, launching a full-featured, dime-novel sneer, made a loud remark about the right of the lower animals to ride with human beings.

In a half-second the workman had dropped his pail and let fly at him. Unprepared, Samuel took the blow neatly on the jaw and sprawled full length into the cobblestone gutter.

"Don't laugh at me!" cried his assailant. "I been workin' all day. I'm tired as hell!"

As he spoke the sudden anger died out of his eyes and the mask of weariness dropped again over his face. He turned and picked up his pail. Samuel's friends took a quick step in his direction.

"Wait!" Samuel had risen slowly and was motioning them back. Some time, somewhere, he had been struck like that before. Then he remembered—Gilly Hood. In the silence, as he dusted himself off, the whole scene in the room at Andover was before his eyes—and he knew intuitively that he had been wrong again. This man's strength, his rest, was the protection of his family. He had more use for his seat in the street-car than any young girl.

"It's all right," said Samuel gruffly. "Don't touch him. I've been a damn fool."

Of course it took more than an hour, or a week, for Samuel to rearrange his ideas on the essential importance of good form. At first he simply admitted that his wrongness had made him powerless—as it had made him powerless against Gilly—but eventually his mistake about the workman influenced his entire attitude. Snobbishness is, after all, merely good breeding grown dictatorial; so Samuel's code remained, but the necessity of imposing it upon others had faded out in a certain gutter. Within that year his class had somehow stopped referring to him as a snob.

III

After a few years Samuel's university decided that it had shone long enough in the reflected glory of his neckties, so they declaimed to him in Latin, charged him ten dollars for the paper which proved him irretrievably educated, and sent him into the turmoil with much self-confidence, a few friends, and the proper assortment of harmless bad habits.

His family had by that time started back to shirt-sleeves, through a sudden decline in the sugar-market, and it had already unbuttoned its vest, so to speak, when Samuel went to work. His mind was that exquisite *tabula rasa* that a university education sometimes leaves, but he had both energy and influence, so he used his former ability as a dodging half-back in twisting through Wall Street crowds as runner for a bank.

His diversion was—women. There were half a dozen: two or three débutantes, an actress (in a minor way), a grass-widow, and one sentimental little brunette who was married and lived in a little house in Jersey City.

They had met on a ferry-boat. Samuel was crossing from New York on business (he had been working several years by this time) and he helped her look for a package that she had dropped in the crush.

"Do you come over often?" he inquired casually.

"Just to shop," she said shyly. She had great brown eyes and the pathetic kind of little mouth. "I've only been married three months, and we find it cheaper to live over here."

"Does he—does your husband like your being alone like this?"

She laughed, a cheery young laugh.

"Oh, dear me, no. We were to meet for dinner but I must have misunderstood the place. He'll be awfully worried."

"Well," said Samuel disapprovingly, "he ought to be. If you'll allow me I'll see you home."

She accepted his offer thankfully, so they took the cable-car together. When they walked up the path to her little house they saw a light there; her husband had arrived before her.

"He's frightfully jealous," she announced, laughingly apologetic.

"Very well," answered Samuel, rather stiffly. "I'd better leave you here."

She thanked him, and waving a good night, he left her.

That would have been quite all if they hadn't met on Fifth Avenue one morning a week later. She started and blushed and seemed so glad to see him that they chatted like old friends. She was going to her dressmaker's, eat lunch alone at Taine's, shop all afternoon, and meet her husband on the ferry at five. Samuel told her that her husband was a very lucky man. She blushed again and scurried off.

Samuel whistled all the way back to his office, but about twelve o'clock he began to see that pathetic, appealing little mouth everywhere—and those brown eyes. He fidgeted when he looked at the clock; he thought of the grill down-stairs where he lunched and the heavy male conversation thereof, and opposed to that picture appeared another: a little table at Taine's with the brown eyes and the mouth a few feet away. A few minutes before twelve-thirty he dashed on his hat and rushed for the cable-car.

She was quite surprised to see him.

"Why—hello," she said. Samuel could tell that she was just pleasantly frightened.

"I thought we might lunch together. It's so dull eating with a lot of men."

She hesitated.

"Why, I suppose there's no harm in it. How could there be!"

It occurred to her that her husband should have taken lunch with her—but he was generally so hurried at noon. She told Samuel all about him: he was a little smaller than Samuel, but oh, *much* better-looking. He was a bookkeeper and not making a lot of money, but they were very happy and expected to be rich within three or four years.

Samuel's grass-widow had been in a quarrelsome mood for three or four weeks, and, through contrast, he took an accentuated pleasure in this meeting; so fresh was she, and earnest, and faintly adventurous. Her name was Marjorie.

They made another engagement; in fact, for a month they lunched together two or three times a week. When she was sure that her husband would work late Samuel took her over to New Jersey on the ferry, leaving her always on the tiny front porch, after she had gone in and lit the gas to use the security of his masculine presence outside. This grew to be a ceremony—and it annoyed him. Whenever the comfortable glow fell out through the front windows, that was his *conjé;*

yet he never suggested coming in and Marjorie didn't invite him.

Then, when Samuel and Marjorie had reached a stage in which they sometimes touched each other's arms gently, just to show that they were very good friends, Marjorie and her husband had one of those ultrasensitive, supercritical quarrels that couples never indulge in unless they care a great deal about each other. It started with a cold mutton-chop or a leak in the gas-jet—and one day Samuel found her in Taine's, with dark shadows under her brown eyes and a terrifying pout.

By this time Samuel thought he was in love with Marjorie—so he played up the quarrel for all it was worth. He was her best friend and patted her hand—and leaned down close to her brown curls while she whispered in little sobs what her husband had said that morning; and he was a little more than her best friend when he took her over to the ferry in a hansom.

"Marjorie," he said gently, when he left her, as usual, on the porch, "if at any time you want to call on me, remember that I am always waiting, always waiting."

She nodded gravely and put both her hands in his.

"I know," she said. "I know you're my friend, my best friend."

Then she ran into the house and he watched there until the gas went on.

For the next week Samuel was in a nervous turmoil. Some persistently rational strain warned him that at bottom he and Marjorie had little in common, but in such cases there is usually so much mud in the water that one can seldom see to the bottom. Every dream and desire told him that he loved Marjorie, wanted her, had to have her.

The quarrel developed. Marjorie's husband took to staying in New York until late at night, came home several times disagreeably overstimulated, and made her generally miserable. They must have had too much pride to talk it out—for Marjorie's husband was, after all, pretty decent—so it drifted on from one misunderstanding to another. Marjorie kept coming more and more to Samuel; when a woman can accept masculine sympathy it is much more satisfactory to her than crying to another girl. But Marjorie didn't realize how much she had begun to rely on him, how much he was part of her little cosmos.

One night, instead of turning away when Marjorie went in

and lit the gas, Samuel went in, too, and they sat together on the sofa in the little parlor. He was very happy. He envied their home, and he felt that the man who neglected such a possession out of stubborn pride was a fool and unworthy of his wife. But when he kissed Marjorie for the first time she cried softly and told him to go. He sailed home on the wings of desperate excitement, quite resolved to fan this spark of romance, no matter how big the blaze or who was burned. At the time he considered that his thoughts were unselfishly of her; in a later perspective he knew that she had meant no more than the white screen in a motion picture: it was just Samuel—blind, desirous.

Next day at Taine's, when they met for lunch, Samuel dropped all pretense and made frank love to her. He had no plans, no definite intentions, except to kiss her lips again, to hold her in his arms and feel that she was very little and pathetic and lovable. . . . He took her home, and this time they kissed until both their hearts beat high—words and phrases formed on his lips.

And then suddenly there were steps on the porch—a hand tried the outside door. Marjorie turned dead-white.

"Wait!" she whispered to Samuel, in a frightened voice, but in angry impatience at the interruption he walked to the front door and threw it open.

Every one has seen such scenes on the stage—seen them so often that when they actually happen people behave very much like actors. Samuel felt that he was playing a part and the lines came quite naturally: he announced that all had a right to lead their own lives and looked at Marjorie's husband menacingly, as if daring him to doubt it. Marjorie's husband spoke of the sanctity of the home, forgetting that it hadn't seemed very holy to him lately; Samuel continued along the line of "the right to happiness"; Marjorie's husband mentioned firearms and the divorce court. Then suddenly he stopped and scrutinized both of them—Marjorie in pitiful collapse on the sofa, Samuel haranguing the furniture in a consciously heroic pose.

"Go up-stairs, Marjorie," he said, in a different tone.

"Stay where you are!" Samuel countered quickly.

Marjorie rose, wavered, and sat down, rose again and moved hesitatingly toward the stairs.

"Come outside," said her husband to Samuel. "I want to talk to you."

Samuel glanced at Marjorie, tried to get some message from her eyes; then he shut his lips and went out.

There was a bright moon and when Marjorie's husband came down the steps Samuel could see plainly that he was suffering—but he felt no pity for him.

They stood and looked at each other, a few feet apart, and the husband cleared his throat as though it were a bit husky.

"That's my wife," he said quietly, and then a wild anger surged up inside him. "Damn you!" he cried—and hit Samuel in the face with all his strength.

In that second, as Samuel slumped to the ground, it flashed to him that he had been hit like that twice before, and simultaneously the incident altered like a dream—he felt suddenly awake. Mechanically he sprang to his feet and squared off. The other man was waiting, fists up, a yard away, but Samuel knew that though physically he had him by several inches and many pounds, he wouldn't hit him. The situation had miraculously and entirely changed—a moment before Samuel had seemed to himself heroic; now he seemed the cad, the outsider, and Marjorie's husband, silhouetted against the lights of the little house, the eternal heroic figure, the defender of his home.

There was a pause and then Samuel turned quickly away and went down the path for the last time.

IV

Of course, after the third blow Samuel put in several weeks at conscientious introspection. The blow years before at Andover had landed on his personal unpleasantness; the workman of his college days had jarred the snobbishness out of his system and Marjorie's husband had given a severe jolt to his greedy selfishness. It threw women out of his ken until a year later, when he met his future wife; for the only sort of woman worth-while seemed to be the one who could be protected as Marjorie's husband had protected her. Samuel could not imagine his grass-widow, Mrs. De Ferriac, causing any very righteous blows on her own account.

His early thirties found him well on his feet. He was associated with old Peter Carhart, who was in those days a national figure. Carhart's physique was like a rough model for a statue of Hercules, and his record was just as solid—a pile made for the pure joy of it, without cheap extortion or shady

scandal. He had been a great friend of Samuel's father, but he
watched the son for six years before taking him into his own
office. Heaven knows how many things he controlled at that
time—mines, railroads, banks, whole cities. Samuel was very
close to him, knew his likes and dislikes, his prejudices,
weaknesses and many strengths.

One day Carhart sent for Samuel and, closing the door of
his inner office, offered him a chair and a cigar.

"Everything O.K., Samuel?" he asked.

"Why, yes."

"I've been afraid you're getting a bit stale."

"Stale?" Samuel was puzzled.

"You've done no work outside the office for nearly ten
years?"

"But I've had vacations, in the Adiron—"

Carhart waved this aside.

"I mean outside work. Seeing the things move that we've
always pulled the strings of here."

"No," admitted Samuel, "I haven't."

"So," he said abruptly, "I'm going to give you an outside
job that'll take about a month."

Samuel didn't argue. He rather liked the idea and he made
up his mind that, whatever it was, he would put it through
just as Carhart wanted it. That was his employer's greatest
hobby, and the men around him were as dumb under direct
orders as infantry sub-alterns.

"You'll go to San Antonio and see Hamil," continued
Carhart. "He's got a job on hand and he wants a man to take
charge."

Hamil was in charge of the Carhart interests in the South-
west, a man who had grown up in the shadow of his employer, and with whom, though they had never met, Samuel
had had much official correspondence.

"When do I leave?"

"You'd better go to-morrow," answered Carhart, glancing
at the calendar. "That's the first of May. I'll expect your report here on the first of June."

Next morning Samuel left for Chicago, and two days later
he was facing Hamil across a table in the office of the Merchants' Trust in San Antonio. It didn't take long to get the
gist of the thing. It was a big deal in oil which concerned the
buying up of seventeen huge adjoining ranches. This buying
up had to be done in one week, and it was a pure squeeze.

Forces had been set in motion that put the seventeen owners between the devil and the deep sea, and Samuel's part was simply to "handle" the matter from a little village near Pueblo. With tact and efficiency the right man could bring it off without any friction, for it was merely a question of sitting at the wheel and keeping a firm hold. Hamil, with an astuteness many times valuable to his chief, had arranged a situation that would give a much greater clear gain than any dealing in the open market. Samuel shook hands with Hamil, arranged to return in two weeks, and left for San Felipe, New Mexico.

It occurred to him, of course, that Carhart was trying him out. Hamil's report on his handling of this might be a factor in something big for him, but even without that he would have done his best to put the thing through. Ten years in New York hadn't made him sentimental, and he was quite accustomed to finish everything he began—and a little bit more.

All went well at first. There was no enthusiasm, but each one of the seventeen ranchers concerned knew Samuel's business, knew what he had behind him, and that they had as little chance of holding out as flies on a window-pane. Some of them were resigned—some of them cared like the devil, but they'd talked it over, argued it with lawyers and couldn't see any possible loophole. Five of the ranches had oil, the other twelve were part of the chance, but quite as necessary to Hamil's purpose, in any event.

Samuel soon saw that the real leader was an early settler named McIntyre, a man of perhaps fifty, gray-haired, clean-shaven, bronzed by forty New Mexico summers, and with those clear, steady eyes that Texas and New Mexico weather are apt to give. His ranch had not as yet shown oil, but it was in the pool, and if any man hated to lose his land McIntyre did. Every one had rather looked to him at first to avert the big calamity, and he had hunted all over the territory for the legal means with which to do it, but he had failed, and he knew it. He avoided Samuel assiduously, but Samuel was sure that when the day came for the signatures he would appear.

It came—a baking May day, with hot waves rising off the parched land as far as eyes could see, and as Samuel sat stewing in his little improvised office—a few chairs, a bench, and a wooden table—he was glad the thing was almost over. He wanted to get back East the worst way, and join his wife and children for a week at the seashore.

The meeting was set for four o'clock, and he was rather surprised at three-thirty when the door opened and McIntyre came in. Samuel could not help respecting the man's attitude and feeling a bit sorry for him. McIntyre seemed closely related to the prairies, and Samuel had the little flicker of envy that city people feel toward men who live in the open.

"Afternoon," said McIntyre, standing in the open doorway, with his feet apart and his hands on his hips.

"Hello, Mr. McIntyre." Samuel rose, but omitted the formality of offering his hand. He imagined the rancher cordially loathed him, and he hardly blamed him. McIntyre came in and sat down leisurely.

"You got us," he said suddenly.

This didn't seem to require any answer.

"When I heard Carhart was back of this," he continued, "I gave up."

"Mr. Carhart is—" began Samuel, but McIntyre waved him silent.

"Don't talk about the dirty sneak-thief!"

"Mr. McIntyre," said Samuel briskly, "if this half-hour is to be devoted to that sort of talk—"

"Oh, dry up, young man," McIntyre interrupted, "you can't abuse a man who'd do a thing like this."

Samuel made no answer.

"It's simply a dirty filch. There just *are* skunks like him too big to handle."

"You're being paid liberally," offered Samuel.

"Shut up!" roared McIntyre suddenly. "I want the privilege of talking." He walked to the door and looked out across the land, the sunny, steaming pasturage that began almost at his feet and ended with the gray-green of the distant mountains. When he turned around his mouth was trembling.

"Do you fellows love Wall Street?" he said hoarsely, "or wherever you do your dirty scheming—" He paused. "I suppose you do. No critter gets so low that he doesn't sort of love the place he's worked, where he's sweated out the best he's had in him."

Samuel watched him awkwardly. McIntyre wiped his forehead with a huge blue handkerchief, and continued:

"I reckon this rotten old devil had to have another million. I reckon we're just a few of the poor beggars he's blotted out to buy a couple more carriages or something." He waved his hand toward the door. "I built a house out there when I was seventeen, with these two hands. I took a wife there at twenty-one, added two wings, and with four mangy steers I started out. Forty summers I've saw the sun come up over those mountains and drop down red as blood in the evening, before the heat drifted off and the stars came out. I been happy in that house. My boy was born there and he died there, late one spring, in the hottest part of an afternoon like this. Then the wife and I lived there alone like we'd lived before, and sort of tried to have a home, after all, not a real home but nigh it—cause the boy always seemed around close, somehow, and we expected a lot of nights to see him runnin' up the path to supper." His voice was shaking so he could hardly speak and he turned again to the door, his gray eyes contracted.

"That's my land out there," he said, stretching out his arm, "my land, by God—It's all I got in the world—and ever wanted." He dashed his sleeve across his face, and his tone changed as he turned slowly and faced Samuel. "But I suppose it's got to go when they want it—it's got to go."

Samuel had to talk. He felt that in a minute more he would lose his head. So he began, as level-voiced as he could—in the sort of tone he saved for disagreeable duties.

"It's business, Mr. McIntyre," he said. "It's inside the law. Perhaps we couldn't have bought out two or three of you at any price, but most of you did have a price. Progress demands some things—"

Never had he felt so inadequate, and it was with the greatest relief that he heard hoof-beats a few hundred yards away.

But at his words the grief in McIntyre's eyes had changed to fury.

"You and your dirty gang of crooks!" he cried. "Not one of you has got an honest love for anything on God's earth! You're a herd of money-swine!"

Samuel rose and McIntyre took a step toward him.

"You long-winded dude. You got our land—take that for Peter Carhart!"

He swung from the shoulder quick as lightning and down went Samuel in a heap. Dimly he heard steps in the doorway and knew that some one was holding McIntyre, but there was no need. The rancher had sunk down in his chair, and dropped his head in his hands.

Samuel's brain was whirring. He realized that the fourth fist had hit him, and a great flood of emotion cried out that

the law that had inexorably ruled his life was in motion
again. In a half-daze he got up and strode from the room.

The next ten minutes were perhaps the hardest of his life.
People talk of the courage of convictions, but in actual life a
man's duty to his family may make a rigid course seem a
selfish indulgence of his own righteousness. Samuel thought
mostly of his family, yet he never really wavered. That jolt
had brought him to.

When he came back in the room there were a lot of worried faces waiting for him, but he didn't waste any time explaining.

"Gentlemen," he said, "Mr. McIntyre has been kind
enough to convince me that in this matter you are absolutely
right, and the Peter Carhart interests absolutely wrong. As far
as I am concerned you can keep your ranches to the rest of
your days."

He pushed his way through an astounded gathering, and
within a half-hour he had sent two telegrams that staggered
the operator into complete unfitness for business; one was to
Hamil in San Antonio; one was to Peter Carhart in New
York.

Samuel didn't sleep much that night. He knew that for the
first time in his business career he had made a dismal, miserable failure. But some instinct in him, stronger than will,
deeper than training, had forced him to do what would probably end his ambitions and his happiness. But it was done
and it never occurred to him that he could have acted otherwise.

Next morning two telegrams were waiting for him. The
first was from Hamil. It contained three words:

YOU BLAMED IDIOT!

The second was from New York:

DEAL OFF COME TO NEW YORK IMMEDIATELY CARHART.

Within a week things had happened. Hamil quarrelled furiously and violently defended his scheme. He was summoned
to New York, and spent a bad half-hour on the carpet in Peter
Carhart's office. He broke with the Carhart interests in July,
and in August Samuel Meredith, at thirty-five years old, was,

to all intents, made Carhart's partner. The fourth fist had done its work.

I suppose that there's a caddish streak in every man that runs crosswise across his character and disposition and general outlook. With some men it's secret and we never know it's there until they strike us in the dark one night. But Samuel's showed when it was in action, and the sight of it made people see red. He was rather lucky in that, because every time his little devil came up it met a reception that sent it scurrying down below in a sickly, feeble condition. It was the same devil, the same streak that made him order Gilly's friends off the bed, that made him go inside Marjorie's house.

If you could run your hand along Samuel Meredith's jaw you'd feel a lump. He admits he's never been sure which fist left it there, but he wouldn't lose it for anything. He says there's no cad like an old cad, and that sometimes just before making a decision, it's a great help to stroke his chin. The reporters call it a nervous characteristic, but it's not that. It's so he can feel again the gorgeous clarity, the lightning sanity of those four fists.